Translations
of
Beauty

ALSO BY MIA YUN

House of the Winds

Translations of Beauty

A NOVEL

Mia Yun

ATRIA BOOKS

New York London Toronto Sydney

I dedicate this book to the immigrants of New York and to their struggles and triumphs.

To speak the truth is one thing, but the whole truth, that cannot, must not, be said.

—Colette, *The Vagabond*

The house where you are born is but a nest. It is a way station to which you have come. It is your point of entrance into this world. Here you sprout, here you flower. Here you are severed from your mother, as the hip is struck from the stone.

—Aztec

PROLOGUE

In my dream, I am in the back of a taxi, speeding to Kennedy to catch my flight to Italy. We slip in and out of the sun-dappled shadows of the Manhattan Bridge, a steel-caged tunnel, and hurtle on, almost flying through the air. The foot-tall deep orange turban elaborately wound about the head of the driver, a Sikh, an actor in a Bollywood epic, floats up like a lotus bloom, almost touching the ceiling of the cab before floating back down. Then, suddenly, I am flying out the open window of the taxicab, and before I know it, I am airborne, riding on a magic carpet. The wind, pregnant with a faint sea smell, whooshes by, its fingers spread. Below and around me, pelted with sunlight, everything seems throbbing and throbbing with new life. The East River shimmers like the iridescent silver scales of a million fish. Lower Manhattan, turning and shifting and flying back and shrinking to the size of a postage stamp, is sparkling like a newly built city. Tree branches writhe and stretch like birds sprouting wings. White pollen balls bloom in the sunlight into a zillion tiny flowers, drifting like confetti over Manhattan. I am thinking it's unbelievably fantastic. Like flying through a Chagall painting. I wake up screaming and laughing from sheer terror and excitement.

Of course, it turns out to be what Koreans call a "dog dream," because nothing like that happens when I go to Kennedy today. Instead, Mom's waiting outside the Alitalia check-in counter with a suspicious-looking bag and a huge old ugly suitcase sporting two electric blue pom-pom tassels Mom tied to the handle (as extra insurance, as though the double strips of iridescent gray packing tape weren't enough) so, she says, I won't have trouble spotting it at the luggage claim in Venice. Then at the last minute, from the plastic bag, she produces a humongous bottle of kimchi she made for Inah, my twin sister. It's her favorite kind, made from radish leaves.

I know I didn't expect this would be a glamorous, jetsetter's trip, but neither did I imagine it to be a mule trip. The sight of the kimchi bottle, as big as a ten-gallon cowboy hat, makes me nearly hysterical. Of course, Mom has anticipated my reaction. Undaunted and with the practiced eagerness of an insurance salesman, she assures me it won't leak. She points to the mouth of the bottle, swaddled thickly like a mummy with the same gray packing tape she'd used to disfigure the suitcase. I am not convinced. I might as well travel donning a dunce cap. Mom knows and I know and every Korean knows that traveling with kimchi is almost as dangerous as traveling with a live bomb. Once it starts fermenting, the juice will bubble up to the top and spill out, ruining everything in the vicinity and, as delicious as it is, the smell, to say the least, is not that pretty. It could be as awful as the most pungent kind of cheese.

I am sure that's what does it. Later, alone at the gate waiting to board my red-eye flight to Milan, I am all distracted and nervous. I find myself worrying about everything: Mom's kimchi bottle I deliberately lost in the bathroom, leaving it by the trash bin; switching planes in Milan; and whether Inah will really be there waiting for me at the airport in Venice. She is known to be rather unpredictable, to put it mildly. I know she could easily change her mind and not show up. The thought really terrifies me. It's one scenario I hadn't entertained until now.

I try to tell myself it's traveling alone that makes me so nervous. Who knows. Maybe in the back of my mind, I still associate flying with nagging uncertainties and new situations. Maybe I still carry that undefined fear that transplanted people never seem to be able to lose. People who uproot themselves and plant their feet on new soil. People who are permanently marked by memories of another terrain. Immigrants.

But then I remember the first time I called Inah in Rome to suggest the trip. How she'd screamed and hissed and hung up. I think she had been there nearly two months then. I'd had no idea what she was up to. At the end of her five-month backpacking trip through India, instead of coming home as she had promised Mom—even if for a short visit—Inah had gone to Rome. Maybe it had been as good a place to go as any. Vague as always, Inah hadn't offered much of an explanation. All she had said was that she would be staying with a friend. A girl, she'd added, in case we wondered.

Maybe that was why. That was why Inah had so vehemently protested the idea of my coming to see her. For she had yet to explain it and many, many other things. Like what it really was that had made her abruptly abandon her doctoral studies at Oxford seven months earlier and take off to India. Maybe there had been no particular reasons. She thought she would travel for a while—that's what she'd said to our parents when she'd eventually called home from New Delhi and broken the news. According to Mom, she'd said it so casually that, for a second, it had sounded perfectly reasonable.

But it was typical Inah. It wasn't the first time she had done something like that. Making an important decision seemingly on the spur of the moment. Never bothering to consult anyone in advance. Over the years it had become a kind of pattern as she'd transferred from school to school and moved from city to city. Changing states and even continents. Turning into an academic junkie, a perennial student and an intellectual wanderer. Inah simply dispensed facts later. Just skeletal facts, only after they had become unalterable, irrevocable facts. Inah was someone who constantly climbed a slippery hill; she could fall off at any time. Mom lived in a constant state of trepidation. And yet we remained helpless spectators. Out of a sense of guilt and pity, we let Inah get away with almost anything. Like her five-month trip through India.

While she backpacked her way across India, Mom, of course, worried and fretted, biding time, waiting for her to end the trip and come home. She couldn't stomach the idea of Inah traveling alone. Whenever there was bad news out of India—natural disasters like landslides or flooding, or a bomb exploding on a train in the south or fighting in Kashmir—Mom would call me. Her voice always thick with worry and fear.

Mom knew I was tracking Inah's trip through the occasional postcards she was sending like afterthoughts. (It seemed a miracle each time that as flimsy a thing as a postcard would find its way from India to my apartment mail-box in Manhattan.) But I was never sure where she was at any given time, as the postcards would arrive weeks after the postmark stamped on them. They came from exotic-sounding places like Goa, Madurai and Bodh Gaya (where Sakya-muni achieved enlightenment, Inah remembered to note). Each invariably filled with a few pretentious-sounding, poetic lines she'd scribbled in her slithery handwriting. I couldn't really explain why, but at the sight of her handwrit-ing, I always felt a little anger rise inside me. Even though it would pass soon enough, scattering like a wispy trail of smoke, afterward, I'd feel a little like a scrooge. I guess I just wasn't willing to admit it, but I begrudged Inah her freedom and luxury of "traipsing around."

But I wasn't being fair. For one thing, she couldn't have had much money with her. She had to be traveling on a shoestring budget. Probably surviving on rice and beans, traveling on buses and "hard-seat" trains, and staying at yoga ashrams and dirt-cheap, filthy hostels with communal rooms. After a while, it must have been only grueling. And lonely, although she would never have admitted it. One could travel like that only so long.

The thing was that she kept extending her trip. After a month and a half of making her erratic way down south, from New Delhi, through Rajasthan down to Bombay, stay-ing close to the coast of the Arabian Sea, Inah resurfaced in Calcutta, on the other side of India, on the Bay of Bengal. Then after nearly two months in Calcutta, she was moving again, heading north through Gaya, Varanasi, on to Kash-mir. I got the impression that there was no clear plan. That it was more a day-to-day thing. That she was just playing it by ear. Winging it and making decisions based on passive impulses. Like someone following a rumor mill. It was as if she wanted to see where it would lead her. Maybe she was looking for a reason to end the aimless wandering, a motive to return but finding none. And I began to wonder.

It was only when Inah failed to show up after her trip despite her promise (she was a slippery fish that got away every time) that Mom convinced herself that something was very wrong. She could feel it, she insisted. She started asking me to go and see Inah. She practically begged me. So worried and desperate to maintain the tenuous link to her wandering daughter, a forever-shifting island. That was how the idea of the trip, really just an excuse to spy on Inah, was hatched. In Mom's overactive imagination, Inah was a lone star, roaming and catapulting and hurtling toward the earth. Adrift and lost. Before she fell and crashed and burned without a trace, we had to catch her. And, of course, I was the one who could do just that. If anyone possessed the power to perform such a feat, it had to be me. I was Inah's twin. I would be able to divine her thoughts and guide her back home. Once again, I had to turn myself into Mom's movable bridge.

The problem was that Inah just wouldn't hear of it. I kept pestering her, and she kept resisting. I must have called her a half dozen times. I have to admit that by the second or third call, I was so blindly in love with the idea of a free trip to Italy that I conveniently forgot the whole point of it. (I wonder if I would have pushed as hard if she had been in someplace less tempting, like Lithuania.) I was no longer thinking about Inah or the potential consequences of the trip or the responsibilities it would entail. The more she resisted, the more tantalizing and desirable the trip, or rather the idea of it, became.

So I persisted. And eventually, Inah gave in. She couldn't stand my bugging her anymore. Reluctantly she agreed to meet me in Venice, and from there, we would make our way down to Rome, stopping in Florence and Siena on the way. Maybe she figured she would put up with me for two weeks, play my travel guide and flick me off. And I was too ecstatic to be scared. Until now.

When I board the plane, a steward looks at me and says, "It couldn't be that bad." It's Inah. She has a way of burrowing into my thoughts, and once she's there, she stays put, refusing to budge. It's only then that I realize how wholly absurd all this is. The very idea of going and "saving" her for Mom. Across the Atlantic; a new ocean, not even our ocean of separation, the Pacific. But there's not a thing I can do about it now. Nor about the butterflies that start flapping about in my stomach. It's all too late.

On the runway, the plane sits idling for a long time. Outside, the afternoon is stalled in a soundless vacuum. It's the fuzzy sunlight; everything looks a little surreal and slightly skewed as if in a Daliesque landscape, even the late April sky that hangs lackadaisically over the low-slung terminal buildings in laminated blue. I remember how, growing up as sullen teenagers on Ash Avenue in Flushing, a spring afternoon like this used to bore us to death.

Then suddenly, as though having finally mustered up enough courage, the plane barrels down the runway and takes off in a rumble. Lifting its nose to the sky. Levitating. Shrinking the earth below. Up and up, climbing the sky that suddenly resembles the scorched, chalky sky of summer. Flying over the sparkling blue Jamaica Bay bathed in a reddish glow, and a Long Island girdled with frosted white beaches.

Soon, we are over the slate blue Atlantic, where we will fly through an abbreviated sunset. The red disk of the sun plunges like a dropped ball behind the horizon, leaving a sliver of orange rind at the hems of the azure sky. It turns a deeper and deeper indigo, pitching a swollen tent of Prussian blue all around, toward the horizon. Then, it's nothing but an endless sea of black tinctured with pearl and zinc. All night, we will be chasing the sun across the Atlantic, and I rather like the idea.

PART ONE

Mostly and usually, babies are born one at a time to ensure that they get all the attention they deserve. But Mom dreams of a glossy full moon over a mountain peak splitting in two, and soon afterward Inah and I arrive in this world together as "winter twins." Already a year old by the way Koreans count age. We come in a hurry, barely ten minutes apart under the flood of cold, green fluorescent light in an overheated room at a university hospital in Seoul. Red and wrinkled and tightfisted and kicking feet, each no bigger than a hammerhead, and issuing the shrill cries of a squealing crow. Indistinguishable other than the greenish Mongolian spots we carry on our bottoms, which will fade in time. It's January 1973, but still 1972 by the lunar calendar, the Year of the Rat. Wet snow falls all night.

We are the first children and will be the only children born to our parents. Mom is a twenty-five-year-old novice teacher at a primary school. Pretty mostly from her youth and her open moon face blessed with beautiful, pale, dewy skin. Daddy is forty-four, considered too old to be a first-time father or, for that matter, even a second-time father. He weeps as he holds his newborn twins in his arms. He can't help himself.

Afterward, every Saturday, Daddy hurries home for the weekend from his teaching job in the eastern city of Choonchon, Spring Stream, and spends hours sitting next to us twins, transfixed, never tiring of looking at us, lying side by side, babbling and dribbling, sleeping and dreaming, he's sure, the same dreams. Noticing things like new feathery hair sprouting all over our warm heads. Our faces filling out from Mom's breast milk. His dark lips open, and smiles leak out. He talks in whispers to us twin girls. He tells us how we will always have each other as a companion on the road of life. How lucky we are.

Time flies, leaving us with no apparent memories. A year passes. Then two, three. We know these stories because they are told to us later. In careless repetition by tired Grandma at our bedtime. We are now four years old. Wispy little things. With spindly legs and arms. People in our old neighborhood at the foot of Nam San, South Mountain, where traditional, tile-roofed Korean houses run shoulder-to-shoulder along the narrow alleys crisscrossing each other in a seemingly endless gridlock, now refer to our old Japanese house as "the twins'" instead of "the Japanese house." On the street, strangers, whom Grandma never fails to meet when she goes out with us in tow, stop and marvel and say we look as if stamped from the same mold. Laughing, they pat us on the head and ask Grandma how she could tell us apart. Every time, Grandma imperiously declares to the curious and always rapt audience, "You wouldn't guess it, but they *are* different." Pointing to me, she claims I am the quiet one of the two, a watcher, and then, pointing to Inah, she says, proudly, "She is the spirited one."

It's true. Already such a self-absorbed and self-involved thing, Inah is feistier and more vociferous. She leads, and I follow. Inah thinks out loud and I listen. Inah will try everything a little harder. She even talks faster, as if in a race. Almost in a stutter. In her slightly high-pitched tone. Impatiently repeating words. Stumbling and tripping over them because her mind races faster than she could string them up together and give them voice. Waving her arms. Anxious to keep the attention from slipping away. Her bright, sparkling eyes become two black rambling seas of emotion. It's as if she knows and is in a hurry to grab what fun, love and attention she can.

Shoving past Grandma, Inah runs after Mommy across the courtyard. Her feet are barely inside her silver, fur-trimmed shoes, and on top of her head, from the elastic bands holding her feather-brown hair in two rabbit ears, the plastic cherry-colored beads jump and go *click-clack* like abacus beads, and the balloon sleeves of her jacket (iridescent green on one side and iridescent blue on the other; the colors of peacock feathers) go *swish, swish* making the sound of wind in the trees.

All the way out to the damp alley, where winter mornings always smell like soot, Inah hangs on to Mommy's coat sleeve until Grandma grabs her, firmly planting her by her side.

"Say good-bye quick to your mother and get inside," Grandma says, all bundled up like a snowman. "It's cold." Inah pushes off the scratchy sleeve of Grandma's gray wool sweater that smells like salted oily fish and turns up her bun face to Mommy and asks if she's coming home early. Mommy assures her that she is. What time? Inah asks. At four o'clock maybe? Maybe. Promise? Mommy hooks her baby finger to Inah's, but Inah still looks unsatisfied.

"Bye, Mommy," Inah says finally, looking dejected.

"Bye," Mommy says, pretending not to notice the tears brimming in Inah's eyes. She pats us on the head, first Inah and then me. Resigned, Inah watches Mommy walk down the narrow alley in her long tea-colored winter coat as the sound of her shoe heels, soft clucking tongues, drift away like melodies of a slow song. Then, just as Mommy reaches the end of the alley, Inah, stretching all of her wispy four-year-old frame, belches out one more time, "Bye, Mommy!"

"Bye, Mommy!" I repeat after her, copying even her slightly aggressive tone.

Mommy turns, smiles and waves back with her hand in a black leather glove. And then she is gone, turning the corner. Suddenly, the sunless alley, hemmed in on both sides by the stone walls of the houses, feels empty and desolate. Inah, sad-faced and looking puzzled, stares at the gray space where Mommy has just disappeared. Then, even as she is being pulled away by Grandma's cold and cracked hand, Inah looks over her shoulder just one more time, wistful.

For the rest of the day, Inah waits, and I watch her wait. When noon comes and passes and the sunlight that floods the house in the morning pulls out, leaving the old, dank Japanese house dark as a cave, time slows down, and the afternoon drags on interminably long as uneven hours and minutes accumulate and play tricks. Inah and I, confused with our still hazy sense of time and not comprehending the arbitrary nature of it, play, eat lunch and take a nap, and constantly ask Grandma how many hours before Mommy comes home and count and recount, folding and unfolding our small fingers. We never get tired of this daily repetition of waiting because of the sheer shiver of excitement that punctuates the end of it.

Then finally comes Saturday, and Daddy, a college art teacher, is back home for the weekend. How anxiously Inah and I wait for Saturdays. Sharing that aching thrill, and holding on to the memory of his warm voice and unique smell, so familiar, so recent but nonetheless fading. With none of the certainty that accompanies our daily waiting for Mommy. But with the fierce affection we reserve only for him. Every time he walks in through the door, Inah and I simply soar and fly to heaven. Ecstatic and breathless and momentarily shy and very much relieved, we rush and dive into his wide-open arms.

The next morning, even before sleep falls from our eyes, we rush to our parents' room to wake him up so unceremoniously, pulling off the cover and shaking his arms. Jostling each other, Inah and I beg him to get up and play with us. Our hearts skip when he finally opens his blurry eyes, looking a little confused and sorry at the memory of sweet sleep, and massaging his sour morning stomach through his loose pajama top. But he's ready to oblige us twins, who are climbing onto his lap, competing for his attention.

Soon, we get him on his hands and knees and climb up to his back and go on a horse ride. Out of the room, across the *maroo*, the slippery, varnished wooden floor, cold as ice in the winter, and then down the dank hallway splashed with morning sunlight. First in a halfhearted trot but soon in a full gallop, he goes carrying Inah and me on his back as we shout, "*Iri-yah, ggil-ggil!*" to get the Daddy-horse to hurry up even more. After a while, Daddy-horse gets angry and raises and tilts back his head and hisses and jumps up and down (we can see his splayed hair on the crown ripple like black waves), threatening to toss us up into the air. Inah and I shriek and scream, scared out of our wits, desperately clinging to his long, skinny back, wiggling and rolling.

Then, reaching the other end of the hallway, at the foot of the wooden staircase, Daddy-horse stops full and refuses to move. But we shrilly order him to climb up the steps and take us to the big, mildewy tatami-floored room upstairs, his painting studio, shut up for the winter. He pulls up his neck and cries for our mercy, but we shake our heads, laughing and giggling. He turns and asks us how we would like it if Daddy-horse grew wings on his shoulders and became a flying horse and carried Inah and Yunah to the sky over the river and mountains instead. No, no, no! We will be too scared! Just take us upstairs, Daddy-horse, we say. Crawling, he scales just a couple of steps before he collapses, out of breath. We scramble off his back fast, and bend down over Daddy-horse, sprawled on his back over the steps with his eyes shut tight and his long arms dangling at his sides. Terrified, we plead, "*Apa! Apa!!* Wake up! Open your eyes!" But he doesn't wake up or open his eyes. Inah places her sticky thumb and forefinger on one of them and tries to pry the lid open, but it closes right back when she lets it go.

Now convinced Daddy is really dead, Inah and I are ready to burst out crying. That's when he suddenly springs back to life. Opening his eyes wide, he bolts up, spreading out his arms and roaring over us, "Woo-waah!!" Inah and I jump up like two beans on a hot pan and run for our lives, screaming and squealing. Grandma looks in, loudly clucking her tongue, and says what a beautiful sight it is: an "old man" about to turn fifty in just a couple of days, horsing around with his two little girls. Fiercely protective of him, Inah hates Grandma so for that brief second, but Daddy just laughs.

By late afternoon on Sunday, though, Daddy is gone, and Inah and I start waiting and counting out loud for the next Saturday all over again. In our unerring conviction that the future holds only more fun and excitement.

TWO

It's another Saturday, but Daddy still hasn't come home when Inah and I change into our tutti-frutti pajamas. Mommy tucks us under the covers and reads us a story from the book of Korean folk tales; a story from long, long ago when "food grew on the Food Tree, and clothes grew on the Clothes Tree . . ." We know the story by heart.

After Mommy leaves, Inah and I lie in the dark with Grandma in the middle, tall as a haystack, all bundled up in her scratchy sweater and padded dungarees. I can't see Yunah, Inah complains from the other side of her, and Grandma says just close your eyes and go to sleep. What's there to see in the dark anyway. You saw Yunah all day and isn't that enough. I can't get out of my clothes yet because I will have to go out and open the door for your father, in case your mother falls asleep and doesn't hear.

"Ha, he'll like that," Grandma says. "I don't ever say one

nice thing to him and always show him a scowling face. Ha, ha."

"How come you don't like Daddy, *halmoni*?" Inah asks.

"How come? How come! He stole my baby daughter. That's how come. It wasn't just any daughter. It was a daughter I got at forty-five years of age, already old as a witch. Whoever heard of a woman having a baby so old?! Certainly, I hadn't. My first daughter I had at nineteen was already married by then. Your mother was a miracle baby. So what if it was a girl? I didn't mind it a bit. It was your grandfather who minded it. He had left me years before for that fat concubine of his because I didn't give him a son. That's what he said, I didn't give him a son. Like I was being spiteful to him. Well, he got his wish, for he got a son all right. Only he turns out to be dim-witted in the head. Then as a bargain, he gets three more daughters from her, one after another and another like it's harvesting season. That should be the end of the story, you'd think. But no. One time he comes back, don't ask me why, and plants me a baby. He then waits around hoping it will be a son, but should he be so lucky, it's another girl. So he turns around and walks out for good. Huffing mad. He goes back to his fat concubine who's now grown as big as a hippo. I said they deserved each other. But that's another story. No one knows how I raised your mother. Alone. But I wouldn't have given her up for all the jade and gold in the world. I did everything I could for her. Now, after all that, do you think I was planning to give her away to any man who came along? Certainly, not to an old bachelor, a dauber at that with nothing to his name. Now you know. It's nothing personal. Your father certainly knows why I am so mean to him. Oh, to think that I used to be a number-one man-worshiper, too!" Inah and I giggle, covering our mouths.

"What are you two giggling about? As if you understand a thing I am saying!"

Soon Grandma is snoring, blowing out a whistling noise through her parted lips. And trees whistle too in a thin voice outside. A beam of light slides in through the rice paper door and climbs to the ceiling. I hear Mommy in the next room. She's still awake. On the other side of Grandma, Inah is wide awake, too. She tosses and turns. She's thinking and thinking in her busy little head.

"*Halmoni,*" Inah whispers in the dark after a long while.

"I thought you were sleeping," Grandma says in her tired, scratchy voice.

"How come Daddy hasn't come yet?"

"He should've been home a while ago. It must be the snow. If there's a snowstorm, he won't be coming with all those roads running through the mountains. Don't stay up waiting. You can see him in the morning. Why aren't you tired, anyway? You should be from gibbering all day like two noisy birds."

But we're not sleepy. We watch the ceiling where the beam of light is slithering across like a snake.

"*Halmoni,* tell us the story again, the time we were born," Inah says, turning to Grandma.

"Yes, *halmoni,* tell us that story again," I say.

"Don't tell me you are awake, too," Grandma says in her surprised voice. Inah and I giggle. "And haven't you heard the story enough times?"

"But we want to hear it again. I was born first. Before Inah. Tell us how I popped out of Mommy's belly button and cried and cried."

"You weren't just crying. You were all fussy, kicking your legs and screaming. All squished and red in the face. And then Inah followed. Very calm, not like Yunah. So your father thought, oh, she's going to be the calm and patient one, and named her Inah, the Patient One. The first one he named Yunah, the Sparkling One. But if you ask me, I'd say it should have been the other way around. Because it turns out that Yunah is the quieter one of the two of you. And let me tell you, I don't think there's one patient bone in Inah." Inah giggles proudly.

"Grandma, when we were born, Daddy cried. Right?"

"Sure he did. The first and last time I saw him cry. He was so happy. But all I could see was a hardship gate open wide in front of him. Now, go to sleep! It's getting very late. And if you don't, you know who might come for a visit."

"The Japanese girl ghost?!" Inah and I whisper, listening for that *psst, psst* foot-padding sound the Japanese girl ghost makes as she wanders around at night, up and down the hall outside our room and the stairs. She's lost and looking for her mother.

"That's right. She will open the door to see who's talking and talking in the room so late at night." Shrieking, we cling to Grandma like two monkeys and bury our faces in her scratchy wool sweater. "Aggggh!" Grandma hisses and shakes when Inah's cold hand slips in under her shirt, groping for her old hang-down breasts that are wrecked with wrinkles and have two dried jujubes for nipples. They are the same dried-up nipples Inah and I used to suck after Mommy painted her ninnies with iodine, and cry because no milk would come out. We were two years old. Too old for Mommy's breast milk.

"Now go to sleep," Grandma says. "Both of you."

In sleep, I slip into Inah's dream and together we fly on the back of Daddy-horse, who has grown big white wings on his shoulders. Up and away. Soaring and soaring into the sea-blue sky. Inah and I are so happy and excited, we raise our hands and shout and laugh.

THREE

Inah thought I should be able to see the snow-capped Alps as we approach Milan. But instead, it's a sea of fog we fly into. It's the kind of fog—white, opaque and dense as steam—that conceals everything from view. It closes in on us in a billowy wall as we descend blindly through the interminably gray space over Milan airport.

It's barely six in the morning. The transit area where I wait for the connecting flight to Venice is all but deserted. The airport snack shop is just opening. At the service counter inside, two Italian men in crisp dark blue uniforms are chatting over their coffee in their scratchy morning voices. Outside the steel-framed glass wall, the somber sky hangs flat, like a hammered-out sheet of tin. The morning sun, unseen.

I read for a while and then give up, distracted by the new and old worries hatching like schools of tiny fish in my head. I notice the Italian man who sat next to me on the plane. He has taken refuge in the seat by the glass wall. (During the time it took to cross the Atlantic and change continents, we didn't exchange a single word.) On the orange seat next to him sits his striped burlap bag. Like another person, a traveling companion. Mute and faithful. It's the way he sits so still, slouched over, wrapping his big bent head with his thick, stubby, nicotine-stained fingers, he looks like a monk in penance. He isn't a man good at waiting, but a man who is forced to the life of waiting. It never stops chipping away at him: waiting.

I wonder what he does, where he's going, to whom, and who will be welcoming him back at the end of the flight. When we were kids, Inah and I would often wonder about these things. Especially riding in the back of the car. We would wonder aloud where all those people were going—those people inside the cars that flooded the roads in endless streams. The ceaseless motion of people. Where does it come from? This perpetual impetus to move.

Dad would always laugh at our philosophical waxing, tilting his head back. When he was a boy growing up in a small, mountain-locked village in Korea, he used to go up a hill every afternoon to watch the train that would pass by, once toward the north and once toward the south each day. In a long line of black steel cars. Leaving smoke blooms against the blue sky. It was while watching the train scissoring through the rice paddies from the hill that Dad nursed his unnameable yearning for places unknown to him. He knew that one day he would head somewhere, anywhere, aboard the same train. For it's the dreaming that takes us to places. Trains, cars, buses, jets and our feet, they are just tools of our yearnings and dreams and desires.

The electronic clock now shows that it's ten minutes to the departure time, but there is no sign of imminent board-

ing. Instead, a vague announcement comes on through crackling static; they are waiting for the arrival of the plane from
Venice. The announcement instantly unhinges me. I get up
and pace about. Growing nervous at the thought of Inah
waiting at the Venice airport, glum-faced and grumbling.

The small plane I finally board for Venice looks Spartan and
a little tattered at the edges. It takes off in a noisy drone, and
sunlight floods in. Exhausted, I doze off right away.

In my dream, I am back at my parents' house in Flushing, standing in the hallway upstairs outside the door of
Inah's room. For some reason, the door is varnished black
like a coffin. It is open, so I slip inside. The room is empty
with all the furniture gone: Inah's old desk with nicks and
scratches, the ugly bed Dad painted for her in buttercup yellow, and the baby blue dresser. And on the wall where the
window used to be hangs a huge poster. I recognize it right
away: It's a blown-up cover of *The Lost Steps*, the Alejo Car-
pentier novel Inah once sent to me from college. The picture in iridescent silver overlapping blackish gray looks like
a film negative of a Manhattan scape, with the steepled
Chrysler and the UN jutting above and over the forest of
buildings. It's capped not by sky but by an aerial view of a
gray-greenish forest, where a silver river or road snakes away
below the patches of floating clouds.

What catches my eye is a pair of paper-cut emerald
green butterflies that seem caught in the jungle of buildings.
When I touch them, to my great surprise, the emerald
wings instantly crumble and disintegrate into silver-flecked
black dust and fall through my fingers.

I wake up from the dream with a long string of drool on
my chin. The hot, sun-drenched plane is already descending. Below, dusted with gauzy veil-like golden sunlight,

Venice lies flat, like a faded ancient map; intricately patterned with interlocking waterways and marshlands, all silver and ash. It's the most surreal landscape I've ever seen.

The dream hangs in the back of my mind like a tendril when I step off the plane onto the hot steaming tarmac. It's hazy, and the light is glaring. A bus ferries us to the airport building, which is surprisingly small and drab. I am the only Asian face in the immigration line. Unconsciously, I keep checking my American passport.

"*Arrivederci!*" the immigration officer booms when I present my passport. He's handsome, like a young Clint Eastwood. At Kennedy, as I went through the metal detector, Mom called out to my back and warned, "Watch out for Itaeri (Italian) men!" As if she could just picture all these Italian men waiting for me with their mouths open like sharks. "From Korea, eh?!" he says, smiling when he returns my passport. (My American passport shows that I was born in Korea.)

I pick up my luggage and pass through customs and head for the door. To my great relief, I spot Inah right away. So it was another "dog dream."

"Inah! Here!" In a fit of excitement, I shout and wave my passport over my head. Embarrassed by my exuberance, she barely acknowledges me. Closing the book she has been reading, she slings over, as slow as a slug. Without even a pretense of hurrying. Cool as ever. Her wardrobe hasn't seen a change: the usual oversized white T-shirt, loose-fitting khaki jeans and beat-up sneakers. A dark blue "Kipling" backpack hangs all the way down to the small of her back. I wait, frozen. And as Inah gets closer, my heart sinks a little further. She looks awful. Thin and appallingly pale. Almost dingy. Her white T-shirt is grayish and wafer thin from too many washes. Her hair falls limply over her shoulder, and her bangs badly need a trim. And the burn scars on her face somehow look worse than I remember. But then they always do, and each time it's a shock. I can't explain the flash of anger. I guess I am disappointed. It's just all too familiar. Nothing ever changes.

Coming over, Inah gives me a quick look-over. Not missing a thing: my long hair, which I put up at the airport in Milan, my knee-torn blue jeans and tight tie-dye T-shirt and the Miu Miu sandals. (At Kennedy, Mom, so unhappy with the way I was dressed, tried to make me go to the bathroom and change.) Without uttering a single word, Inah still manages to make me feel defensive.

"Inah!" I grab her, wrapping my arms around her bony shoulders and squeezing them. She smells a little sweaty and dusty, like a child who's been out playing on a hot, sticky summer afternoon. She grudgingly endures my claustrophobic arms, then pulls away.

"How was the flight?" she asks, but I know she doesn't mean it to be a question; it's just sort of a defensive bumper she throws around her perimeter.

"So-so. Just a little tired," I answer. "I hope you're not pissed off waiting." Inah doesn't say anything. She has only now noticed the ugly dinosaur of a suitcase sitting at my feet. She looks at it disapprovingly. Somehow, it looks even more hideous than it did at Kennedy.

"Sorry, Inah. Mom brought it to the airport and I couldn't say no. It's for you, although I don't know what it is. I had to lose her kimchi, though. She brought it in a huge bottle duct-taped like an Egyptian mummy." But she barely listens. She couldn't care less. "Mom kept begging, saying it was your favorite radish kimchi," I continue obtusely. "I left it at the bathroom at Kennedy. By the trash bin. I bet someone called in a bomb squad. Anyway, if Mom asks you about it, I am afraid you'll just have to lie to her."

"Whatever," Inah mutters, shrugging her shoulders. "Wait here. I am gonna go and get the bus tickets." She takes off.

I see the Italian man from the plane. Carrying the blue-striped burlap sack in one hand and a brown battered suitcase held together with a cloth belt in the other, and flanked by a short, plump woman and a cherubic, rosy-cheeked boy with splayed brown hair, he's heading for the door. Beaming, no longer chipping away at waiting but in a happy hurry to get home.

FOUR

Daddy doesn't come home that weekend because of the snowstorm that blankets the mountainous eastern region. On Monday morning, Inah wakes up all cranky and tails Mommy around the house like her little shadow, all fixated on her. Begging and pleading with her to stay home and play with her.

"Go tomorrow," she begs again for the tenth time when Mommy sits down in front of the vanity mirror. "Stay home and play with me."

"You know I can't," Mommy says. "But soon, when school closes for the winter, Mommy will stay home and play with you every day."

"But I want you to stay home today," Inah insists.

"Haven't I told you to leave your mother alone and come and eat?" Grandma yells at her again. "It's not like she doesn't feel bad enough already, and I tell you I am not going to chase you around the house with a rice bowl and a spoon. Like an old slave." Inah looks at Grandma uncertainly, angrily turns her head away and sits around with a sour face, pulling at her hands. Then she notices Mommy's handbag lying on the floor, and her eyes light up. She springs to her feet, grabs it and runs out of the room. It's all right, Mommy says when I tell her. Soon Inah rushes back, and she doesn't have Mommy's handbag with her anymore.

"*Umma*," she says, sticking her head over Mommy's shoulder, making her eyes big and putting on a surprised look. "I don't know where your handbag is!"

"Not to worry. I am sure we'll find it," Mommy says, powdering her nose.

"No, no! I am telling you. It's gone. You can never find it!" She squeals fanatically, but Mommy just smiles. Looking dejected and miserable, Inah impatiently watches Mommy inside the mirror, coloring her lips with her lipstick that she swivels out of a shiny black tube.

Out in the alley dark as a rainy day, Inah whimpers and hangs on to Mommy's coat. Grandma asks her what's the matter. Let go of the coat and say good-bye. Only Inah clings on to Mommy even more desperately, clutching her coat with both of her hands. Mommy pats her on her head and tells her to be good. She will bring her favorite walnut cookies later. Inah shakes her head hard and says she doesn't want walnut cookies, she only wants Mommy.

"Good, then Yunah can have all the walnut cookies to herself," Grandma says, and Inah bursts out crying. Mommy is frustrated; she's going to be late. She asks Grandma to hurry and take the twins inside before they catch cold. Grandma peels Inah off Mommy, and Mommy hurries down the alley. Inah shrieks, shakes off Grandma's hand and runs after Mommy all the way to the end of the alley where the narrow strip of gray sky unfurls into a curtain. But Mommy doesn't stop or look back. The fluttering hem of her coat turns the corner after her like a flag, and she is gone. Inah squats down in the middle of the damp alley and bawls.

"*Umma! Umma!*" squeals Inah. Her cries bloom in echoes and escape like frightened birds into the narrow sky above. Don't know what's wrong, Grandma says. She has never done this before. Grandma starts toward her, and Inah gets hysterical.

"Go away!" Inah screams, flailing her arm.

"Stop crying!" Grandma yells. "People will think your mother's dead or something!" Grandma comes back, takes my hand and says we are going in without Inah. Let her stay here and cry all day, all alone, until she's hoarse and sick in the throat and frozen stiff like a winter pollack. No one's going to come but the alley ghost to carry her away on his back.

"No, no, no," Inah shrieks and screams.

"Stop crying then! How long are you going to cry? Can't you see I am too old for this? If you don't like to be with your old grandma, tell your mother to quit school and stay home. I've been taking care of you two long enough. I've had it. I'd much rather spend my days in the country watching the clouds roll in the sky."

Grandma pulls my hand and pretends to walk away. Inah bolts up as though on a springboard and runs after us, screaming and stamping her feet. "No, Grandma! No!" But as soon as we stop, she squats right back down and sobs on hoarsely between jerking hiccups. She's freezing. Her face is goose bumped. Her nose drips like a faucet. Her lips are blue and purple. She trembles and shakes. Grandma runs back and angrily grabs her arm and yanks her off the ground.

"Stop crying! How many times did I tell you? How many times? You cry the first thing in the morning, it brings nothing but bad luck!"

"I hate you, Grandma, I hate you," Inah cries.

After a nap and lunch, though, Inah is in a good mood again. Sprawled next to me on her stomach like a starfish, she's looking at our baby pictures in the little blue vinyl pocket album. Turning the pages back and forth and finger-rubbing the pictures, she sings and talks and laughs and kicks her legs in the air.

"You see that?" Grandma says, stabbing and pulling back her knitting needles. "Some kinds of moods she has! They change more often than the summer monsoon sky."

After a while, Inah sits up and blankly stares at the picture I am drawing—Mommy in a red coat with a big toothy smile and a blue flower in her hand.

"*Halmoni*," says Inah, turning to Grandma.

"What's the matter? Are you already bored looking at the pictures?"

"I am hot," Inah says.

"It's not so hot. Keep your clothes on if you don't want to catch cold."

"But I am hot," she says again, but Grandma just grunts. Inah gets up and goes over to the toy chest and pulls out a xylophone and a drumstick. She brings them over and sits down and starts banging away. The jangled notes she plucks out fly and spatter the walls and spray the warm and stuffy room like broken pieces of glass. On top of the potbellied iron stove, flared up in a red shimmery glow, the barley tea that Grandma sips all day like a fish starts boiling again in a big dented yellow aluminum teakettle. Coughing up clumps of thick white steam, hissing and shrieking like a stoned bird and rattling the lid in a rhythmic *click, clack.* The gray sky outside the window swells and sags lower and lower, and the room grows warmer and stuffier and gloomier. Glassy-eyed and looking sweaty and flushed in the face, Inah, peeled off down to her undershirt and long johns, recklessly bangs away at the xylophone.

"You're making a racket!" yells Grandma, getting up, as if she is hearing it only now. After turning on the light switch, Grandma goes over to the stove and pours cold water into the teakettle: Right away the shrieking bird goes quiet. Inah throws down the drumstick and asks Grandma if we're going to the bus stop to wait for Mommy.

"Look at the sky," Grandma says, picking up her knitting. "It's going to dump snow any minute."

Inah looks up at the window and says, "*Halmoni!* Look! It's snowing already!" Excited, Inah claps her hands. Grandma glances up at the window, where tiny snowflakes land, sticking.

"A few dancing flakes, that's all," Grandma says. "They will just dust the ground like dandruff and melt right off." Inah and I sit and watch white snowflakes float down. They get bigger and bigger, and soon they turn into a wet, dizzy flurry, pelting and streaking the window.

"*Halmoni,* it's snowing harder," Inah says. Grandma looks up again and says, "*Aiigoo!* I must be losing my mind! I've forgotten all about the laundry." She puts down her knitting, gets up and reties the belt around her ballooning *chima.* "I am going to bring the laundry in. Don't run around, and stay away from the stove!" Winding the knitted scarf around her neck, Grandma hurries out of the room. The door settles behind her with a tremble.

On the floor, Grandma's knitting on three bamboo needles rests like a squirrel, the ball of mauve yarn attached to it like a tail. Inah looks about and spots a doll's arm sticking out from behind the toy chest. She goes over, pulls it out and holds it up in front of her.

"You're a dirty, dirty baby," she says to the doll in her high-pitched voice, mimicking Mommy. She wets her finger and rubs at the doll's face, which is smudged all over with magic pen makeup.

"It's OK. I will take her to the bathhouse," I say, pulling at its torn jacket, which Grandma stitched up from an old scrap of cloth. The jacket falls apart at the seams and easily comes off in my hand.

"No, no, no! *I* am taking her to the bathhouse," Inah says, pulling back the doll. I grab its arm and yank at it hard. It comes off at the socket. Surprised, Inah looks at the now one-armed doll, turns around and darts up, clutching it. I throw down the arm and run after her.

"Give her to me! I want it," I shout.

"No, it's mine!" she shouts back. "She's *my* baby." Dragging the doll behind her, upside down, she runs to the other end of the room, turns, circles around the hissing and blazing stove. Shrieking and shrieking every time I come close to catching her. Going around and around in circles. Stopping once long enough to push the hair away from her sweaty face. Before long, I am hot and out of breath, and my head swims, and cheeks throb, but I keep running after her, strangely fixated on the doll Inah carelessly drags behind her along the floor. With her plaited black hair undone, her wide-open brown eyes fixed to the ceiling, and the one arm, twisted up and backward, scraping the floor, the doll looks miserable and frightened. She seems to be pleading for my help as she is being dragged away, and I am determined to rescue her.

But suddenly, a strange thing happens. I am stopped in

my tracks by a pair of clawed hands grabbing my ankles. I falter a little around my tangled feet. And then, I can't move. It's as though my feet are glued to the floor.

It happens the very moment Inah trips on the metal tray placed underneath the blazing iron stove. And all I do is just stand there frozen and watch as hot and cold shivers shoot up through my head in millions of tiny sparks of fireworks: Inah falling and tumble-landing on her knees as if after a bad somersault attempt; her hair flying out and over her.

As I watch, another thing happens. Like a fuse blowing out, a soft pop goes off in my head and everything goes very quiet. All the sound is lost and gone. And I keep standing there, watching and watching as everything in the room shifts. All at the same time. In no particular order. In a chaotic and jumbled but also very slowed-down and drawn-out movement. The aluminum teakettle holding the boiling barley tea atop the stove comes unhinged, as if tossed from underneath, and flies off into the air. It then slowly drifts back down. Bouncing in an undulating motion. Vomiting into the air jet-stream gulps of brown, steamy liquid, which jump in splashes of breaking waves and scatter in particles of a waterfall.

Then just as abruptly, sounds return again. The kettle crashes onto the floor, making a simple and light clanking sound. The fired metal of the stove hisses madly, burning off the black water marks, shriveling them fast in jagged patterns of worm-eaten leaves. The stovepipe above snaps at the joints in a loud thunder-crackling noise and comes crashing down only to halt at midway, dangling from a steel wire like a badly broken arm. Finally, the smell of something burning. Meat. Wool. Hair.

I look down. Next to the doll spread on its back, Inah is sitting crunched on the floor. Her small body is tightly curled over her knees, and she's frantically flailing her hands and arms about her face, which is covered with hair and spattered with scalding hot, brown barley tea. And she is howling and howling. It is the most awful sound I will ever hear—the howls she spits out. Ferocious, piercing and jagged-edged, they seem to be exploding out of her little bent-around body. Not out of her mouth. Splitting and tearing open her skin. I coil in terror, yet my mind still can't grasp what is happening. Just seconds before, we were two happy kids, the "winter twins" who will never catch cold, playing and running around the room.

Just at that moment, the door flings open, and Grandma charges in like a gale of wind. The armful of frozen laundry she carries falls and litters the floor like stiff dead bodies as she bounds across the room. She seems to be floating, although below her cotton-padded pants, her small feet paddle furiously. Her wrinkled walnut face is all bunched up, ugly and dark. From her eyes, red sparks shoot out. Her mouth hangs open as if her jaws are stuck. Her chalky white hair spreads out from her head like fine steel shreds. She is screaming and calling out to Inah, but all sound is lost to me again.

Grandma reaches down, scoops up howling Inah into her arms as ferociously as a vulture snatching its prey, and flies out of the room. Spilling the ends of the blanket she has piled on Inah. Forgetting to put on her shoes. Forgetting to close the door. Forgetting the whole world but Inah. Crying and screaming, I run after them, out of the room, out of the house to the snowy alley. But there is no trace of either one. It is as if Grandma has flown off into the narrow sky above. Carrying Inah in her thin, old, ropey arms.

FIVE

On the bus to Venice from the airport, Inah isn't much in the mood for talk. After a perfunctory "How's Mom and how's Dad?" she is silent as a wall. She keeps her head averted, her squinting eyes fixed on the murky, sun-shot bus window, which frames blurry pictures of single-story brick houses with flowerpots and small wrought-iron-fenced-in gardens.

Something about the scenery reminds me of the outskirts of Veracruz, where I spent a miserable week the first summer at NYU. Across the aisle, two middle-aged American couples, the only passengers other than us, are talking—they have that twangy Texas drawl—and laughing with that peculiar gaiety people on vacation develop. They are all dressed like plumed birds, even the men, in intense polyester pinks, turquoises and yellows.

"Oh, darn, Jimmy, I don't care what you think," says the thin, middle-aged woman whose bleached white hair is gathered up into a feather duster. She has a shrill, pinched, nasal voice that is grating to the ear. "Julie and I ain't gonna leave Venice without a gondola ride. I hear those gondolier boys are so darn cute!" They burst into laughter. Inah rolls her eyes and grunts.

The sun has all but burned through the morning fog when we get off the bus at Piazzale Roma. The narrow roads that peter away from the circle are throttled with noon traffic, and the air chokes with fumes. A little dazed by the heat, I hang back while Inah militantly heaves out Mom's ugly suitcase from the luggage compartment of the bus. She plunks it down and looks on impatiently as I adjust the straps of my backpack. Just then, out of the corner of my eye, I notice a stocky man in a tricolor shirt striding over in our direction.

"Miss, want water-taxi ride?" he says in a booming voice, raising his arm. He has a dark, sun-grizzled face with a bulbous nose punctuating the middle. Inah flashes me an angry, black look as if it were my fault. "Promise! You enter Venice like queens!" he declares in his oddly Brooklyn-accented English. What a great line, I think. Borrowed from an opera? But aren't we in Venice? Confused, I look at Inah. I can tell she isn't terribly impressed. She has heard that exact same phrase before. More than once.

"Don't be gullible, Yunah. It's BS. And we're walking," she says.

"What hotel you stay?" he says again. "Just tell me."

"No, *grazie*," Inah blurts out tersely and picks up the handle to Mom's suitcase. It must have been the glare of the sun. He is only now seeing Inah's face. A look of surprise flashes through his eyes. Then, as if he can't help himself, he briefly stares at her face, turns around and takes off up the road. Without another word. Huffing. I almost expect him to spit.

His blatant display of hostility catches me completely off guard, and I stand dumb and speechless. It doesn't matter how many times I've been through this sort of thing before. Indeed, how many times? More than enough. And I haven't forgotten any of that. I was there, wasn't I, when mean kids called Inah every imaginable name? And haven't I seen the looks on the faces of people, the hostile stares and furtive glances? But none of that helps, and it's something I never get used to. I am never prepared for the next time, and the hurt is always fresh. I am stunned, taken aback, helpless and angry. But more than anything, I feel stupid.

I manage to collect myself quickly enough, but Inah's already gone. I see her crossing the street, recklessly dragging Mom's suitcase by the handle through the swirling traffic and cacophony of horns. I can tell she's mad. Mad at herself for letting me talk her into this trap of a trip. Mad at me. I scramble and catch up with her at the foot of a high, arched bridge, encased in wooden scaffolds. She is furious. She can hardly bring herself to look at me.

"Inah, I . . . ," I fumble.

"Don't!" Inah blurts out with disgust in her thin splintery voice. "Just don't say a word." She grabs Mom's suitcase and hauls it up the steep steps of wooden planks. Halfway over the bridge, in despair, I stop and watch her stomp away. Black clouds follow her, hovering like seagulls tagging a fishing trawler. I know I shouldn't have come. But then I knew all along this was what was waiting for me. I knew we would fight because, with Inah, it's something as inevitable as death. But I was wistful. Just like Mom. And it's all too late. I can't simply turn around and go back home. I will just have to endure her. I asked for it.

I walk over to the side of the bridge to compose myself.

But how improbable! Suddenly, I realize I am looking at the famous Grand Canal. Belatedly feeling dizzy from the ceaseless motion of the water around me, I quickly swallow down the thick, sea-tangy air. And then, hypnotized, I stare at the vista that unfurls in front of me, so dazzling and so utterly unexpected; the listing and decaying buildings along the canal, the onion domes and orange rooftops, the boats and bridges, indescribably beautiful and splendid, awash in the sunlight, so opulent and yellow, and complemented by the sky, so immense and pastel blue; it's a painting drawn on a gigantic air balloon leisurely floating in the breeze. Leaning over through the scaffolds, I greedily drink up the sight, having forgotten Inah, the intense anger and the despair of just a moment ago.

"Are you coming or not?" Inah's impatient voice pulls me out of the delirious state of enthrallment. She has stopped at the end of the bridge. She looks listless and exasperated. Reluctantly, I walk over.

"Inah, it's the Grand Canal, isn't it? I wish you had told me."

"Well, what did you think it was?" she says, trying hard not to sound too mean, and starts down, recklessly pulling Mom's dinosaur of a suitcase behind her in a loud clunk. Off the bridge, not bothering to wait, she walks ahead, up the crowded embankment along the noisy canal, constantly bursting with the hiccups and groans of motors. The sun, a red, combustible flame, has now climbed to the center of the sky as if on a ladder, eating up all the shadows, and it's a carnival of golden sunlight. Everything looks phosphorous, the moving crowds, the green-and-white striped parasols shading the tables of sidewalk cafes and orange and yellow and blue streamers hanging outside the souvenir stalls. A warm, wet breeze lazily drifts over from the canal carrying a sharp

whiff of gasoline. Alongside Inah, Mom's mammoth suitcase rumbles and rattles on like a disgruntled child, threatening to career off on a broken wheel. Annoyed, Inah stops
and gives it a quick, violent jerk, as if that will do the trick.
She's still mad. It's going to be a very long trip.

SIX

There's no more gibbering and gibbering Inah. It has been like that for days, although I don't know how many because, without her, everything has become a shapeless blur. Now, in the morning, Grandma hastily stuffs my see-through vinyl bag with crayons and coloring books and picture books and snacks, and hurries me up the crooked alley to a two-leafed wooden gate. There she delivers me and my bag into the hands of a woman Grandma calls *wolnam ajooma*, Vietnamese Auntie. Then looking dazed but determined and galvanized, she hurries away back down the alley, stuffing back her slithery muffler, which is escaping from the collar of her coat. I don't know where she goes. I am too scared to ask her. I am too scared to ask about Inah or about Mommy and Daddy, who never seem to be around anymore ever since that snowy afternoon Grandma disappeared with Inah in her arms.

Every time Grandma hurries away, my head gets all

foggy and I get all breathless. I am scared that she will never come back to get me. I have to try very hard not to cry when I follow the Vietnamese Auntie inside. The wooden gate closes with a solemn squeak, and the auntie helps me over the high threshold of the sliding wooden door fitted with two milky glass panes, and we enter a rectangle courtyard, paved over in gray cement that smells like the wet moss on the cement tub at home in summer. It has the typical layout of a traditional Korean house, so everything looks very familiar, as if I've been here many times before; the tiled roofs, wooden beams, the shiny yellow color on the varnished wood, and the rice-papered doors with intricate wood patterns.

Before climbing up to the floor, the auntie helps me take off my silver shoes trimmed with fur, and I follow her into the dim room where a curtain printed with yellow flowers and spiky green leaves hangs over a small window. It's the room where I play alone every day and where I woke up the afternoon Grandma disappeared with Inah and cried and cried, making myself dizzy until the whole room was turning: The walls swelled out like a big skirt, and the ceiling spun up and down and up and down, slowly first and then faster and faster, making a whooshing sound.

The Vietnamese Auntie gently pulls me down to the floor and opens my see-through vinyl bag and takes out the coloring books, the box of broken crayons and a bag of marble-shaped cookies with peanuts inside that Inah likes so much. She pushes the things toward me. She looks stiff from cold. (She's not used to the cold, Grandma says, coming from a hot country.) Her hand is purple just like her lips on her face with dark, pitted skin, and her big, brown eyes seem sad from the memory of the hot sun.

She says something with a soft voice that has a pleasing

lilt. Maybe she's telling me to play. Even though I don't know what she's saying, I nod my head. I don't speak, because if I do, I will feel like crying, and once I start crying, I won't be able to stop. She pats me on the head and leaves the room, and I am all alone. Everything in the room is still. The corners where the walls meet, dark. The wall clock *tick-tocks* ceaselessly. Now and then, from the courtyard outside comes the muffled sound of the auntie's footsteps, the kitchen door sliding open and closing, basins clanking and water running. And once in a long while, someone passes by the lane outside, making that *psst, psst, psst,* sound of the Japanese girl ghost padding up and down the hallway at night in our house. And then it gets all quiet again. The quiet swells and grows and grows into a din, and then through it, I hear Inah screaming and screaming. I squeeze and twist the tin foil cookie bag, making the crinkle-and-crackle sound so I don't have to hear the swelling quiet of the room and Inah crying and screaming.

At some point each afternoon, the sun hits the window, flooding the dim room, and the curtain suddenly turns into a rippling green field specked with tiny yellow flowers. I spend a long, long time staring at the sun-splashed pasture. Then I fall asleep and dream of playing hide-and-seek with Inah in the very same field, magically expanded into a huge, rolling green meadow carpeted with buttercup-yellow flowers.

Inah has hidden herself, and I walk around and around looking for her among the clusters of flowers and dense leaves. At last, the sun starts going down, but Inah is still nowhere to be found, and I am getting more and more scared. I put my hands around my mouth and shout at the top of my voice: "Can't find you, *que-kko-ri!*" *Que-kko-ri* is the name of a Korean warbler, and that's what you are supposed to say when you can't find someone during hide-and-seek. Inah is then supposed to come out from hiding, but she doesn't. It's just me lost in the middle of the empty and darkening meadow. I wake up crying in the dark room. The sun has moved away from the window.

There are many more dreams. In one of them, Grandma takes us twins to the dumpling house, the one that's out on the boulevard, a couple of doors past the movie theater. She gets us a table wedged between a wall and a window that looks out onto the street, and orders our favorite steamed dumplings, stuffed with minced meat and clear noodles.

Soon, they arrive steaming in a bamboo basket shaped like a tambourine, lined with a cotton cloth. As we eagerly reach for them, Grandma gets up and says, "Eat slowly. I will be back soon." By the time we finish the dumplings, though, Grandma hasn't come back. We wait and wait. Then we go stand behind the window that looks out at the busy sidewalk. Next to the aluminum newspaper kiosk, a man sells plastic sandals. A grandma (not ours) is squatting on the sidewalk with a brown-beaded rosary draped over her hand, waiting for a bus that never comes. But no Grandma. So, Inah and I count the buses and taxis and sedan cars passing on the road, and wonder and wonder where she is.

After a long, long while, the dumpling house auntie comes over and asks us when Grandma is coming to get us. We don't know, we tell her. The auntie shouts toward the open kitchen in the back where her dimple-cheeked husband, his hair gone white from the flour dust, is beating and kneading a big lump of flour dough. The old lady must be in her second childhood, she says to him: She has forgotten all about her granddaughters.

After some more waiting, Inah and I tell the auntie we

are going home. We know the way, we assure her. Then you must walk straight home, she says, not stopping anywhere. Holding hands, Inah and I walk out and head up the sidewalk, turning into the side street by the theater, where it smells like wet papers and garbage. Back out in the street, we pass a dry cleaner, a hardware store, and the store where Grandma sometimes buys us strawberry milk in paper cartons and yellow melons in the summer. At the third alley to the left, Inah and I turn and race to the wooden kitchen door that opens right smack into the lane, and bang at it, making the milky panes rattle. We wait and then pound at it again. Finally, from inside comes the sound of Grandma's shuffling feet in her rubber shoes.

Grandma drags open the kitchen door, looks at me and shouts, "Why are you alone?! What did you do with your sister?" I turn around. Inah is not there.

SEVEN

One morning, instead of packing my see-through vinyl bag, Grandma asks me if I would like to go see Inah. She's all dressed up in her brown wool coat, and a shiny, slithery scarf, printed in brown and silver swirls, is wound around her neck. I don't say anything because I am not sure if I would like to go see Inah. But Grandma doesn't really care. She doesn't care whether I would like to do anything, because she's all scrambled in the head. That's what she says, she's all scrambled in the head when I ask her about anything: Don't bother to ask me about anything, I am all scrambled in the head.

Grandma brings over my coat and stuffs my arms into the sleeves. Then she says she can't find my mittens, so I will have to wear Inah's instead. But I don't want to wear her mittens. She is fussy about not mixing our things. She will get mad when she sees me wearing them. And I don't want to get her mad. She will throw a temper tantrum and cry. I don't want to ever hear her cry again.

"Tough!" Grandma snaps. "I can't spend the whole morning looking for them. They look the same anyway. Inah won't know." But she is wrong; Inah's mittens are attached to a blue string, not to a red one like mine. "So you take them off before you go in to see her. That way, she won't see you wearing them. How's that?"

'No, no," I protest.

"I'm telling you you are not going without them," Grandma says. "It's freezing outside. If you catch cold, whom do you think your mother's going to blame? Me! And as it is, I've got enough blame to last me a lifetime."

After a sharp spanking or two on the bottom, I sniffle all the way to the bus stop. It's bright and cold. Big icicles are hanging from the eaves of the shops we pass. They look like glass swords and sparkle plenty in the sunlight. Inah likes to lick them, pretending they are ice-cream sticks.

At the bus stop, Grandma takes out her coin purse and counts out our bus fare into her dry, cracked palm. She's not wearing gloves. She wipes her nose with the white, wrinkled ball of a handkerchief and puts it back into her coat pocket. Down the street, on the sunless, black sidewalk in front of the movie theater, cart vendors stand all scrunched, stamping their frozen feet.

"Keep your mittens on," Grandma says when we settle down inside the unheated bus. Soon, Grandma is sleeping to the jolting rhythm of the bus, her arms folded over and her wrinkled mouth hanging open. I pull my hands out of the mittens, letting them hang down the front of my coat on the string. I climb up the seat and watch the buildings, cars, people and gray, bare trees fly by the bus window, slipping and sliding backward, practicing the moonwalk, as if they are all wearing soft-soled shoes. Grandma's snore roars up like thunder, and then she's quiet again.

The bus turns and joins the sea of traffic circling around the East Gate. Through the bus window, the roofed gate pirouettes round and round, as if on a rotating plate. I slide back down to the seat and look at Grandma. She's still sleeping.

"*Halmoni,* wake up!" I shake her arm as the bus jolts to a stop, sending us lurching forward. Grandma flings her eyes open like push-out windows and looks out.

"*Aiigo!* We're getting off!" Grandma grabs my hand and dashes up the aisle toward the front door. "Watch your step!" she says, picking her way down the steps. I hop down and jump, landing behind her. The automatic bus door shuts with a *whoosh* and I feel a quick tug at the mitten's string, slung around my neck. I turn and look: One of the mittens is caught in the door of the bus, slowly pulling away from the curb. I tug at the string but quickly let go, shrinking at the sharp burning on my palm. And the other mitten is gone too, flung off my shoulder. I then stumble around my tangled feet and land hard on my palms, scraping the cold cement curb.

"*Halmoni!*" I scream, pointing at Inah's mitten on a string, flying along the speeding bus like a kite, like a small waving hand. Grandma turns around and bleats. Suddenly, her arms are all over, pulling and dragging me up to the sidewalk.

"Are you hurt? Are you hurt? Tell me!" Grandma shouts in her frantic, shrill voice. She jerks me around, checking my face and hands. I shake my head even though my palms are raw and throbbing. "Are you sure? Look at me!" I look up at her. Her face is whiter than white chalk, and she's trembling.

Grandma is still shaking and muttering when we start across the road. Her muffler has spilled out of her coat collar and hangs down the front. And she is squeezing my hand so tight that she's going to break my fingers. After crossing the street, Grandma stumbles toward the bottom of the steep hospital driveway and collapses against the low stone wall hugging the hospital garden. She is all scrambled in the head again because she has that look in her eyes when she pulls me into her arms. "*Aigoo, aigoo!*" she squeals, sobbing over my head smothered inside her arms. "Why don't I die? Why don't I die now? If I live any longer, I'm going to end up having both of you maimed or killed. . . ."

We stand there a long, long time against the icy stone wall. Dwarfed by the tall, crooked pines, the hilly hospital garden, and the bright, blue sky. It's so cold, it hurts to breathe, and inside my fur-trimmed shoes, my toes are turning numb.

"Don't say anything to your mother," Grandma says when we are finally walking up the driveway to the hospital. "She doesn't need one more thing to worry about."

From the doorway, Inah in the hospital bed looks so very tiny. Like a leaf floating in a sea of white. White sheets. White walls. White metal frames. White is the color of snow.

"Go in," Grandma whispers sternly, nudging me on the shoulder, but my feet are stuck again, glued to the floor. I see Mommy sitting on a chair by Inah's bed. I haven't seen her for days. She comes home late every night, long after I go to bed, and leaves again early in the morning before I get up. She must hear Grandma because she turns her head. She looks strange, puffy in the eyes and all stiff in the face. She waves me over. Only she doesn't smile.

I walk, making small, careful and tentative steps. It seems to take forever to reach Inah's bed. Bit by bit, Inah's face comes into focus and I see it's all bandaged up, except an eye and the tip of her nose and a sliver of her lower lip. They have her hands tied to the bed rails in gauze strips so she won't touch her face. There are reddish bruises on her wrists where the cloth rubs against them.

I inch closer and stop by the bed rail. I am barely tall enough to reach over it. Inah looks over, steadily fixing her one exposed eye on me. Her long black lashes are wet and hold tiny dewdrops at the tips. I feel anxious and shy. The room is a vacuum with all the air and sound sucked out. I can't think of anything to say to Inah. It scares me. Her one eye. Staring and staring. Unblinking. It's a dark black button on her bandaged face.

"Your sister is here." Leaning over, Grandma tenderly whispers to Inah in her raspy voice, "Remember you asked for her?" Inah lets out a sad whimper. "You want her to come later?" Grandma asks, and Inah turns her head away, bleating, and jerks her arms, pulling at the straps and shaking the bed rail. I am frightened. The sound of her crying sends me rolling and tumbling back into a sea of thick, black fog. Mommy leaps to her feet. She bends over Inah, pats her, trying to calm her down. Inah cries on anemically in a weak, scratchy voice. She won't look at me again. Mommy says we better go. Inah's upset. She's not ready to see Yunah.

Grandma grabs hold of my hand and pulls me away. She rushes me out of the room and into the hallway with gray linoleum floors and lime-colored walls and on to the waiting area, where the sunlight is blinding. Without ever letting me stop. Outside the window, the sky is a speckless bright blue. Blue is Inah's favorite color, I remember. I remember all of her and our favorite things.

PART TWO

ONE

On a hazy, steady-rain afternoon in June, Inah and I are planted in the backseat of a lemon-green Hyundai taxi, plowing through the traffic and rain puddles to Kimpo International Airport. Just seven years old, toothpick skinny, and swimming in our stiff, brand-new clothes from the South Gate Market in Seoul: bumblebee shirts, jelly-bean red pants and blue jean jackets.

Mommy sits in the front with the driver, who resembles a sea captain in a white shirt, white cotton gloves and a white cap. (On his white, blade-lined shirtsleeve, an epaulette is stitched, saying MODEL DRIVER.) She is stiff-shouldered like a mannequin and looks tense, tightly clutching the half-circle handles of a paisley-patterned fake Gucci bag on her lap. Staring hard into the blank page that is the future, through the rain-streaming taxi window where busybody windshield wipers work nonstop, clearing a twin set of folding fans. Ahead of us, the squash yellow Hyundai

Pony with Daddy crawls through the traffic, carrying our
rain-splattered brand-new suitcases in the trunk. We can
see the lid, held down with a rope, bounce up and down,
dripping water, like a crocodile's jaw clamping down on its
prey.

We're emigrating to America. Leaving everything
behind: the old Japanese matchbox house; the one Mommy
calls "the bad-luck house"; Grandma at the apple orchard in
the countryside; and all the good and bad memories that
will take years to congeal. Severing all ties, as if that were
possible. Putting all the persistent and insistent memories
on hold. We are leaving. For many new beginnings. For a
spit-shined bright, everything-possible, desires-to-reality
future. In America. Foremost and all, for Inah, whose face
below the straight paintbrush bangs is permanently disfig-
ured with burn scars. Because a girl like her has no future in
Korea. In America, she will go to the best schools, and
become all that she can be. Definitely NOT in the U.S.
Army, but an astronaut, maybe, in a silver-white space suit,
a scientist, maybe, in a sparkling lab, and even a veterinarian
in a zoo! But most of all, in America, kids won't call her
names (there are only good kids in America) and people
won't stare at her face on the streets and cluck their tongues
in pity. And in "God-blessed" America, the land of uncom-
mon miracles, she might even get a new face. Mommy says
all this, whispering, lest any jealous god or ghost might hear
it. And as if it's not yet safe to voice hopes.

But Inah and I, who inhabit a tiny world made up of
small, concrete and immediate-resulting things, don't grasp
the meaning of leaving. We are just two impressionable,
moldable, formless children excited about a plane trip to
America. Too young for regrets or sorrows. Too young to
have a sense of history, of belonging and of country. Even

the memory of all that has happened for now is all but forgotten, too, pushed into the place where memory goes for a
long hibernation to reemerge later.

Instead, with a child's delight, we marvel at the imposing
sight of the huge tanks parked around City Hall plaza in
downtown Seoul where the fountain is spewing up tall gray
columns of water. Unaware that it has been a bloody spring
in Korea and that, barely a month ago, the lives of hundreds
of people were ruthlessly snuffed out in a horrible bloodbath
in a city called Kwangju in the south—a place more remote
in our consciousness than America. And blessedly oblivious
of that sense of fear and foreboding that hangs over the wet,
grainy capital under martial law, slip-sliding by the rain-
spattered taxi window.

To Inah and me, for years to come, 1980 will simply
mean the year we left Korea and emigrated to America.
Until we start to remember and begin to understand and
sort out the meaning. Only then would we guess that at that
very moment, Daddy, in the other taxi, wasn't feeling
excited like us, but very sad. Leaving the country where he
was born and had lived for fifty years on account of such
small, selfish reasons: mere personal gain and happiness.
Fleeing the country others were willing to give their lives
for. To live like a refugee in another country, one eye always
looking homeward the rest of his life. How as the taxi
passed the Ducksoo Palace, Daddy was thinking of us, how
Inah and I would never get to grow up and appreciate the
beauty of the tall, very tall, vermilion wooden gates and the
swirling roof lines; the beauty that every Korean should
appreciate without trying, as it runs in our blood.

Inah gets excited as we get nearer to the airport. Now, on
both sides of the rain-slicked highway, it is miles of nothing
but rice paddies, a carpet of vivid green in the rain, disap-

pearing toward the foggy horizon. Inah loudly wonders how our plane will find its way. The sky doesn't have paved roads or traffic signals or road posts arrow-pointing to America. She worries that our plane might fall down from the sky when it gets too tired after staying up there too long.

Inside the airport building with tall gymnasium ceilings, in a mad confused rush, Inah and I fly alongside Mommy across a huge room flooded with pale green fluorescent lights, past steep-slide escalators, rows of identical seats, automatic open-shut doors, parades of moving feet and ginger-ale-colored faces. Anxious, and disoriented by the zinging microphone voices and the bee-in-the-sac hums. Daddy wheels a cart where mammoth-sized suitcases crammed with everything we own perch precariously on top of one another, dwarfing him behind it.

"Stay close," Mommy says in her unreal-sounding voice that escapes us like pieces of ripped paper thrown in the wind. Instinctively, Inah and I reach for each other's clammy hands and hook our fingers. Daddy parks the cart at the tail end of a long line where a crush of people and suitcases and carts spread out like wiggly octopus legs.

Later, standing outside the departure gate, ringed by relatives and family friends who have come to see us off, the corners of Mommy's mouth crumble, and before we know it she is sobbing.

"Why does she cry, Daddy?"

"She is sad."

"Oh?!"

Mommy sobs on, and her shoulders jerk. Puzzled and anxious, Inah and I tightly clutch her crepe de chine skirt, which collapses in our hands like puffed-up, hollow-inside bread.

"No more tears! You're scaring the children," scolds

Mommy's brash cousin with a stiff bouffant hairdo, pushing up her brown-tinted butterfly sunglasses way too big for her face. She hands Mommy a stiff white handkerchief that reeks of naphthalene mothballs. "It's not like you're going to a place of no return!

"Besides, it's now the jet age. Not like the old days. Everything's easy now. You can always come back for a visit. And you're leaving for your children. You should be happy instead of being sad like this." Mommy tries to smile, but her mouth crumbles again. Daddy looks away.

"How true! Wipe your tears and go in before it's too late and you miss the plane. I'm not coming out to the airport to see you off again! Traffic is so bad. Ha, ha." Mommy jabs her eyes dry with the stiff handkerchief.

"Now you, Inah and Yunah. You have to grow up to do great things and make your parents proud. And don't ever forget you're Korean." We nod. Daddy says we should get going. Mommy pulls at the innocent straps of our book bags, which are loaded down with books she picked for us from our *Complete Children's Collection of Great People's Life Stories:* of Helen Keller, Madame Curie, Joan of Arc, Florence Nightingale and Yu Kwan Soon, the Korean girl patriot. Mommy turns and waves and waves until the automatic door shuts on her face. Then as we hurry through the departure ramp in a last-minute dash, her eyes start brimming with tears again.

Somewhere over the Pacific, the novelty of flying for the first time wears off for Inah and me, and the restless long hours turn into a blur. Leaving only fragmented memories of the striped airline blankets and the scratchy pillows, slipped off and lying scattered and bunched at our feet; of the blue plastic meal trays that come with minipackets of salt and pepper and Coffee-mate; of the vaguely nauseating smell of warmed-over meals; of the *ding-ding* sounds that go off with the seat-belt signs; of Mommy's puffy eyes; and of Daddy tossing and turning, trying to get comfortable in his sleep.

By the time the plane touches down in Anchorage for a stopover, Inah and I have completely lost all sense of time and place. (This lack of a sense of place will follow us for years.) Disoriented and carrying our buzzing heads and wobbly legs, we walk with Mommy and Daddy around the Anchorage Airport. We stand in front of a tall glass display case and point at the gigantic roaring Alaskan grizzly bear. At the snack bar, we make Daddy spend precious dollars for tempura udon to fish up a few fat, bloated strands of noodle from the Styrofoam cups with the splintery wooden chopsticks. Then we troop upstairs to the lookout lounge. Outside the tall glass wall, predawn Alaska stands as an immense blue sky and majestic walls of snowcapped mountains. Windswept. Still in prehistoric time. Moonstone blue, cerulean blue and periwinkle. Inah and I stare out in awed silence.

For the rest of the flight, from Alaska all the way to New York, Inah and I sleep, dead to the world. Squished like insects between Mommy and Daddy, breathing in the sour sweat smell of the striped blankets. Dreaming no dreams. Floating through a sea of blue. When Mommy wakes us up, we're circling over rainy New York. Mommy says it's midnight, and we'll have to hurry. She fusses over us, combing our hair and smoothing out the wrinkles in our clothes. But Inah and I can barely keep our eyes open.

Dazed, after the hurried walk through a long, endless corridor in tight-feeling shoes, after the immigration and the customs inspections, Inah and I follow Mommy and

Daddy and the luggage out of the automatic sliding door. Never noticing the famous Emma Lazarus poem engraved on the bronze panel that graces the wall we pass by. The poem Inah and I will later read out loud through the murky and scratched Plexiglas partition, and puzzle about its meaning as we wait for our jet-lagged relatives to arrive from Korea (with bird-nest spots on the back of their heads, missed in the last-minute combing, and the smell of stale airline food and bathroom cologne on their clothes just like us, but carrying genuine Gucci bags with them and dressed in much nicer clothes than us):

Give me your tired, your poor,
Your huddled masses yearning to breathe free,
The wretched refuse of your teeming shore.
Send these, the homeless, tempest-tost to me,
I lift my lamp beside the golden door!

TWO

In Venice, it rains every day. In intermittent downpours and soundless drizzles. Everything turns damp and soggy; the mildewed walls, crumpled sheets and wrinkled clothes. Venice transforms into a water-clogged, dank and dark and moody catacomb, floating in the lurching and churning, sloshing and murmuring water. At the flooded Piazza San Marco, tourists are seen wading around in knee-deep water.

I am afraid Inah's mood isn't much better than the weather. One minute, as though holding inside her a whole angry black sea, barely containable, she is tense, irritable, bristling and sarcastic, and the next, paralyzed with lethargy, she's glum and quiet and looks as alive as a gutted fish. She still resents it, the trip Mom and I literally forced on her (she acts as if it's the last thing she wants to be doing), but it has to be more than that. It is something she isn't willing to put, or capable of putting, into words. So she is just going to make it maddeningly difficult and torturous for both of us.

I knew better and should have known better, but it's still such a huge disappointment to me. To find her at the same struggling place. I'd thought and hoped, in my naiveté, that after all that traveling and wandering she would have found some peace, having arrived at that inner place of calm. Obviously, I was wrong. If anything, her struggle seems even more tortured and intense.

So stuck together and with nothing better to do, Inah and I chug on joylessly in rainy Venice. Under the limp and water-smudged sky. Shapeless in rain ponchos we buy from a store on busy Lista di Spagna. Tracing and retracing our steps, over rain-streaked bridges, up and down the echoing, cold and shiny marble stairs of museums and palazzi, and entering and leaving dim, musty churches. Trying to concentrate on the exterior and not to get on each other's nerves. Like a long, unhappily married couple who grudgingly put up with each other's nonsensical behavior just to keep peace.

But it doesn't always work. In the morning, after a shower, Inah slips into a T-shirt, jeans and soggy sneakers, and she's ready to get out the door. So she sits and fumes over having to wait for me. She can barely hide her contempt at the way I dress, or the makeup I put on. Are you really wearing that, she says, or rolls her eyes when I dab lipstick or apply a quick coat of mascara. I laugh it off. Just to keep the peace (which has quickly become my mantra in Venice). It goes more or less the same way for the rest of the day, with her goading and kneading and uttering sarcastic and curt remarks. She just can't help herself.

That's what I find most depressing—that no matter how hard she tries or we try, there's no escaping from what happened. There is going to be no ending to this struggle Inah's locked into. And it's as though I've come all the way here merely to reconfirm that.

But sometimes, walking with her across a rain-drumming piazza or standing on a vaporetto traversing the swollen and gray Grand Canal where rain is sometimes like fog, the reality hits me with such crushing sadness that all I want to do is just disappear. Run away from her. As far away as I can. Because it's too much to witness her struggle up so close. But running away is not even an option for me. I simply have no right to do that to her or Mom. So I will just have to stay and take whatever she gives me. It's the price I have to pay. Again and again. But isn't it such a small price to pay compared to what she has gone through and is going through and will go through?

THREE

Flushing is a sea. A baptismal sea that churns out New Americans. It admits a constant influx of new people, not so much from other parts of America as from the rest of the world, people who come from other continents across seas and deserts and rivers and over mountains. You see them everywhere in Flushing. On the subway. On the street. At stores. The new people. You can always tell them right away from the way they dress or wear their hair; or from the language they speak or the subtle scents they carry; or from other such myriads of small things. Some carry their villages in their walk, and others wear the terrain they come from on their faces. As unmistakable as their hard-to-erase accents.

It never ceases to amaze me that they all find their way and manage to build a new life here. It seems a miracle that they all somehow survive. Some of them come here with nothing. Nothing but memories and a dream and a will. Some smuggled in as stowaways on a ship. So awfully unpre-

pared. But even they manage. Most of them, anyway. They
find places to live. They find work. They put food on the
table for their families. They buy their first TV set. Their
first dining-room table. Their first car. Their first apartment
or house. And their children start school, and are on their
way to becoming Americans. It's nothing special. Really. As
they say, people do it every day. And so many people have
done it before them. And so many will do it, long, long after
them. And after all, we did that. There's no mystery at all.
Remember? Once we were that new people on the street,
shopping for our first whatever, and once we were the kids
on the street in our fresh-off-the-boat clothes. But I don't
remember how we did it. It was our parents' responsibility to
put food on the table, to buy that first TV set and the first
house. All Inah and I had to do was grow up.

The summer we arrived in America, we temporarily stayed
with Uncle Shin's family in their white house in Bayside.
That's where we had our very first July Fourth. I still
remember the hazy afternoon. The backyard with the sloping green lawn edged by a huge rhododendron bush. The
sticky heat. The hot sun. The smell of smoke and the mari-
nated beef sizzling on the grill in the deck off the swimming
pool. The smoke hung in the warm afternoon air, mingling
with the sound of us kids running around barefoot and frol-
icking and screaming in the swimming pool.

Everyone was there, everyone who would form our
loosely connected American family. Us and Uncle Shin's
family. There also was Auntie Minnie, a distant relative
from Daddy's side, her husband, Uncle Wilson, and their
eight-year-old son, Jason Wilson. By then, Uncle Wilson, a
sleepy-eyed, scrawny, electric-pole-tall twenty-one-year-old
GI with a towering Afro in their wedding pictures from

more than a decade before, had become huge, at least it seemed to us, having steadily spread sideways since his GI days. He was a subway conductor with the appropriate voice that boomed like a blaring trumpet. Inah immediately took a shine to him that day, for the pure novelty of him being the only *real* American among us, and to girl-pretty Jason Wilson latching on to them like a leech.

Inah shimmied around Uncle Wilson, getting a ride on his shoulder, *heh-heh*ing. And when she climbed onto the tongue-shaped blue rubber float, lying flat on her stomach bloated with the Coca-Cola she'd downed all afternoon from a tall cylindrical plastic glass, Inah, without knowing how to speak English, somehow enlisted Jason to push the float for her from behind while she arm-paddled around the pool. Squealing with delight and shouting, "Oh-kay, Oh-kay," and dodging Cousin Ki-hong and Cousin Ki-sun—they spoke funny, chopped-off Korean—who were playing treasure-hunting divers wearing Day-Glo goggles and black rubber flippers.

In a picture taken that day, all the children, a motley crew of nine, are gathered in the front row. Blue-lipped and teeth chattering, Inah, in an orange-and-yellow-swirl two-piece swimsuit, has squeezed herself next to Jason Wilson. She's wearing white-rimmed plastic sunglasses, far too large for her face, and a big toothy grin. Next to her, Jason stands, looking squashed, his smooth, olive-skinned face solemn and serious. Behind her, Uncle Wilson towers like a big oak tree. His two big hands are placed on Inah's shoulders to stop her from fidgeting. And next to Jason stand Uncle Shin's two sons, Cousin Ki-hong and Cousin Ki-sun, in wet swim trunks sticking around their legs. And then finally me, in shorts and a tank top, squinty and looking confused, barely making it into the frame.

That's what I mostly remember about our very first summer in America: being confused and disoriented. Maybe it was only natural, having been suddenly yanked away from familiar surroundings. Maybe it had to do with the fact that it was summer and we were yet to start school. Hot and sunny days went by, loosely strung together in a shapeless medley, and I felt haunted with this sensation of slowly floating toward nowhere, which of course I couldn't even begin to articulate. I remember, though, constantly asking Dad or Mom where we were and where we were going, like someone who had suddenly lost all sense of direction.

And it seemed we were always going somewhere that summer. On foot. Following our parents around Flushing, where the crowded streets looked strangely somnolent on hot afternoons. And in Uncle Shin's shiny, black, air-conditioned Cadillac with everything automatic and plush blue leather seats that smelled new. Inah wouldn't miss the chance to ride in it for the world. Whenever Uncle Shin came to take Dad to look at used cars that summer, elbowing me in the arm, Inah would climb into the back.

Then on the way, she would listen in as Uncle Shin—he was even then a self-appointed expert on America—explained to Dad how things worked here, saying how in America, we do things this way and that. Then he would hold up his tubby thumb and say how in America, money is king and without money, you are nobody. Dad would always quietly listen to him and say, smiling, "You have an incurable American disease." Inah, all razzle-dazzled, would break into their conversation and chirp, "Uncle this" and "Uncle that," ingratiating herself.

Later, walking around the steamy used-car lots, squinting in the sun, among the rows of glinting and immobile used cars between Uncle Shin and Dad, Inah would ask them how they liked this car and that. The prices marked on the scratchy windshields in Magic Marker, of course, had no actual meaning to Inah or me. Uncle Shin, who had a big head, mostly bald except for a few strands of long hair that he'd carefully comb across the shiny pate, and a big puffy red face that made him look like he was a little short of breath, always carried a small brown leather bag, which dangled from his pinkie as he walked around with his arms behind his back. And for some reason, in the summer heat, he wore a turquoise-and-pink iridescent jogging suit. It made swishing noises as he strolled ahead of us, leaving behind a trail of the too sweet smell of the eau de cologne he was known to apply liberally. Inah followed him and giggled, covering her mouth every time he pointed at a car with his chin and said it was nothing but a "*tong cha*," literally a "shit car."

A few times that summer, Auntie Minnie and Uncle Wilson took us and Jason sightseeing in their big, old, faded electric blue Bonneville. It was trimmed with shiny chrome fenders, and I remember the afternoons when we returned home, all hot and tired, in the back of the baking car, which Uncle Wilson drove like a sailboat, sitting sloped sideways at the steering wheel, his left arm leaning out the open window. Often soul music was droning on drowsily from the car radio. And from the backseat, I could always smell Uncle Wilson's musty aftershave and Auntie Minnie's menthol cigarettes, which she smoked one after another, holding them pinched between her two fat fingers tipped with press-on nails, all the while patting down her frizzy, bleached permed hair pinned to the top of her head, spread out like bird plumes.

We must have been coming back from the Bronx Zoo the afternoon Auntie Minnie pointed out Central Park and the horse carriages we were passing. In the sky just over the tree lines of the park, a huge August moon, full, hazy and orange, was hanging. I remember sticking my head out the window and watching it follow us, slipping behind the tall glass buildings and out again in the slivers of sky between side streets as cars, honking, bumped past us like a stream down the wide avenue. Tall buildings with flags, and yellow and red, sun-melted, Jell-O–like windows flew by. People swelled like waves along the sidewalks cut by deep, black shadows.

No matter where we went that summer, the terrain was always new and unfamiliar. The sounds ambivalent and the smells foreign. It was as though I was always seeing things through haze: Everything looked somewhat blurry and fuzzy, disjointed and jumbled. And so puzzled that Inah's face had remained the same, I'd obsessively and compulsively check it. I had been sure that it was going to become new the moment we stepped off the plane in America. Like magic. We would say abracadabra and Inah's face would be new again. Just like that. I don't remember what it was that made me finally realize that, even in America, she wasn't going to get a new face.

But Inah was a happy and chirpy and intensely animated presence that summer. She was so relentlessly upbeat that Uncle Shin even nicknamed her "Sunshine." And, she was in love with Jason. The late afternoons when we returned home from sightseeing she always sat in the middle, between Jason and me, and played endless rounds of paper-scissors-rock with him, being thrown about, sliding up and down the oatmeal-colored, cracked backseat. Her bony back always obstinately turned to me, she would pull at his arms and beg him, "Play, play," and repeat, "Oh- kay? Oh-kay!" Jason, looking hot and all bothered and tired, would finally scream and bury his face in his hands and say, "No, no, no."

But Inah, laughing and giggling and still undaunted, would climb onto his back and try to pry his hands away, singing to him, "Yes, yes. Play. Oh-kay?"

I always felt vaguely sad and rejected during the ride back home. That must be why I still remember it so vividly: row houses with small backyards and quiet and deserted tree-lined streets, and tall buildings with their windows on fire from the sun that I saw flying past the car window. And a big blue sky with white feather clouds that floated along. In endless reels.

That summer, Inah was also what they call an ass-kisser. She would try so hard to ingratiate herself to everyone around her. Okay-ing and kowtowing. Strangely docile even to Cousin Ki-hong and Cousin Ki-sun, who seemed to decide it was more fun to scare her than to play treasure-hunters in the pool.

They would repeatedly dive in and roar out of the water behind her like sea monsters, and Inah, squealing with fright and delight, would furiously paddle away on the float. Then Cousin Ki-hong and Cousin Ki-sun would catch up to her, grab the end of the float and push it around, this way and that, shaking it and jiggling it. Inah, trying desperately to hang on, would say, in her fake, singsong voice, "Oh-kay! Oh-kay!" and they would make fun of her, saying, "*Anyah,* OK," "Not OK," and cruelly flip her over, repeatedly dumping her into the pool.

Inah, who couldn't swim, would go down and come up, frantically flailing her arms and spitting water out of her mouth. From the look in her eyes, I could tell she was scared out of her mind, but she wouldn't scream or make any sound. She would just try to stay afloat, blinking her eyes and gurgling. Trying all the time to look like she was having the time of her life. I would run along the edge of the pool, screaming to Cousin Ki-sun to get her out of the water. Cousin Ki-sun would pretend he didn't understand me. He would put his hand behind his ear and say, "*Moo-soon mal?*" "What are you saying?" and laugh. I would keep screaming and hollering and stamp my feet as Inah desperately struggled to stay afloat.

Finally, Cousin Ki-sun would grab her by the scruff of her neck like she was a drowning puppy and push her to the edge of the swimming pool. Frantic and looking like a sewer rat, she would scramble and climb out, dazed, her face plastered with wet dripping hair, her lips blue, and her eyes red. As Inah stood doubled over, retching and coughing, all goose-bumped and her teeth chattering uncontrollably, Cousin Ki-sun would stagger around holding his skinny, ripple-lined belly, laughing and laughing and pointing at her. But Inah was willing to go through it all over again. Just so she could paddle around on the float.

Then we moved to our own place in an old apartment building on Bowne Street in Flushing. We had hardly any furniture, and the rest of the summer we lived out of suitcases and ate and slept on the floor, Korean-style. Mom seemed to be constantly cleaning, scrubbing down the walls and floors, turning the old apartment inside out. In the living room, Dad often sat cross-legged on the old parquet floor, hunched over the Korean newspapers he'd go out and buy. We'd hear him saying, "Hmm, hmm," as he drew circles here and there with a leaking ballpoint pen in the Help Wanted section.

Inah, so excited about living in an apartment, would ride the elevator up and down or go to the hallway and ring the doorbell, calling in her trilling voice, "Hullo. Hullo." She would also spend endless hours with her elbows planted on the sill, looking down at the street below from the window of our eighth-floor apartment. Kicking her legs and humming. And every afternoon, on top of the kitchen counter, like a tireless parrot, the portable cassette player blared the "Listen and Repeat" English conversation lessons we had brought from Korea. We hardly listened to them, but Mom never stopped putting them on.

Some time that summer, we rode along with Dad in the noisy, mini, plum-colored, dented Ford his driving instructor drove. It was a sweltering afternoon, but we couldn't open the windows as all the handles were missing, and for some reason, the seats in the back where we were riding were ripped up and the springs kept poking at our legs. The instructor, a Korean man who wore extra-thick-lensed glasses that kept slipping off his skinny nose, was a self-proclaimed devout Christian. In the car, he kept a picture of Jesus nailed on the cross. It dangled from the rearview mirror, and Inah and I couldn't help notice it, because every time the car hit a bump, Jesus seemed to writhe in such terrible pain. Dad wasn't too fond of him because, like so many other Koreans he'd meet in Flushing, he tried to talk him into becoming a Christian, a God's child, as he called it. One day Dad finally told him he was a Buddhist, even though he wasn't really. After that, he talked to Dad only when it was necessary to teach him how to drive.

He drove us to a flat, low-lying area in the shadow of the electric-purple Shea Stadium. It was intersected with gritty, industrial-looking streets lined with body shops and used auto parts yards that sold hubcaps and used tires. It must have been Sunday afternoon, because the streets were completely deserted and all the shops were closed. As we drove by, behind the padlocked chain-link fences, vicious-looking, sharp-fanged dogs jumped and barked. Inah and I had to get out of the car and wait at the curb of a stinky, oil-blackened street, blasted by the white afternoon sunlight, while Dad practiced left, right and U-turns, up and down the street. It would be a while before it would dawn on us that Dad wasn't going to be driving a black, shiny Cadillac like Uncle Shin. At least, not any time soon.

Then one day, our first summer in America came to an abrupt end. It was the day Auntie Minnie and Uncle Wilson took us to see the Statue of Liberty. Inah was super-hyper, and mean all day, pushing and pinching, as we waited in the long lines in the blistering heat.

On the ride home in the afternoon, Inah and Jason fell asleep in the back of the car. I remember that Inah was wearing a sleeveless blue dress that day, ruffled around the armholes and skirt hems, and she looked like a crumpled blue flower, sleeping slumped like a half-empty barley sack with her hot, sweaty head crushed against my arm. Next to her on the other side, slouched sideways with his head on the hot window, Jason was out cold too, with a frown on his soft and smooth brown face, prettier than any pretty girl's, like he was having a bad dream. I remember sitting very still and trying to stay awake so as not to disturb Inah. Then, I too fell asleep.

Some time later, we all woke up to the sound of Auntie Minnie and Uncle Wilson arguing in the front of the car. To my sleepy head, it sounded like firecrackers going off, the way Auntie Minnie was yelling and screaming. And then suddenly, it was Uncle Wilson whose thunderous roar made us jump up like jackrabbits, disoriented and frightened. Not knowing English, we had no idea what the fight was about. We just sat without a peep, hoping it would stop, while they went on arguing at the top of their voices. Instead, Uncle Wilson began hissing and pounding the steering wheel with the palm of his hand, and Aunt Minnie went on yelling and cursing in Korean and English. All at the same time.

Jason sat hunched over, his hands pressed over his ears and his eyes tightly crushed shut. Scared, Inah and I held on to the edge of the cracked vinyl seat, melting in the sunlight that was blasting in through the window. Traffic was heavy. We could hear cars honking. Then outside the window, we saw the Korean furniture store where, with our parents, we had gone to look at a dining table once. We were almost home!

But just as we turned onto Bowne, Auntie Minnie angrily rubbed out the cigarette in the car ashtray, picked up a tissue box from the floor and threw it at Uncle Wilson. I remember Uncle Wilson swerving the car toward the front of our apartment building. He flung the door open, jumped out and stomped around. Terrified, Inah and I fast-peeled our sweaty legs off the seats, scrambled out and ran to the doorway of our apartment house. When we looked back, Uncle Wilson was trying to pull Auntie Minnie out of the car, and she was fighting him off like mad, screaming and cursing and kicking her sandaled feet like busy pedals.

Jason was still in the back of the car, glued to the seat with his head down, as if melted by the sun. Inah ran back down and gestured and shouted to him in Korean to get out of the car, but he wouldn't even look up. I went back down and joined her. He was weeping now, holding his pretty shaved head, sparkling with sweat beads. His neck was shiny, too, with sweat. Auntie Minnie was still screaming and cursing at Uncle Wilson, who had her arm in his hands. Her skirt had climbed up her plump white legs, almost all the way to the hip. I wanted to go and pull it down for her, but I was afraid.

Inah turned around and ran into the apartment building

to get Mom. With my heart pounding and pounding, I stayed put on the sidewalk, where a small crowd had gathered. They stood around and watched Uncle Wilson and Auntie Minnie fight, as if it were a show. And poor Jason was still weeping like a baby in the back of the car.

Soon Inah ran out of the building with Mom at her heels. Mom pulled Jason out of the car and handed him over to us, and we took him up to our apartment. Inah made him sit on the floor, and stayed with him, holding his hand. I got him a glass of water and a wet towel. Jason took just a sip and sat sniffling and twisting the wet towel in his hand as Inah rubbed the tears off with her dirty hand, leaving smudges all over his smooth cheeks.

"Oh-kay, oh-kay," Inah whispered to him.

After a while, we heard the apartment door fling open, and Mom sailed in, followed by Auntie Minnie, hissing and cursing in Korean. Her hair was down in a frilly mess and her makeup was all smudged in sweat. Mom looked very upset and out of breath.

"If you two want to fight, go somewhere else and fight. Of all places, why do you have to do it right at my doorstep?" Mom said to Auntie Minnie.

"I'm not in the mood to be preached to!" she yelled at Mom. "So what are you going to do? Now everyone knows you got a relative married to a blackie!" Then, pulling Jason off the floor, Auntie Minnie sailed out of the apartment with him. Inah ran out after them, calling, "Jason! Jason!"

FOUR

(I)n the morning of our first school day in America, Inah and I pose for Mommy's camera in front of our redbrick apartment building. We are scrubbed clean, and dressed in matching twin outfits Mommy picked out from the suitcase full of brand-new clothes from Korea. From our necks, two sets of nylon cords hang, one with a name tag, the other with a steel bicycle whistle. Inah fidgets.

"Stand still," Mommy tells her, stepping backward and bending her knees. Squinting in the bright morning light with our arms dropped stiffly at our sides, we stare and stare at the camera, trying not to blink. The big white bows decking the fronts of our cutie-pie, blue-and-white checkered dresses already start to droop like the tongues of panting dogs.

"Smile! Don't frown," Mommy says, and the camera goes *click, click*. Twice. Inah blinks hard. She hates taking pictures.

But in no time at all, we hate going to school. Every day, during the recess, Korean kids chase us around the playground like a flock of mad birds, pushing us at the back and pulling at our way-too-uncool dresses, and shouting and singing, "One so pretty! One so ugly!" and "Monkey see, monkey do." And they call Inah "Ghost Face" and "Devil Face" and "KFC." (It takes us a long time, like a month, before we find out what "KFC" means: Not Kentucky Fried Chicken as we'd thought but Korean Fried Chicken.)

White kids are no better, even though some look like angels with their yellow curly hair and blue eyes. Pointing at Inah's face, they chant what sounds to us like, "Cha-na-chi! Cha-na-chi!" We ask Jessica Han what's "Cha-na-chi." She says they are saying "China Witch." But we're not even Chinese, Inah says, looking puzzled. Jessica says it doesn't matter. After that, whenever kids call her "Cha-na-chi," Inah barks back and says, "You stew-peed! I not Chai-nee!" They laugh because, as Jessica says, they don't care if we are Chinese or Korean. They pull their eyes up and say, "You all same same."

Inah screws her face hard and sticks out her tongue at them, and they laugh like they have never seen anything so funny. "Catch me or catch you," they say, making her chase after them around and around like a merry-go-round. They wait until she comes close and pretend they are oh so scared (but they aren't) and run off, screaming. But they are having the best time in the world. "Witch, you watchee!" they sing in pidgin. "How about a watchee for a peachee!"

I don't fight back, although I know I should stand up for Inah. But it's not that easy. Every time kids pick on us and call us names, my tongue gets tied and my face turns as dark red as the ripest plum. I only wish I could make myself invisible, or grow wings and fly off to the sky. I wish we didn't have the same pageboy haircut and wear matching clothes. I wish we didn't go to the same school. I wish Inah didn't tag along after me everywhere like a shadow. I wish I could lose her even if just for a day. And I wish she didn't fight back like mad, because it only makes everything even worse.

When we walk home from school in the afternoon, kids from Bowne stalk us like an army of ants on a march. Up the street, around the corner, giggling and mouthing off bad words and crushing their faces into odd shapes and peeling down their eyes with their sticky fingers. It doesn't matter that Mommy is with us. There's not a Korean kid up and down Bowne who doesn't know her by now. They know she's just a paper tigress. With no bite.

"Mommy!" Inah indignantly tugs at her arm, looking up at her imploringly. If only she would catch every one of those bad kids and beat them up real good, but she could go to jail for that in America. So Mommy can't do anything about them. Too bad we aren't in Korea. Because in Korea, she could scold them good and no one would think it wrong.

"Don't look. What did I tell you?" Mommy says as Inah turns her head, trying to take a peek at the kids. "Just keep walking." Ignoring Inah's protest, Mommy propels us forward, faster and faster, tugging and squeezing our hands, safely imprisoned inside hers. Almost forcing us to fly in and out of the patches of sun and shadow along the sidewalk.

But Inah can't help it, even though she'll only encourage them more, just as Mommy says. Busily pedaling alongside Mommy all the while, she manages to swivel her head now and then and stick out her tongue at them. The kids giggle and roar, feeling safe by the distance. Emboldened, they trail us closer and closer. Then when they least expect it, Mommy spins around to confront the gaggle of bad kids. Caught by surprise, the kids freeze up, dead in their tracks. Like swatted flies. Too startled to run, they gape at Mommy, mouths hung open, almost expectantly. At last, to Inah's great disappointment and squandering the perfect opportunity for revenge, Mommy asks them what they are doing. And of course, one of the bold kids lies and says, "We are only walking home." Then all too fast, the rest of the insolent kids chime in and say in a triumphant unison, "Yes, we are only walking home."

FIVE

One afternoon on the way back from a supermarket with Mommy, Inah spots Piggy outside his apartment building. (Kids call him "Piggy" because he's soft and pudgy all over.) He's got a new buzz cut, and on his round head, every strand of hair is shooting straight out like chestnut fur.

Inah, salivating, points him out to Mommy, telling her how he's been calling her "Bug Face." Piggy notices Inah pointing at him and starts slowly back-stepping, keeping an eye on us. Mommy waves him over, asking him to come and talk to her. Instead of coming over, though, he makes a quick U-turn. But before he can escape up the street, Mommy catches up with him. Nonplused, Piggy places his right hand behind his back and gives Inah and me the Korean finger by inserting his tubby thumb between his fore- and middle fingers. He's lucky Mommy doesn't see it.

Mommy is nice and gentle with him, though. She asks him if it's true he's been calling Inah names. It's not a very nice thing to do; what does he think? Piggy doesn't look like he's in the mood to answer her questions. He sullenly glances up at her out of the corner of his narrow eye to see if she is serious. He then quickly drops his porcupine head. If it weren't for her hand firmly placed on his round, sloping shoulder, he would try to run off.

"It's all right," Mommy says, "just look at me and answer honestly. Maybe you didn't know it was wrong. Everything will be forgiven if you now apologize to Inah and promise not to do it again." But Piggy doesn't look up or apologize. Instead, he stares at the ground and sulks. His mouth is out a mile. And his perfectly round, flat, dish-face is getting redder and redder.

Mommy doesn't know what to do, so she finally says, "Do you know I was a teacher in Korea?" But that doesn't get his attention, either. He shows no sign whatsoever that he will budge soon. Inah and I watch, having stationed ourselves by the doctor's office sign outside the basement office entrance of his apartment building. Up the sidewalk, kids stand in a cluster and watch Mommy and Piggy in a standoff.

"All you have to do is answer," Mommy assures him, jiggling his shoulder, which is sagging further and further. "Do you think it's a nice thing to do, to go around and call people names? Do you like it when kids call you Piggy?" Piggy sullenly stabs the toe of his splayed sneaker into the crack of the sidewalk. He's got an attitude problem, anyone can see that.

After what seems like an eternity, Piggy finally seems to realize that Mommy isn't going to let him off the hook easy. He crushes his doe eyes and squeezes out big drops of tears. They roll down his fat cheeks and fall to the sidewalk, drawing dark, knuckle-sized circles on it.

"Chicken shit," Inah says.

Mommy finally gives up and warns him, "If I ever hear again that you called Inah by that name, I will have to talk to your parents. Understand?" But he doesn't seem to understand that at all. As soon as Mommy releases him, he turns around and dashes into his apartment building, bellowing and crying for his mommy as if he's been manhandled. Mommy shakes her head. Inah's delighted. But I am worried because Mommy can't be with us all the time.

After school, we stand at the top of the steps, waiting for Mommy to pick us up. It's dazzlingly bright and hot. Inah scratches her scarred cheek and wiggles her arms out of her green jacket. I drape it for her over her book bag.

"It's Friday, so it's frying hot," Inah says smartly.

"True, but Saturday is very satisfying because we can sleep late," I say, stepping into the shade.

"Sunday is sunny," Inah says, following me into the shade. "So we can lie on a sundeck and get a perfect suntan."

"Eating ice-cream sundaes!"

"They are yummy, says Mummy."

"Monday is called Moon Day in Korea, but it's Money Day in America because we get pocket money for the week."

"It's a pity that we can't think of a word that rhymes with Tuesday."

"True. So true."

"And then it's Thank-God-Wednesday for we get to go to Wendy's!"

"On Thursday, we are oh-so-thirsty because Mommy makes us kimchi fried rice."

"That makes up a whole week."

"It's a merry-go-round for poor us!" We giggle. I wiggle out of my jacket, too, and tie it around my waist. Inah points to my ponytail, and I pull off the rubber band around it, letting my hair fall to the shoulders. I don't want Mommy to see how I hate to wear the same hairdo as Inah.

We go down the steps and join Jessica Han who is sitting slouched at the bottom step. She's waiting for her older cousin she calls "*unni*," "big sister," whom kids say is a little loony in the head. She speaks in tongues, they say, but we don't know what that means. Still, it sounds kind of mysterious. And if you are to believe what Jessica Han says, when her cousin speaks in tongues, she sounds like a quacking duck and her body sways like a tree in the wind and the whites of her eyes show. Otherwise, she is normal, Jessica says, sounding so sure. But she's strange for sure. Even though she's very pretty and has shiny black hair that hangs all the way down to her waist, she looks like she's just woken up from a dream. When she looks at you, you know she isn't looking at you but through you. That sort of thing. It's a pity she has to be so very pretty. It's like letting good food go wasted, bad boys say.

Jessica sees her cousin coming around the gate, jumps up and dashes across the ground. Inah and I follow her. And soon, we are out of the school and walking down the street, surrounding Jessica's cousin like three small trees around a tall one, skipping and stamping our feet. Luckily, *unni* doesn't say we should stay and wait for our mother. She doesn't say anything or ask any questions at all.

When we are near Bowne Playground, Inah and Jessica Han tear down the street and run through the gate toward the swings. They throw their book bags and jackets to the ground and climb onto the swings and kick them up. I follow *unni* to a nearby bench and sit down with her. Her white-socked feet peek out from her flower-printed skirt. Her feet are as small as a child's.

She asks me why don't I go and ride the swings, too, like she wants to be alone. I don't ride swings when I have a skirt on, I tell her, because anyone can see my undies. She says it's all right as long as my undies are clean. I laugh. She smiles, staring at the distance.

Inah, the fearless, kicks the swing hard, flying higher and higher against the blue sky dappled with white cotton-ball clouds. The chains clink and squeak and creak as she swings up and down, drawing arcs. Her blue pleated skirt blooms like a morning glory and folds down like an umbrella. After a while, she stands perfectly still on the swing, letting it slow down. She has a strange look in her eyes. I turn and see several boys ambling toward us from the direction of the basketball court. They are from Bowne and Sanford. Sometimes they hang around Weeping Beech Park, but they prefer Bowne Playground because it's got a basketball court. And holy of the holy, one of them is Piggy's big brother, Hoon.

My heart starts beating loudly. Unlike Piggy, Hoon, who is two grades ahead of us, is willowy and has a pretty, girl-like face, so smooth and pale, like white chocolate. And moreover, he's got the kind of slitted, smiling eyes I like. (Jessica Han—at eleven, only a year older than us, but already showing the hints of bosoms of thy-kingdom-come—likes him too. She says when he flashes you a smile with those eyes of his, it kind of makes you feel like you have to go to the bathroom!)

"You, the screw face," Hoon says, pointing at Inah with his pointy chin.

"Why do you call her that? She's got a name like everybody else," I say, hoping to sound fierce, but instead I end up sounding meek.

"Huh? Yeah, I know. Like Fuck Face? Ha, ha." My face burns. Jessica Han scrambles down the swing, picks up her book bag and jacket and slings away. "Anyway, who said I was talking to you?" he says, a little sheepishly. "You girls are twins. Right? So what happened to your sister's face?" Tongue-tied, I just stand dumbly, getting red and redder in the face. Just then, Inah jumps off the swing, landing real close to him. He steps back, a little startled.

"What do you want?" Inah says challengingly. Hoon looks tickled. He turns to his entourage of kids. A straggle of assorted Asian boys, no more than a year or two older than us.

"Did you see that? The screw face talks." Then he turns back to Inah and says, "You talk tough, so why did you snitch on my brother Piggy to your mom, huh? I know all about it. So what if your mom was a teacher in Korea? It's not like we give a rat's ass about that. And you're lucky it's Friday because you got till Monday to bring me a whole box of Choco-Pies. Bring it to the basketball court. Right after school. Got that? And another the Friday after. Until e-ter-nutty."

"Why should I?" Inah says bravely.

"Because I tell you so," he says. The other kids giggle. Inah stares him down, fixing him steadily with her eyes. Like she is memorizing every detail of his face. But the crushed, bunched eyelids make her look like she's crying. I can't stand it. I hang my head.

"Stop staring, you spooky face," he says and flicks his thumb, launching a rubber band. It sails over, swats Inah in the right eye and falls. It must sting bad because Inah squeals and bends over, covering her eye with her hand. My heart races real fast. I look around for Jessica Han and her cousin, but they are nowhere. I furiously debate what to do—whether to jump him—when out of the corner of my eye, I see Mommy flying through the entrance. She must have been looking for us all over. She looks like an angry dragon. Hoon, Piggy's brother, sees Mommy, too, because he slowly takes off toward the basketball court, followed by his cowardly entourage. Inah and I scramble to gather our book bags and jackets. Mommy strides over. Her face is set all tight. She doesn't seem to notice the red welt on Inah's eyelid.

"Go home!" she says. We speed out of the playground. We know we are in deep trouble because she doesn't say a word all the way home. Then as soon as we get inside the apartment door, she grabs my arm and starts spanking me on the bottom. Not Inah!

"I'm late a minute and you just walk off! What am I to think when I don't see you two?" Her palm rains down in frenzied succession. It stings bad. I squeal like a cornered mouse. If I try to get away, I know it will only get her angrier, so I just dangle at her arm, hoping she will soon get tired, forcing her to move in a circle, chasing my bottom. We go around and around, and Mommy's face turns beet red.

Inah, who has been standing stiff, like a borrowed broom, smarting in the corner, finally feels sorry for me. She comes over, gets down to her knees and wraps Mommy's leg with her arms. She swears never to do it again, so stop. She's so sorry. With the two of us clinging to her, Mommy gets quickly exhausted. She lets go of my arm, and I plop down to the floor and sniffle through hiccups. Mommy is already sorry, though.

"Don't ever do it again," she says, getting all choked up. "What if something happens? It would just kill your mother."

SIX

Usually, at some point every afternoon, rain clouds break up and blow out to sea, and the sun emerges, if only for a brief spell, for an hour or so, but unambiguously, to douse Venice with a million tons of gold powder. But when we come out of the Palazzo Ducale in the afternoon, the steady morning drizzle has left a dense pall of gray mist all over, and it looks very unlikely that the sun will ever make it through.

"Well, still want to go?" I ask Inah as we head down to the Piazzetta di San Marco. She's been talking about going to see the Lido beach from Thomas Mann's *Death in Venice*. And today is her last chance, it being our last full day here. "You know it might just start raining again," I add, hoping to discourage her. Squinting, Inah looks out at the gray choppy water, hardly distinguishable from the opaque gray sky hanging low over it.

"If you don't mind, I'd like to wait a little and see."

"Whatever you want." Zipping open her backpack, Inah pulls out her wrinkled rain poncho and spreads it on the step, and we sit down facing the water. Before long, she's completely lost in her book.

To my relief, Inah's mood has improved, if not dramatically. It probably has to do with the rain: It mutes the lights, rounds off jagged edges and calms frayed nerves. Maybe she simply realized that I wouldn't be going anywhere, not for a while, and resigned herself to the fact that she was stuck with me whether she liked it or not. Still, I haven't been able to talk to her at all. (Notoriously evasive, she hasn't offered any chance, either.) I guess I just didn't have the heart to bang up on her so soon, seeing her still struggling so. But the real reason is fear. Being with Inah is like gingerly walking through a minefield. A step in the wrong direction, a thoughtlessly placed foot, will detonate a bomb, and shrapnel will be flying before you know it. I'm not sure if I can handle that. Yet. So I think I will wait, earn back her trust. Until then, I will stay out of her hair. I will just try to maintain the tenuous, fragile, hard-earned calm. Who said it— Don't be afraid of going slowly; be afraid of standing still?

"What are you reading?" I ask.

Inah simply holds up the cover of the flimsy pocket-sized book for me. It's *Goethe's Letters from Italy*. Strangely, that's what excites her most about Venice. The idea that Byron, Goethe, Henry James and countless other great artists were here at one time or another.

Inah hands me the book, pointing at a paragraph in the open page. It reads:

> . . . at five in the afternoon of the twenty-eighth day of September in the year, 1786, I should see Venice for the first time as I enter the lagoons from

the Brenta . . . this beaver-republic. . . . Venice is no longer a mere word to me, an empty name, a state of mind. . . . At last I can really enjoy the solitude I have been longing for, because nowhere can one be more alone than in a large crowd. . . ."

I remember how growing up, Inah always armed herself with facts and details to deflect any unwanted attention from her and her face. That it's still true amazes me and depresses me at the same time; her capacity to absorb them and dispense them, no matter how minuscule.

I give the book back to her. It looks like the sun is going to come out after all. The upper sky over the water is clearing in pale blue denim.

"So, are we going then?" I ask.

"Yes, we are going," Inah says, snapping shut the book and springing to her feet. We grab the rain poncho and the book and backpacks and make a mad dash across the quay to catch the vaporetto just leaving for the Lido.

On the boat, Inah is quiet and pensive. I know what it is. It has belatedly occurred to her as it has to me—the irony of going to see the beach in the book that is essentially about the power of youth and beauty, and the great length to which one is willing to go in pursuit of them. But of course, we don't and can't talk about it. (Inah's face is a snag you catch at every turn.) But what is beauty? How do you define it? What did Keats mean by "Beauty is truth, truth beauty"? And what about Inah, who will never know the privilege of being beautiful and the power that's blindly bestowed to the one who possesses physical beauty? But there is so much beauty everywhere. So many kinds of beauty. Why does it have to matter, how you look? Of course, it matters. Sometimes, it seems that's all that matters.

There's a great, inspiring passage in *Death in Venice* that I once memorized in college but now can't quite remember. It goes something like this: " . . . nearly all the great things that exist owe their existence to a defiant despite: it is despite grief and anguish, despite poverty, loneliness, bodily weakness, vice and passion and a thousand inhibitions, that they have come into being at all." The passage always made me think of Inah. With some hope.

Of course, aside from the warning in Inah's guidebook that the Lido is not what it used to be, it's not at all what we expected or imagined it to be like, at least not from the novel. But it's still disappointing. There are few things that even remotely evoke the moods of the book. And no "Hotel des Bains," and no "white-blossoming avenue." Inah drily states that we've come only about a hundred years too late. And as Dad, our family mystic, used to say, everything that once has the privilege to exist is destined to be gone one day.

But still, Inah is happy to have come. She says she would have always kicked herself otherwise. It's better to be disappointed than to live with regrets. I agree. We each scoop up a fistful of wet, coarse sand and throw it out to the wind. On the far sky, dark billowy rain clouds are gathering again.

SEVEN

In America, home-alone kids are taken away and placed in foster homes. So when Mommy starts working for Liberty Tours, the travel agency on Main Street, after school, we head to Auntie Minnie's hair salon instead of home. Mommy is so very sorry that we have to spend the afternoons cooped up at the salon, but we don't mind it at all. For one thing, we no longer have to sit down with her for our daily math study and spelling test.

We are supposed to go straight to the salon, but, if we are in the money, we stop at the Korean bakery, O-bok, Five Blessings, which is just a couple of doors up from the salon on Union Street. Usually, we get a couple of red-bean-filled doughnuts or cream-filled buns, at sixty cents each. But our favorite is *bing-soo*, which comes in a pretty glass bowl, heaped with shaved ice and sweetened red beans, and sprinkled with dried fruit on top. When we are there, we also like to look at the birthday cakes that sit behind the glass display case. One can be ordered in advance, and we would very much like to when Daddy's birthday comes. That's if we're in the money. We will ask them to decorate it with blue and white roses, since he loves flowers.

But if we're not in the money at all, we go to the Korean stationery store on Roosevelt Avenue, where they sell Made-in-Korea fruit-scented erasers, fancy pencil cases with magnetic covers and Hello Kitty sticker pads. We finger them and smell them until the Korean uncle comes over and says if we're not going to buy them, we shouldn't touch them so much. If they get to be old-looking, who would buy them?

In the back of Auntie Minnie's salon, there is a small curtained-off room, and that's where we spend the afternoon. It's got a sagging brown leather couch, perfect for a couch potato or two. And there is also a minifridge, a boom box, and a coffee table, where stacks of old Korean beauty magazines and hairstyle magazines sit, their spines broken and pages thumb-harassed into tatters. The minifridge is stocked with our favorite red bean bars, *Bing-grae* yogurt in miniplastic containers, and a big family-size bottle of Coca-Cola that keeps us wide awake for the rest of the afternoon on a caffeine high. After hurrying through our homework, Inah and I play Monopoly and tic-tac-toe with the boom box on. I like Kiss FM. Inah likes 1010 WINS. News every ten minutes. With traffic and weather updates.

When I get bored, I go out to the salon and sit in one of the pink swivel chairs and watch Auntie Minnie snip and snap hair off her customers and blow-dry it and set it with plenty of hair spray, which she pumps out in clouds of mist from a can she wields like a magic wand. Auntie Minnie's customers are mostly "aunts," not "misses," because "misses" go to the salons that have track lighting and play piped-in music, and those are not even called salons but a "hair lab" or a "hair studio" or a "hair science," and in those places, beauticians are called "hairstylists" and they wear silver lamé vests over black mesh uniforms. But Auntie Minnie has plenty of business. She talks a haircut customer into being a perm customer. She gives a free manicure or free hot-oil treatment to any highlight or dye or tint customer. Highlights and tints soften the look, Auntie Minnie says, for she's got an opinion or two on everything and everyone. Black hair makes you look harsh. Blond hair is softest and easiest to cut. White women's skin wrinkles easy because it's so fair. Asian women have yellow skin tone. A regular facial massage—twice a week—keeps skin young. And a peel-off pack shrinks pores. Besides shampoo and hair rinses and hair gels, Auntie Minnie also sells cucumber massage cream that comes in white plastic jars, and Aloe Vera & Herbal soap that comes in three-bar sets. She's also taking permanent tattoo makeup lessons and is thinking of applying to become an Avon representative. She says, no one calls them Avon Ladies anymore. I say, Oh.

Did you know, Auntie Minnie asks me one day, that I used to sell Amway products when I had a salon in Brooklyn? No, I didn't know that. Almost all my customers were black women, she says. And they are the best customers in the world. And to tell you the truth, I like black people better than any other people. Better than Koreans. Then how come you and Uncle Wilson are getting a divorce, I ask. And how come Jason lives in Brooklyn with Uncle Wilson and Grandma Wilson, not with you in Flushing. It's a long story I haven't got time to tell, and even if I did, you wouldn't understand, she says. But I still go to my old black church every Sunday. All the way to Brooklyn. Why do you think that is? I don't know. Do you know, she says, Koreans call me a *yang-gongjoo,* "western princess," because I married an American GI? Uh-uh, I shake my head. Not only that, they look down on me even more because I married a black GI. Oh, I didn't know that. Now you know, she says.

When Auntie Minnie is extra busy with more than one perm customer, I help and sort out a pink plastic bucket full of perm rollers, dripping with solution. The smell makes me fuzzy and happy in the head. Every time I help out, Auntie Minnie promises a free pin curl, but when she's finally free, she lights up a cigarette instead, sits down in one of the pink chairs and watches what she calls "soaps" on the mini TV that perches on the counter. Pulling at her cigarette and blowing out smoke through her nose, she asks me if I notice how all the soap actors and actresses have perfectly beautiful hair. Instead, I notice the sunlight pulling out of the scratched linoleum floor like a magic carpet, and I yawn.

But Inah doesn't ever hang out at the salon. She doesn't like all the mirrors, where her scarred face multiplies. It makes her feel stuck inside a magic glass. That's what she says. Besides, customers always stare at her through the mirror. They just can't help themselves. And then they want to know how her face got that way. They ask Auntie Minnie what happened. Then they find out that we're twins and feel double sorry for Inah. Sometimes, I wish someone would feel sorry for me, too, but no one ever does. They cluck their tongues again and again. They look at me, and say such a pretty face Inah lost too. They say all this in front of me and Inah, making us blush and squirm and feel so dumb and bad.

Inah rarely gets bored, anyway. She likes to read. That's all she does every afternoon after finishing her homework. No more Monopoly or tic-tac-toe. Instead, she sits crumpled at the far end of the sagging brown leather couch and reads for hours with her nose buried in whatever she can lay her hands on. Just like Daddy, when she's reading, she doesn't hear anything or notice anything.

In a way, Inah is even worse than Daddy. Wherever we go, right away she looks around to see if there's anything to read. Her eyes greedily zero in on a book or newspaper or whatever happens to be lying around. And then she gets so caught up in reading that she becomes oblivious of everything else that goes on around her. When we go to Jessica Han's, as soon as she shakes her shoes off her feet, she heads straight to the bookcase. It's full of medical books that belong to Jessica's father, who is a doctor with a ground-floor office in the same building. She then sits on the floor and pores over one of them for hours. Jessica Han says she's such a bore.

I know for sure Inah doesn't *really* understand all the stuff she reads. It's just a fixation. She just has to devour anything and everything. She likes to read newspapers most of all. Advertisements. Stock market reports. Horse racing results—from Belmont and Yonkers and even the Kentucky Derby. She knows all the names of the racehorses, like Surpassed by None, Simply Fabulous, Unbridled Delight, Soaring Lark and Belle Indeed. And she keeps asking Daddy to take us to a horse racing track but he never has time to because he works all day as a stock boy (even though he's too old to be called a "boy") at a warehouse in Long Island City and then goes to English classes at night. Anyway, I don't think they let children into those horse racing places.

On Easter weekend, we go to Dobbs Ferry to visit Dad's college friend from Korea. He's a doctor who cuts up dead bodies to find out why and how and when and what they died of. But he doesn't look scary. He even looks normal. They live in a big house with a thick woodland behind it. After the Easter meal of Korean food and turkey meat we've never eaten before, all of us kids go out to play. Only Inah doesn't want to, so Mommy shoos her out like a fly, saying, "Go out and play. Get some fresh air." The air is real fresh in Dobbs Ferry.

We play hide-and-seek. When it's Little Sam's turn to seek, every kid scatters into the woods to hide. But he's too scared to go in because it's so quiet and dark there. So he just wanders around the edge, finding no one, and we get bored stiff waiting for him. Finally, David, the oldest kid, goes out and sneaks behind him and squeezes Ernie, someone's squeaky toy that says, "Hi, my name is Ernie." It scares Little Sam out of his wits. Screaming and crying, he runs as if his behind is on fire, and we laugh and laugh. He says he doesn't want to play anymore. Inah jumps at the chance as though she's been waiting for it and takes him back inside.

A while later, Mommy comes out and tells me to get Inah because we are leaving. But she's inside, I tell her, but she says in turn, no she isn't. I go look for her all over. She is not in the den, where the TV is. Not in the basement, where the Ping-Pong table is. Not in the living room, which is full of people. Not in the backyard that sits empty. Not in the darkening woods, where birds I can't see shriek. Not even in the garage, where we are not allowed to go because we might push the automatic door button by mistake and get crushed underneath. Inah is playing Alice-in-Wonderland again.

Soon everyone in the house is looking for her. We go around, calling, "Inah-ya!! Inah-ya!!" Outside, it's starting to get dark, and Mommy is scared. She is sure Inah wandered outside by herself and got lost. And having never been up here before, she would never be able to find her way back. Mommy asks Daddy to call the police. Daddy's friend says, "Before calling the police, let's look around the house one more time."

And guess where she's found? Upstairs, in the room of Daddy's friend's son who's away at college. Daddy and I find her sitting crammed under a desk, doubled over a thick, heavy college textbook about human social behavior or something that sounds very boring like that. Lost deep in a *sam-mae-kyong*, a blissful state of absorption people are supposed to fall into while reading, she doesn't even look up until Daddy gets on his hands and knees to crawl in and shake her good. The way she looks at him, you can tell she has no idea where she is or what's going on. She looks like someone who's been sleepwalking.

On the way home in the car, Mommy berates Inah, saying she still can't believe she didn't hear everyone calling her name. But Inah insists she didn't. Mommy says it's Daddy's fault. He makes a bad example. Daddy finally says that's enough. It's not like she's been caught doing something bad. If that's the only trouble parents have with their kids. . . . Isn't it surprising, though, that she finds such a difficult book interesting? Did you even understand what you were reading? Inah shrugs her shoulders, and he says she might be a genius. I don't want that kind of genius, Mommy says. Don't you know, he says, all the geniuses are a little strange.

But Daddy doesn't know how bad it really is because he's long gone and not around in the morning when we get ready for school. He has no idea what kind of battle we go through just to get Inah out the door. When she's supposed to be brushing her teeth and washing up, she's spread on the bathroom floor with Daddy's Korean newspaper from the night before, or his new book or some junk mail salvaged from the garbage bin. I tickle, pinch, poke and even kick. She just grunts and keeps on reading. Then, in the last-minute mad scramble, she sprinkles token water on her face and hands. Thanks to her, we are always rushing and always running late. Every morning, flying out the door with shoes hardly on our feet. Book bags dangling and jackets dragging.

Inah's fixation gets so bad she can't function normally. Life for her is an obstacle course. So says Mommy. She seems to be constantly stumbling on a new book or newspaper or magazine. Then, so distracted, she can't do anything until she has read the very last word. Mommy has to literally rip it away from her hand before she staggers out of her zombie state and begins to focus on things. Mommy yells, cajoles, threatens and even cries, but nothing works.

One day in school, Mrs. Warshofsky notices what looks like a black ring of dirt crusting around Inah's scrawny little bird's neck. She calls her over and asks if she can take a look at the back of her neck. But Inah squirms so, shrinking her neck like a turtle, making it impossible for Mrs. Warshofsky to get a good look. So she asks her if she regularly takes baths at home. Your neck seems very dirty, Mrs. Warshofsky says. Inah doesn't get fazed that easily. No, not at all. She's got the chutzpah—that's what Mrs. Weiss in our building says Inah has—to say that it is only a tan. She plays a lot outside and she gets tanned easily. Are you sure, Mrs. Warshofsky asks skeptically. She's got the voice of a thrush so it always sounds pleasant even when she doesn't mean to. Inah cheerfully assures her that she's sure. Inah reports all this back to me like she's proud, but she doesn't let me take a look at her neck, either.

"Promise not to tell Mommy," she asks, holding up her pinkie.

"Promise you will wash good," I say, wondering how come so much shampoo is gone after she takes a shower. We hook our pinkies and shake them hard.

"How is school?" Daddy asks as soon as we sit down for dinner. He always asks the question before he opens the Korean newspaper he brings home.

"Oh-kay," I say. Daddy nods and looks at Inah, expecting more or less the same kind of answer.

"Oh-kay, Daddy."

"Speak Korean," Mommy says, ladling out the rice into a stainless bowl. The rice is hot and steamy and smells sweet.

"Being good students? Good!" Daddy crackles and spreads open the paper, and soon his face disappears behind it.

"Oh, I forgot about Mrs. Warshofsky's letter," Inah blurts out. Then she looks at me and covers her mouth. I don't know anything about Mrs. Warshofsky's letter.

"What letter?" Mommy asks, looking very alarmed. She puts down the chopsticks she has just picked up. They settle on the table with a sharp chime. "Where's the letter? Bring it over right this minute!" she says. Daddy slowly and reluctantly folds back the paper and puts it down and tells Inah it's all right, go ahead and bring it. Oh, we are in deep doo-doo for sure.

We are then sent to our room so fast that we're still chewing mouthfuls of rice. Inah sits at the edge of the bed, dangling her legs and looking scared and nervous and chewing her thumb. She won't look at me either because she knows I am hissing mad at her for dragging me into trouble all the time, and getting Mommy and Daddy into fights. We can hear Daddy shouting at Mommy to quit her job if she can't even send us to school clean. She's doing everything wrong. She has forgotten what's important and why we came here. How, how could she not know Inah goes to school unwashed and dirty? Forget the job, and that church she goes to every week, twice a week. "So religiously too!" we say in hushed unison, completing his sentence. If she can't even send the children to school clean, we all might as well pack up and go back to Korea, Daddy says, rephrasing. Right now! We jump a little when we hear the door slam. Daddy is gone.

Soon, Mommy sails into the room and tells me to go and fill the bathtub with hot water.

"And you, stay right there!" she yells at Inah. I slide past Mommy and escape to the bathroom. The tub is nearly full with scalding hot water when Mommy marches in with Inah in front of her like a hostage. Inah looks terrified.

"What are you doing in the bathroom every morning and every night? Do I have to keep an eye on you every second? Hold straight! Keep your arms up!" Mommy angrily pulls the shirt over her head. Inah folds her arms right over the two little buds on her chest. Mommy slaps them down, but they come right back up.

"What are you trying to cover? Nothing there," Mommy says, slapping her hands down again. Inah stands stiff as a frozen broom out in the January cold. I giggle, and she gives me a black look.

"And you!" Mommy shouts, throwing Inah's clothes into my arms. "Where do you carry your eyes? How come you don't notice anything? Letting your own sister go around looking like a beggar living out of a cave! Inah's Inah, but at least you should know better."

Mommy tells Inah to turn around and gasps. Every crevice of her body—at the ankles, the knees, the back of the knees, the elbows and the neck—is crusted with about

an inch thick of dirt. I'm exaggerating, but still, it is so
ingrained with dirt that the skin looks leathery. Like
cracked crocodile skin.

"The shame! The shame!" Mommy hisses and says she
hasn't seen anything like it since the Korean War. Inah
sheepishly wades into the tub full of scalding hot water and
squats down, wincing. I squirt bath gel and lap up mounds
of foam around her with my hands. Mommy rolls up her
sleeves and lathers a washcloth with soap and scours her all
over. Inah whines and yelps. Roll after roll of black dirt falls
off, revealing pink, scrubbed-raw skin below.

EIGHT

During the weekdays in the summer, Jason is staying with Auntie Minnie. But all of his friends are in Brooklyn, and that means he's often bored stiff. So every afternoon, he comes and waits for us outside the YWCA where Inah and I attend summer school only to make Mommy happy.

"Yo," Jason hollers when he sees us filing out the door. He has on a yellow mesh Magic Johnson basketball jersey that reaches all the way to his knees. Below it and his half-pants, his skinny shanks disappear into the high-top Nike shoes that look huge.

"You look like a scarecrow," Inah says.

"What's that?" Jason says, and Inah giggles, covering her mouth with her hand.

With Jason leading, we slowly walk in a single file to Weeping Beech Park. No one's around because it's so blazing hot, without a dot of shade anywhere. With the whole park to ourselves, we horse around, wrestling and pummeling one another like chimpanzees in a zoo, and then play jump-over-the-back and tag until we are red in the face and sticky as melting caramel.

Out of breath, we stagger after Jason and sit slouched on the seesaw. In the red sunlight, Jason's face sparkles in golden amber. Inah's face, cooked red, looks like raw sirloin steak under cling wrap at a supermarket meat counter.

"Jason, what do you want to be when you grow up?" Inah asks, cooing.

"Oh, no! Not again!" Jason rolls his eyes, smacks his own forehead and crosses his eyes. Inah giggles. She loves to play the stupid rhyming games over and over again. Never ever getting tired of it. But Jason is oh-so-patient with her. Not so much with me. Maybe because she kisses up to him so. He even tells her to let him know if anyone ever bothers her and calls her names. He will kick butt. Be it yellow butt, white butt or black butt. He likes to sound tough, but he's only twelve and a half, still soft-skinned and skinny as a calf.

"Jason, Jason, guess what? Inah wants to marry you when she grows up!"

"No, I do not," Inah says, flinging me an angry look.

"You do! Remember?"

"Like when?"

"The summer we came from Korea. When Uncle Wilson and Auntie Minnie took us sightseeing with Jason. In the car, you always sat next to him, saying oh-kay, oh-kay, because that was the only English you could speak. And you were always touching him, too, so Auntie Minnie told you to leave Jason alone. If he were a bar of soap, you would have worn him out many times already."

"I did not!" Jason makes a snorting sound, and Inah giggles.

"So, Jason. Tell me again what you would like to become when you grow up. Please," begs Inah, cooing like a baby dove. I walk behind Jason and try to pull him off the seesaw.

"Let's go get fruit bars," I say.

"Soon, Yunah," Jason says, and Inah smiles happily. I stick out my tongue at her and slouch down between them. My head throbs from running around in the heat.

"You want to be? . . ." Inah swivels her head and smiles expectantly at Jason.

"A magician maybe. Or a musician maybe," Jason recites. "Definitely a sensation with a reputation. But not a politician or a physician."

"That's sooo good!" Inah says adoringly. "Oh-kay, now my turn," she says, sitting up. "When I grow up, I want to be a pomologist or an anthropologist or an archaeologist. But not a capitalist or a Baptist. A Buddhist maybe, but surely not in Budapest."

"What's a pomologist?" I ask. "I bet butt you don't know and if you don't know, you can't become one."

"Yes, I do," Inah insists.

"Do not," I say.

"Do too," she says and turns to Jason. "Do you want to hear a poem I made up?" Jason snorts and falls back, rolling himself off the seesaw. He lies on his back on the ground, spreading his arms and legs in a capital letter X.

"It's short! Ready?"

Jimmy is a baby
Plump as the purple plum in his plump hand
He plunks the purple plum into the toilet
And the plump plum gets stuck in the toilet

So they call the plump plumber
Even though they say he's got a pea for a brain.
The plump plumber comes
Wearing a hat with a purple plume
Carrying his toolbox
That's been sitting in the puddle
Left by his white poodle!
He tries a plunger, tries flushing
To no avail!
The plumber is pissed
So he says his piss of a son is a punk
That's why he works till he smells like a skunk.

"How do you like it, Jason?"

"Uh, not bad," he says, lying on the ground, blinking his eyes.

"Now your turn," Inah says. "Do that one about Brooklyn."

"No, Inah! I've done it a zillion times already!"

"But it's so good!" Inah gets off the seesaw and goes to Jason and tickles him. He rolls around the sand, squirming like a centipede and squealing like a girl.

"All right already!" Jason climbs back up to the seesaw and closes his eyes. Inah sits at full attention, supporting her chin with her clammy hands. I am so mad at her, I feel like kicking her in the butt. And Jason goes:

There's not a brook in Brooklyn
That anyone can see
Clean or dirty or otherwise.
Some call Brooklyn Crooklyn
'Cause it's got plenty o' crooked corners
Where there's not a tree for a shelter

Where pigeons go crook, crook
Looking for crumbs
Clean or dirty or otherwise
All day long, sunny day long
Brooklyn is no Brookhaven
It's more likely a Crookhaven
He's a crook for sure,
The bookie with the crooked teeth
One or two capped with gold.
He hangs around the corner all year long
Crying and laughing
For no good reason.
Cooking the books 'round the clock
All day long, sunny day long
Calling me a gook when I walk by
"Yo gook!" he says,
"Got a lo mein to go?"
"Got a chow mein to go?"

Inah claps appreciatively.

"Now can we go?" I ask.

"All ready," Jason says.

We file out of the park, sweaty and clammy and smelling like dust. It's still sunny, and we carry three extra-long shadows with us. When we reach the corner of Sanford at the crosswalk light, a white pickup comes up the road and slows to a stop at the red traffic light. The driver is a white man in a blue T-shirt, its sleeves rolled up to hold a cigarette pack. His freckled, beefy arm, covered with reddish curly hair, rests at the edge of the rolled-down window. It's sunburned red and peeling bad in tattered sheets of dried glue. The light changes to Walk, and we start to cross. Inah calmly walks over to the pickup and yanks at the peeling skin on his arm. He jumps in his seat and Inah runs past us across the street, shrieking like a bugle. Scared, Jason and I dash across and up Sanford, pedaling our hot feet as fast as we can.

"Hey, kid!" the man swivels his head and shouts at Inah, running up the sidewalk. "You get over here!" he yells. I am so scared that I think I am going to wet my pants. The light changes and he rolls the pickup along, glancing at the sidewalk where we run for our lives. Jason steers Inah onto Roosevelt Avenue. I turn and look for the pickup. It has stopped again at a red light. He's still straining his head to get a good look at us.

"Holy mackerel shit, Inah. What did you do that for?" Jason asks when we finally stop, out of breath and gasping for air.

"I couldn't help it," Inah says, looking at her hand.

"No shit! You're so weird!" Jason says, scratching his head. I am still too scared and out of breath to say anything.

The hair salon is empty, and the only person we see is the shampoo lady, Yolanda, sitting behind the cash register, worrying with her brown eyes. When she sees us file in, she puts her finger to her lips and rolls her eyes toward the back room. We tiptoe in and peek through the curtain. Auntie Minnie is on the couch, all made up as usual like an Asian Dolly Parton, her Ivory-soap-pale short legs folded one on top of the other. She's pulling at the cigarette madly smacking the air with her other hand, armed with pointy press-on nails. The ashtray on the coffee table is littered with butts freshly stained with her fuchsia lipstick.

We also see Uncle Wilson by the minifridge, where he has rooted himself like a tree. His brown wrestler's arms are folded over his barrel chest. He sees us and smiles with his big, hooded eyes.

"Hey son," Uncle Wilson says to Jason in his thick, boom-box voice. "Where you kids been?" Inah and I hang back, not sure if it's oh-kay to be friendly with him. We know Uncle Wilson is soon marrying Cecilia, his black girlfriend. Afterward, they are moving down to South Carolina. They are taking Jason with them.

"You no fool them," Auntie Minnie sneers at Uncle Wilson and waves us away. We go and sit on the swiveling salon chairs, spinning to the left and to the right, letting our dangling legs fly. Auntie Minnie's voice is rising and rising like the voice of an opera singer, and soon she's spitting out cuss words. Jason looks at us with a here-we-go-again look and covers his ears with his hands.

"Everyone know you butterfly me plenty, you madda fucka! It your fault, no my fault we divorce. But I no care. I no give no damn you marry that ugly black mama. I no make it my business. But Jason, he no black! You lie to him, I know. You say to him he black but he no black. You no can fool Jason. You no can fool me. You think he want to go live with you and black mama?"

"Oh, yes, he does. Just ask him. And let me tell you, mama, Jason is as black as Jesse Jackson and no more Korean than I am. You know what I'm saying? If you don't believe me, show me one Korean who thinks Jason is Korean 'cause I am yet to meet one damn Korean who does. Anyway, you Koreans are all goddamn racists to begin with. I ain't stupid, mama. I've seen them treat you like shit just because you're married to me, a black man."

"What that got to do with Jason? He my son, that all I care!"

"I am not denying Jason is your son, but he's my son, too. That's a fact and don't you ever forget that!" Uncle Wilson walks out to the salon, and we all jump out of the chairs and stand at attention. Auntie Minnie runs out and lunges at Uncle Wilson, pounding his broad back with her tiny, closed fists. She looks like a teddy bear trouncing on a grizzly. Uncle Wilson turns and grabs her by the wrists, trying to keep her hands away from him.

"You madda fucka!" Auntie Minnie curses. "I no can live without Jason. He my life," she cries, hammering at his chest. "Before you take him, kill me first!"

"Get the f . . . away from me, mama," Uncle Wilson says, peeling her off him like she's a sticky wad of gum, but she lunges right back like she's connected to him by an elastic cord. Jason tries to get in between them, but Uncle Wilson tells him to stay away. With his big hands, Uncle Wilson grabs Auntie Minnie's shoulders, and she screams as if she's hurting. "Call police!" she yells to us over her shoulder. Inah and I look at each other. We feel ashamed and sorry for Auntie Minnie. We don't know what to do. We just stand there, stamping our feet. "What's gonna happen?" Inah cries.

"You want the police? What for? You want to get arrested or something? Go ahead, call the police, mama!" Uncle Wilson peels her off him again and gives her a quick shove, sending her spinning. Auntie Minnie loses her footing, hits the back of a swivel chair and falls down. Jason starts crying. Inah and I are frantic. The shampoo lady, Yolanda, runs out of the salon, not knowing what else to do. Auntie Minnie gets back up on her feet and reaches for Uncle Wilson's face with her press-on nails. Inah and I rush over, squat down and wrap our arms around each of Uncle Wilson's huge legs, holding on to them desperately. We are so scared, we crush our eyes shut.

When we finally open them, Uncle Wilson is looking down at us. He seems surprised to see us down there on the floor holding on to his legs. He throws back his head and bursts into a roaring laughter like he has never seen anything so funny. Jason quickly goes over and puts his skinny arms around his mother's round waist from behind. Auntie Minnie shouts at Jason to let go of her, ranting in Korean and in English and flailing her arms. Her wrists are red and welted. But Uncle Wilson can't stop laughing. He laughs and laughs and wipes his eyes.

NINE

Saturday afternoon, the day before Uncle Wilson's wedding, Daddy takes us to the Flushing Meadows Corona Park. That morning, because Auntie Minnie wouldn't, Mommy took Jason to Caldor's and bought him a black polyester suit, a white penguin-tailed shirt, a black bow tie and a pair of shoes, so he could go to his daddy's wedding looking clean and decent.

At the park, we pick out two bicycles at the bike rental. Inah climbs onto the back of the one Jason will ride, and off they go. Daddy props me up on the other one and shows me how to steer the handlebars. Afterward, with him walking alongside, I take off in a zigzag, stiff and tense with the fear of falling. After just a few feet, the bike careens off and I end up ditching it. Daddy wants me to try again, but I don't feel like it. Jason and Inah, though, are having a great time together, going around and around the sphere fountain. Laughing and hollering. Getting sprayed by the spewing mist. Daddy takes out the camera and snaps pictures. Inah and Jason. Riding the bike together.

But Daddy can't get them to laugh when we sit down on the bench later outside the scrubby flowerbed, where roses are wilting in the heat. After tomorrow, after the wedding and the banquet, Jason will be moving down to South Carolina with his dad and new mommy. And that makes everyone so sad.

Daddy puts his arm around Jason's hot, sad, sagging shoulder and gives him a squeeze. And then they sit quietly, both squinty-eyed in the glinting sunlight. In Jason's hand, the soft chocolate ice-cream cone Daddy got him from the Mister Softee truck is fast melting.

"Jae-son," Daddy says, calling him by his Korean name, "after tomorrow, you leave your mommy and go far away to live with your dad and his new wife. So it's natural you are very sad. Everyone sad. Especially, your mommy. She most brokenhearted. She say things and hurt your feelings, but don't mind too much what she says. She may been here many years, but her thinking is still Korean sometimes. She can't help it. She think less with her head and more with her heart. That can be good and bad. But she loves you. Even more than her own life. You most important to her. You don't believe? Ahh, this uncle knows what Korean mommies are like. Better than anybody. They love too much and sometimes, it can feel like burden. But you very lucky to have a mommy like that. And I know you are upset because she says you are Korean and your dad says you are black. But you both. No more one thing and no less the other. And we not blood related maybe, but we are like family. Korean. Black. It not matter. Look at Inah here. She loves you. You are her favorite person in the whole world. But it's not just Inah, we all love you. Remember that for me?

"And I know you love your mommy. You don't have to say. Maybe it so hard for you now, but so long as you don't forget she loves you, everything will be OK. You understand? Good!" Daddy pats him on the shoulder. And Jason's mouth fast crumbles at the corners, and soon he's sobbing with his head down. The soft ice cream melts and flows down in chocolate rivers between his fingers. Daddy wipes it off for him with a paper napkin. Inah is so sad that she doesn't even try to comfort him.

The next morning, Auntie Minnie brings him over. She's been crying. Her eyes are all swollen and red. But Jason looks gorgeous, like a prince in the new suit and tie, but he is so quiet that you'd think he'd been born mute. Inah tries to cheer him up, but he doesn't want to be bothered. He just sits on the couch in the living room, staring at his hands. Auntie Minnie hides in the kitchen because she can't stop crying. It's like a funeral parlor, Mommy says. She goes over to Auntie Minnie and scolds her. "This is how you're going to send him away? How would he feel?! Think about that."

It's time for Jason to go. Daddy and Inah and I stand by the apartment door waiting for Auntie Minnie to release him. But she holds on to him, smothering him with her face flooded with tears. She can't talk, and her body shakes and shakes like Jell-O in a cup. Finally, Jason pats his mommy and wipes his eyes with the back of his hand. It's all so very sad.

"Who's the child here?" Mommy scolds her, but her eyes have turned red, too. She pats Auntie Minnie's back and says, "Go ahead, you cry." And Auntie Minnie wails, holding Mommy's hand: "I no can live! How I live?!" Jason has never looked so miserable, standing there hanging his head.

"It's OK, Jason. You go!" Mommy says, waving her hand to him. Daddy goes and brings him over, and we all go out.

From the hallway, we can hear Auntie Minnie cry, calling after him.

Inah and I sit in the backseat and Jason in the front with Daddy. No one says anything. It's another hot, sunny day, and the shadows are extra black. After passing the Brooklyn Academy of Music, Daddy pulls the car next to the sidewalk, where cracked bricks are caving in and weeds and garbage hem the smashed chain-link fence of an outdoor parking lot. It's the sun that makes the street look so desolate and desperate and sad. Up a couple of blocks lined with old and shabby-looking brownstones, we can see the tower of the russet-colored, old stone church rise against the blue sky. Once Jason brought us an old creased paper fan from the church. It had Dr. Martin Luther King's portrait on the front and a Franklin Street funeral home ad on the back. We didn't know then who Dr. Martin Luther King was, and Jason explained, "He's the greatest of all of us black people ever lived."

Jason wants to walk the rest of the way to the church by himself. So Daddy shakes his hand and says, "Jason, I know you're going to grow up to become a great man." Jason opens the car door, quickly glances back at us and gets out. We watch him amble up the weed-infested sidewalk in his new suit. Skinny and narrow-shouldered under the peppery-hot sun. The white shirttail spills out the back of his trousers and he doesn't even know it. He looks like a black-plumed bird with a white tail. Daddy slowly drives the car up the road, to make sure he gets to the church. We stick our heads out the open window.

"Jason!" "Bye-bye!" Jason turns only the slightest angle, and with the hand he pulls out of his trouser pocket he gives us a quick, stingy, little flick. Like he doesn't want people to see him waving to us. We drive past the church. The sidewalk and the church steps are crowded with black ladies and girls, all dressed up in crisp and cool summer dresses, and black men and boys looking sharp and handsome in suits. Watching Jason walk up, a large old black lady in a peach-colored muslin dress and a wide-brimmed, cream-colored hat breaks into a broad smile. She looks as inviting as a big old tree that throws a cool shade on a hot summer day. She pulls him into her arms and pecks his cheeks twice, one then the other. Daddy says she must be Grandma Wilson.

As Daddy drives up the road, Inah and I turn our heads, craning our necks for one last look at him with his grandma on the crowded sidewalk. And look how he makes a nice picture next to her, handsome and bright and festive as any summer flower. Her skin so dark, almost gray, and his skin, half a shade lighter, complementing each other. It looks as though he has always belonged to that place on the sidewalk full of happy people. He has already become a stranger. We're puzzled and sad.

TEN

When I wake up in the morning, Inah is already packed and sitting by the naked, gray window, lost in thought, her diary open facedown on her lap, like bird wings. I pack quickly and take a shower.

"So are we calling Mom and Dad?" Inah says as I put on my clothes. Every time I've asked her, she has answered it with the garden variety of "not in the mood," "not now," or "later." I have given up.

"If you want to," I say, trying to sound nonchalant. I look at my watch on the night table. It's past one in the morning in New York, but I know Mom won't mind. She has probably been waiting by the phone every day.

Mom's voice answering the phone is thick with sleep, but she vehemently denies that I woke her up. Dad went fishing with Uncle Shin in the morning, she says, as if letting me in on a secret. Thankfully, she doesn't grill me on why we haven't called until now. I talk to her briefly, then hand the phone to Inah and slip into my sandals. I don't feel much like listening in on their conversation. Mom and Inah have always had that special something between them. That tense and tangled bond I was and will never be a part of.

"Don't forget what I said about the kimchi," I whisper to Inah, and she impatiently waves me away. I walk out of the room, shutting the door carefully not to make too much noise.

It is drizzling outside. The narrow lane, strewn with rain-fallen leaves, looks even shabbier this morning: The gray brick walls are listing, soft and swollen with rainwater and soggy paper boxes lie around with bloated cat food still in them. On Lista di Spagna, a man sits on a soaked piece of cardboard, holding up a tiny, shaggy, wet, black puppy on the palm of his outstretched hand toward passersby as if it were a precious offering. It's much too early; the cliniclike store where we've been stopping by every afternoon to get bottled water and occasionally Parmalat milk is yet to open.

It's strange how quickly one gets used to a place. (And yet, it feels like ages ago, the sunny afternoon I followed unhappy Inah up the Lista di Spagna and through the leafy lane to our pensione.) It makes me a little sad to think that German tourists will still be sitting around the same flimsy white tables outside the tiny beer hall off the Scalzi, looking out at the drizzle just as they did every afternoon when we returned to our pensione, tired in soggy clothes. That it will be other tourists who will cross the same small courtyard of our pensione, open the same creaky, semicircular wooden door into the same dim-lit lobby. That they will be handed the same key attached to the heavy, pear-shaped bronze knocker by the same old lady, whose powdered, bone-pale face, emphasized by a great, masculine, aquiline nose and dull orange hair severely swept up into a stiff helmet of a pompadour I will never forget. And then for several days, every afternoon, resting on the same impossibly high Venetian bed, they will hear, as we heard, the gondoliers sing on the canal, in clear, high-pitched, and lush voices, like those of certain birds. Their songs will travel across the water, the Lista di Spagna and the lane and reach them, as they reached us, in distant, yet clear, echoes as though from a dreamland. And how sad that no one will ever remember our brief presence here.

I cross the street and walk out to the edge of the canal by the pink Hotel Principe. The water is murky, gray and listless. The buildings across all have lights on with the windows lit in warm orange glows like rectangular moons of August. In one of them, a woman is walking about with what looks like a water jug in her hand. A battered green motorboat heads up the canal, carrying a man and a wet, gray-haired dog, and an old couch, a TV and chairs, half-covered with a blue tarpaulin. They are moving in the rain.

Then a vaporetto chugs down. Looking sluggish. It is crowded with people going to work. From the crowd, my eye instantly picks out a man in a beautiful dark blue suit standing behind the railing. He carries a long black umbrella and a brown leather briefcase in his hands. He is very elegant. Like an actor. Immediately, I think to myself: a man at home. There is that beauty about him—that intangible and yet immutable beauty that grows around only such a man. The kind that stems from a life lived in continuity, rootedness and rituals. A proud, self-assured sort of beauty you find in an ancient tree standing on terra firma.

After the vaporetto is gone, taking him with it, leaving a churning trail of waves behind, I stand there awash with pangs of envy. I just know Dad would have liked to have lived such a life. In Korea. Instead, he has been living the life of a transplanted tree, only half-rooted at best in a mutually rejecting foreign soil.

When I come back to the room, Inah is getting dressed. Her hair is wet from the shower. I can tell she has been crying. Her scarred face is blotched, and there are wads of dark clouds hovering about her. I take her soggy sneakers and put them out on the windowsill, knowing they will never have a chance to dry before we leave. I then hand her my spare pair of sandals. Inah takes them without protest and slides her feet in. She doesn't say anything about Mom or the phone call.

PART THREE

ONE

Daddy hates our Bowne Street apartment. He calls it a box in the sky. He says it's unnatural for people to be living so far off the ground. Stacked on top of one another like chickens in cages, waiting to be sold at a marketplace. Maybe he says these things because he misses Korea. He's always telling us stories about him growing up in the country: pulling out a radish from the dark brown dirt and eating it right there, sinking his teeth in; how fragrant it smelled, like earth itself and how sweet and juicy it was; or walking miles through pouring rain to his country school, wading across streams and up and down the muddy mountain paths with the smell of rain and earth and grass and trees all about him. Inah and I cock our heads when Daddy talks about these things.

That's why we move to Ash Avenue. Because Daddy, whom Mom calls "the poet," hates living in the apartment and misses living in a house with the smell of living and breathing soil. But we are moving only ten minutes' walk away. Nonetheless Inah is excited. Every morning, she checks the wall calendar hanging on the bathroom door where Daddy marked our moving date by drawing a five-pointed star with a blue Magic Marker.

On that morning we get up so early that it is still dark outside. The streetlamps are still fluttering on feebly, like fading moons, and most of the apartments across the street have dark windows. In her shrunken Betty Boop pajamas and splayed hair, Inah flits about the apartment like a spring swallow, tripping over the piles of boxes. Mom yells at her for getting in the way, but she doesn't care. Then Daddy steps on a thumbtack on the floor and Auntie Minnie has to come and drive him to Flushing Hospital for a tetanus shot. He comes home limping a little. Mom's all frustrated.

Later, in Auntie Minnie's car, we follow Daddy and the graffiti-ridden moving truck he's riding in. When the car turns off Kissena Boulevard onto Ash Avenue, Inah drapes herself on my back like a lizard, trying to look out my side of the window where a neat row of identical-looking houses slip by. Boxy, and white and cream-colored, standing shoulder to shoulder, they look as if made from cake icing.

But soon the block of neat row houses ends, and from its right side Ash Avenue bleeds away into an oval circle of Syringa Place and Magnolia Place. After that, the street turns noticeably shabby. Lining either side, flush on the narrow sidewalks, detached from one another, stands a hodgepodge of old and dilapidated houses, looking weary, like disgruntled stragglers who wandered in and, too tired to move, decided to stake a claim there. That's what Auntie Minnie says.

Just then, up ahead, the moving truck pulls up at the curb, and we hear a loud belch. Auntie Minnie turns to

Mom and says, "Is that it?!" She sounds disappointed. We eagerly follow Auntie Minnie's finger pointing to a tiny stone house.

Little do we know then that it will be the only house we will ever live in before we leave home. That we will stay put here while other Korean families we know move away over the years to rich suburbs in Long Island and Westchester and New Jersey. That we will never leave Flushing, not in any true sense. That Flushing will become our American hometown.

Inah and I stare out the window at the demure stone house dwarfed between a ramshackle clapboard and a rambling gable-roofed dark brown Victorian. It wears a sun-bleached green asphalt-tiled roof and hangs a palm-sized porch like an apron pocket in the front. There is no driveway or garage. Just a short, cracked cement path running to the porch from the sidewalk. It looks just like a camping lodge.

The cab door of the truck opens, Daddy climbs down and waves to us. Instantly recovering from the disappointment, Inah and I stumble out of the car and run up the steps to the porch and file inside after him. The house is stuffy and smells like mildew. Inah shoots up the hallway and runs up the steps, shaking the walls with her thumping feet. We go around, opening every door and peeping into the empty, gloomy-looking rooms. In the upstairs hallway, Inah pulls off cracked sheets of paint from the wall and flings them to the floor. Mouths open, we stare up at the ceiling where water stains spread in spiderwebs, as if deciphering puzzles. In the bathroom, taking turns, we yank at the chain; water roars down, making the walls shiver, and tumbles into the toilet bowl with a thick brown water ring and disappears.

"We live in Flushing, flushing the toilet," Inah says, and we laugh.

When we go down into the kitchen, Mom and Auntie Minnie are inspecting the cupboards. "Hallelujah," Auntie Minnie whoops sarcastically, shrinking back from the mouse droppings she finds under the sink. Through the open kitchen door, we can see Daddy walking around the scrubby backyard, where grass is ankle-deep.

"Whoever lived here was a stranger to cleaning," Mom says. "Look at this, too." With the toe of her foot, Mom scrapes at the burn marks on the bubbly linoleum floor, and sighs. "It will take years to clean up and fix things."

Daddy walks in through the kitchen door from the backyard and asks us how we like the house. "Don't you think it beats living in the box in the sky?"

"Amen!" Auntie Minnie says in her thunderlike voice. Mom just sighs and sighs. Inah tells Daddy that Mom is not so happy. Your mother's got the Flushing blues, that's all, he says.

After Auntie Minnie leaves to get back to her salon, Inah and I make ourselves comfortable on the couch in the middle of the tiny living room, surrounded with mountains of boxes, and eat potato chips from a bag. Munching, Inah says, "Salty, salty, naughty, naughty." It is cold and her teeth are chattering but she goes on, "Salty, salty, naughty, naughty."

TWO

"Isn't it good to live in a house instead of in that little box in the sky?" Daddy is standing on a wobbly ladder, hammering a nail on the wall. We stand below him, steadying the ladder and holding up a tray of nails and hooks for him. It's about the hundredth time he has asked the question, and Inah and I nod our heads. A little puzzled. "And we have a backyard now! How about that?!" But we know that the backyard is just a sorry-looking scuffed lawn with a weather-beaten wooden fence listing sideways as if from years of exhaustion.

"I know it's not much of a backyard now. But just wait and see. Your dad is going to turn it into a beautiful Korean Zen garden!" We don't know what a Korean Zen garden should look like, though.

On the weekend, with Daddy, we go to paint stores and hardware stores, where he stocks up on gallons of paint and garden tools; a shovel and a rake, garden gloves and rubber boots, a wheelbarrow and a sieve, a tin watering can and a green rubber water hose, coiled like a snake.

The weekend Daddy paints our room in Robin Blue and the kitchen in Egg Yellow, rollers and pans are lying all over the floor, which is covered with plastic sheets. Whenever Daddy takes a cigarette break, we tail him out to the back-yard like midget bodyguards, blowing out huge pink balloons with our wads of Bazooka bubble gum. Daddy, with a cigarette dangling from his mouth and covered with millions of yellow and blue dots of paint from head to toe, walks around and around in a warped circle, his arms behind his back, squinting his eyes and tapping the ground with his feet. Like a geomancer!

In the afternoon, Uncle Shin stops by with a cold Miller six-pack, which they take out to the backyard and drink standing side by side with the grass up to their shins. Daddy tells Uncle Shin how he is going to get rid of the lawn and the brick barbeque pit by the white birch and build a beautiful Korean Zen garden. Uncle Shin, an American expert, says no, no, leave the lawn alone. Just replace it with new sod. You can't be a home owner in America without a lawn to mow. Daddy says it's one of the dumb things Americans do. The trouble they go through to keep their lawns manicured! Moreover, lawn mowers pollute the air. Uncle Shin shakes his head and tells us your father will never become an American. Uncle Shin and Daddy stand in the spring afternoon sunlight and laugh, shaking their heads. From the beer, their faces are the color of a ripe plum.

The April sky is spotlessly blue, and the sun is shining. Daddy's boots and pant legs are all caked with mud. Half of the lawn is already all ripped up, and every time Daddy sinks the sharp blade of his shiny new shovel to the ground, yellow dust rises and joins the cloud of dust hanging in the air in a long, trailing swath of yellow. It's a carnival for Inah. In her shiny, buttercup yellow rubber boots, she drags the tall rake around behind her, singing like a broken record, "'Mary, Mary, quite contrary, how does your garden grow? With silver bells and cockleshells and pretty maids all in a row.'" Once in a while, Daddy stops, wipes his forehead and leans over the handle of the shovel and sniffs at the air. "Ah! Nice!" he says, smiling and closing his eyes. "What's so nice, Daddy?" Inah asks. "Why, the smell of dirt!" "Oh!" As Mom says, Daddy is a funny man.

Mom sticks her head out the kitchen window and says it looks like a storm has passed through the backyard. Come in, lunch is ready. We hose down Daddy's dirt-caked arms and hands and his rubber boots and pelt him with the hand towel he wears around his neck, to shake loose the dust on his clothes. We leave our muddy boots outside and file in, and Mommy says we look like street urchins. We have spicy noodles and, after that, slices of apple.

The sun has shifted, and it's cold in the shade when we go back out. Daddy sets up a sieve on four wooden pegs, and we walk among the clumps of dirt lying around wearing bits of grass on them like so many severed heads. After Daddy finishes sieving the first batch of soil, we load the stones in a wheelbarrow and dump them along the foot of the listing fence. It's a lot of fun. And we are the world's best little helpers, that's what Daddy says, fishing out the mini spiral notebook he carries in his shirt pocket and the pencil stub he carries behind his ear. Inah peeks at the notebook, where he is busy jotting down notes, and wants to know what's that he's writing down.

"Oh, some new ideas about the garden. Daddy's going to

plant bamboo trees there," he says, pointing to the ground by the listing fence. "And Korean tree peonies here."

"That's all, Daddy?"

"That's all? That's plenty! In a Zen garden, the empty space should be the focus." Inah and I stare at him, perplexed. Daddy squats down and draws an S-shaped line on the ground with his nicotine-yellowed forefinger. "See this? An unbroken empty space flowing, what does that remind you of? A river! That's what it will look like in the moonlight. A white river. Wouldn't that be beautiful! A white river flowing around the patches of flowers and bamboo groves!"

But they don't sell any Korean tree peonies at the garden centers we visit. They don't have any books on Korean tree peonies at the public library on Main Street, either. So we bring home books on flowers and plants and gardening. Sitting at the kitchen table, Inah thumbs through the books and asks Daddy if we could have dahlias, or hyacinths, or gladioluses or cannas. And a little pond, too, with water lilies and lotuses. And goldfish in it. But Daddy says it will be really nice to have wisterias. Hanging wisteria blooms, so beautiful. And they give a nice cool shade in the summer. Mom clucks her tongue and says if people overheard us talking, they would think we have a huge yard. Daddy laughs and tells Mom to wait and see. It's going to be beautiful when it's done. Mom says Daddy has to be the happiest man in Flushing with his scrubby little backyard and his dream of a Korean Zen garden.

On Sunday, while Mom is belching hymns and praying to God at the Siloam Reformed Church of New York, Daddy and Inah and I walk all the way to the Queens Botanical Garden. It's the wedding season. Everywhere at the garden we see newly married couples: Koreans, Chinese,

Indians and Hispanics; brides in white or ivory wedding gowns with trellises and bouquets, and grooms in black tuxedos and new haircuts. They are trailed by tripping cameramen, sweating and lugging videos and cameras, and their families and friends and guests and bridesmaids, in flowing saris and matching satin dresses that swish and dance at their feet. While Daddy and Inah walk around looking at the plants and flowers, I park myself outside the rose garden and watch newly married couples pose for the cameras at the arch of the white gazebo, all lovey-dovey and doe-eyed and bursting with smiles. Their teeth are dazzling white pearls in the sunlight.

The next Sunday, on the way back from the Japanese garden, we pass a winding-down garage sale on Quince Avenue. Inah moseys over and picks up a couple of old mildewed books sitting on the sun-splashed lawn. It's a two-volume set called *The Little Nature Library: Dedicated to the Glory of the Outdoors.* (Volume one is about wildflowers: *Wildflowers Worth Knowing,* and Volume two is about trees: *Trees Worth Knowing.)* There are lots of color illustrations in them. Inah asks Daddy to get them for her. Please Daddy, she says, cradling the mildewed books in her arms. The old lady with a silver doughnut-shaped bun tells Daddy it's only one dollar each. Practically free. She could have cut out the illustrations and sold each easily for a buck, but she wouldn't ruin good books like that. Daddy counts out two bucks from his wallet and pays the lady. Oh, then, I want to get something too. I notice a V-shaped piece of driftwood sticking out of a cardboard box. I pull it up and show it to Daddy. It's carved with bulging bird eyes and wings and covered with a cobweb. Daddy looks at it, turning it this way and that. It looks scary, Inah says. The old lady says it's from Indonesia.

"Oh? From Indonesia?" says Daddy, giving it another look over.

"Yes, it's nice, isn't it? You can have it for five bucks."

"Oh?!" I say. "More expensive than the books?"

"Of course, it comes all the way from Indonesia. And I think it's old." Daddy asks me what I am going to do with it. Do you really want that? I am not so sure. Daddy peels out a five dollar bill and hands it to the lady, and I am already regretting it. But the lady says enjoy it. I carry the carved driftwood, and Inah, the old mildewed books. So very happy, Inah skips and dances. Daddy says it takes so little for her to be happy.

"Are you that happy to have the books?" Daddy asks Inah.

"Yes, Daddy," she says in her singsong voice.

When we get home, Inah torpedoes through the door and runs straight to the kitchen to show the books to Mom, who says but they have mildew all over. Inah says, it's okay: She needs them because she's going to become a botanist when she grows up. That's news. What has happened to the astronaut? And I am not even sure what a botanist does.

"But you go to Harvard first," Mom says.

I wash the driftwood in the bathroom sink and put it out to dry in the backyard against the wall. After dinner, sneezing and sniffling and rubbing her red itchy-eyes, Inah spends hours looking at the books, turning the mildewed, yellowed pages that are stuck together. In the book about trees "worth knowing," she reads all about the trees after which the streets in our new neighborhood are named. She says ashes, maples and elms are deciduous trees that bear winged seeds, and that magnolias, dogwoods and hollies are fruit-bearing trees, and are known for their showy flowers. Does she know what *deciduous* means? I bet she doesn't.

Well, I don't know either. But what Inah likes most in the books are the color illustrations of wildflowers and their names: New Jersey Tea, Indian Pipe, Ghost Flower, Indigo Broom, Shooting Star, Poor Man's Weather-glass and Gold-thread.

"When I become a botanist," Inah says out loud, "I am going to discover wildflowers and give them names like Blue Tangles, Red Flute, and Snow Shoot."

"You have to discover the flowers first before you can give them names," I say.

"But I know already what Blue Tangles look like. Like blue satin ribbons you put on a gift box!"

THREE

The early morning train pulls out of the dank termini, and memories of Venice recede like a low tide into the back of my sloshing mind. And the details of my old life that have stayed in the background—blurry and abstract, like so many smudged watermarks on rice paper—rush in and demand my attention. I feel anxious, as though emerging from a long amnesia.

Picking up speed, the train lurches on, simulating the movement of water, and I fall asleep. When I wake up, Inah is still poring over the beat-up guidebook with her legs pulled up like a tent on the seat across. Next to her, her spiraled notebook is lying open, the entire page filled with a long list of must-sees in Florence. It puts me in an inexplicably bad mood.

Groggy and shivering—as if I am still in damp clothes—I watch Inah, her engrossed, expressionless face, her straight black hair falling over it. It still puzzles me. The way we have turned out. The way Inah has turned out. Whatever happened to the Inah who used to flit about the Bowne Street apartment in the morning in her favorite flint-balled, shrunken and threadbare Betty Boop pajamas she wouldn't part with? Relentlessly upbeat. I still remember the giggly and hushed and breathless falsetto voice she used to use when, at bedtime, lying in our narrow bunk beds Cousin Ki-hong and Cousin Ki-sun generously bequeathed to us, we whisper-talked in the dark.

Inah had just discovered that she could make up anything in her head. "Let's pretend we live on the beach in California," she used to say, her Tinkerbell voice ringing with such a thrill. And that very instant, together, we would leave behind our small Bowne Street apartment and fly to some far-off places, away from crowded Flushing, bulging with people from all over the world. To the Real America we'd glimpse on TV. For we knew (even though Dad would tell us that Flushing was where miracles happened every day), Flushing was not real America. That, just as Uncle Shin said, it was just a temporary holding pen of immigrants like us, a stopover place on the way to the Real America. If we stayed too long, we would get stuck here forever to become Flushing ghosts.

And there we were in an instant. On the sugar-white beach (in California) where seagulls fly, spitting out throaty, noisy cries. Inah walking a fluffy-eared brown dog she pretended (just because she could) was hers. The dog had a real American name like Margie or Max, and she/he knew just how to catch a star-spangled Frisbee every time she sent it flying in a perfect arc. (These pictures she drew were at once vivid but fuzzy and blurry at the outer edges, from her lack of experience.)

I blankly stare out the train window at the grass fields flecked with red poppies, freshly tilled brown land, and blue-green hills flying past in splashes of bottle green, ruby red and myrtle brown. Inah finally looks up.

"Listen to this," she says. With her wet thumb, Inah rapidly flips back the pages of the guidebook. "Visiting the magnificent Chiesa di Santa Croce, the French writer Stendhal experienced this overwhelming sensation which left him unable to walk for days. . . . It's called 'Stendhal-ismo' or 'Stendhal's Disease,' and symptoms include sweating and giddy faintness. It's said that Florentine doctors treat up to twelve cases a year."

Well?!

My bad mood persists, and I feel almost paralyzed with inertia when we walk out of the Santa Maria Novella station into the blazing Florentine afternoon. The sudden blast of sunlight is unnerving. And just like that, I know I will hate it in Florence.

Inah uncertainly looks out into the big mad swirl of traffic circling the station and consults her map, turning it around this way and that. Finally, she concludes that it should take us no more than ten minutes to get to our hotel. Of course, she means by foot. But I am in no mood to drag Mom's suitcase around in the stifling heat.

"Well, you are the boss," I say instead.

"You are in a good mood," she mutters. "Anything the matter?"

"No, Inah," I say. "Everything's real swell." Sighing audibly, Inah grabs the strap to Mom's hideous suitcase and redistributes the weight of her tubelike, dirt-slicked backpack.

"We better cross the street here," she says. "Otherwise, we'll have to walk all the way down and back up."

"I don't see any sign of a crosswalk," I say. Inah goes ahead anyway, hurling the suitcase over the guardrail. She then squeezes herself through the space between the rails, obviously placed there to prevent just that: pedestrian crossing. She stands dangerously close to the passing cars.

"Come on," Inah hollers to me because I am still dawdling behind the rail. Then, seeing a lull in the traffic, she dashes across the street, dragging the suitcase behind her. Just then I see a tiny green Fiat speed around the circle. It's obvious that Inah doesn't see it because of the blind spot the sunlight creates. The Fiat speeds up and comes to a loud screeching halt. It all happens in a matter of a split second. I am in a sudden blackout. In my head, I hear the echo of a silent scream. It's all so sickeningly familiar; the sudden suspension of time, blurred vision, slowed-down motions, the horrible dread and the slow crash landing to reality that follows. My heart thumps so loudly that it feels like it's going to explode out of my chest.

I force myself to look up. The Fiat has come to a stop after nearly sideswiping Inah. And Inah stands in the middle of the road next to the Fiat, as if frozen. But looking more disoriented than frightened. And then I see the head of the driver of the Fiat poke out the window. Gesticulating wildly with his hands, he starts spitting out infectious streams of curses at Inah. Stunned, she stands mum, docilely taking the shower of verbal abuse. Enraged, I squeeze myself through the rails and dash toward the middle of the road where Inah's standing mute and frozen. I hear myself screaming at the Fiat driver. In English and in Korean. He has no idea what I am saying. His head jerks toward me, but even this close, all I can make out is his dark, curly hair and his face shaped like a sledgehammer. Cars honk wildly. And in the periphery of my vision, I can see a crowd gathered on the sidewalk, gawking.

Suddenly, as if woken up from a sleepwalk, mortified and petrified, Inah pulls me by the arm. "Yunah! Come on, let's just go," she says. "It's my fault."

"I don't care whose fault it is. You're not a damn door-mat, Inah!" I hiss, shaking off her hand. "Goddamn speak up and defend yourself. You don't deserve his tirade."

"But you're causing a scene!" Inah says. "People are star-ing. You're not in New York, you know." Dragging Mom's suitcase, she steers me up to the sidewalk.

"So what!" I yell. "What are you so afraid of? Let them stare. I don't give a damn. I don't believe in enduring, over-coming and suppressing like you and Mom. Do you know how many Koreans die of *han,* from suppressed regret and anger?" Inah stares at me like I am nuts. Bewildered by my outburst. So out of proportion. I feel like giving a good swift kick at Mom's suitcase sitting there on the sidewalk. I really can't believe how ugly it is. It seems to represent everything that's wrong with my life.

"Can we go now?" Inah asks, exasperated.

"I hope next time I try to defend you, you either side with me or just shut up."

"I hope you wait until I ask next time," she says, looking surly and thoroughly fed up.

"Oh, forget it. Why should I expect you to be loyal!"

"How does it have anything to do with being loyal?"

"Just shut up and tell me where to go. It was your fault anyway."

"Bitch," Inah grumbles.

"Butch," I hiss, and speed down the street, feeling ugly with anger, fighting the crowd clogging the narrow sidewalk and sopping with sweat. I hate everything. Inah. The heat.

The crowd. And I don't need any convincing: The Italian sun is poisonous. It can kill.

Of course, we end up lugging the suitcase and backpacks all over, circling and back and forth across the same piazzas before finding our hotel. So much for "Stendhal's Disease."

FOUR

Inah's bent over at the foyer, fussing over her sneaker laces. Daddy's looking up at the sky, holding the door open for her. "Now all ready, Daddy!" Inah says, unfurling herself like a plant, and together we run down the steps to the sidewalk, smudged dark from the early shower. Daddy comes down, stops and sniffs the wet air. "Ah! Isn't it so nice out?" he says. We giggle, and Daddy's dark face, old as long as we remember and as familiar as the face of a penny, blooms in a sad kind of happiness.

Inah and I greedily present our hands for him to take, and off we go for our after-dinner walk. Daddy, in his favorite white Sperry Top-Sider canvas shoes and a brown *jamba,* jumper, that Mom says makes him look like an old Korean grandpa. Down the wet sidewalk, dizzily strewn with cherry blossom petals felled by the shower. With Daddy in the middle, like a tall, skinny tree.

In Inah's arm, Mom's fancy black meshed nylon bag

from Korea dangles like an empty fishnet. It's got two shiny black plastic rings for handles, and Inah, the future botanist, calls it her "botanizing bag." In it, she carries home tree leaves and flower petals and whatnot and presses them in the pages of *Webster's Dictionary*. When they are all pressed nicely, flat and delicately brittle, she pastes them in her sketchbook with Scotch tape or Krazy Glue and writes down all the botanical facts about them in the margins, copying from *The Little Nature Library* and *Webster's Dictionary*. Her favorite so far is a whole dandelion she pulled up from the sidewalk outside our house one day; its spiky leaves and yellow flowers and roots and all. Later, she glued it to a sketchbook page and taped it on the bathroom door upstairs.

DANDELION FACTS
(ACCORDING TO *WILDFLOWERS WORTH KNOWING*)
A/K/A: Blowball, Lion's-tooth or Peasant's Clock
Distribution: around the civilized world!
From a poem on dandelion: "Dear common flower
    that grow'st beside the way / Fringing the dusty
    road with harmless gold . . ."

We follow the thick tangled green wall of tall forsythia shrub and turn to Magnolia Place. There, the shrub breaks briefly into a narrow opening where a winding redbrick path runs to the door of the kitchen of an old gable-roofed house. Inah and I call it "the Chinese house," because from Ash Avenue, we see yellowed and rain-stained Chinese newspaper placed behind the broken pane in the upstairs window. But we have yet to see anyone who might live there.

Curious, as we always are, Inah and I stop and peek at

the back of the house, a dark shingled hulk sitting in a spooky hush, veiled in the evening mist and grizzled with the shadows of tall pines with droopy, scraggly branches. The ground around is thickly padded with pine needles, and above the kitchen door, from a naked lightbulb, yellow light burns feebly, sputtering a misty halo around it, and we can almost hear it hum.

"Daddy, who lives in the house?" Inah asks. "How come we never see anyone?"

"Hmmm . . . ," Daddy says, stroking his chin. "It looks like a haunted house, doesn't it?" Shuddering, Inah quickly pulls back her head and runs down the sidewalk, flinging her "botanizing" bag, pretending she's scared to death. She then trips and falls but gets up right away. "I am OK, Daddy," says Inah, rubbing her scraped palm to her legs.

"Ha, Inah, be more careful. Daddy likes everything about you, except you should try to be more thoughtful and calm."

"Okay, Daddy," she says.

On Beech, we turn and head down the street. The forsythias and magnolias have already bloomed and dipped, and trees are getting thicker every day. In the pale streetlights, dogwoods and cherries in bloom look blurry and iridescent, as if covered with wet snow, and the warm, damp air drips with faint scents of the flowers. Inah and I expect at any minute Daddy will drink the air and say how it's hard to believe we're only five minutes away from the dirty and crowded and noisy Main Street and how it's almost like the country. And, of course, Inah is all ready to say, never missing a beat, "Quite contrary!" Daddy then will laugh, pushing his head back, "Hah, hah, hah."

We also know that at the corner of Cherry, we will pass the Chinese Buddhist temple: a shabby, weather-worn, old wooden house, where, up the rickety wooden steps, outside the door, sun-bleached red plastic lanterns that, in rain, look like overripened tropical fruit ready to fall, hang like full red moons at night. There we'll hold on to Daddy's arms, rippling with lean muscles, and peer through the picture window to take a look at the huge golden Buddha, with his placid face and thin, wispy curlicue of a mustache and red lips, sitting aglow in a lotus position inside the smoky living room. Looking a little too cramped: The tip of his cone-shaped head almost touches the white plaster of the low ceiling.

We will then walk as far as Quince, up Oak (another nut-bearing tree) and then down Poplar (water-loving trees like willows) before turning back. Past houses with hanging pots of geraniums and petunias, and small front lawns, where a faded pink plastic hula hoop or a child's tricycle with streamers patiently endures its temporary abandonment in the lingering light of the dusk.

And then, gradually, adrift in a dreamlike world, we will forget everything, and instead, it will be the mysterious and undefinable swelling and lulling night world, full of muffled voices, faraway sounds of barking dogs, soft echoes of doors opening and closing, that will have our full attention. Flanking Daddy, Inah and I will float through the night streets, our feet on automatic pilot, fascinated by the way the plain, somber-looking houses that we pass without ever noticing during the day go through nocturnal transformation: each house, like a plant that folds inward at sundown, shutting itself in, creating an island with its own rhythms and rituals and mysteries. Offering its softly glowing windows to the world like movie screens where people soundlessly move about like shadows and televisions flicker endlessly.

But the glimpses of intangible America we get only in fleeting doses will never quite satisfy us but only convince us that people in those houses are different from us. That, unlike us, they are "real" Americans.

"Daddy, is it true Americans eat steak every night for dinner?" Unable to articulate the puzzle, Inah, as though waking up from a dream, will ask a stupid question like that. But Dad will know what she means and explain to her and to me, too, how people are the same everywhere: how they get hungry just like us when they don't eat; how they are sometimes happy, sometimes sad; how they fight, make up and fight again; and how they all want to be happy. Just like us.

In the afternoon, though, walking home from school, we hardly remember to give a second look at these same houses, now sitting hushed, unambiguously lacking in character. But Ash Avenue always manages to surprise us a little. The way it waits for us, empty and quiet and looking strangely vulnerable in the afternoon light, showing all of its shabby walls and old paint jobs, and patched-up roofs and untrimmed hedges in its worn-out nirvana. (By Ash Avenue, we mean just the short shabby stretch where our house stands with six others. Across Parsons, Ash continues on, but we hardly ever go there.)

Ash Avenue hosts very few kids. Now and then, the chubby Korean girl who lives on Beech comes around, walking her yapping Pomeranian on a white studded leather leash. Her name is Jin-joo, which means "pearl" in Korean. But she's stuck-up. Whenever we try to pet her dog, Sparkle Plenty, she says he is going to bite us, so be careful. Now, Inah just snubs her.

That leaves the kids who live in the low-slung ranch

house on Syringa Place, across from "the Chinese house" on Magnolia. Every afternoon, behind their low, undulating, gray wall, trimmed white at the top, the three brothers play hoops, their bowl-cut blond hair flying, or ride their mountain bikes around the oval circle. They don't ever talk to us or say hello, but they zip past real close on their bikes as if they are following an invisible track, and when we squeal, they make faces. On weekends, their blond-haired father, in khaki shorts and T-shirts and bare feet, washes down their old car outside. He doesn't ever say hello to us either.

Many an afternoon, bored stiff, Inah and I aimlessly walk around the deserted streets. Inah, carrying her "botanizing" bag, and I, carrying nothing but my feet. Inah muttering and yakking like a loony bird and saying things like, "Aw, dang," "Gosh," "Shucks," "Aw, jeez," and "O damn," just to see how they sound out of her own eleven-year-old mouth. (She picks them up from boys at school.) We walk to Parsons and peek through the black iron gate of the Nichiren Shoshu Temple, the most mysterious of all the houses of worship in our neighborhood that is full of them; five churches and three Buddhist temples, and other kinds we don't know anything about. We stare at the white building at the end of a winding stone path bordered by lawn. With black glass slits for windows (which makes it impossible to look in—or out, for that matter), it's as though a spaceship has landed. (We wonder why, of all places, in Flushing, Queens.)

But it, too, gets boring, and we wander off again. More often than not, the only person we come across is the Chinese grandma out hunting for mugwort, which grows in the shrubs and bushes. She's carrying the same old tattered blue canvas bag with a pink daisy appliquéd on it, and is wearing the same black cloth shoes, gray men's pants and a flower-printed blouse. She smiles at us and says, "*Hoa, hoa,*" and her face blooms with wrinkles that crisscross her face like intricate lacework. We feel sorry for her that she has to go around looking for mugwort.

But come Sunday, Ash Avenue turns into a thoroughfare, overflowing with church-goers, temple-goers and mosque-goers, from all the houses of worship in our neighborhood. All day long, the narrow sidewalks are crammed with families with children in tow; silver-haired and white-robed Muslim men with embroidered caps on their heads (Inah says they are Pakistanis, but what does she know?); Korean grandmas in *hanbok,* carrying golden-edged hymn-books and red-edged Bibles; and gaggles of kids from Sunday schools playing tag up and down the street as if, Mom says, they are in their own living rooms.

And still, not even a hint of life at "the Chinese house." Then, one Saturday, on the way home from the store with a bottle of sesame oil for Mom, we see a rusty pair of gigantic scissors going *snip, snip* along the top of the tangled, tall forsythia hedge around the rambling "Chinese house." And just the flat top of a head, where thick silver hair stands up like grass in the freshly mowed lawn. Inah and I crouch a little and poke our heads through an opening of the hedge to see who is behind it. A short old grandpa looks at us. He's wearing cotton gloves with their palm sides painted red. It looks like his hands are bleeding badly.

"Do I know you?" he says, closing the scissor hands, which look like Alaskan king crab legs.

"No, but we live next door," Inah says, pointing to our house. "That one."

"Huh!" he says, as if that's the most surprising thing he has ever heard for a long time. "You Chinese?"

"No, we are just Korean. And she's my sister."

"Oh?!" He looks at me and then at Inah.

"We're twins," Inah says.

"I can tell you're twins," he says.

"Really?" Inah says happily.

"And you how old?"

"Eleven. But twelve in Korean age because in Korea when a baby is born, they say it's a year old already."

"Ha!" he says, looking at the scissors in his hands.

"Do you need our help, Grandpa?" asks Inah in her hopeful voice and points to the ground around him, strewn with leaves and snipped-off branches. "We can sweep them off for you." I give her a quick shove, but she just ignores it. A sucker for a fast buck, she's always rushing over to an old lady carrying a grocery bag or two on the street. She got a quarter only once, but she remains eternally hopeful. The Chinese grandpa considers Inah's offer and says OK. I myself am not so sure, but Inah's already walking around the hedge. She shuffles after the grandpa to the alley and helps him drag out two big plastic garbage cans. He hands us a tall broom and a short broom. We work fast. Like two little peasants out gathering firewood.

"Good, good," the grandpa says after we help him fill up the two big black garbage bags. We tie them up, put them in the garbage cans, drag them and line them up at the Magnolia side entrance.

"Thank you, thank you," he says to Inah, now standing expectantly with her arms at her sides. "You like come in?" he says, taking off the gloves. But we are not even supposed to go around talking to strangers, let alone following them into their houses. Although the grandpa doesn't look scary at all. Still, I want to think it over just because the house looks so spooky and dark, but Inah blurts out yes. She knows the chance to get that buck is much better that way. Reluctantly,

I shuffle after her and the grandpa through the back kitchen door. It is real dark and stuffy inside. All the windows are shut tight and drawn with venetian blinds, discolored to egg-yolk yellow. The musty hallway leading to the living room is cluttered with tall piles of Chinese newspapers tied up with strings and rickety stacks of cardboard boxes holding empty cans and jars. Several years later, Inah and I will read the novel *Housekeeping* and think of this very house.

"Come, come," the grandpa says, picking his way through the clutter. Inah looks insanely happy. She's almost shaking with excitement and trying hard not to squeal. We tiptoe after him into the living room, a little expectant. But it's nothing like what we thought it would be. The living room sits quiet in grainy, diffused, dusty strips of sunlight pushing through the slats of the venetian blinds. It looks like an old movie set that hasn't been dusted or disturbed for years.

It's a while before we notice a narrow metal-framed cot standing against a wall. On it, under a crumpled blue sheet, a small lump rises. Oh, it's an old lady's head that lies on the bed where the blue sheet ends. It looks like someone has placed it there. Her face, shrunken small like a dried chestnut, is all bones and rigid and gray, like it's molded out of gypsum. Her eyes are shut in two zippy lines and gummy in the corners. Her mouth has only traces of lips. On her forehead, her gray, coarse hair is arranged like a little girl's bangs. It hasn't been washed for a while. It looks all matted, like old, dirty wool. If it weren't for the slow rising and falling of the sheet and the whizzing sound, like an asthmatic cat, coming from her chest, we would have thought she was dead.

"Is she your wife, Grandpa?" Inah asks boldly. The grandpa nods and looks at the grandma on the bed.

"She sick from old age," he says. "Can't no more go up and down the stairs."

"How old is she?"

"Oh, old." The grandma makes a sigh, as though telling us she has heard it.

"Do you have children?"

"One. Son. He no more child, though. He live far."

"In California?"

"No, no. Not that far." Inah and I feel very sorry for the grandma and the grandpa. In Korea, children take care of their parents when they get old. We don't know if it's the same in China. But we live in America. Still, we will surely take care of Mom and Dad when they get old. We won't leave them all alone and sick in a big spooky house with a broken window and unmowed lawn. The grandpa waves his hand and points at the big brown corduroy couch. "Sit. Sit." Right away, Inah saunters over and hops onto the couch, sending up a cloud of fine dust around her.

Suddenly, her eyes are shiny with greed. She has noticed the chess set sitting on the coffee table. She picks up one of the ivory chess pieces and fingers it admiringly.

"You like?" Grandpa asks her, as if he finds that unusual. Inah nods and smiles. When she does this, the scar tissues, with paraffin-like sheen, pull the muscles in odd ways and make her look like an old, sly, wicked woman. Embarrassed for her, I look down at the floor, where a strip of pearly light slithers across my foot like a long, slow-moving snake. I move a bit, letting it fall back flat and straight on the floor. I know Inah's going to hang around awhile. She has what Mom calls a "heavy butt." I try to signal her, but she won't meet my eye. I go over and sit down next to her, shoving her a little.

"I'm gonna go," I say. "You coming?" Then I remember

the sesame oil and ask her what she's done with it. Inah's eyes
light up. She has left it out on the sidewalk in a bag. I get up.
Inah puts down the chess piece and reluctantly gets up.

"Grandpa, we have to go home. Our mom's waiting."

"OK. You go out the back door." I run out the kitchen
door and around the corner to Ash. The sesame oil is still
sitting there in the middle of the sidewalk in the brown
paper bag, on the very spot Inah left it.

FIVE

During the summer, Ash Avenue acquires a Buddhist
temple, Golden Lotus, and the Unification Church. Golden
Lotus is the first one to open. In the redbrick Colonial house
right across the street from us. On a drizzling morning, from
our living-room window, Inah and I and tongue-clucking
Mom spy on men hoisting up a sign—a fancy wooden board
engraved with gold Chinese characters and red dragons—
tied by ropes over the entrance of the house. Mom says, it's a
Chinese temple, as if that's better than a Korean one.

Then a couple of weeks later, the Unification Church
moves into the old rickety clapboard at the corner of Ash
Avenue and Parsons Boulevard. One afternoon, Inah and I
take orange Popsicles from the freezer and post ourselves
across the street in stifling heat, a safe distance away, as
we're not supposed to go near it. (They might turn us into
Moonies and make us go sell roses in restaurants.) Slurping
and licking the fast-melting Popsicles, we watch an army of

people sprucing up the house, crawling all over it like ants. The air buzzes and zings with the sounds of hammers and chain saws and a lawn mower.

"It's very literary," Inah says.

"What is?"

"The whole she-bang!" she says, hoping it sounds way cool. But to her huge disappointment, no one ever pays any attention to us. Getting bolder, each afternoon, we post ourselves a little closer, and then, finally, we cross the street and stand right outside the picket fence. The dingy, old, rickety house is now a picture-perfect, American dream house. With a fresh coat of snow white paint, the house and the picket fences are blinding to look at, and the zinging lawn mower has turned the weed-infested lawn into a mint green carpet. Now the rest of the houses on our block look even shabbier and more dilapidated.

Every time we sit down to dinner, Mom complains about the new Buddhist temple. All the people coming and going, day and night. And that smell of burning incense that lingers over the street "like a ghost." Daddy jokes to us that they must have known Mom was a Christian. Don't complain, he says. It could have been worse. Mom asks how. Well, imagine if it were a Christian church. Ha, ha. Mom says Buddhists are nothing but idol worshipers. Daddy says, you don't know what you're talking about. Buddhism is the gentlest of all religions. If only all other religions were as gentle as it. All it teaches is that life is suffering and illusion, and that happiness is achieved through a state of nothingness. How bad could that be?!

"So naive!" Mom says. But we wonder what a "state of nothingness" is.

"All right. If it bothers you that much," Daddy says to Mom, winking at us, "we will move."

"Why should we move?" she says. "Then they win!"

"See?" Daddy says to us. "You mom makes a bad example of a Christian. With her narrow-mindedness and intolerance. There's nothing uglier than a religious turf war."

"I just don't want to be assaulted by the sight day and night," Mom says.

"It's the same thing. Why do you go to church, anyway?"

"I like sitting there in the church. I feel good. Peaceful."

"But Daddy, why do people have religions?" Inah butts in.

"Why? Because they are lost and confused. Through religion, they hope to find contentment and peace of mind."

"Oh?!!" A grain of rice falls out of Inah's mouth. "You don't have peace of mind, Daddy?"

"Don't talk with your mouth full," Mom tells Inah. "Do you think your father knows what he is talking about? He should have shaved his head and gone into the mountains a long time ago before he made a mess of things in this world." Ha, ha, ha, Daddy laughs and says, "Your mom is a comedian."

Instead of moving, Mom hangs heavy double drapery over the living-room window. I guess we will stick it out in Flushing. But Inah still dreams of living in California. One day. Some day.

After summer, school starts, and what do I get but a crush on Brad Chung. He's Piggy's big brother, Hoon, who once launched a rubber band at Inah in the Bowne Playground. He's now called Brad, American-style. I am extra nice to Inah so she won't blab her mouth off. Anyway, she thinks I have a fat chance. I am not *that* pretty. Besides, all the plump, braces-wearing seventh- and eighth-grade Korean girls have a crush on him, too. I am merely one of them. But I don't care. I can't help it. I get a flighty feeling and goose bumps all over just thinking of his side cowlick, which sends his jet-black hair spinning in a circle. Simply passing him in the school hallway, I get all dizzy and stupid. Moreover, he has the kind of eyes that become slits when he smiles or laughs. (Salina Ong says Richard Gere has the same kind of eyes, but neither Inah nor I knows what Richard Gere looks like.) But it's not that easy to make Brad notice *me* out of all the giggling girls. Especially when I get dizzy and stupid just passing him in the school hallway.

One Friday after school, at the public library, Inah and I get a book of love poems and find one called "Sally in Our Alley." We change a few words around, and in less than five minutes, come up with a song that goes like this: "Of all the boys that are so smart, there's none like pretty Brad." Every day at school, we sing "the Brad song" and giggle every time Brad Chung walks by, and we pretend to swoon when he beams at us, eyeing us sideways.

But that's all that will ever happen with me and Brad because by the time the dark and dull green leaves of summer start turning into bright yellows and reds and russets, I no longer have a crush on him. I have found out that he has a girlfriend. A white girl. With a name like Naomi or Ashley. We saw them hanging around together on the steps in front of the post office building on Main Street. She was trying to tickle him. Ugh!

But Inah is so very happy about that. She says it's better not to have any crush on any boy because boys are fickle. Anyway, I should wait until I am in high school. I say in high school I will change my name to Leslie or Donna. She says just don't get big boobs. Ha, ha.

Now no more goose bumps. No more of that floaty feeling in the head. Instead, on our way home from school or the library in the afternoon, Inah and I scoop up the leaves from the sidewalk, where they lie in deep piles like soggy scraps of cloth, and have a leaf fight. We bring them home stuffed in our backpacks, and with a needle and thread sew them together into long leis and hang them on all the doors and on our bedroom window upstairs.

Then one afternoon on the way home, we notice a FOR SALE sign outside the Ash Avenue entrance of "the Chinese house," and wonder what's happened to the grandma and grandpa. We go around to Magnolia Place. Inah drops her book bag on the sidewalk, tiptoes her way to the kitchen door and knocks and calls, "Hello, Hullo." She waits for a long time. Nobody comes to the door.

But the other Chinese grandma is back after having been gone the whole summer. In the evening, when the light turns sapphire blue, she comes around with a skinny, splay-haired Chinese man carrying a long wooden pole. Whenever they spot a female gingko tree (deciduous, according to *Trees Worth Knowing,* gingkos live over a thousand years) where the leaves have turned bright electric yellow, the man with splayed hair parks himself under it and shakes and knocks the branches with the pole. The stinky gingko nuts fall to the sidewalk in a noisy hail, and the Chinese grandma bends down, half-squatting, and busily, happily and greedily gathers them. They all disappear into her blue canvas bag with the daisy appliqué.

One evening, she sees us coming down the street with Daddy, and she picks herself up. She pulls at Daddy's arm like it was a door knocker and smiles and points at her bag and shouts something as if he is hard of hearing. Daddy nods and smiles, stretching his lips sideways. She makes a face at him, though, and shakes her head. She knows he is only pretending to understand her. She dips her hand into the bag and pulls out a fistful of gingko nuts and pushes them into Daddy's hand, making a big flurry of fuss, and waves him off with her toothless smile. We still feel sorry for her that she has to go around gathering stinky gingko nuts with a skinny man with splayed hair.

SIX

We've come to Florence at the peak of its tourist season. It's thoroughly trampled by, and infested with, tourists. In this claustrophobic museum filled with its jealously guarded treasures, I feel hopelessly trapped.

And then, of course, there's Inah. Relentlessly driven by this strange inner frenzy and insatiable need to see everything, quietly and stoically, she puts up with my bad temper and constant nagging, endures the relentless crowds, the long, endless lines, and suffers through the stifling heat. Without even a peep! Trudging from piazza to piazza, from church to church, from museum to museum, from one long, endless line to another. Pounding the narrow, heat-trapped, mobbed streets through blistering heat with near regimental discipline. So joylessly. Glum and sullen. Methodically and obsessively consulting and checking off the must-see list in her notebook pages. Hardly ever looking people in the eye or talking to them, as though they are mere moving shadows and forms around her.

After a day or two of this with her, I am ready to fold the tent. I feel like I am being force-fed very rich food, much too fast. One by one, my sensory devices shut down. It's futile, the effort. Really pointless. Yet Inah shows no sign of slowing down. Does it really matter, Inah, if you saw another Caravaggio, Donatello, Botticelli or Michelangelo? The infinite versions of Annunciation with the Magi, Madonna, the Child, saints and angels, the endless, mind-numbing human forms and religious symbols, don't you ever get tired of them; what do they speak to you? Inah hardly reacts. She simply shuts herself up, withdrawing even further behind the thick, opaque wall she builds around her, as though that's the only way she can cope with me and the world.

I begin wandering off, leaving her engrossed and still in front of a fresco or a painting, and I skip through the gilded rooms of palazzi, every inch decorated like a most elaborate cake, and rooms of museums filled with painting after painting, and hushed churches where images of suffering doggedly reinforce the immutable fear of hell. Trying to shake off the nagging suspicion and fear that it is just Inah's body standing there and that her mind is somewhere else, roaming some other terrain. On a landscape so remote, impossible to reach. That she is just floating through it all. Unconnected. Unnoticed. Unseeing. Lost in her own world. Moving as stealthily as unseen wind. And I am getting weary and tired of that silent, stoic Inah. That pale, drab, dingy, cool and poised Inah. That Inah who hides behind oversized T-shirts and loose jeans and a plain, stringy bob. That Inah who obliterates every trace of femininity. I am afraid that she has become a hidden fossil buried deep inside a rock, dead and unreachable.

SEVEN

Daddy rustles us out of bed early in the morning. It's a long drive to the Adirondacks, and we have to get an early start. It's our first ever sleepover vacation in America, but Mom's not even here. She's still in Korea, where she went to see sick Grandma. Only Grandma died before she could get there. Mom was still on the plane, somewhere over the blue-rippled Pacific. So it turned out she went there only to bury Grandma. Then she found herself unable "to just turn around and come back." Her feet felt stuck, that's what she'd said on the phone when she'd called from Korea. Inah and I had puzzled over this statement, but Daddy had said Mom was just being poetic. She must have been homesick and hadn't known it until she'd gotten there.

Inah and I make sandwiches to take with us, slapping up canned tuna on white bread and packing them in Ziploc bags. Mom would have made us *kim-bop*, Inah says wistfully. Without Mom, we've been eating badly. Our dinner has been just rice and kimchi and cold mackerel from cans, or soggy fried rice Inah and I make with soy sauce and egg. Daddy doesn't even know how to cook rice in the rice cooker.

Inah's the designated "map reader." So she rides in the front with Daddy and the I Love NY State map he sent for. Early in the summer, she had another dermabrasion, so even in the car she keeps on her pink floppy hat, pulled low over her face, greasy with the thick sunblock cream she finger-smeared on. She looks like a Raggedy Ann on a car trip.

Not long after passing Albany, we drive into a heavy thunderstorm. It starts with a swirling in the sky over the far horizon. Soon, the sun slips behind the clouds, and the air turns dusklike gray-blue. Then the winds come, blowing straight toward us, bending and swaying the trees along the road in green waves, and sending the leaves and broken branches in a spiraling whirl over the road. We can hear the crackling noise of thunder traveling closer and closer. Suddenly, the sky over us breaks up with jagged lightning, and with a loud peal of thunder, thick, driving rain pours down, pounding and pelting the roof, and the din of the hammering rain fills the car. Almost instantly, the road turns into a raging river, and the rain fog closes in on us in a thick gray wall. The blurry red taillights of the cars in front of us swim and float like extraterrestrial bugs. The red emergency indicator blinks steadily, as if warning of impending doom.

Daddy, who is having a hard time seeing through the rain-bleared windshield, now all fogged up, hunches over the wheel and fiddles with the buttons, but the defogger doesn't seem to be working. So Daddy tries to hand-wipe the window. Inah pitches in with a bunch of tissues she grabs from the tissue-box I hand to her, but she ends up making it even worse. Scared, we sit stiffly, holding on to the door handles because we know we could easily get hit by a blinded car behind us. I wonder if God is angry because we're going on a vacation so soon after Grandma died and for not even feeling sad.

Crawling along, Daddy manages to make it to the next exit, and we get off the highway. A few minutes later, looking out at the earth-pitting rain, coming down in heavy, slanted ropes of silver, Daddy and I and Inah stand under the dripping eaves at a closed village gas station and auto garage. A car passes by, splashing through the flooded road that winds up a hill and disappears through wet trees. Across, on top of a steep, green slope, a rain-streaked, turquoise crackerbox house stands all by itself on a lonely vigil.

Daddy and Inah and I are all quiet, thinking about Mom in Korea and wondering what she's doing. Daddy says it's August 15 in Korea, *Gwangbok-jeol,* Independence Day. "Oh," Inah says, peering out from under the pink floppy hat. She fingers her greasy cheek, healing in shiny red patches, and wipes her fingers on her shirt. I smack her hand, and she yelps.

"Too bad your grandmother didn't get to see you two again," Daddy says. "She probably died with her eyes open." We don't say anything. We feel bad because we don't even remember her face very well. It has been more than five years since we saw her for the last time. We were seven and it was just before we left Korea. Mom and Daddy took us to see her. We took an express bus from Seoul to the village where she lived with her older daughter and her family. We remember the trip mostly in pictures: green rice paddies and farm villages nestling at the foot of pine-tree hills, and dark blue mountains beyond that, slipping past the bus window; the winding, yellow dirt road we followed to Grandma's vil-

lage hiding in a narrow valley, walled by mountains; the sad-
looking farmhouses we passed on the way, closed down after
their owners had left for cities.

Grandma lived in an old, gray, tile-roofed house with
crumbling walls around a sunken courtyard, shaded by a
bamboo grove and an old fruit tree with gnarled branches. I
remember walking in through the half-open wooden gate.
Grandma was sitting alone on the veranda floor, and she
didn't even seem to recognize us at first. Mom went to get
Auntie and Uncle at the apple orchard, and Daddy and I
and Inah sat with her on the veranda floor. It was late afternoon and thin birds' cries floated down from the hill, where
groves of tall, skinny trees and islands of pine broke the
green monotony of the terraced rice paddies and vegetable
patches.

When we left the next day, Grandma held our hands and
cried like a sad old bird. She thought America was as far as
the sky is from the earth. She didn't think she would see us
again. Outside the crumbling stone-and-mud wall, where
white and pink flowers were blooming on tall green velvety
stalks, Daddy took a picture of us with her. Afterward, she
pointed at the flowers and said, these are *Neng-son-wha*.
Look at them well, she said, and whenever you see these
flowers in America, you think of your grandma. The flowers
were opaque and lusterless, as though they were folded out
of thin rice paper. (In America, they are called hollyhocks,
but we didn't know it then.)

When the rain becomes just a lazy drizzle, we file into the
car and get back to the highway. Soon the sun peeks out
from the storm-passed, thin, blue-skinned sky and floods
the car with watery light. In the backseat, slouched sideways, Inah sleeps, hugging her pillow. The gray road rushes

over and vanishes underneath in endless, monotonous and repetitive rhythm. It's as though Daddy and I are the only people awake in the whole drowsy world.

Then, bit by bit, as if someone is cranking up a huge screen in a drive-in movie theater over the flattop of the road, dark green hills and blue-gray mountains with shadows and overlapping lines slowly float up.

"Ah, see that, Yunah? We are now getting closer to the mountains," Daddy says, his scratchy voice waking up in excitement. "We will be there soon. . . ." Daddy's voice drifts off into a faraway murmur, and I am outside Grandma's house in Korea. Along the crumbling wall, dusty, lusterless hollyhocks are in bloom, just like that summer we went to see her. Suddenly, one of the tall stalks turns into Grandma. Her hair is flour-white, and her *hanbok,* too. White is the color of death and mourning in Korea. "*Halmoni!*" I shout, surprised that she isn't dead.

"Why did you come?" she yells in a surprisingly loud voice. "After you ruined your sister's face for life?" She then raises her cane as if she is going to hit me with it. I shrink away, screaming.

"Yunah! Yunah, wake up!" It's Daddy's voice. I open my eyes only to close them right back; the bright light hurts. Daddy says I must have been having a bad dream. I sit up. Inah is still sleeping, dead to the world. Rubbing her greasy, sunblock-cream-covered face on the pillowcase.

In the morning I wake up in the upper bunk bed in our cabin at the Blue Mountain Lake Inn. In the bed below, I hear Inah talking to Daddy in her sleepy voice. I let my head dangle down. On the picture window filled with tree trunks, the morning is gray.

"A-ha, lazy Yunah is finally up," Daddy says. He's already

all dressed. "Get ready for breakfast. Daddy will show you the lake on the way. It's very pretty."

Shivering in the cold drizzle, and a little breathless from the wet, thin mountain air, Inah and I wade after Dad through the tall, wet grass.

"Look, Daddy! The lake!" Inah points to it, a blue oval mirror. In the middle of it, a small craggy island is marooned, and it holds a tall, thunder-struck pine with jagged stumps. Inah and I rush down to the edge, where wet, empty canoes rest, looking forlorn.

"Isn't it pretty, huh?" Daddy says. Inah and I nod, like two Alices in Wonderland. With his hands, Daddy screws our wet hair turning frizzy in the drizzle.

Inside the nearly empty cafeteria, everyone is wearing a poncho or parka. We sit down at a table by the window so we can look out at the lake, and the sage green hills and the gray-blue mountains beyond, fuzzy and grainy in the rain mist. Inah and I shovel in cornflakes in cold milk. Daddy munches on white-bread toast and sips hot coffee, and leafs through all the guide booklets and pamphlets he collected from the rack at the doorway. If it rains all day, we can't go hiking, he says. We will have to find something else to do.

"Hi!" I turn around and see a round-faced Asian girl in a lavender dress printed with yellow flowers gazing up at me, moving her thumb around inside her mouth like it's a lollipop. I wonder where she's popped out from.

"Hi," I say.

"My name is Chang-mi," she says. "It's a Korean name. Are you Korean?"

"Yes, I am. I know your name means rose."

"Uh-huh," she says, nodding. "But you know what? My whole name is Phoebe Chang-mi Wilkinson."

"That's a long name for a little girl like you."

"Uh-huh," she says again. Suddenly, her thumb inside her mouth stops moving. And she stands very still. She is staring hard at Inah. In turn, Inah swivels her head around me, screws her face at the girl and says in her cold, cutting voice, "Nice meeting you. Bye now!"

"OK. Bye." But she doesn't go away. She just stands there, examining Daddy (who doesn't seem to notice or hear anything as usual) and me and then Inah again.

"Daddy?"

"Uh . . ." Daddy looks up and, surprised to see her, says, "Oh." She smiles at Daddy expectantly.

"*Apa*, she's Korean. Her name is Chang-mi."

"Oh, pretty name," Daddy says. "Where's your family?" Chang-mi half-turns and points to a table across the room. We turn to look, and they all wave. Her family is white.

"That's my mom and daddy and grandma. And my baby brother, he is Korean like me," she says. "His name is Daniel."

"Like we want to know," Inah blurts out.

"Huh, Inah! Be nice!" Daddy says.

"Why should I?"

"She's happy to meet other Koreans."

"How come she's so ugly?" Chang-mi asks, pointing to Inah.

"Huh, like you're so pretty yourself. You *shi-gol-te-gi*," says Inah, calling her a country bumpkin in Korean. Chang-mi looks at Inah uncertainly, turning red in the face. She then turns around and dashes off.

"What did you do that for?" Daddy scolds Inah. "You're not very nice!"

"But she's the one who called me ugly first," Inah says sullenly.

"She's a little girl. She doesn't know any better. But you're older. Daddy always thought you were a good-hearted person. Never knew you could be mean like that! Next time, think before you talk." Daddy glares at Inah, and she just hushes up, shocked, because he hardly ever raises his voice. Daddy doesn't say anything more, but he still looks mad, the way he stares out the window. Pulling at her hands nervously under the table, Inah steals quick glances at him from the corner of her eye. She knows she has disappointed him. Daddy waits and waits for her apology, but it doesn't come. Finally, folding up the pamphlets, he gets up.

"Let's go," he says. Inah looks like she's going to burst out crying.

It rains on and off in drizzles the rest of the day, and Inah's kind of quiet. From the Adirondacks museum, Daddy drives us to a mountain peak. It's windy and cold enough to make us wish we had heavier jackets. Daddy and Inah and I stand for long minutes, shivering and whipped by the wind, looking at the clouds moving in billows over the ash-colored Adirondack Mountains; craggy slopes and crooked spines, spreading in every direction like a dead sea. It feels as though we are standing atop the world.

The next morning the sun is out, but it's a weak, diluted sun. After breakfast, Daddy rents a canoe and we paddle around the glacier blue lake. And then we spend the rest of the day hiking, following the trails that run through the woods of furs and pine, spruce and ferns and moss. Daddy often makes us stop and feel the tree bark and the smooth green moss spreading on the fallen trees, and he points out the way sunlight plays on everything, changing the colors and shapes and the way it glides over the moss-covered rocks. We stop to drink in the fragrance of the forest, filling our lungs and listening to the sounds of the woods: leaves rustling in the wind, birds flapping their wings as they take off from the trees and tree branches falling in soft, dull sounds. In the middle of the hushed woods, where trees shoot up in clean, straight lines, skyward and pointy, we tilt back our heads and follow the lines of tree trunks up and up until our eyes water, through meshes of branches and leaves, to the canopy top, where the sunlight pours through the dense foliage in powdery gold dust before splintering into thin, arrow-straight pencil lines.

But it's not like it used to be, when Daddy used to take us on day trips to the Harriman State Park, Bear Mountain and the Catskills (which he thought looked just like Korean mountains) and when we used to cling to his every word. Inah does everything perfunctorily, just to please him. She's not even interested in botanizing and has left all the Ziploc bags she brought from home at the inn. Daddy keeps asking us if we're having a good time. Yes, we are, Daddy, we answer. But he knows we are being less than honest, and is disappointed. We're growing up and changing.

EIGHT

On the way back from hiking, Daddy gets lost and we miss the dinner service at the inn's cafeteria. At the rec room, where we see Chang-mi and her little brother trying to get a Ping-Pong ball going across the table, a woman says the only place to eat for miles around is in town.

Tired and hungry, Inah and I trudge out to town on foot with Daddy. The sun has just set. The light is blue all over, and below the far sky, where feathery slivers of orange and purple are barely traceable, mountains and hunkering hills are turning into blue-black silhouettes. Not a single car passes by on the newly paved, serpentine black road, fringed with the skinny fall cosmos and painted rocks giving off a metallic gleam in the blue light. From the roadside bush, even a fall cricket makes only a tentative attempt to try out its vocal cords before going quiet. Then all the way, it's just the sound of our footfalls in the hushed, empty blue world.

We find the town wholly devoid of people or traffic. Inah races up the stone steps to the restaurant, which is built like a chalet. "Daddy?! It's closed!" she shouts back, pointing at the sign on the door of the town's only restaurant. "It says, 'Sorry, we are closed for the season.'"

"That's too bad," Daddy says. "It looks like a nice restaurant, too." Disappointed, Inah comes back down the steps. She's known for getting all cranky when she is hungry.

"How hungry are you?" Daddy asks.

"I might just die," Inah replies, exaggerating. Daddy laughs.

"And it was your fault we missed the turn," I say. "You're supposed to be the map reader."

"No it wasn't. Are you blind?!" she says.

Tailing Daddy, we cross the street and head down to the town's only general store. The parking lot in front of the store is empty. And, as we feared, we find the store, even if only for the day, closed. Inah, unconvinced by the WE'RE CLOSED sign, peers through the glass door of the store, longingly staring at the bags of chips and cookies in the rack. She finally gives up, turns around. It's now inky black all over and the sky has expanded and risen into a high, immense, sapphire-colored dome.

Not knowing what to do, Inah and I and Daddy stand there outside the closed store, spattered by the white and grainy, misty lamplight. As if stranded in a puzzling dream. Having traveled a zillion dream waves away from Flushing. Shivering in the rapidly cooling mountain air and vaguely sensing that something is being forever lost that very fleeting moment.

All of a sudden, without warning, crickets start in the black clumps of bushes up the street in a bold, dreamy chorus.

"Daddy?!" Inah tugs at his arm as if waking up from a strange but brief dream.

"Uh . . ." Daddy looks down at her and says, "Not to worry. Daddy won't let you go to bed hungry."

"But everything's closed!"

"How about we go back to the inn and go out in the car? There must be a place to eat somewhere." Inah murmurs and whines. We walk back to the inn and climb into the car. As Daddy drives, we stick our faces out the window to the cool wind that rushes by, grabbing our hair and whipping it back to our faces in sharp needle sprays.

"How about singing?" Daddy says, but we can't think of a song for the world of us. Not even Inah, the nonstop chatterbox who loves all the groovy songs. We are starving, and we miss Flushing, home and Mom.

"Daddy, look!" Jumping back to life, Inah points to a building sitting atop a hill above the road we have just passed. On the huge, floodlit banner that's slung across the front of the building, we read beer, pool and pizza. Daddy makes a quick U-turn and drives the car up the steep, dirt driveway. We can tell the building has been hastily put together for the summer season: It sits on a plot of red mud claimed from the waist of a scraggy pine hill, and part of the outer walls are still exposing Sheetrock. We notice, too, that it's all pickups and flatbed trucks that are parked there in the muddy ground.

Out of the car, Inah and I follow Daddy through the door and stand facing a big room with a long bar to our left. Pool tables are scattered around the rest of the room where, in the lamplights, smoke clouds drift like dirty yellow fog. To our right, a small attached dining room sits empty with a few tables.

Inah and I jump a little when the door belatedly shuts

with a clack behind us. Suddenly, every head turns, and the room goes very quiet. The men stare at us, practicing the same silent, fixed look as the stuffed deer heads mounted on the wall. They look like lumberjacks we've seen on TV. We stand there, silently stared at like swatted flies on the wall. No one comes over or talks to us.

"Let's go sit down," Daddy says, pointing to the dining room, and, as if that's exactly what we've been waiting for, Inah and I start for the room. We pick a table against a wood-paneled wall and sit down. Daddy goes over to the service window, where a sign above it says it serves pizza and salad only, and he orders a large pizza pie and three cans of 7 UP. The men at the bar are still staring. Daddy comes back to the table, and we wait. Self-conscious, Inah and I sit as stiffly as cardboard cutouts, as if that's what is expected of us. Then Inah, like an insect that is tired of pretending to be dead, starts fidgeting, sliding down the seat and up, trying to make the staring men disappear from the range of her sight. Finally, she slouches down, resting her chin on her folded arms on the sticky table. From a pool table, balls break in a *click-clack,* and it's quiet again.

"Daddy?" Inah says pleadingly, slinging a furtive glance toward the bar.

"It's OK. Sit up," he says. Amazed and dumbfounded, Inah and I stare at him. How does Daddy know? He's sitting with his back to the bar. We thought only animals carry eyes in the back of their heads! "And Inah, now that you're inside, take off your hat." Inah reluctantly sits up and pulls down her pink floppy hat. We sit and sit, staring at our hands and the wall.

"Why don't we study the map while waiting?" Daddy suggests.

"But I left it in the car," Inah says. When Daddy gets up

to go out for it, she looks scared. She jumps in her seat when the door closes after him. It's the first time I've ever seen her afraid of anything.

"Like to play husband-wife-concubine?" I ask Inah, trying to sound normal. Inah shakes her head. She has seen one of the men at the bar stand up. He's slowly heading toward the dining room where we are sitting, scared to death. Inah looks frantic, and flushed in the cheeks. My heart is racing so loud that I can hear it thump. Tense and with strange anticipation, we sit and wait, watching him from the corners of our eyes.

In a flash, I remember the story Cousin Ki-hong told last Christmas, home from Stanford University. Over Thanksgiving, with his friend, Cousin Ki-hong motorcycled down to Baja California, Mexico. One scorching afternoon, they found themselves in a small fishing village. Feeling thirsty and hot, they walked into a dark, dirt-floored bar. As soon as they stepped inside, all the Mexican men turned their heads and stared at Cousin Ki-hong, a Kiss fan, in long, shaggy hair, tight black jeans hugging his skinny rocker legs, a tiny silver hoop earring in one ear, and his friend, a stocky Korean guy who was built like a brick house. Nobody moved, and nobody said a word to them. They just stared and stared. Like in a silent movie. This went on about several long minutes until a man at the bar got up, walked to a jukebox standing against the mud wall and slipped in a coin. To their amazement, a Yoko Ono song flew out of the jukebox. (We: Who's Yoko Ono? Cousin Ki-hong: Wow, is this a generation gap or what? You girls live in a cultural wasteland, don't you?) Ha, ha, ha. Soon everyone in the bar was laughing and clinking beer bottles.

When Cousin Ki-hong told us the story, he hinted at some dark danger avoided. He said that it's always a little dangerous to travel in this continent when you are an Asian. It's a lot like rolling dice. The word *dicey* means just that. The key is never to ingratiate yourself and never show them you're afraid. Inah and I, so impressed, later looked up the words *dicey* and *ingratiate* in our *Webster's Dictionary*.

I see the man's feet in heavy mountain boots, the toes all curled up. They stop. Inah can't help it: She turns bug-eyed when he puts his hands on the back of the chair where Daddy has been sitting. I steal a quick look at him while his eyes slowly tour Inah's scarred face, blotchy and waxy. He is a little cross-eyed, and his eyes are pigeon gray, as if faded from blue. His oatmeal-colored hair hangs in stringy strands, and below his cutoff sweatshirt sleeves, his Captain Cook arms, sunburned to salmon color and full of freckles and curly gold-flecked hair, are as thick as trees. He looks a little like Jesus Christ in the picture hanging on the living-room wall in Jessica Han's apartment.

Inah doesn't dare to look at him. In her hands, her pink floppy hat is being twisted and twisted into a tight knot. Suddenly, he turns to me and catches my darting eye, and I think I am going to burst with fear.

"Yo kids happen to speak English?" he says in a surprisingly warm voice. Inah springs back to life and eagerly nods, as if she has turned into a yo-yo. "Well, then, yo kids mine tellin' yor daddy, when he gits back that is, we not too crazy seeing Chinks or Japs here in dis part of the country." Inah snaps to attention and sits up. From the look, I just know she's going to tell him we are neither Chinks nor Japs, and he will ask us what we are then and say it makes no difference anyway, that we are gooks. I pinch Inah's leg so hard that she jumps in her seat. Instead, we say nothing and sit curled and still like two stepped-on worms. To our relief, he starts to walk away. Then, as if having a second thought, he turns his head and says, "Yor folks ain't goin' find no place serving rice around here, either. Better off goin' back where yo come from originally."

When Daddy comes back with the map, we don't say a quip about the man. The pizza comes, sizzling with thick, melted cheese. We stuff ourselves so fast that when we get back in the car later, we can still feel the big lump of under-cooked dough of the pizza sitting inside.

As Daddy drives, Inah and I quietly watch the lonely night road run away, chased by the high beams, slithering and climbing and descending, bending and then straightening itself out like an unfurling ribbon. Trees forming black, ragged walls on both sides of the road swish by. We enter and leave black night that seems endless.

"Look at that," Daddy says, slowing down the car. He turns off the high beams and points toward the edge of the black woods, where fireflies are zinging around soundlessly, beaming on and off in blue-green lights. They are more beautiful than green stars that buzz in the summer sky.

"Ah, it's been a long time," Daddy says, in a voice syrupy thick and encrusted with the sudden rush of longing. "When Daddy was a farm boy growing up in Korea, they would be out all over on a summer night . . ."

"Daddy, but we like Flushing better," Inah says, shaking with a hiccup.

"Why? It's so clean and beautiful here! What's so good about dirty and crowded Flushing, you can't wait to go back?!"

Suddenly, heaving, Inah flies to the window, pushes her head out and throws up. The pizza and soda shoot out of her mouth in thick, sticky streams and disperse and scatter into the thin, pine-scented mountain air. I hand Inah a bunch of Kleenex and rub her back. Daddy asks her if she wants to stop. Inah wipes her mouth and hangs her head out for fresh air. No, Daddy, she says, curled over the window ledge, trembling and shaking. Keep going, I feel better already.

NINE

Florence that numbs me during the day, induces dreams at night. Feeding on my fears and longings, my restless mind regurgitates as I paddle through sluggish sleep. I dream a thousand dreams: I am standing on Ponte Vecchio, leaning over the side. There, there is a body, down there, floating on the jade green Arno River. My heart jumps into my throat: It's Inah, the body afloat facedown. It's her hair, a black loosened mop. It's her khaki jeans and white T-shirt, swollen bags. I scream and scream.

I am inside the empty, dark and echoing Duomo, walking up the aisle. Inah is somehow missing. Suddenly, a snow white pigeon flies out from behind a pillar and shoots straight up toward the dome, beating its wings, and disappears. I look up: Inah is looking down from the cupola, her arms spread, ready to jump. Don't, Inah, don't. Choking with fear and throbbing with hot panic, I run, climbing up the narrow and dark and endless semicircles of stairway laid out in foot-worn, smooth, cold stones. Desperately trying to reach her before she jumps. Stumbling and slipping. Getting nowhere.

I am wandering through the rooms at the Uffizi Gallery, looking for that beautiful Florentine youth with dark brown eyes, hooked nose and black curly hair in one of the portraits. Feverish with longing. In and out of endless rooms. Finally, in despair, I walk out to the sun-flooded hallway, and he's there. Smiling. But there's Inah behind him, watching me with her cold, mocking eyes. I turn around and walk away, ashamed and brokenhearted.

Inside the entrance of a small church, in the nook of the wall, stands a porcelain statue of the Madonna. She is wearing a sky blue robe, and her head is draped in white. As I look up at her, her face turns into that of Inah's, and she starts weeping silently. Her teardrops roll down her white porcelain face and fall to the floor and calcify into red glass beads. I pick them up, and they melt back into blood in my hands. I run out of the church screaming and holding up my bloodied hands.

I wake up from these hideous, phantasmagorical dreams dry-mouthed, sweaty and exhausted, screaming voicelessly under the tangled sheet, only to find Inah sound asleep next to me. I drift back to sleep, where more dreams await.

In another dream, I am back with Mom and Inah in the old Japanese house in Korea Mom used to call "the bad-luck house." Mom is standing near the kitchen door, dressed in silk *hanbok:* short water-blue top and long, streaming azalea pink skirt. Next to her, little Inah stands, holding one of those lotus lanterns they string along in temples on Buddha's birthday. On her face, she is wearing an elaborate mask of a rouged Korean bride, leaking a sly smile out of her painted lips. I wonder why she is wearing a mask when

Mom and she turn around and walk through the sliding kitchen door to the alley outside. The light from Inah's lantern throws shifting shadows around her. Not wanting to be left behind alone, I try to run after them, but my feet won't move.

The dream is so vivid that when I wake up, I can still see the tiny, delicate creases on the pink-dyed rice paper of lotus petals. I realize the mask Inah was wearing in the dream was the same mask Dad made for her on our first Halloween in America. Inah and I helped him tear up a whole stack of old newspapers, which Dad soaked in a bucket of water. Later, he pounded them into a pulpy mess, mixing in the flour glue he'd cooked up on the stove. Inah trembled with excitement when her hand-molded mask was finally dry, and Dad brought out the paints and brushes to draw a face on it.

That Halloween evening, Inah was a Korean bride and I was the gatekeeper of hell seen on temple gates in Korea. My mask boasted big, bulging eyes and sharp fangs pushing out of the blood red mouth. In my right hand, I carried a *samji-chang*, a three-pronged sword Dad made out of crushed aluminum foil, and in my left, a plastic jack-o'-lantern.

But it was Inah who made a big hit. In her Korean bride mask with that sly expression and in Mom's Korean silk apron tied around her chest, she looked so comical. We went knocking on every door in our Bowne Street apartment building, belching out the tongue-twisting phrase, "Trick or treat!" after Jessica Han, the cat, and her baby brother, the Superman. Inah always got the most attention. Oh, she's so cute, everyone said. Cute! Cute! Cute! How pretty! So adorable! The old Jewish ladies put all of their pennies into Inah's jack-o'-lantern, and later even her apron pockets started sagging with mini Milky Way bars and Hershey's Kisses. Jessica Han's baby brother threw a jealous temper tantrum and I followed Inah, poking her behind with my aluminum-foil-wrapped sword, but she was having so much fun, she couldn't care less. In fact, she loved the attention so much that for days afterward, she'd walk around the streets with the mask on. To her thrill, on the street, people would stop, look at her and laugh. It tickled her that people couldn't see her real face. It was a different kind of attention for a change, and she loved it.

There is something very depressing about the dream of Mom and Inah, and I can't go back to sleep. I try to remind myself that it's just the time of day when life energy dips to the lowest level and everything appears much bleaker than it really is. But it doesn't help. My head keeps churning out images, and my mind keeps wandering off.

Finally, I give up and slip out of the bed. I tiptoe to the window and open the green plastic shutters. The light bothers Inah. She groans and stirs in bed, turning and kicking off the sheet. Then slowly rearranging her long, lean, boyish legs, she folds and refolds her arms around the pillow, trying to get comfortable. Mesmerized, I watch the way her body languidly moves itself in the heaviness of sleep and the way the small of her back above her narrow hips cups like a porcelain bowl. In her white cotton tank top and white panties, the body Inah hides like a secret, like shame under oversized T-shirts and baggy pants, looks unbelievably exquisite and sensual in the morning light, which gilds her skin taut and smooth, like a water-rounded pebble.

How it used to terrify Mom. The idea that Inah would grow up and become a woman one day only to be denied the joy and the pain of loving and being loved. But no matter, she has become a woman. A twenty-eight-year-old sexual being with a beautiful body that must feel desires. And how hard Inah must have tried all these years to become a stone incapable of thoughts of love, longing and yearning. Even in her dreams. If not to allay Mom's fear then to spare herself the humiliation and indignity of not being wanted or desired.

Soon, Inah is still again, immobilized by sleep. Her body is again that pristine and unexplored and untouched virgin territory. It looks as innocent and pure as that of a prepubescent girl. It's as if she's regressing back to the child she once was. Before she became a prisoner of the immutable fear. I can almost believe that when she wakes up, she will be again that happy and relentlessly upbeat chatterbox.

PART FOUR

ONE

Saturday afternoon on the July Fourth weekend, we are in the car, driving to Staten Island for Uncle Shin's house-warming party. Northern Boulevard already looks like a parking lot with tangles of cars. Mom fiddles with the car air conditioner, sputtering and purring like the wings of an injured bird, but after a while, she gives up.

In the back, Inah and I sit at opposite ends, leaving a wide Demilitarized Zone in the middle. Inah is quiet and sullen, as usual. She's got a pink jean skirt on because Mom wouldn't let her wear her usual uniform of an extra-large white T-shirt and baggy khaki jeans. She fidgets and fidgets as if she doesn't quite know what to do with her pair of bare legs, skinny and pale as beansprouts. Although she has added almost three inches since last summer, at fourteen, she's still the same flat-chested, straight beanpole with no apparent signs of curves or boobs.

Inah shifts in her seat, lifts her legs and folds them under her butt. I give her straying foot a smack. She turns, glares and hisses.

"Your feet are dirty," I say.

"Like it's your business," Inah says. "And you got zits."

"You're swearing."

"Not!"

"Yes, you are!"

"BS."

"See, there!"

"Ugh!!" Mom turns and shoots me that don't-you-dare-start-a-fight look.

"See?!" Inah says. I sneak a hard pinch on her skinny leg, and she swiftly responds with a kick to my leg. She's lucky, because if it weren't for Dad, she would have had it coming to her. As for Mom, I don't really care. She always sides with Inah anyway, and I always end up getting the bum rap. More so ever since Inah got into the coveted Stuyvesant High, one of the two best public high schools in the city. Now Mom treats her more like a celestial queen. She's exempted from all the chores. She doesn't have to lift a scrawny finger at home.

"You go up and study," Mom says to her as soon as she puts down her spoon at the dinner table. It means it's always my turn to do the dishes. So just to rile her up a bit, I say, "Go ahead, Inah. The road to Harvard can't be that smooth." It never fails to annoy her.

"You're twisted, you know that?" She hisses, glaring at me, like she would love to swallow me down whole. And then before we know it, we are swearing and cursing, calling each other every kind of abominable name we can think of. I call her a geek, a dyke, a butch, a creep and some other names I would never utter under normal circumstances. She calls me a meatball, a cow, a hare-brain, an egghead, a fathead, a bonehead, a moron and a bimbo. Luckily, Mom doesn't know what the worst of those words mean. If she did, she would kill herself. As it is, she says we act like sworn enemies.

In the middle of every fight, though, Inah storms off to her room and locks herself in. She does it because she knows it gets me mad like nothing else. And what do I do? Bubbling and boiling with rage, I follow her and park myself outside her room. Banging at the door and jiggling the doorknob, I scream and yell at the top of my lungs, telling her to open the door. According to Mom, a pig being slaughtered wouldn't sound as ugly and horrible. Of course, Inah is no fool. She isn't ever going to make me happy by opening the door. She taunts me from behind it while I rant on and on "like a maniac." It's a good thing she locks herself in the room, because otherwise she might just end up missing a limb or two.

It's a matter of pride. I can't ever bring myself to back down. After a while, I just change my tactics, turning the tables. Through the crack of the door, in my little-girl voice, I call out to her, using her various nicknames: Pootz, Pootzy Poot, Pootzy Pringle, Pootzeroon, Whoopsie Daisy, Rap Scallion, Sparkle Plenty and so on.

"Come on, Pootz, Pootzeroon, Pootzy Poot, open the door," I croak. That sends her off to the roof. Incensed, she will grab a book or something and throw it at the door. Screaming, "Go away, you freak! Why don't you take a long walk off a short pier!" Or something incredibly stupid like that. And I holler back, "Oh, why don't you drop dead, you geek!"

Not wanting to be accused (by me, of course) of taking sides with Inah, Mom waits and waits patiently, hoping we will stop. But when she's had it, she will race up the stairs, her face all flushed, and haul me downstairs and herd me into the kitchen so we will be out of Inah's earshot when she and I have a talk.

Then I have to stand there and listen to Mom saying things like how she'd rather die than see us fight like this all the time. She won't let me put in a word. Every time I try to explain the situation, she just shushes me. It doesn't matter who's right, she says. Let Inah win. To keep peace. Do that for me, Mom asks, if you can't do that for Inah. Another favorite line of Mom's is that after she and Dad are gone, Inah will be all I have. But really, what kind of logic is that? All I ask Mom is just to be fair. I don't think she has ever listened to what Inah says to me. I mean, what right does she have to call me a slut just because I put on a tight T-shirt? Why do I have to constantly look over my shoulder? Why do I have to live like this? Mom can't and won't answer these blazing questions of mine.

And so, while Inah sulks and wallows in self-pity and gloats in her warped sense of victory behind the locked door of her room, Mom and I go back and forth, arguing; Mom, in her rapid-shooting Korean, and I, in my rude and insolent-sounding English Mom just can't stand. The whole point lost in translation. It is like shadow boxing. Frustration galore.

But I am not that dense. I know, and I think Mom does too, that all these fights and skirmishes we have are not really about these petty things. It's the onset of our puberty, and fear. Naturally, in the confusion of fear, every little thing gets snowballed into an epic struggle. But the way Mom sees it, I have the face Inah lost. Isn't that enough of luck and fortune? What more could I want? I should try to put myself in Inah's shoes. Instead, all I do is stir up the pot. Rubbing it in. Rubbing what in? For one thing, try not to pay so much attention to how you look, Mom says. I can never win. If I put on a tight-fitting T-shirt, it's to flaunt it. But I do what other girls do at my age. Is it such a bad thing, wanting to experiment with simple lip gloss? But nothing I do will ever seem innocent to Mom (or to Inah). But I can't do what Mom wants me to do: She wants me to cloak it and hide it. Just as Inah does. As if that's going to do it.

The day I got my first period, Mom rushed me to the bathroom, locked the door and kept saying in a whisper, "Already?!" She seemed more scared than I was. Not for me but for Inah, who had yet to start her period. I remember squatting on the toilet with a bad cramp. Mom asked me not to tell Inah about it. Why, I asked, puzzled, and Mom said she didn't have to know about it. As if it might give Inah a wrong idea. That's when I realized how Mom was so frightened of the idea of Inah growing up and becoming a woman. Shunned and ignored. Mom couldn't bear to imagine the pain of rejection Inah would have to go through.

But there's nothing Mom can do to stop me or Inah from growing and changing. Inah doesn't live in a cocoon. She goes out every day. She sees and hears and thinks. That's why she's getting so quiet and withdrawn. She has known for a long time that being smart isn't enough. Out there. In the real world. Mom can't shield Inah from what's inevitable. Still, she tries. In her blind hope. But how is Mom going to stop Inah from becoming a woman? She can't spare her the pain. Still, Mom can't help herself.

Inah must feel and smell the fear that burns and scorches Mom. The fear that emits short, hot waves and stokes up such anxiety. That's why her body hardly changes. Fourteen years old and all she's got are narrow hips and small buds for a chest. Even though we are identical twins, our bodies couldn't be more different. It's as if Inah wills her body to stay that way. To quell Mom's fear.

"You will see. It's a mansion," Mom says out of the blue. She's back to the topic of Uncle Shin's nouveau riche house she's been telling us about for weeks. We already know all about the marble-floored bathrooms, whirlpool baths, cathedral windows and big oval-shaped swimming pool. Mom's voice is thick, poisoned with envy. It's the voice she uses when she talks about other people's cars, other people's houses and other people's kids. When she says other people, she means other Koreans. We know Dad hates it when she does that, but he doesn't say anything. Inah sighs audibly.

The anemic air conditioner suddenly spurts back to life, and whizzes and purrs, blowing out musty air. Dad shuts it off. Inah and I roll the windows all the way down, letting in the sticky, warm air. Mom obliviously goes on, saying how some people move upward in life and others she knows—we know whom she means—stay in the same place, like going through a revolving door.

"Mom?!" I whine.

"What?" she says. "Have I said something wrong?" She casts a sidelong glance at Dad and adds, "Don't worry. Your father, as usual, hasn't heard a thing I said. If you don't believe me, ask him."

"Dad, is it true?" I ask.

"Uh? What's true?" Dad says, looking at me in the rearview mirror. Mom grimaces and clucks her tongue. It's now as hot as an oven in the back. Inah, who's been trying to tune Mom out, pulls her propped arms in from the windowsill and stares at the back of Dad's seat. I grab the *New York City Five Borough Pocket Atlas* Dad keeps in the car and flip through the pages.

"Did you know there are zillions of cemeteries in Queens?" I ask Inah, effectively annulling the fact that we're in a cold war. "It's got to be the world's capital of cemeteries." I notice her right leg has strayed into the DMZ.

"So?!" she says tersely, putting back down her leg.

"Look at all these cemeteries: Calvary. New Calvary, Mount Zion, Mount Olive, Lutheran, St. John's, Mount Hebron, Flushing, St. Mary's . . ." I point at them, shaded in lime green. "What do you think it is about Queens that attracts all the immigrants and the dead?"

"The land is cheap in Queens," Inah states drily.

"Like you should know!" I put the *Pocket Atlas* back onto the ledge behind the backseat. Inah slides her hands under her butt and, slouching, stares out the window with a faraway look, listlessly peeling her sweaty legs off the seat. The sucking sound drives me crazy, but I don't say anything, not wanting to be blamed for starting another fight.

I notice we are passing the dark underpass curve that climbs out and merges into the westbound B.Q.E. near the Kosciuszko Bridge. The bridge marks the border of Queens and Brooklyn, and the traffic is always heavy there. In anticipation of merging, Dad puts on the left-turn signal. Then, just as we slowly merge into the traffic on the B.Q.E., the old clunker gasps and purrs, and we notice a thick gray column of steam spewing out of the front hood. It quickly turns into blackish clouds outside the windshield.

Mom immediately starts to panic. Because of what happened to Inah, she can't stand the sight of fire or smoke. It doesn't help that she hasn't a clue as to how a car works (not that we do). She's so sure that the car is about to blow up any minute in a fireball, tossing us into the air, blown apart in bits and pieces.

"Get out of the car! Quick!" Mom yells at us in her frantic, fear-stricken voice. Mad at Mom, Dad screams at her that she is going to get all of us killed.

"Stay in the car! Stay in the car!" Dad shouts, trying to maneuver the car back over to the shoulder. Inah and I push our heads out the windows and frantically wave, trying to warn the cars behind us. All the while, paralyzed with unbearable fear, Mom sits with her eyes crushed shut and her hands closed in tight fists.

"No good! It's dead!" Dad announces. "Get out of the car and go over to the shoulder. Watch out!"

Inah and I scramble out the back door and help Mom out. And then, holding her by the arms, we make a dash toward the shoulder like border-crossing aliens. Gripped with fear, Mom can barely move. But Inah is absolutely calm. It's morbid, but even as I dash toward the shoulder with Mom and Inah, in my head I can almost see our mangled and twisted bodies lying on the road and Mom crumbled over us, wailing.

Dad's face is drenched with sweat when he finally makes his way over to join us. Our car, an old dung-colored Oldsmobile, sits in between the two merging lanes, belching out black smoke from under the propped-up hood. Mom asks Dad what's wrong with it and what we are going to do. We know for sure we are not going to make it to Uncle Shin's for the housewarming party, and won't get to admire his nouveau riche house. Dad says we will have to wait for the tow truck. But it doesn't look like it's going to happen any time soon. The traffic is already backed up for miles. And the other side of the B.Q.E.—bottlenecked by the new asphalt-laying work—looks as bad if not worse. We can see a long swath of a yellowish-gray smoke trail hanging in midair like clouds.

Peering up and down the road, Dad paces restlessly.

Against the corrugated, rusting rail, Inah and I stand around Mom. It's almost surreal. The glare of the sun. The boiling heat. The humidity. The dust. The hot air, reeking tar. The constant *ping, ping* metallic hum coming off the bridge. Miles of snarling traffic without end.

Dad finally says he's going to go and look for help. Inah and Mom try to talk him out of it, but he takes off anyway, down the hill, heading toward the Meeker Avenue exit. Mom, recovered from the initial shock, gets all mad. She says she knew something like this would happen sooner or later. She has been telling Dad to get rid of that "junkyard" car for months. Inah and I, crushed by the heat, keep our mouths zipped.

"At least the view is great," Inah mutters ironically. But it's really true. We have miles of unhindered view stretching all the way to Manhattan. The spot is any photographer's dream. Below us, the stagnant Newtown Creek lazily coursing away like worn, relaxed yarn looks oddly pastoral; its oily surface, glossy and flat like a black mirror, reflecting the hazy summer sky dappled with white clouds, and the smokestacked, rusting, industrial buildings. To the right, the sprawling Calvary Cemetery looks like an immense, hunkered-down lion, gasping and panting, impaled by a million corroding, blackened stones of the dead. Suffering from its own traffic jam. Even if only a muted one.

"Mom, look at the view!" Inah pleads, trying to distract her, but she's too shaken, too hot, and too upset to give a hoot about the view. We know that if she could, Mom, being a true-blue Flushing bourgeoise, would bribe God with everything she had just to be about any place in the world except here. She's most probably worried about being seen—by people we know and she knows, like people from her church who may just happen to go by—standing huddled in the heat like a bunch of refugees, and our car, the ugly, rust-eaten Oldsmobile (Uncle Shin calls it "Oz-mo-bill") sitting there in the middle of the highway like a war relic, belching smoke.

"Now everyone knows," Mom says, reacting inappropriately as usual, as if anyone gives a hoot about what kind of car we drive. Inah mumbles to herself that she didn't know it was our best-kept secret.

"Knows what, Mom? And who's everyone?" I ask.

"Why, the people passing by. They can see," Mom says, wiping the rivers of sweat on her forehead with a ball of tissue.

"So what? It's not like you're famous. And what do you care? You are not ever going to see these people again. And you always tell us not to care about what other people think."

"Shut up, Yunah," Inah says. "You always have to make it worse."

"And you don't," I hiss.

"And you two have to fight even here," Mom says, worryingly and anxiously peering toward the Meeker Avenue exit. No sign of Dad or a tow truck. From every car that crawls by, people still gawk, rubbernecking. A beat-up, acid-burned Mustang rolls by with several tattooed, beefy guys in it. (Remember? Dad once wanted a Mustang!) They shower us with catcalls, banging the sides of the car with their hands. Inah sticks her tongue out and I give them the finger. Horrified, Mom yells at us to turn around and stand facing away from the traffic. But it feels really indecent standing like that. Like we are mooning the whole world.

Inah glumly gazes at the skyscrapers of Manhattan far away: steeples of steel and glass soaring like cliffs along the East River; a twelve-paneled screen, shimmering in silver and white and blue. After a long while, Inah heaves a sigh and says, "I can't wait to go to college. I can't wait to leave home." She says it almost in a whisper, as if she is saying it to herself. "And I am going to go far away, too. And never come back to Flushing." I am too scared to say anything.

"You heard me, Yunah," Inah says.

TWO

*A*fter a late lunch, Inah and I head up to the Boboli Gardens. The cone-shaped hill rises continuously in steep angles, and it makes an arduous climb in the thick heat. Above the hill, the sky around the sizzling sun is all bleached salt white.

At the hilltop, we wander into a small, lovely garden. Its one end overlooks the low, rolling hills below, dotted with olive trees and dark green cypresses shaped like tall candle flames. At the other end stands a small, rococo-style fountain resembling a fancy tiered wedding cake, very different from the ones we've seen so far in Florence. It's being repaired. In the shallow, green, scummy pool, a half-dozen hot-looking men are standing around, conducting a loud heated debate, we assume, about how best to go about doing the job at hand. Then all of a sudden, the debate escalates into a shouting match, and one of the men, in disgust, throws up his arms and walks out of the pool. We figure it's time to leave.

It's then, following Inah back down to the wrought-iron gate, I notice the low green bushes in the flowerbeds. No flowers, but I instantly recognize those dark green, waxy leaves with serrated edges. They are peony trees. Who knew. There are peonies in Italy. For some reason, I've always associated them with Asia and Korea. And with Dad and his affair. I hurry out, hoping Inah hasn't noticed them. I don't know exactly why.

Outside, discouraged by the heat, we agree to forgo the walk to the Forte di Belvedere and slowly meander our way back down the hill. Halfway down, we spot a bench in the shade and sit down. Around us, the sluggish afternoon stands breathlessly still, and there's not even a hint of a breeze. Below us, from the huge, onyx-colored marble fountain, which we find absolutely hideous, gray columns of water soar silently. And beyond, through the thick, hazy heat, the gray-blue hills lapping away into the far distance seem to shimmer and shift. The only other people around are two shirtless, gangly American teenage boys loudly playing chess at a nearby bench. Their American accents couldn't sound more foreign here. We couldn't possibly come from the same country.

I leave Inah on the bench and move to the grass under a tree and sprawl on my back. Inah makes herself comfortable and opens up a book. (It's the kind of book found in the parapsychology section at bookstores.) I close my eyes, and instantly I am drifting down a slow-moving river. Soon, germinated by this and that, thoughts crop up in my head, and smothered images spring back to the surface and grow branches before I can snuff them out. (Is it the peonies I just saw?) Miles and miles away, but life back at home still follows me. With all its cluttered details. Dad. Mom. My job at the Legal Aid Society. Other people's troubled lives I deal with day in and day out. And even Tai, whom I broke up with months ago. Back home, they are all waiting to claim me back. Home that Inah strenuously avoids talking about. Because she knows it will be like punching a hole in a dam. But she must know she's missing everything. The family that is getting older (and getting younger) all the time. Shrinking and expanding like the moon. But she doesn't want to be any part of it. She wants to run away until she's undefinable, unknowable and unreachable.

By now everyone's used to Inah's absence from family scenes. Her name hardly comes up anymore. She doesn't figure in at family functions. Sometimes, it seems she has never existed. I remember Cousin Ki-hong joking, "I hear Inah's in India. Do you think she's gonna come back a vegetarian?" Ha, ha. He thought he was being funny, but his casual remark had a bite.

It was Cousin Ki-hong's second daughter's first birthday, and we were standing on the kitchen deck at his parents' house in Staten Island. Barefoot and in shorts and a black Polo shirt, he was dangling a donkey piñata to the gaggle of excited kids down below in the backyard lawn where white kids, Korean kids, black kids, half-Korean, half-white kids formed a mini United Nations. It was hard to believe, but Ki-hong, once our idol, the Kiss fan who used to be a skinny, earringed rebel in black jeans with a Hispanic girlfriend, had married a Korean girl and long become a suburban family man, bloating in domestic bliss, driving around in a baby-seat-strapped Saab. I was sure the hole in his soft earlobe had long closed up.

Mom and Dad were there, too, that day. I remember how Mom looked so wistful, watching Jennifer Kim, Cousin Ki-hong's wife, lumber their bun-faced girl around in a rainbow-sleeved Korean costume. And every time I looked into the den off the kitchen, Dad, alone and sleepy-eyed, was watching lions in the African tundra on the muted TV.

In the living room, as usual, Uncle Shin held a noisy court from the fancy rococo-style couch preserved like bones under a vinyl cover. (Dad used to teasingly quiz him if it was Louis XIV or XV, and Uncle Shin would always answer good-naturedly, "Just Louis.") At one point, I even overheard him quote his favorite old Korean saying, "Work like a dog, live like a nobleman." He was rehashing the old story of his wig-peddling days in Harlem. "And think that I never even been near a college gate in Korea. They must mean a man like me when Koreans say, 'A dragon rising out of a gutter.' America is a great country or what?"

When I later went to say good-bye, Dad turned off the TV and said he would go for a walk; he had eaten too much. Mom was nowhere. The living room was empty, too. In the bedroom upstairs, where I went to get my bag and jacket, Jennifer was changing her baby on the bed. I sat down and helped her with the powder. Then she left to go to the bathroom, and her baby went into a frantic cry. She returned in a fussy flurry, unbuttoned her blouse, whipped out her milk-swollen, white moon of a breast and slid the dark nipple into her girl's mouth, putting an immediate stop to the crying.

I remember sitting there, a little shocked. Maybe because Jennifer (she was our age, but she seemed so much more mature than either of us) did everything so casually and nonchalantly and expertly. Maybe because it was a picture in which I had never placed Inah or myself. It didn't seem then and doesn't even now that we would ever arrive at such a stage in life.

Jennifer looked adoringly at her sleepy-eyed baby, suckling and playing with the pearl strand around her neck, and she dabbed off the milk dribbling down her daughter's chin and giggled. "Isn't she so amazing?" she said, her voice ringing with that simple, pure joy. I felt sick. I couldn't believe she could have pulled off such a miracle. The song says, people do it every day, but it still seemed a miracle.

"God, Yunah, I love her so much," she moaned and solemnly added, "it's almost scary." She meant it. "Although when I first saw her, I was a little surprised," she said. I must have looked confused.

"You know," Jennifer said. "Her face, it was so Korean!"

"What did you think she would look like?" I asked, incredulous. "You and Ki-hong are both Korean!"

"I don't know. Big blue eyes. Not-so-flat nose. And blond hair?" I laughed, but she wasn't entirely joking. "Remember?" she continued. "The surprise? Growing up? Your face in the mirror? The flat Asian face that stared out at you? Like a stranger? I don't know about you, but it surprised me every time that I didn't look anything like white kids. You see white faces every day, day in, day out, at school and on TV, you start to think that you look like them, too. I used to have a real complex."

"So you're just one more banana. White inside, yellow outside," I said.

"Aren't you one? Even my mother's so used to seeing white people on TV, she no longer thinks Korean faces could be beautiful."

I had never thought I would ever envy Uncle Shin's family, but that day, I did. Not for their nouveau riche house or money, but for their ability to be happy. They harvested the fruit of life so effortlessly. What was their secret?

I look at Inah. Her face grizzled with the dappled shadows of leaves, she sits still, her book left open on her lap and her eyes pinned to some faraway hill. The sensual Inah earlier, with her pristine body sheathed in the morning light, is now traceless. She is again the plain Inah, with the marred face framed with stringy hair and her exquisite body encased in loose clothes. I always thought that I knew the answers to and causes of Inah's actions and nonactions: her face. But a week with her has left me more confused than ever. I am not sure about anything.

I sit up, and she turns to look at me. I toss off the grass I pull up. It drifts down lifelessly. Inah follows it with her eye and looks away. I feel the chance to talk to her is fast slipping away. If I am anxious, it's because talking to her is never a spontaneous event. It's so hard to gauge her mood and harder still to predict her reaction. And more than anything, I hate having to watch every word I say. So often the effort itself turns into an insurmountable impediment. I know that even if I come up with just the sort of an opener that might chip away at the impassive wall Inah has built around her, it is not going to be enough. It will only end up sounding like a contrived, rehearsed pep talk.

"Inah, you know Mom's worried," I say simply in the end. I have no backup words or contingency plans. The muscles on her face visibly tighten. "I don't know what you talked about on the phone with Mom and whether you told her why you quit your studies. I do know she was upset for a while, but I think she's OK now. She just wants to make sure you're OK." I know it's only half true. Sometimes I blame Mom for Inah's wanderings. Mom, who greedily bore all the guilt for what happened to Inah's face, always pushed her hard. Setting the bar so impossibly high. Always an excellent student, Inah skipped grades and stayed on honor rolls. But it was never enough for her. What followed next was more important. Inah's little successes were mere stepping stones to reach the Zenith. Mom refused to see her scarred face as an impediment. Just the opposite. She just couldn't understand that in the end, it was Inah's choice and Inah's life. She kept raising her expectations. Until it became impossible for everyone. The years after Inah left home, Mom resolutely stood facing her, fixated on the daughter who kept breaking her heart. Mom hardly ever seemed to notice me, even long after Inah became her sun that failed to shine.

Still, when it was time for me to leave, I stayed instead. Mom didn't have to ask. I chose NYU because it was just a bridge, a river, a subway ride away. I could always return. At a moment's notice. I became a good daughter. Not that Mom ever appreciated that. She took me for granted. I had the face, even considered pretty, the same face that had been snatched away from Inah. I would live a normal life, have plenty of chances to be happy as a woman, she must have thought. I don't know whether Mom was ever secretly disappointed. I don't think I ever mentioned one of my boyfriends to her, so unsure how she would feel about it. Sometimes, I felt I lived a double life. But I was always there for her, as her gal Friday so that she could turn to me for help. But I can't rescue Inah for her. I am not capable of such a feat. And I am getting tired of playing a good daughter.

Inah isn't going to help me out. She just sits silently. "Inah, don't get me wrong, because I am not telling you what to do. You know, no matter what, Dad and I will always support you, but there's Mom to deal with. I guess she worries more because you're always so far away. You know how she goes through these emotional highs and lows. All depending on what you're doing at the time. Now she's got this picture of you aimlessly drifting around. And to be honest, I can't deal with Mom anymore. Just tell her what your plan is. You must have one, no? Even if it's tentative? Like how long you are going to stay in Rome. Anything. So I can relay it to Mom. She deserves to know that much."

"I wish I knew," Inah says, her voice trailing off like a wisp of smoke. After a long while, she adds, "I just can't live the life Mom wants me to." I don't know why I get the impression that Inah is still resisting. That she has just bypassed the real thing and instead delivered an empty shell. A universal truth rather than the personal truth. Disappointed, I mull over what she has just said. What kind of life does Mom want her to live? I am not sure I know. Mom's worried. Simple. All she now wishes is that Inah would carve out a form of life. Nothing so colossal. Time has a way of humbling a planner and a dreamer like Mom. All of us have been finding out how elusive even an ordinary life with ordinary dreams can be. That seems to come by so easily, effortlessly, to other people. To people like Uncle Shin and Cousin Ki-hong. Their families grow and prosper. They dream simpler dreams. They make practical plans. They are happier. Somewhere I once read that it is happiness, not unhappiness, that ruins us. But a line like that no longer comforts me. I want us to be happy. For a change. I don't know why our life still threatens to fall apart. Where do you go to get the stamps of ordinary life?

"I don't think Mom expects you to be an Einstein or a Madame Curie," I say. Inah hoots, spitting out air through her lips. I look away, not wanting to see the way her scarred lips pull, crunching the rest of the face. "Come home, Inah. Even if it's just for a while until you know what you are doing. It doesn't have to be to New York. I know you don't want to be too close by. Just show your face. You know Mom and Dad would be real thrilled to see you. You can't go on like this forever. What are you doing in Rome? How about money? What are you living on?" I know I am still beating around the bush. What I really want to ask her and what I really want to know is more abstract. I want to know what it is, that elusive something she is searching for.

Inah sighs. She doesn't want to promise anything. Maybe she doesn't know what she is searching for, either. Maybe she is swimming in the dark like the rest of us.

The sky over the hills is starting to turn dark purple-blue. I hope for a rainstorm.

"Remember, Inah? Dad always said that rain comes from the east." Inah simply smiles.

THREE

The afternoon of Dad's birthday, Mom calls from the travel agency and asks me to meet her in front of Kum-wha, the "Golden Flower" Korean supermarket. She needs me to help her shop.

August is nearly over, but outside the sun still feels prickly hot. Down Ash, the sidewalk, patched with splashes of sunlight and shade, looks like a quilt. Behind the gray wall of the house on Syringa Place, sunflowers, huge and bright and combusting yellow against the dazzling blue of the sky, hang their necks from tall, velvety green stalks. The gray, diamond-shaped seeds embedding the centers have turned dark brown, as though they have been slowly dying all summer from self-immolation. Soon they will be pulled out and discarded on the sidewalk, the roots and the floppy leaves and all, and the summer will be over.

It has been a strangely quiet summer. Inah, working on some science project at a biology lab in Manhattan, has rarely been home. Mom's been working six days a week all summer, as it's the busiest season at travel agencies. Even Dad, still out of work, has seemed to manage to spend very little time at home. The house usually sits empty when I come home in the afternoon from my summer job at the YWCA, where Jessica and I work as camp counselors. At some point during the summer, I began to dread coming home. I hated walking into the empty house. It always made me furious for some reason.

Mom looks hot in the sun standing outside the supermarket. She asks me why it has taken me so long, and I just shrug. Sometimes, Mom is just too much of a dose of reality. Inside, at the fish counter, I hang back as she pokes and fingers the long, silver tails in the ice bed. It's Dad's favorite fish and I've seen them only in Korean markets. Mom lifts up a couple of them and puts them back down. She smells her fingers and makes a face and says, "The fish isn't that fresh." The man behind the counter doesn't seem too happy with the way Mom molests them, but she just ignores him. Finally she picks two.

Carrying the grocery bags, I sulk all the way home. Distracted by her own thoughts, Mom doesn't even notice it. Inah has come home while I was gone. She opens the door, takes the grocery bags from Mom and carries them to the kitchen. Mom takes out the fish from the grocery bag and hands them to me. I carry them to the sink to wash and salt them. But the fish stink something awful when I unwrap them.

"Mom, I think they're spoiled," I say, holding my nose. She comes over, saying, "I knew it." She pokes at the skin and angrily rewraps the fish. "Take it back!" she says, handing the package to me.

"Now? Mom, it's kind of far," I say.

"Go with Inah," she says, as if that makes sense. I know better than to argue with her. Inah and I go out and walk all the way down to Kissena, where we chuck the fish into a garbage can. We then walk back through Beech just to kill time. I ask Inah if she got a present for Dad. She shakes her head and mumbles, "Like it's very likely Dad remembers it's his birthday."

"So what? You do!"

Inah doesn't say anything. At Magnolia, we pass "the Chinese house." On the ground off the kitchen, a big green garbage Dumpster is sitting. And someone also has cut all the shaggy branches off the pine trees. We rarely come around this way these days. It's been months, too, since we last went for a walk with Dad. It was sometime in June when the printing company he worked for went bust and Dad lost his job.

Dad still leaves home every morning, but we have no idea where he goes and how he spends his days. When he comes home at night, he has often eaten, too. With someone or another. No one we know—a man he met at his college alumni association, he says when Mom asks. Inah and I kind of suspect that he just goes somewhere and spends the day killing time because he doesn't want us to see him idling at home. Because he doesn't even seem to be trying to get a job. We know it's not that easy at fifty-eight.

For a while during the summer, though, Dad seemed busy. With a Korean man he had met, he used to drive out to masonries and granite quarries. Sometimes, they even went on overnight trips as far as Massachusetts. From the trips, he would bring home little pieces of granite samples in Ziploc bags, and glossy leaflets and Korean books on stonework filled with pictures of traditional Korean stone pagodas and lanterns and step-by-step illustrations. But it just stopped as abruptly as it had started. Another time, after going to see a Korean man who owned a motel in the Catskills, he floated the idea of getting into the motel business. But Mom torpedoed the idea. So everything kind of fizzled out. One way or another. From lack of feasibility or money or both. Or Dad would eventually lose interest.

Then as the summer passed, we noticed how Mom and Dad talked less and less to each other. If they ever did, it was usually about something trivial like taking out the garbage or fixing the dripping faucet. Even then, it was like a shuttlecock match, their conversations flying and bouncing off, as they would never sit down together, face-to-face. They were always doing something else. Mom at the sink. Dad reading a Korean newspaper at the dining table or on the couch in the living room. Sometimes, I wondered if they remembered each other's face.

"Back already?" Mom says when I walk into the kitchen. She's rolling out meatballs on the flour-dusted cutting board at the dining table. "Got the money back?" I nod. Inah, who has snuck up to her room to get the money for the fish, comes in nonchalantly and puts it in the drawer. I wash the vegetables and peel and mince garlic and ginger. Inah mops the floor and goes out to the backyard and brings back a bunch of red roses from the climbing rosebush Auntie Minnie brought when we moved here. The petals are almost black. Inah sticks them in a Sunkist bottle and places it in the center of the dining table. Mom is growing quieter and quieter.

With the dinner all ready, we sit around the Formica-top dining table in the kitchen. The clock on the wall shows it's past eight, but it's still sunny outside. The kitchen throbs with heat and the smell of rice, garlic, ginger and sesame oil. Inah's got her nose buried in a book. Mom keeps glancing at the clock and gets up to adjust the flame under the stainless pot of the birthday seaweed soup.

When Mom comes back to the table, Inah puts down the book and spies on Mom's face.

"Did your father say anything this morning?" Mom asks us.

"Like what?"

"Like he's going out to dinner with someone?"

"No. You mean Dad doesn't know it's his birthday? You didn't tell him, Mom?"

"I forgot," she says.

After a while, restless, I get up and scrub the sink clean with a new Brillo pad. Outside the kitchen windows, dusk is slowly spreading its blue sheath. The low peony trees look like black umbrellas. The predatory bamboo makes a thick, shaggy, unruly grove by the wooden fence. And in the barrels along the flagstone path, white and pink and deep purple petunias—their colors almost livid in the light of the dusk—are blooming profusely, cascading down the sides of the barrels. Over the years, the Korean Zen garden Dad once envisioned has gone through some modifications.

I remember how excited Dad was the day the peonies he had ordered from a catalogue arrived from a farm in Connecticut. Just in time for fall planting. It didn't seem to matter that the three-year-old, bare-rooted plants had come from China. Dad was like a child who opened his first ever Christmas toy. He couldn't wait. That evening, he went out and dug up big holes and planted them. In the spring, he spent hours and hours in the backyard, squatting like a Korean farmer, mulching and improving the soil and also laying down the flagstone path. He coddled them like babies and constantly talked about peony blossoms as a man talks about a beautiful woman he couldn't hope to attain. He would read up on everything about them, looking them up in his English-Korean dictionary, and in his spiraled mini notebook would write down all the characteristics and the fancy names of Chinese peonies: Taoist Stove Filled with the Pills of Immortality; Coiled Dragon in the Mist Grasping a Purple Pearl; and Purple of the Sung Dynasty.

It took two springs before the peonies decided to send out blooms and reward Dad. It was May. They seemed to bloom all at once, bursting out in luscious hues. Each petal as flawless as a piece of new-spun silk. Each blossom a perfection of beauty. Dad went out and bought oiled-paper umbrellas from a Chinese shop and kept the "thousand petal" blossoms shaded to prevent the colors from fading in the sun and being stained in the rain. Under the shading umbrellas, they looked like ravishing beauties coyly waiting for their lovers. They waited and waited until dusk and then floated away into the night, softly padding away. But the season of peony blossoms turned out to be so fleeting. After just two weeks or so, the best of them were all gone, and Dad quietly mourned their passing.

I go back to the table and sit down. Inah complains of hunger pains. Mom repeats we aren't eating without Dad. It's his birthday. I look at Inah. I can tell she isn't going to swing into action.

"Dad might be at the *kiwon*," I casually spill the beans. Inah angrily pinches me at the back.

"What *kiwon*?" Mom wouldn't have looked more surprised had I said "house of prostitution." Although she looks more disappointed than upset. She knows it's more than just a place to play a few games of *badduk*. Men who frequent the place are either old, lonely or out of jobs, and all have lots of idle time on their hands. Inah and I even code-named it the House of Lonely Men. It's a small

Korea, a refuge men seek from the outside world: America.
To Mom these men are failures.

"I didn't say Dad's there, Mom. I just thought he might
be there, and if you want, I'll go and look." Mom doesn't
answer or look at me. Instead, she gets up and turns off the
gas and walks out of the kitchen.

"Are you coming?" I ask Inah. She just hisses. I go out to
the foyer and slip into my rubber thongs. It is nearly dark
outside but still muggy. I hurry down, making my thongs
sing. The *kiwon* is on Union Street, across Northern Boulevard, and it's at least a fifteen-minute fast walk.

I am hot and almost out of breath by the time I reach
Northern Boulevard. As I cross the street, I remember the
Chinese girl I knew in sixth grade. Her grandfather got
killed crossing the street at the very spot, hit by a car. Mom
gave me a ten-dollar bill in a white envelope to take to
school when we collected money because she didn't have a
father and her family couldn't afford the funeral expenses. I
thought ten dollars was way too much and debated about
replacing it with a five-dollar bill. But in the end I didn't,
because I was afraid that I would go to hell when I died.
Auntie Minnie and Mom always talked about going to hell.

The stairwells of the *kiwon* building smell like hot spices
of *jambong* from Mi Mi Hyang, the Korean-Chinese restaurant downstairs. It sends me into a sneezing fit. Outside the
kiwon door upstairs, I hesitate a little before giving it a careful push. To my surprise, it gives in easily, and I slip inside.
A yellow-faced man at the counter looks up from the newspaper. I stammer a little. I must have said that I've come to
look for my father. I know it's saying it in Korean that
makes me feel ashamed. He nods and goes back to the
paper.

I look around the big, rectangular room, to which the

fluorescent lights and thick cigarette smoke give a seedy, cavelike feel. Hesitantly, I head down the aisle. On the elevated floor along the wall, men sit on cushions, cross-legged, across yellow *badduk* tables, where black and white buttonlike stones make up quizzically beautiful patterns. The sounds of *badduk* stones hitting the boards echo through the room like errant hammering. To my relief, no one pays any attention to me. Halfway across the room, though, I suddenly realize something: I don't want to see Dad here, slouched over the edge of the floor, observing a game. Not on his birthday. I turn around and quickly slip out of the *kiwon*. The man at the counter never looks up.

FOUR

Two months after his birthday, as October winds down, Dad goes AWOL. For years, that's how we will refer to his affair as "Dad going AWOL." As if it were a joke. Saying to each other, "Remember the time Dad went AWOL?" As if that way we can somehow wipe out the bad memory that will linger like a black spot in our vision or make it less hurtful.

I don't know if Inah and I could have ever guessed it. Dad just wasn't someone who would have an affair. If there were clues, we never picked up on them. Everything was usual that morning. When I left for school, Dad was getting ready to leave for work just like any other morning. Although later I would remember smelling on him the Aramis aftershave when he walked into the kitchen that morning. Inah and I had chipped in and bought it for him the past Father's Day, but he rarely wore it. That night, Dad didn't come home, and Mom told us he was staying the night at the house of his friend whose mother had died. So we thought nothing of it. I wonder if Mom knew.

When Dad went AWOL, things were getting better, too. At the end of the listless summer, after months out of a job, Dad started working again. He went to work for Uncle Shin, who owned an importing company and a wholesale store in Koreatown, Manhattan. We know working for Uncle Shin was something Dad had avoided as long as he could. He didn't want a job handed to him. It was just somehow too easy. But there had been other reasons. Some things about Uncle Shin always irked and rankled Dad. Like his politics. Dad knew he couldn't, without losing his temper, deal with him on a daily basis. He didn't want to end up losing him, unable to separate the Uncle Shin he loved like a brother from the one he disliked: a proud Staten Island Republican and a generous campaign contributor, whose mantra was "in America, money is king"; who freely admitted that he despised the weak and thought the poor were lazy; whose business dealings often seemed, if not criminal, a little shady and just barely legal.

Several years later, when the L.A. riot would break out, they would nearly have a falling out. They would have a heated argument in front of the TV, where surreal scenes of the riot splashed on the oversized screen in the den of Uncle Shin's house: buildings going up in flame; rowdy, festive mobs looting the stores and beating motorists; and Korean business owners perching on the rooftops in military prone position with their machine guns and rifles. Uncle Shin would declare that under the same circumstances, he would do exactly the same thing the men on the rooftop were doing. He genuinely believed every man has a right to make a living without fear and, if it were needed, to protect his livelihood in any which way he could. Even with a machine gun.

Dad would remind him of his early days in America as a wig peddler in Harlem, the story Uncle Shin often proudly rehashed. The fact that he once made a living off black people. So what, Uncle Shin would say. I didn't steal. I didn't live off welfare. I worked like a dog. I am not ashamed. I am proud. That day, Dad would end up calling him a capitalist pig. And he, accusing Dad of being a socialist and a communist and saying Dad didn't deserve to live in America, enjoying its freedom. Dad, furious with him, would break his wooden chopsticks into pieces, bolt up and walk out of the room.

But Dad seemed fine. In fact, after he went to work for him, Dad started spending a lot of time with Uncle Shin. Often at the end of the day, Dad would call home from Manhattan and tell Mom not to expect him to dinner as he was going out with Uncle Shin.

Then one Friday night, not long after Dad had started working for him, Mom came in and woke me up. It was just past two in the morning. Almost two hours since Uncle Shin had called to let Mom know that he had just put Dad in a livery cab Koreans refer to as a "call taxi." Dad should have been home long ago, Mom said. Something must have happened.

On the way to our parents' room downstairs with Mom, I went into Inah's room and woke her up. She grumbled plenty but followed Mom and me downstairs. But as soon as we were in our parents' room, she burrowed into Dad's side of the bed and went right back to sleep. Mom, unable to sit still, kept pacing around the room.

I must have dozed off because the next thing I remember is jumping up at the loud ringing of the doorbell. Inah catapulted out of the bed, and we hurried to the door after Mom. At the door, it wasn't Dad we found, though, but a skinny, bespectacled Korean man we had never seen before. He wore a white short-sleeved dress shirt, dark blue slacks, and brown leather sandals over his sockless feet. He bowed to Mom and, pointing at a dark limo parked down at the curb, said he had a certain Mr. Hong in the car. We knew right away it was Dad. As we followed him out, he told Mom how he had been driving Dad around Flushing for over an hour. Apparently, Dad had refused to tell him where he lived. Every time he'd asked him for his address, Dad would holler, "Ah, uncle, I told you to take me to Seoul, Korea. You come from Korea. You must know how to get there, don't you?" Eventually, Dad had gotten tired of the game.

We found Dad sitting slouched in the plush backseat of the Lincoln. He had never been a big drinker, and he wouldn't touch the hard stuff. With Uncle Shin, though, you never knew. Uncle Shin was known to think nothing of ordering a whole bottle of Rémy Martin or Johnnie Walker Black. And often Korean men drink as if it were a game of daring, an endurance test. Glass to glass. And no one was more Korean than Uncle Shin. Making money, having fun, there was no difference to him. He worked on both very hard.

"Ah, *yeobo*," Dad blared, peering at Mom through his bleary eyes. "I had a couple of drinks, is that all right?"

"Only a couple and you can't even remember where you live," Mom said sharply. Even though Dad was much older, Mom would sometimes treat him like a child, chiding and cajoling. It was her way of letting him get away with his gaffe.

Dad looked at us and said, "Oh, you're all still up!"

He wouldn't let us help him. Instead, he pulled himself out of the car and stood on his wobbly legs. He apologized to the driver and saluted him in military style. And then, as we helped him up the steps, he launched into the Korean anthem: "Until the water of the East Sea dries up and the Mount of Baekdoo wears off. . . ." Inah and I giggled. Mom said he was going to wake up all the neighbors.

When we went down to the kitchen the next morning, Mom was making *boog-uh-gook*, dried fish soup, for Dad's hangover. Obviously, he was still in bed. On the kitchen counter, we noticed a fancy "room salon" matchbook. The black laminated cover showed a picture of a woman in silver silhouette holding a red-cherry-topped martini glass.

"Mom, where's this from?" Inah asked, holding it up. Mom said it had fallen out of Dad's shirt pocket while she'd been helping him undress. We knew it was more likely that Mom had searched all of his pockets.

"Dad went to a room salon last night?" I asked.

"Uncle Shin must have taken him. Your father can't afford a place like that."

"So, what's a room salon anyway?" Inah asked innocently.

"With a name like that, what do you think?" Mom said. "*Kaya,* House of the Night!"

FIVE

Dad's absence is so palpable, that's all we seem to notice somehow. In fact, Dad in his absence dominates our life at home. All over the house, we keep stumbling across the visible and invisible traces he left behind. Like his shed skin. His empty seat at the dining table, his favorite pair of white Sperry Top-Siders sitting in the corner of the foyer, the white canvas stiffening and yellowing, his toothbrush with splayed bristles poking out of the holder at the bathroom sink, his frayed blue terry-cloth bathrobe hanging on the hook of the bathroom door and his gardening book sitting on top of the hamper, open and facedown. They remain exactly where they were the day Dad went AWOL. Untouched and unmoved. We just go around and around them, as the void grows and grows, stealthily, and steadily like a spot of mildew.

Now every night after dinner, after the dishes are done,

Mom locks the doors and turns off the lights, and we go scattering around the house to our separate rooms. For the rest of the night, the house sits all quiet except for the sound of the refrigerator humming and burring. No longer the muffled sounds of our parents talking downstairs, the scuffing sound of Dad's slippered feet down the hall to the bathroom or the kitchen storm door closing with a soft click as he goes out to the backyard to have a cigarette.

And for days and days, waking up in the morning, it's the first thing I listen for—Dad in the backyard and the familiar sounds of morning: the water can clinking and clanking as it's being filled with water; Dad clearing his throat and his feet scraping the flagstone path. The sounds of Dad enjoying the quiet morning hour, his hour, before the whole house wakes up, converging into the kitchen for a hurried breakfast, colliding in the hallways and at bathroom doors, with his hands on his back, strolling and pausing to look up at the sky and bending down to pinch off the withered leaves. But everything's still, and I remember that Dad is no longer here. It always makes me a little sick in the stomach.

Not surprisingly, Inah, the geek and the prude, is in a state of deep, deep shock. Home from school, she pads around the house, moping and sulking and looking funereal. Whatever thoughts she may have, they sprout and wither in her own head, never expressed. I can't even wring a fight out of her; her interest soon flags. Instead, it's at Mom and at her moods that all of her sensory antennas are now aimed.

Inevitably, Inah and I pick up all the sordid details of Dad's affair. Whenever Mom's on the phone, there we are eavesdropping on her, lurking in the hallway outside the kitchen, shushing and glaring at each other. That's how we learn that Dad's lover used to manage one of the "room salons," expensive "hostess bars," in Manhattan, where Uncle Shin used to take him on their nights out on the town. On the phone, Mom invariably and disparagingly refers to her as "that madame" or "a woman like that!" Gritting teeth. Sounding hateful. Apparently that's what goads Mom most—that Dad got himself involved with "a woman like that." As if she wouldn't feel half as bad had Dad's lover been a rocket scientist or a suburban soccer mom with a family van full of screaming kids instead. But at least, as Auntie Minnie points out, Dad didn't run off with one of those young hostesses they call *young-gyes,* spring chickens.

In front of us, though, Mom tries not to let on, pretending everything is fine. She doesn't once mention or bring up Dad's affair. But she can't eat. At dinner, oblivious of us floating anxious and furtive glances, she sits there pushing the rice around and around in the bowl with her thin, slippery stainless chopsticks, endlessly counting and recounting the grains. Struggling to contain the anger, roiling, bubbling and percolating noisily inside her, threatening to spill out at any moment.

This goes on for days, until one night I am more than ready to confront her. But it doesn't look too promising. At the dinner table, she doesn't say a word. She scoops the rice into the bean sprout soup and then puts down her spoon as if it weighed too much for her.

"Mom, you not eating?" I say, exasperated.

"I can't eat," she says, getting up. "The rice tastes like pieces of stone." She then quickly gathers her rice bowl, spoon and chopsticks and carries them to the sink. Inah freezes up and then, looking helpless and aghast, watches Mom standing at the sink, motionless like a statue, letting the water run as if waiting for her anger to be washed away, down the drain.

Springing to my feet, I nudge Inah with my elbow. Reluctantly, she peels her butt off the chair and makes a face as if it hurts. We stack up all the dirty plates, carry them to the sink and stand crowding around Mom.

"Mom, we'll do the dishes," I say. But she won't even look at us. She just snatches them away from our hands.

"Mom, please!"

"Don't worry about the dirty dishes and go to your room and study. Both of you!" she yells, her voice bursting with anger. Nonplused, we return to the table and plop back down. Inah leans over her arms and chews her thumbnail, staring into space. It's been getting dark earlier. Outside the light-reflected kitchen window, the night seems coal-black and without boundaries. The kitchen feels like an airless vacuum.

Mom finally finishes loading the dishwasher and pushes the Start button. But she doesn't come back to sit down with us as I hoped. Instead, she slams open all the cupboard doors. Inah looks at me with that here-we-go-again look. Whenever Mom's upset, she cleans, storming through the house. She will raid the cupboards and drag out perfectly clean pots and pans, and spends hours scrubbing them until they are as spotless and shiny as mirrors. That's her way of dealing with anger. By cleaning.

Mom stares into the cupboards and walks back to the sink and just stands there with her back obstinately to the world. I get up, walk over to the sink, shut off the faucet and stop the dishwasher. Mom turns and looks at me, a little surprised. Then, she angrily turns the water back on and picks up the Brillo pad.

"Mom?!"

"What?!"

"How long are we going to live like this? Are we ever going to talk about it?"

"Talk about what?" Mom burns me with such a withering look that I shrink like a dry leaf tossed into a flame.

"It's not like we don't know," I mumble.

"So what?! It doesn't concern you," Mom snaps.

"How can you say that? Don't we at least have a right to hear it from you?" Mom drops the frying pan into the sink. Soap bubbles float up in white clumps. I look over at Inah. She is pissed off. She glares at me, bunching up her eyelids in yanking pleats. I realize I have bitten off more than I can chew, and I have no idea how I am going to patch things back together.

"You American kids always talk and talk and talk about your rights!" howls Mom. "You have no right to shame your parents!" I am dumbstruck. I have never thought about it that way. Mom looks as though she is about to break down and weep, but she quickly steels herself. I know I should stop right there, but I have to push my luck.

"Mom, I'm not trying to do anything," I venture cautiously. "I just want to know what we are going to do about it."

"Who's we?" asks Mom. Her eyes are furious. "Since when are you so concerned about your parents? Your father and I fed you, clothed you and sent you to school. Isn't that enough? Go to your room. You're not going to do anything about it!" What she says doesn't make any sense to me. No logic to it at all. Mom angrily pulls off her rubber gloves, shuts the faucet and walks out of the kitchen. I stand, a little flabbergasted. Inah kicks her feet and noisily pushes her chair back.

"Why did you have to bring it up?" Inah looks at me

with murder in her eyes. "Thanks a bunch for the wonderful evening!" She marches out of the kitchen.

"You're welcome. Not that you were any help!" Soon, the doors to our parents' and Inah's rooms shut in consecutive loud slams downstairs and upstairs. I stand at the sink, running my hand through the soap bubbles. After a while, I hear Mom come out and the front door open and close. She is running away to her church. To be alone with her Jesus. She finds us American kids pretty much useless in times of crisis. After cleaning up, I turn off the kitchen light. It is so quiet that I can almost hear the plants breathe in the backyard.

On the way to my room, I try the doorknob on Inah's room. As I expected, it is locked.

"Inah, will you open the door?" No answer. I go back down to the kitchen and return with a stainless steel chopstick. I've done it hundreds of times before; I pick the lock easily, like a professional thief. I could always make a living as a locksmith. It's a comforting thought.

Inah is lying spread on the bed on her stomach, her face buried in the pillow. I flick the light switch on, and she hisses and digs her face deeper into the pillow. I sit down on the bed next to her. The box spring sags with a sigh and settles. Inah's breathing and the *tick-tock* of the bowl-shaped clock on the desk fill the room.

I know Inah is much, much more disappointed with Dad than she has been letting on. He has always been the bumper and the balancing force between her and Mom, who always pushes Inah along with a relentless drive, out of guilt. If Mom's love was the breathing-down-on-you kind of love that singes you and brands you, his was the warm breeze kind of love. Mom stirs the water and Dad calms it, tipping the scale back, giving Inah much needed breathing room and equilibrium. And more than anything, Dad has always tried to show Inah that there are many, many beautiful and wonderful things to appreciate in life other than the obvious things the self-absorbed world makes her believe count. He was special and different. But now, of all people, it is Dad who has let her down.

I look at Inah, lying on the bed. Under her T-shirt, her shoulder bones form cliffs and jut up sharply. Suddenly she looks so fragile and vulnerable. It is no longer the Inah I resent: Mom's perennial pet, who always so effortlessly gets all her attention; the brilliant Inah who has breezed through all the subjects and skipped a grade; the Inah who, I assume, will go to Yale or Harvard, get a Ph.D., become a celebrated scientist by inventing a way of growing artificial skin from a single pig cell or something like that and get nominated for a Nobel Prize in science; the Inah, Mom's hope, who will make it all worthwhile for her. It is just unhappy, miserable, teenage Inah in her stupid, plain, over-sized T-shirts.

"Inah, come on."

"Go away," she simpers, hoping I won't. I wonder whether she, too, lies in bed at night and thinks about Dad and his affair. Whether she draws all kinds of romantic pictures in her head as I do, desperately wishing Dad's affair to be a romantic one because it is too hard to bear any other way: Dad at the wheel, speeding away on a winding country road, arched by trees, no longer green, his coy lover next to him, her long black hair and a red scarf blowing in the winds. Wet leaves whirring and falling after them like so many colored, festive confetti.

After a long while, Inah turns over and fixes her eyes to the sky blue ceiling, where, the spring we moved into the house, Dad climbed a ladder and spray-painted lavender roses of Sharon, Korea's national flower, surrounded with serrated dark green leaves. Inah and I shared the room then, and at night, with the lights out, from our beds, we would observe the flowering ceiling transform, in the faint light coming through the window, into a sort of half-realized, misty Oriental Eden, shifting and drifting, and imagine lying in the sky under a floating garden. It was so hypnotic that it was like gliding weightless, falling asleep.

"Why did Dad have to do it?" Inah says, her voice cracking and splitting in a sudden spurt of anger. I don't know if she is wondering whether Dad consciously made the choice. Her over us. I remember reading somewhere how life is all about making one choice after another. Connect those dots and see what kind of picture emerges: a portrait of a life.

"I don't know, Inah. Maybe Dad was lonely," I blurt out and instantly realize that it makes perfect sense.

"How could Dad have been lonely?" Inah springs up like popped corn, as if I'd said something outrageous. It simply has never occurred to her that Dad, too, just like us, has an emotional life, that he might be lonely now and then, and that more than simple daily worries might occupy his mind. To Inah, things are much more black and white. Despite all of her voracious reading, she remains puzzlingly innocent and rigid. She probably thinks sex is dirty, too. Anyway, when you're an angst-ridden teenager, you don't think there's a bigger crisis than your own. And your parents? You sort of develop blind spots. You think they are immune to temptations. They should be. They forfeited those rights long ago. They should behave.

"Isn't it obvious? He ran off with a woman," I mutter, suddenly feeling impatient and a little cruel. I probably sounded worldly and jaded to Inah, who could easily win Triple Crowns if there were contests for Miss Clueless, Miss

Prude and Miss Innocence. Disgusted, Inah screams and throws her pillow at me. It is just too hard for her to digest the idea of Dad running off with "a woman like that." It sounds so cheap and so vulgar.

After a while, Inah slides back down and says, "I don't want to see Dad ever again." She sounds more sad, though, than defiant.

SIX

Inah and I walk to a trattoria on Via dei Neri for dinner. It's that time of day, just before dusk when the lavish, gold-flecked and iridescent rays of the sun cast spidery webs, turning the buildings along the narrow, curving side streets into thin, pencil-line sketches, when the large and small piazzas, moped-terrorized, dusty narrow streets and stately boulevards all slowly turn up empty, and when Florence magically transforms into the pastoral Renaissance town in the paintings.

Then, as we wait for a table at the tiny, treeless triangle piazzetta outside, the light turns blue all over, deepening into intense sapphire blue. And suddenly, it's as if we are standing in the middle of a movie set. It's not just the blue light or the austereness of the piazzetta, or the straight lines of the buildings around it but it's also the craggy-faced middle-aged Italian man standing against the trattoria's open doorway. (With about two days' worth of stubble on his chin and in a blue sports jacket that is unraveling at the hems, he has that elegantly disheveled look.) It's the way he uses his hand (his other hand holds a glass of white wine) to expertly excavate raw green peas out of pea pods and pop them into his mouth at regular intervals. The sagging pockets of his blue jacket hold an infinite supply of them, because his long-fingered hand digs up some more and still some more. And all at the same time, in his condensed baritone, he conducts a long-running, casual, public conversation with the horse-faced man busily pulling at the espresso machine inside, peppering it with short, guttural laughs and issuing contemptuous grunts.

It's absolutely mesmerizing and hypnotic to watch. The way his fingers expertly and nimbly excavate the lime green peas and pop them into his mouth. . . . And the contrast of the vivid green of the pea pods and the deep brown of his hands.

That's it. In a flash, the long puzzle is solved. I know why Inah travels. Traveling is like dreaming. In travel, your real life is put on hold. As long as you travel and keep on moving, you can defer it forever. You are safe from reality. Loneliness being the only consequence. You are not asked to participate. You observe and move on. You are forever a stranger and an outsider. It involves no emotional entanglements. You can just go on experiencing the moments of green pea pods in the brown hands of an elegant man. Is that what Inah's been doing? Deferring life? Running away from reality? But how could I blame her? How could I begrudge her anything? I want her to go on, if she could, experiencing the magical moments of green pea pods in the brown hands of an elegant man. Anyway, aren't we all living in the sustained illusion that life is worth living? Otherwise, we will have to give up sooner or later.

*   *   *

Then everything goes wrong. We end up sharing a long table with a group of American art students studying in Florence. I can tell right away that Inah isn't too crazy about the arrangement. But it's clear that our squat, no-nonsense, mustachioed waitress isn't about to let herself be bothered with such a trivial thing as a seating preference. She throws down the menus on the table with that take-it-or-leave-it look and walks away. "Butchsky," Inah mutters to her back with surprising malice.

As we reluctantly settle into our seats, one of the students turns and says, "Hope you guys don't mind sharing the table with us. With the exception of myself, these guys are real animals." A roar of laughter erupts, and I laugh.

"Yeah, I can tell," I say, and Inah floats a disgusted look toward me.

"Peter," he says. "Where are you guys from?"

"From New York," I answer. Peter explains that they are all NYU graduate students and that he's an art history major and has been in Florence for three months. He's kind of cute, but not my type really. A little too sunny and eager. Anyway, for some reason, I omit revealing the fact that I am an NYU graduate myself but instead tell him that I live on Thompson Street. We then joke about how NYU is now more like a mighty corporation and is taking over the Village by putting up ugly dormitory buildings all over. Inah's finally had it. Exasperated, in a show of displeasure, she lets the menu slip from her hand to the table and rolls her eyes. She hates people who gush.

"Sorry, Inah," I say, a little embarrassed and suddenly self-conscious.

"Why don't you go ahead and narrate your entire life story?" she says sarcastically.

"Don't be stupid, Inah," I say, regretting it right away. "Know what you want? If you are ready, let's order." But she has already slipped into one of her black moods. She won't look at me.

Throughout the dinner, she keeps her eyes glued to the plate and barely breathes a word. And against my better judgment, I ignore her and talk to Peter and a couple of other students around him. Once or twice, I do try to draw her into our conversation, but she flatly refuses.

In fact, she can't wait to leave. Turning down dessert, she asks for the check and takes off to the bathroom. That would have been the end of the story, but no. When she comes back, she looks absolutely furious. She sails over, slaps down two ten-thousand lire notes on the table and walks out blurting, "See you outside." I realize that on the way back from the bathroom, she saw Peter handing me a piece of paper (where he wrote down the names of "great, cheap places to eat" in Rome) and completely misinterpreted it.

It could not have been more than five minutes later when I go out, but Inah isn't there. I quickly scan the length of the darkening street. No trace of her. Cursing, I hurry up the street. At the first corner, I turn right. And just for the sake of it, I peek inside the tobacco shop and bar, where Italian rock music blasts. Of course, she isn't there. As I race up the street, young kids hanging around the parked motorcycles whistle and shout, "Sayonara!"

Then it occurs to me that she might have gone back to the bathroom as I was coming out (but why?) and she might still be there waiting for me. I should go back. I turn down a narrow sloping street, sure that it will take me back to Via dei Neri. In the night glint, the narrow deserted street seems to rise like a staircase out of a deep well of black fog. After about a couple of minutes, afraid I will end up completely lost, I stop. Across the street, inside a brightly lit closed barbershop, I see a white-haired old man sitting all alone in one of the barber chairs, still as a prop, watching a soundless soccer game on a small pink TV. It's all very surreal. I feel as though I have wandered into someone else's dream.

Then it all comes back to me in a rush. All the hideous dreams I have been having: Inah's body floating down the Arno River; Inah up on the cupola at the Duomo, ready to jump; Inah's weeping face on the statue of Mary and her red, calcified tears. What if they were prescient? The old, unspoken fear comes back. Mom's worried face flashes through my hot head. And I start to panic.

I turn around and run back to the intersection. It's only after a long while, walking up and down, that I realize it doesn't make sense at all, roaming the streets like this. The chance of finding Inah this way has to be very slim, if not zero. My best bet is to go back to the hotel. I start walking, roughly aiming toward the railway station. But of course, having no sense of direction whatsoever, soon I am utterly lost. It seems impossible, but I have missed the Piazza della Signoria entirely. Instead, I end up on the deserted and mist-draped Via Cavour. The wide, stately boulevard seems to go on forever. I have to get to the Duomo. At least from there, I know I will be able to find my way back to our hotel. I turn around and walk, as I will realize later, away from the Duomo.

It's past eleven when I manage to find my way to the Piazza Santa Maria Novella. I am exhausted and hot and sticky with sweat but afraid to go back to the hotel. I don't have the courage to walk into the empty room with Inah's things lying about like remains. I head to the phone booths by the newsstand outside the piazza.

It's weird. At this late hour, all the phone booths are occupied. And not only that, outside the booths, there are about six or seven more men and women waiting their turn, rolling around heavy coins with their fingers, stacking and restacking them on their palms. They look like Africans, and they are here probably to call home. I join the end of the line and pace about, getting more desperate each second. Fear feeds on fear. I keep hearing Mom's voice: "Don't fight with Inah." Mom will blame me if anything happens to Inah. And I will just die, too. Just then, a booth door clicks open, and I see a big, handsome woman squeeze herself out, laughing and talking to herself as if she is still carrying on the conversation on the phone.

"Excuse me!" I rush up to the man at the head of the line, just about to walk inside the booth. "Would you please let me go ahead? Please, I will be real fast. Ten seconds!" I beg and gesture. I don't know if he understands me, but I must look so pathetic. He stops and stares at me briefly and says, "No problem." I thank him and fly into the booth before he changes his mind. I drop a bunch of palm-sweated coins and dial the hotel number. A hotel operator answers, and I give him our room number and wait, holding my breath.

"Please, please, Inah, answer the phone!" But it just rings and rings, and with each ring that goes unanswered, my heart sinks further. At about the seventh or eighth ring, I put down the receiver and walk out.

I cut across the piazza, looking shabby and tired in the dim, pallid lamplights. The green-and-white marble facade of the Chiesa di Santa Maria Novella up the piazza looks just that: a facade, painted on a cardboard. At the piazza, more Africans are standing around in small clusters, talking and laughing. They seem so relaxed and content and even festive; so completely contained in their own village, in their own world. Their happy language all vowels. Sung in vibrato. The women have high foreheads that gleam like smooth chiseled onyx, and they wear brightly patterned flowing gowns and matching tall, fancy, and elaborate head wraps. Even in the waxen light, they look beautiful, picturesque and as regal as high priestesses. For a second, I think I am somewhere in Africa, not in Florence. Even the misty night air seems to drip scents of bitter almond oil and orange flowers.

Drained, I slump down on a bench. This is how it works: After anger dissipates, you worry, and then after a while, you get all worked up again. If Inah were here, I could strangle her. I watch the Africans. They look so utterly at home. Together. Wherever they go and however far they end up, instead of letting a place transform them, they transform the place, by creating a piece of Africa, a village. Even in the middle of a piazza in Florence. It's the unshakable pride they have carried with them from home.

I look up at the sky, a luminous sheet of cobalt blue. In sodden Venice, the night sky seemed so macabre. The shade of blackest ash. Nothing bad could happen to Inah under such a beautiful sky. I get up and slowly walk toward the hotel.

From the hallway, I notice a wedge of light spilling out from under the door of our room. Relieved, I literally stagger ahead. I try the doorknob. It's locked. I knock and wait. After long seconds, Inah finally comes and opens it. Not only doesn't she say a word but she doesn't even so much as bother to look at me. She just turns around and walks away nonchalantly. I shut the door behind me and stand leaning my back against it. I can barely move.

She's been packing for her day trip to Siena tomorrow.

On the bed lies her unzipped blue Kipling backpack, looking like an opened-up belly. With my eyes, I follow her
around the room, waiting for her to say something. Just a
few minutes ago, walking back to the hotel, all I wished for
was her safe return. Scared out of my wits that she had done
something stupid, I swore I would do anything to have her
back. But now I am all furious again.

"Are you going to tell me where the hell you went?" I
yell. "I've been looking for you all over. What the hell is
wrong with you?" She doesn't answer. Furious, I bound over
and jerk at her arm. Inah winces but won't look at me.
"Don't you hear me? Why do you have to be such a bitch?" I
scream in rage.

"What do you want from me?" Inah says tersely, in that
flat, calm voice of hers full of disdain.

"Who says I want anything from you, Inah? I don't want
a damn thing from you. Just tell me what makes you think
that you can dictate to me how to behave. As it is, Inah,
whenever I am with you, I feel like I am in some kind of
prison. Always watching what I say or do, afraid to upset
you or displease you. And you know what? I'm not going to
live like that anymore. I'm not going to live in constant fear
that you might not like what I say or do. From now on, I'm
going to talk to whomever I want to and whenever I want
to. And I don't give a damn whether you like it or not." Inah
briefly looks up. In the pale, greenish light, her scarred face
is haggard and gaunt. And her eyes show no sparkle at all.
They are opaque and expressionless and remote. They are
dead.

I realize there's no point. It's hopeless. No amount of
reasoning and talking and screaming would do any good.
She just is not here. As I am about to let go of her arm,
though, Inah angrily jerks it, loosening it from my grip. And

I just lose it. I grab her backpack on the bed and smash it down to the floor. And then violently pushing her out of the way, I storm into the closet and drag out her knapsack. I pull a bunch of her shirts and jeans out of it and hurl them into the air. And her journal falls out, bounces across the floor and lands like a broken wing.

"What are you doing?" Inah screams. "Are you fucking crazy?"

"You think I'm crazy? You haven't seen how crazy I am!" I pick up one of her wash-worn, discolored white T-shirts and rip it open and stomp on it, smearing it with my sandal-prints. And all the time, I feel strangely detached from it all. In my head, I am calmly watching what I am doing, and I even see my own face, all distorted with anger and rage. Inah doesn't try to stop me. Instead, she bends down and starts picking up the shirts and jeans strewn around the floor. I go over and push her away.

"What are you, goddamn stone deaf? How many times do I have to tell you, Inah? You don't need these stupid clothes! Do you have any idea what you look like in these? A goddamn creep, that's what you look like." I tug at the handful of shirts Inah has gathered in her hands. But she isn't about to let them go. She holds on to them dearly, as if it is her last stand. As if those ugly, oversized T-shirts were her lifeline. "How long are you going to hide behind them, Inah? How long? I'm so sick of them. I'm so sick of your clothes, your hair, your glum face. Sick of everything about you!" Inah glares at me, her eyes bright and intense and fierce, giving me a spark of hope that she will fight back. But she just bites down hard on her lip and turns her head away.

"No, no, no, Inah. Don't look away! Look at me! Look me in the eye and say something! Anything! What's on your mind? What do you write in your stupid journal every day? I don't know who you are anymore. What's happened to you? You used to be such a fighter. So feisty and spirited. Remember? Remember those mean kids who used to say terrible, cruel things to you and call you all kinds of names? You used to fight back. What happened to that feisty girl, Inah? I miss that little Inah. I feel I have lost her." I hear my voice break hoarsely. Inah stands still, staring into space. The long fluorescent tubes over the oxide green desk flicker and hum. I am so unbearably sad that I can hardly breathe.

"I know it's hard for you, Inah," I continue, driven by desperation. "But can't you see that it's not easy for me, either? I don't know why it happened. Why it happened to you and not to me. I've asked myself the same question a thousand times. But there's no answer. It's hard not only for you but also for everyone else around you. Try to understand that. No one, no one has it easy. All of us struggle. Isn't life hard enough? We have to just go on as best as we can with what we have. You're never going to solve anything by running away. How about the sacrifices Mom and Dad made for you? Do you remember? It was for you, Inah, that we came to America. Dad gave up everything. His job. His art. His lifelong friends. Do you know he broke all of his painting brushes before he left Korea? He came although he was way too old to start all over again from scratch in America. He gave up so much. For you. For us. Doesn't it count? Even just a little? And we're not teenagers. We are twenty-eight years old, Inah. A little bit too old to blame everything and everyone but yourself. It's time for you to take some responsibility. Time for you to get on with life. I will do anything to make it easier for you. You know that. But I just can't live like this anymore.

"Please, Inah. I am begging you. Why are we here, so far

from home, fighting in this depressing hotel room when we could be having so much fun together instead? Why does it have to be this way? Tell me, because I don't know why." I grab Inah's arms and shake them. "Please, Inah. Say something! Anything! I am begging you. Don't just shut yourself up like this. You must have something to say. No?"

But Inah just stands like an empty sack, like a wilting plant, letting me shake her. She doesn't even try to defend herself. She doesn't even try to fight back. She doesn't even want to prove me wrong. She doesn't do any of that. She just stands there, staring at the floor. Why? What's wrong with her? Whatever I say or do isn't doing any good. I let go of her and throw myself across the bed and sob, fueled with self-pity.

I don't know how much time has passed. When I look up, she is still standing on the exact same spot. By the bed. Noiselessly crying. It kills me.

SEVEN

Dad is not just having a quick fling, although Uncle Shin repeatedly reassures Mom when once a week he drives over from his wholesale store in Manhattan, making a long detour to his home in Staten Island. He brings us samples of custom jewelry, handbags and knit caps his company imports, and also Dad's salary in cash, which he hands to Mom in a white envelope, like the "comfort money" Koreans bring to funerals.

Every time, Mom sends us off in exile, and then when he's leaving, Inah and I go out to the foyer to stand demurely next to Mom while Uncle Shin huffs and struggles to slip his swollen feet into his expensive leather loafers. His square-jawed face is usually muddled red from the *soju* he has had.

"You two, don't worry about anything," Uncle Shin says to us. "Everything's going to be fine. Your only duty is to study hard. Remember that. Your mother and I will take care of the rest." Sometimes, as if on second thought, he pulls out a thick wad of cash from his trouser pocket, wets his thumb and peels off two crisp one-hundred-dollar bills and squeezes them into our shrinking hands as Mom vehemently protests.

"Buy what you need for school," Uncle Shin says and walks out the door. We thank him to his back in our mosquito voices. Mom stands holding the door open, and we watch him walk to his car, his breath frosting, his toes pointing upward and outward, defiantly jabbing the cold air, and we feel strangely safe. Uncle Shin might be greedy and crass and might be the ugly Korean whom America loved to hate for his success, his big house, his expensive car and his money in the bank and for being unapologetic about it, but despite all the faults and bad taste, Uncle Shin is solid and reliable. Every time we watch him walk out into the night, for a wistful second, we wish Dad were a little bit like him and feel ashamed.

Of course, Auntie Minnie is a lot more cynical. She insists Uncle "Sin" relishes it, the chance to take care of us. She knows he has always secretly coveted the role of the head of our loosely connected American family. Not that she articulates it that way.

"Uncle 'Sin' think he godfather! It all show off. He do it because it make him feel good," says Auntie Minnie, blowing out blue strands of cigarette smoke through her nostrils like chimney stacks at a Jersey oil refinery. She is often sleeping over and is already in her frilly pajamas: a turquoise slip-gown with an embroidered laurel of pink rose on the chest.

"So what?" Mom says. "What do you do? You just sit around and talk, talk."

"*Unni*," Auntie Minnie hollers in exasperation. (She's

older than Mom, but she calls her "big sister" in deference
to Dad.) "You not know Uncle Sin! How his mind work. He
never go to university, not like you and uncle. He got . . ."
Auntie Minnie turns to Inah and asks, "You so smart, Inah.
What the word?"

"Inferiority complex?" Inah answers po-faced from the
living-room sofa, channel surfing. "Or carrying a chip on his
shoulder?"

"'Complex,' that the word? Anyway, he think, 'Oh, they
have university degree but they need my help.' That the way
he think. I know it. You wonder why I call him Uncle Sin!"

Inah hates it when Auntie Minnie, presiding over the
kitchen table, doles out outrageous advice and her cheap
opinions to Mom in her "brook-clean" English. Saying
things like, "Think it easy to fall in love? It even more easy
to fall out of love!" or "Everything work. Even love!" or
"Men think with their you know what." Inah usually
responds to Auntie Minnie's pedestrian pop psychology
with frequent eyeball rolling and groans, but sometimes she
can't help it: She falls off the couch, laughing and screaming.

"*Unni,* how the old Korean saying go? 'A house and a
woman, they fall apart if you not take care of them'? So true!
And how about the other one, 'Silver no shine automatic.
You got to polish it.' About time you take care of yourself.
Can't just blame Uncle about what happen. Your fault, too.
All you care about is your kids. This America, not same,
same like Korea! You think Korean way and sacrifice every-
thing for your children. And you think they be thankful?
No. They think they so smart, they did it with no help. And
now look what happen! Uncle run off!! That what I'm say-
ing. Who care you born Miss Korea? Use more makeup!
And if you like, I give your hair highlight. You laugh, but

Uncle no different. He a man, no? And men who say they don't care for flashy woman, they lying! And how you compete with that kind woman? She pro. She come on to Uncle, wagging tail. Uncle no made of stone. He not mind. Who mind? Men all same!"

Finally Inah can't stand it anymore. Hissing, she zaps off the TV, picks up her books and storms upstairs to her room. Not that Auntie Minnie notices.

"You watch too many talk shows," Mom finally tells Auntie Minnie. "And speaking of the old sayings you like so much, how about this one: 'Fanning a burning house'? That's exactly what you're doing!"

At this, Auntie Minnie bursts out laughing, and Mom clucks her tongue, determined to keep her in her place so she won't get too comfortable with her. I guess it's a class thing. Even in Flushing, such a thing as class exists. Mom weaves it into a fine, complicated web.

But it's thanks to Auntie Minnie that we are able to forget, even if only for a while. The nights she's around, the kitchen often looks like a makeshift beauty salon. Every inch of the dining table is covered with her tools of the trade she brings over, along with her aluminum makeup travel case. She hoists reluctant Mom onto a chair with a plastic apron around her for what she calls a "total makeover." After lots of tinkering, Auntie Minnie picks up the sweating gin and tonic glass from the dining table, where, in the ashtray, a cigarette seems to be permanently burning like an incense stick, and regards Mom, sipping her drink and checking the newly plucked eyebrows or the hair job. Mom, growing ever impatient, wants to know then if it's almost done, and Auntie Minnie asks Mom if she ever relaxes and enjoys anything.

Later, hungry, Inah sneaks in for a snack and stands agog

at the chaotic scene. She stomps around the kitchen, reeking with perm solutions and nail polish and other chemical cocktails, coughing and waving away the swirling cigarette smoke, and opening the windows. Then she glances at Mom, who is hoisted on the chair like a hostage, her hair iron-molested and brush-teased, her face turned into a palette of primary colors by Auntie Minnie, and says in her low voice, "Oh mi god. Oh mi god." Alarmed, Mom asks for a look and expectantly searches for her new, transformed self in the hand mirror I hold up for her. Of course, Mom is invariably horrified. "That's it," Mom declares. "No more makeovers. It's just not me!" Auntie Minnie laughs and laughs and asks us isn't it fun, just us girls and says who needs men.

And there's Inah and me and Auntie Minnie, on Wednesday nights when Mom goes to church, sitting around the dining table, playing "go-stop" with a deck of *wha-too*, Korean flower cards Auntie Minnie brings in her overnight bag. "Go-stop" is similar to poker, only much more complicated, and once you get the hang of it, it gets really addictive.

Inah goes nuts because at a crucial and suspenseful moment, Auntie Minnie stops the game, complaining of a hot flash attack. She puts down the cards and sheds her cardigan sweater. This goes on until she is stripped down to just her bra.

"Wait till you have menopause," she says every time Inah grumbles. But that does it. Inah can't stand it—Auntie Minnie sitting directly across the table with nothing on but her bra. She can't help notice the stacks of naked flesh rolling around her middle like lumps of dough, and her ample breasts—two white full moons barely staying put in the bra cups—threatening to spill out.

"Ugh! Ugh!" Prissy Inah keeps hissing in disgust, and Auntie Minnie asks her what's the matter, it's just us girls.

I perfectly understand Inah, though. The undeniable truth is that we are all getting too comfortable and too complacent without Dad around. We used to be a little more careful with everything, watching our words and tapering our behavior. And Inah misses those boundaries that restrained us from straying too far, overstepping the line where an unconscious gesture forms into a habit that is vulgar and ugly.

EIGHT

The way the doorbell bursts so urgently, we know that it can't be anyone but Auntie Minnie. And as soon as we open the door, she charges in like a gusting wind, loaded with bags and carrying with her the smell of winter evening and cigarette smoke.

"Help me take off my boots," she says, clumping down at the vestibule and pushing out her tree-trunk legs in thigh-length boots. It's a mystery how she puts them on to begin with. Taking charge of each leg, Inah and I pull the zippers down, and the imprisoned flesh pours out like rising flour dough. Inah and I then give each boot a quick pull and a jerk, and end up on our butts with a boot in hand. Auntie Minnie scrambles and rushes up the hallway to the kitchen, slipping out of her coat.

"Where is your mother?" she asks.

"In the laundry room in the basement," Inah says.

"Does she know your dad is in Chicago?" she asks in Korean. It's news. Inah and I look at each other.

"*Unni,*" Auntie Minnie hollers toward the basement. "I am here! Leave your miserable laundry and come up!" Auntie Minnie quickly mixes herself a gin and tonic and takes a long sip. Inah and I wait with unbearable anticipation. Finally, Mom comes up carrying a plastic basket full of dried clothes and towels. Auntie Minnie quickly wipes the cigarette ash off the table for Mom to empty the basket. We all pick up something and start folding.

"*Unni,* you find out where Uncle hide in Chicago? You have phone number? You called? No?! I no understand what you wait for! License from God?" asks Auntie Minnie indignantly. "Why you still here anyway? Why not in Chicago? If I was you, I already in Chicago, just to see that shame, shame love nest with my own eye!"

"Is Dad really in Chicago?" Inah cuts in. "How come you didn't tell us, Mom?" Mom ignores her.

"Grab the bitch and drag her out! I tell you. You have every right. That kind woman no understand no nice talk. If you like, I go with you!" Auntie Minnie tilts her head back and blows smoke trails from her nose. "Or you plan to sit here with your high-nose pride and lose Uncle?" Inah throws down the towel she has been folding and gets up.

"He's not a child," Mom says calmly in Korean. "I am not going to drag him back here if his mind is going to be somewhere else. I'd rather live with a scarecrow."

"*Unni!* That just what I mean. You too proud! So what you went to that high-nosed university in Korea, you call Pear Blossom or Cherry Blossom. You just no understand men." Auntie Minnie jiggles the ice in the glass. One of her slip-on nails is missing. She glances at Inah, standing against the counter, sulking.

"If you know men so well, why did you get divorced?" Mom says. "Who's giving advice to whom? I don't need your advice. Don't talk. You open your mouth, nothing but garbage comes out. And is it just any mouth? So pungent, too. You give me nothing but a headache."

"How you say that, *Unni*? You know it not my fault we divorce. He butterfly plenty, that SOB. That the reason we divorce!"

"That's not the only reason! You don't think I have eyes? I saw you scream and curse at him. What man would have stayed? That's not the way Korean women behave with their husbands," Mom says cruelly.

"Aigghhh! No make me start on that black SOB. And you wrong. I not like American women. You know American men no have no balls because women make them cook, do dish and laundry and even go shop grocery. I no did that to him. But that not enough!" Auntie Minnie is nearly shouting, and gesticulating with her hand holding a cigarette. Mom winces. Auntie Minnie lights another cigarette and takes a long drag. She looks at me across the table and sighs.

"Yunah, you lucky, so young and pretty. Good days all gone for you and me, *Unni*," shouts Auntie Minnie to Mom, her voice suddenly shrill. "We like flower already open and close. Golden age, silver age, all gone. Woman, no matter how pretty, she finish after forty. Not worth even shit. For men, it different story. Not fair, but that the way it is.

"I so young and pretty when I marry that Wilson SOB and come to Brooklyn with him. His old friends tease him and say Steady Q back from Korea with China doll bride. They whistle when I walk by in miniskirt and high heel, the fashion at the time. Ugh, but I no like to remember that time too much. Wilson never told me everyone black where we go live in Brooklyn, America. I come and I see whole neighbor around Classon Avenue black. I see no white, no Asian. All black people. I very much shocked. Not the way I imagine America. No big houses with big, nice lawn. No shine plenty, big fancy cars. I just scared. But what point sitting around feeling sorry for me. In Korea, people call me *yang-gongjoo.* GI bride. I no miss that. Beside, Wilson in love plenty then. He so crazy about me, he no can keep his hands off. He all over me daytime, nighttime!" Auntie Minnie crushes her slim Virginia Slims into the Niagara Falls ashtray. She sees my mouth hanging open and laughs.

"Enough!" Mom says angrily. "Some things you just don't say in front of children! I don't understand how you just spit out whatever comes to your mind."

"*Unni,* how old Yunah? Fit-teen? Sick-teen? She no more child. In America, they know everything at that age," says Auntie Minnie, picking a cigarette ash from her lip.

"I don't care what you say. She's not an adult. Besides, can't you see that I have enough to worry about as it is? I'm just not in the mood to sit around and listen to your fungi-ridden old stories." Mom gets up with the pile of folded laundry. Auntie Minnie quickly gulps down the last sip of the drink and tugs at Mom's sleeve.

"*Unni,* sit, sit down," Auntie Minnie says forcefully. "I know what you think. You think I speak nonsense. I maybe not so educated like you, but I not so thick in the head. You look down on me, *Unni,* just like everyone else. Because I *yang-gongjoo,* GI bride. You no respect me. But how you come to America? How everyone come to America? Because of me, *Unni.* Me! GI bride. All relatives see me a ticket to America. But once they come here, they like to forget me. They no want other Koreans know I marry black

GI. I, *yang-gongjoo*. They shamed. Just like you. Just like Uncle Sin. All you treat me no better than a *tong gae*, shit dog, on the street. I Korean but I no like Koreans. That why I don't mind my son, my only son, Jason, think he black, not Korean! You know that?!" Auntie Minnie shoots Mom a truth-or-dare look. Mom is so upset that her face is crimson red.

"What are you talking about? What does it have to do with anything? You're drunk," Mom says. Auntie Minnie puts her face into her hands and starts wailing.

NINE

Why?

The night I learn that Dad is in Chicago, that's the first question I ask myself. Why Chicago, of all places? I can't conjure up even a single image; Chicago is a black hole in my imagination. Even Inah says that she knows more about Mars than about Chicago. Then I remember the Frank Sinatra song "My Kind of Town (Chicago Is)". When we used to live on Bowne Street, we'd go to Jessica Han's for sleepovers, and her father, a Frank Sinatra fan, would always play his songs. I liked the "Chicago" song because it always made me feel like I was somewhere very exotic.

That night, in Inah's room, we pull out the World Atlas map and open it to Illinois State, where Chicago and its expanse, colored red, spread from the southwestern shore of intestinal Lake Michigan like a bleeding ulcer. We stare at it for a long, long time, as if by doing so we could force it to yield some kind of clue. (What kind of clue, we don't yet know.) As though if we stared at it long enough, the map would transform itself into a live city with smells and sounds and people and buildings and streets and houses and cars, and reveal to us the exact spot where Dad is. As though if we studied it long enough, there would come a divine intervention, and we would solve the whole mystery.

But staring at the map, no matter how long, doesn't do it. So every night after dinner, Inah brings her college application forms and books downstairs with an excuse that it's too cold in her room and sets up the low Korean lacquer table in front of the couch. Then she sits there on the floor, her elbows planted on the table and her eyes glued to the TV, channel surfing for all the weather updates.

As it turns out, Chicago is in a siege. Blizzard-bound. The worst winter in a decade, they say. A low pressure, cold front closing in on Chicago like a great wall. Its jagged teeth sharp as barbed wire. One day, the temperature dips to fifty below zero with the windchill. Over the frozen Lake Michigan, snow and ice drift in a great, foggy mass like hot steam out of the spit-fire mouth of a dragon. It shows people bundled up like polar bears and their faces covered with ski masks. Walking doubled over. Struggling against drifting snow and wind. With a strange thrill and twisted elation, we gobble up the scenes on the screen. Staring at the shifting Day-Glo swirls on the weather map.

Every night, shivering under the cold cover, waiting to get warm, I think of Dad trapped in blizzard-bound Chicago. Holed up in a cold, run-down apartment somewhere with "that woman." Probably in some run-down section of the city. On a desolate street where cold shadows draw extra long at night. Isolated from the frozen, snowbound world outside. Living on love, on borrowed time. Money running out. Passion dissipating, I hope, as surely as hot water cools. Dad, lying awake night after night, unable to sleep. Outside, winds whining in high-pitched croaks. The pipes running through the thin walls, rattling and gasping, rattling and gasping all night, keeping him awake. His hard-won sleep only to be disturbed by dreams of us. And then, in that restless and uneasy hour just before dawn, Dad is awake again. Thinking a million thoughts. Wondering what he's doing there. Far from home, in a strange city, in an unfamiliar room.

I am so certain Dad is miserable. He has to be. So miserable, in fact, that he will soon be running back to New York. Leaving his affair behind him like a short-lived fever. But what if Dad never returned? What if our love for him or his love for us proved not to be enough to lure him back? Could our love for him substitute for whatever it was that had lured him away from us to begin with? And I have always assumed only rich people behaved that way. Rich, white people, real Americans, who live in glitzy Manhattan, where buildings are lit bright at night, like elaborate birthday cakes. Flushing isn't America, even Dad himself began to say. It is a way station. A place to shake off the old dirt on immigrant shoes. A place of limbo. One foot there, the other here. Burdened only with duty. Old and new. Dad was supposed to endure, suppress and overcome life. He should have known better than to act on those selfish, ephemeral impulses and improbable passions.

Every evening, I see them, immigrants like Dad, flooding Main Street. Released like so many eels out of an oil drum from the Number Seven train, the Orient Express, from Manhattan, our umbilical cord to America. Men on their way home, to their own section of the Orient, mapped with little Korea, India, China and the Middle East. Spices galore. Except to us, Dad is hardly distinguishable from them. Dad is just one more Asian face in the crowd, struggling to make his way in a new country.

I don't want to believe that love was the reason Dad walked out on us. For love doesn't grow in a hideout, in the shadow. It feeds on the hottest sun. Love should be proud, unashamed. Isn't that what the Bible says? Dad was just looking for proof that he still counted. That he was still capable of change, to stir things up a little. That he hadn't become a paralyzed prisoner in America. Dad, who never seemed to find his way in the new country—or even seemed, at times, uninterested in finding his way—is simply lost and needs to find his way back. And he can't even begin to do so until he's completely lost. I hope and pray Dad gets completely and utterly lost in blizzard-bound Chicago. One day he will realize that he has nowhere to run and hide: Even in vast America, he lives in a tiny world. A-men!

The week Mom's church is holding a nightly *poohung-whe,* revival meeting, I snoop around and find Dad's Chicago phone number in the kitchen drawer where she keeps grocery receipts, emergency candles and batteries. In Mom's handwriting, it's scribbled like a Morse code on a purple Post-it, folded in half.

One night after she leaves, I go to the living room, where Inah has flung herself down on the couch with a book. Inah looks up at the Post-it I display like a war trophy, and says she won't tell Mom if I called.

"You know the call will show up on the phone bill," she informs me helpfully.

"Like I don't know. I am going out and find a pay phone. Wanna come?" Inah shakes her head, not even bothering to look up. I notice it's *The Travels of Marco Polo,* the book she's reading. She, too, wants to run away from Flushing. I guess she couldn't run farther than to Marco Polo's East.

Outside, along Ash, the winter already has the old entrenched feel. The houses look squalid and gloomy. The sidewalks are still patched with old snow that has never had a chance to melt, and the pushed-up snow along the street stands like a frozen wall, its crest jagged-edged and crystallized like sugar. Behind steamed-up apartment windows, early Christmas lights, blurry and dull, lazily blink on and off. I remember how Dad always hated the Christmas season in America for all the commercial frenzy.

At Kissena, I turn and walk down to the pay phone outside the Willow House, a Korean restaurant. But it's missing the receiver, and all that is left is the metal wire hanging loose, like a severed umbilical cord. Then I remember seeing a pay phone outside the Pakistani newsstand at the corner of Roosevelt and Main. As I head toward Roosevelt, the wind picks up suddenly, and I race all the way to Main, cupping my ears and cursing at Inah.

The corner with the newsstand is one of the grimiest and most crowded spots during the day, but it's now completely deserted and in the dim light looks stripped down and desolate. I pick up the receiver and punch in the number on the Post-it. The fistful of quarters I slip in go down in a noisy clang.

At the first ring, my heart starts racing like crazy. I am suddenly scared. What if Dad answers? What am I going to say? I am not even sure if I really want to talk to him. I haven't really thought all this out. I frantically debate whether to hang up, but it's too late, because I hear a soft click cutting off the ring.

"*Yeobo-se-yo?*" "Hello?" It's a woman's voice, that voice on the phone. It's a little tattered and throaty, and it's like a question, her hello. My heart drops. She's Dad's lover.

Say something, ask for Dad, stupid, I tell myself, but my tongue seems stuck at the throat. Just then, I hear what sounds like Dad's voice in the background.

"I don't know who it is," the woman's voice says through crackling static. Cupping the mouthpiece, I turn away from the street to face the grimy newsstand window, where skin magazines are displayed with their covers facing out. One, *Asian Beauties*, catches my blurry eye. I stare at the picture of an "Asian" girl on her knees. She's naked under a floral kimono, its front half open. I can even see she's a little plump in the belly. Her glossy cherry lips parted halfway, she is staring out blankly with her dark brown eyes.

A cold and hot shiver shoots through me. Strangely enough, until that very moment, I have never once wondered what Dad's lover looks like. Her face, it has been, until then, just a blank oval. She isn't real. Just a concept and an idea; "a woman like that," as Mom calls her.

"Ah, *Yeobo-se-yo?*" Dad's low, gravelly voice washes over like a warm wave melting the frozen line. I suck in the frigid air, filling my lungs. My head spins and floats. I am squeezing the receiver so hard that my fingers throb, and my whole body shivers uncontrollably. I want to sit down and cry. Bellowing loudly like a baby. So it is all true. Dad living in another city with a woman, a perfect stranger to us.

Shell-shocked and shivering, forgetting to hang up the phone, I stand, holding the receiver at my side. Across the street, outside a Chinese bakery, the winds pick up and skip by, carrying along bits of newspapers up the sidewalk. Over the elevated Long Island Rail Road track, a night train noisily rumbles past into the cold, black night.

TEN

Inah's gone when I wake up in the morning. She has left a note on top of the bureau: a blue-lined notebook page folded into a square with two tails sticking out. I open it and read it in one breath:

Yunah, I'm taking a six A.M. bus to Siena. I'll be back tonight. And about last night, I was wrong. I am sorry. But it's not like what you think. Not everything has to do with my face. Sure I am not happy about it and, as you said, I don't know why it had to happen. But I've lived with it and know I'll have to live with it. I accepted that long ago and I can only hope that you will, too. And I want you to know that I don't intend to be a burden weighing everyone in the family down for the rest of my life. I must be useful for something and I am going to find out what that is. Until then, don't try to rescue me or save

*me. What I need is time. There's nothing you or Mom or
Dad can do. Or anyone else for that matter. I want you to
go on with your life. One day, maybe I will be able to
catch up with you.*

Love, Inah

I crumple the notebook page, dizzily filled with Inah's
loopy handwriting, and cry. I can't shake off the image of
her last night noiselessly weeping, standing by the bed.

It's almost noon when I force myself to go out. My head
feels dull and heavy, the way it does after too much sun. At
a cafe near Ponte Vecchio, I have a quick cup of cappuccino
and buy a ready-made sandwich and a bottle of water and
head for Piazzale Michelangelo. Without Inah, I am vulnerable and utterly lost. Everything seems all fuzzy, as
though I am merely floating.

To reach the piazzale by foot, you have to hike up the
long, steep road along the Costa San Giorgio. The walk
feels interminable under the midday sun that hardly moves,
as if sewn onto the sky. But it's worth it. The view from the
piazzale is simply breathtaking, and immediately, I regret
coming here without Inah. I remember it was on her must-
see list, but instead we frittered away so much time fighting
and fuming and being unhappy. And Inah would rather be
alone. It's preferable to her. She'd rather be the lonely figure
moving about like a shadow among the crowds. Unspoken
to. And if ever noticed, only for the wrong reasons. But I
miss her in a way I never have before. Even her surly presence. It puzzles me how she has become someone I could
love only when we're apart. From a distance. When the distance is lost, the love turns into something else. Something
petty, narrow and intolerable.

I can only half finish the sandwich. Then I start a letter to Inah that I am not sure I'll ever give to her:

Inah, you're in Siena as I write this. You were gone when I woke up in the morning and not surprisingly, I cried like nuts after reading the note you left. You don't know how sorry I am for all the things I said last night even though it was in anger. If only I could, I would take back all the words and the hurt they must have caused. But as usual, it's too late, and I am filled only with regret.

I know you wanted a day alone without me (and I agreed to give you some breathing room) but I wish I had gone with you. If I had, we would be in Siena together right now, making another memory. Maybe not now but one day, probably old and decrepit, I am sure I would be grateful for that one more memory. What would we be doing then?

Inah, do you remember that gray morning in Venice? (I can't believe how it already feels like so long ago.) We were walking down a moss-covered fondamenta on the way to see some obscure church, its name now I've forgotten. (It had a ceiling painting you wanted to see: The artist as he finished it was killed falling from the scaffolding; how morbid.) I remember it was like a vision from a dream: the sudden appearance of a gleaming black gondola on a narrow, picturesque canal. Framed in the arch of a stone bridge. The gondola's stern was decorated with fresh white lilies. Remember how they were so brilliantly white against the gleaming black of the gondola? And how brilliantly white the starched shirts the gondoliers wore under their red, gold-brocaded vests? I never knew until then that white is such a lavishly beautiful color! That was the one time I wish I had a camera with me; it seemed memory alone wasn't enough.

And you must remember the pretty young girl who looked about seventeen in a simple ivory lace dress. She was sitting on a brocaded seat, next to a middle-aged man, stiff in a blue-gray suit. I assumed, not knowing any better, the man was courting the girl. But Inah, you pointed out how he looked much older than her. And I said, "That's why he's trying so hard to impress her. I bet." Inah, you said it was disgusting. I still don't know what you meant by that. The idea of an old man courting a young girl or my assumption.

Anyway, the gondola glided down the canal and disappeared and we forgot all about it. Shortly afterward, we got lost in the maze of narrow streets, and then after wandering around a while, found ourselves at a piazza facing an old, unassuming stone church. (I seem to remember it had a faded redbrick facade.) In the piazza, there was a large festive crowd of Italians, all dressed in what seemed their Sunday bests, happily milling about. We went inside the church, old but rather plain, and had a quick look around and came back out. By then, the crowd had all converged by the canal. And I instantly recognized the gleaming black gondola with the white lilies. And the girl in that simple, pretty ivory dress. She was being helped out of the gondola by the man in the blue-gray suit. After entrusting her white-gloved hand into his, carefully lifting the hems of her long dress, she stepped out onto the bank. The happy crowd cheered and clapped.

You didn't want to come in, so I left you outside and followed the girl, the blue-suited man and the stream of guests into the church. I couldn't have been more wrong about the man and the girl. Once inside, I quickly put two and two together. You see, Inah, the girl in the ivory dress was getting married that morning. And the man in the blue suit was the bride's father escorting his daughter to the church for her wedding. And at the foot of the steps leading to the altar stood a nervous-looking, red-cheeked young man in a fresh haircut and black suit, watching the girl being escorted up the church aisle by her father.

When I came back out, it was drizzling. I found you standing outside the door. The gondola and the gondoliers were gone and the canal was empty. The rainy piazza stood empty too. No trees. No chirping birds. For a while, we just stood there, silent and looking out at the slanted silver ropes of rain. (Neither of us mentioned the girl in the ivory dress or the man in the gray-blue suit.) I was feeling a little sad as I stood there next to you. I was wondering whether Dad would one day have the chance to hand you and me to the arms of men we are in love with. I wondered if you would ever have a chance to fall in love and marry. I wondered if any man would love you as a woman. I wondered if I would marry if you didn't. I know you hate sentimentality but those questions were swirling inside my head as I stood there outside the church that morning.

Do you want me to tell you, Inah, what I realized at that moment? I realized that I was forever tethered to you as we were once tethered to Mom together through the umbilical cords. By fate and blood and love. And to be honest with you, it terrified me, the idea of being forever tethered to you.

I guess what I am trying to say is that even though most of the time we barely see beyond the fuzzy details of life (we so easily lose perspective), now and then there comes along a moment when you see for once so clearly

that you can see right through your heart. I think it was
one of those moments. Because it also made me see how
much I loved you and how that's what matters most in the
end. I was afraid but also sure that the rest will take care
of itself.

Love, Your twin, Yunah

As I start down from the Piazzale Michelangelo, the sun
slips behind dark blue clouds and the afternoon light turns
into a flat gray. I stop at the Ponte Vecchio over the lan-
guorously flowing Arno River, milky green and as opaque as
melted jade. It's the muted light, everything looks vivid and
clear: the distant hills of dark green olive trees and
cypresses, and the orange-tile-roofed houses into which the
Arno silently disappears, as if strolling away. On the sandy
bank below, a woman sits in a white canvas chair, gazing out
at the river. In a white pants suit and a wide-brimmed straw
hat banded with a flowing magenta ribbon, she looks like a
figure of pointelle strokes in one of Seurat's paintings Dad
once took us to see at the Metropolitan Museum of Art
during the Impressionist exhibition. Inah and I were eleven
or twelve. That was long, long ago.

ELEVEN

Friday evening, I answer the door and find Jessica Han and this Michael O'Connor standing under the yellow porch light. Looking like a pair of wet seabirds blown ashore by a gale wind. Apparently, Inah has sweet-talked Mom into letting their Friday night cooking club meet at our house, promising to deliver her a spanking clean kitchen afterward.

As if struck by lightning and not believing my eyes, I stand there and stare at this Michael. To Mom, Inah described him (he graduated from Stuyvesant the past summer) as an aspiring chef. (Not a cook, a chef, Inah emphasized, saying there's a difference.) Of course, the only chef I know is Chef Boyardee, in that funny chef's hat that looks like a chimney funnel, and a white medic gown straddling over his huge girth. Maybe that's why I expected some nerd with a pimply face, gangly arms and a shocking mop of red hair to show up. Instead, slim and tall and with black hair and a beautiful, pale face, he looks more like a celestial version of Bono of U2 or an Irish version of John Lone, who has that cold, unapproachable and unflappable beauty about him.

A pretty face always does wonders, because Mom makes a terrific fuss over Michael. Whatever reservations she had about him (he didn't go to college) instantly evaporate. She gushes to us in Korean how he looks like a *gui-gong-ja,* a noble prince. I roll my eyeballs, Inah giggles, and Jessica Han, playing her cheerleader bit, tells Mom how these days cute chefs are like rock stars and supermodels, touted around by press agents.

Put off by his pretty face and burning with twisted jealousy, I decide to stay clear of the kitchen. I go up to my room and crawl in bed with my French grammar book. But I can't concentrate. I hear them laughing, and cupboard doors banging in the kitchen downstairs. I lie around fuming.

After a while, I invent a perfect excuse and go down for a hot cup of Ovaltine. The kitchen is in complete disarray. The counter is littered with Hershey's chocolate chips escaping from the ripped bag, and sticky, runny eggshells, and measuring cups, spoons and aluminum tins. The rest of the kitchen looks like a crime scene after the finger dusting; every surface their hands have touched is smeared with some sticky goo and flour dust. And there were Michael and Inah, standing at the counter side by side, whipping up egg yolk in a big glass bowl. Jessica Han has propped herself next to them, like a decorative plant, and is gibbering on the phone, her hand hitching up her shapely hip bone.

"Hey, Yunah!" Jessica sings, waving her fingers and switching the cordless phone to the other ear. She looks really girlie in a tacky way. Her pink, waxlike lipstick seems to have been ironed on permanently, and her long hair is roller-set wavy. She is the Queens version of a California Valley girl cum cheerleader. Inah resolutely ignores me stomping around, banging and slamming the cupboard doors.

Finally Michael says, "You're really welcome to join us, Yunah." With such assumed familiarity! I think I am going to break out in hives.

"No thanks. Cooking is one thing I hope I will never have to do." Inah loudly snickers. I decide to forgo Ovaltine, pour myself a glass of water and stomp out again.

The next Friday night, I am even more obnoxious. But Jessica Han behaves unerringly and unwaveringly pleasant, greeting me in her high-pitched, giggly voice, and Michael not even once betrays a sign that he is irritated by my less than stellar behavior. (That slightly amused look on his face gives me a fit every time.) Inah throws me a sidelong glance now and then but says not a word. I bump into her on purpose and pinch her hard at the arm, just to rattle her a little, but she doesn't even wince, determined not to give me the satisfaction.

"Your mouth is sticking out a mile," Inah informs me in a loud whisper when I brush past her again, using the Korean expression for sulking. I could sock her in the ear.

After everyone leaves, I go down to the kitchen, where Inah's cleaning up. It has been a "chocolate mousse night." (Lots of eyeball rolling here.) On the wooden lacquer tray, little clear plastic champagne cups are sitting, filled with swirls of chocolate mousse. My mouth waters with a sugar craving.

"Want one?" Inah asks. "I'm going to put the rest in the fridge." She hands me a spoon and a cup of mousse. As I shovel in a spoonful, Inah says, "You know it's really embarrassing the way you act so hysterically every time they are here."

"First of all, they've been here only twice. And I have no idea what the hell you're talking about. So if you do, shoot," I say, sotto voce.

"I don't have to say it, do I? It's so obvious," Inah says.

"Okay. I know what you are thinking, but let's just say that it has nothing to do with Michael, the pretty Irish boy."

"Huh!" snorts Inah, looking incredulous.

"All right, Miss Dense. Do I have to spell it out for you? What I don't understand is how you could have this stupid, mindless cooking club shit going. It's not like everything's perfect and worry-free on the home front."

"Mom said okay. You got a problem with that?" Inah says curtly. "And it's not my fault Dad's having an affair."

"Anyway, I bet he's gay," I say, trying to change the subject but unable to resist a dig. "A big pretty boy playing with flour dough and whipped cream and egg yolk. If he isn't, why would he be hanging around with you and that floozy Jessica every Friday night."

"You sure are warped in the head," Inah says.

I don't know if she lodged a complaint with Mom. The next Friday evening, when I stomp out of the kitchen to go up to my room, Mom follows me to the bottom of the staircase.

"Why are you so rude to Michael?" Mom says in an angry whisper. "Did I teach you to treat a guest like that?"

"Mom! He's not my guest. If he is, then how come I don't remember inviting him?"

"Inah did. I did. So you behave," Mom says.

"What do you want me to do? Get down on my knees and kowtow to him?" I sound so insolent, Mom grits her teeth. "All right then. I can't explain it, but I just can't stand him."

"Why, what's wrong? He's so nice!" Mom says, genuinely puzzled. I don't know since when she thought so highly of a man who likes to cook. Korean men never cook, although I am sure that at Korean restaurants all the chefs are men. Dad doesn't cook. Mom doesn't even like him hanging around the kitchen. It's a glaring sign of schmaltziness. What woman likes a schmaltzy man? If Michael were Korean, I am sure Mom would wonder what's wrong with him. Americans are different, that's what she would say if I pointed that out, so I don't.

"What's wrong?! I can't believe you're so gullible. Can't you see what he's up to? He wants to be a chef. He's just using our kitchen because his stepmother won't let him at their home and they got kicked out of Jessica Han's! And I know, too, if Dad were here, you wouldn't let Inah's boyfriend hang around the kitchen, cooking."

"Who says he's her boyfriend? He's just a friend," Mom says defensively. "And what about Jessica? She's here, too."

"He's not Jessica's type! Really, I'll sell you the Brooklyn Bridge. I know you will have a fit if I bring a boy around. But for Inah, the rule is different. You'd be dancing with joy even if it was Pee Wee Herman Inah brought home."

"You can bring your friends any time."

"I'd rather die."

"Anyway, who's this Pee Wee Hermit?" Mom, who tells me how she used to love poems by Rilke and Paul Verlaine (in Korean), has no idea who Pee Wee Herman is. She thinks I am talking about a cartoon character. Not that she's too far off the mark.

Four days after Christmas, Auntie Minnie and Mom and I go to see the Christmas tree at Rockefeller Center. It's Auntie Minnie's idea: Mom needs to get out of Flushing. I go along only because it is the night the stupid "Michael O'Connor Cooking Club" is making its long-talked-about Peking duck, and I don't want to hang around, being the odd duck out, so to speak.

It is already dark when we drive over the Manhattan Bridge and head west. The parking lots we pass all have FULL signs, and the chance of finding a parking space on the street in Manhattan this time of year, to borrow Auntie Minnie's expression, is as slim as going to heaven after a life of debauchery.

Eventually, we park at a lot all the way west near Tenth Avenue and walk back, negotiating the long blocks of the limo-lined theater district, the crowded, light-blazing Times Square, and Radio City Music Hall. It's bitter cold.

It hurts just to breathe. Mom shivers in her thin black wool coat. Her head is bare. She never covers her head, no matter how frigid it gets. According to one of those strange theories only Koreans can come up with, you're supposed to keep your head cold and your feet warm; you get dumb and dumber when you keep the head warm.

"What you gonna do with your high IQ after you freeze dead?" Auntie Minnie says, handing Mom her pair of fur earmuffs, but Mom insists she's fine, this is nothing.

"That must be why Koreans so smart," Auntie Minnie says sarcastically. "And smart people, they give you only headache." After a while, my feet turn numb and it feels like I'm walking on two pieces of stone.

The promenade at Rockefeller Center is packed every inch with a bundled-up crowd. It is next to impossible to see ahead or take a step in any direction. Trapped in moving walls of people, milling about, pushing and shoving, Mom, clutching her pocketbook, holds on to my arm, afraid that we might get separated.

"Hold on to your bag tight," Mom whispers to me, as if relaying a best-kept secret.

"Keep moving! Keep moving!" Auntie Minnie barks like a drill sergeant, militantly shoving Mom and me from behind. She says at the rate we move, come midnight, we will still be standing here in the exact same spot. Mom laughs at Auntie Minnie. It is fun, though. The collective festivity in the air, it's infectious.

Gradually, we inch our way to the railing, close enough to get a peek at the light-flooded skating rink, where people, pirouetting and stumbling, falling and sailing, go around and around the floodlit ice floor, aglow in silver, below the impossibly tall and splendidly decked spruce and the gold Prometheus. Buildings soar around us like chiseled rocks. It is a vertical city filled with noise, lights, more noise, music and laughter and smells of burning pretzels and roasted chestnuts. "Cold as a witch's tit," an old man behind Auntie Minnie says, not unhappily.

"Mom, glad we came?" I ask, hoping Mom has noticed how people do go out just to have fun. Her face is all goose-bumped and greenish yellow in the lights. Mom looks at me and smiles. Her smile says: Of course, what do you think, just like everyone else, I would like to enjoy things and have a good time, too, but I am deferring everything for you kids.

Soon Auntie Minnie is getting antsy to get going. She says her nose is about to fall off her face. As we cross Fifth Avenue, I can feel Mom's mood plunge: Her mind is slipping away to a faraway place. She is thinking about Dad ensconced in Chicago with his lover and about Inah, who is going to leave home for college in the coming summer.

The line outside the Christmas display window of Saks Fifth Avenue department store is long and slow moving. We decide it's way too cold to stand on it and head for St. Patrick's instead. The humming and smoky and echo-filled church feels impossibly huge and cavernous. Auntie Minnie whispers to me that they build churches like this on purpose to stir up fear inside, and to make people feel small. But Mom is quiet. She is squarely back to her crowded life again. In my head, I keep seeing Michael's pale, freckled, pretty face. Smiling. And every time, I feel my stomach churn.

We walk out of the church. It's not yet seven, and Auntie Minnie suggests that we go to see Trump Tower. But Mom wants to go home. "Already! As if you've left some treasure there," Auntie Minnie snickers. We can come back another day, Mom tells her. Trump Tower isn't going anywhere. But we are here, Auntie Minnie protests. How often do we come to Manhattan? Don't you want to see Trump Tower? Mom's lack of interest is genuinely puzzling to her.

"What about you, Yunah?" Auntie Minnie asks me. I am not in a hurry to get home, I reply. I am all for going to see Trump Tower. Outvoted, Mom reluctantly agrees.

At Trump Tower, distracted, Mom gives only perfunctory glances to the shop windows. But Auntie Minnie is virtually salivating. Her eyes literally pop out with unhindered lust. She loves the glitter. And all those goods and goods and goods, pulsating with invisible dollar signs. She looks completely rejuvenated. I bet Ivana can have anything here, Auntie Minnie says, driveling with envy. What does that tell you? she says, poking me in the side. Remember that it's all about meeting Mr. Right, she says, meaning Mr. Rich. Mom looks at Auntie Minnie with pity and clucks her tongue.

At the mezzanine full of glitzy shops, we realize Auntie Minnie is missing. Mom and I look around for her. Where could she have gone? When we spot her, she's pushing the forbidding, heavy glass door into Martha's, the high-priced boutique. Aghast, Mom and I watch her strut in, looking dangerously unstable on the long and pointy heels of her leather boots. Through the glass, we can see an impeccably coiffured saleswoman, all blond and ivory, shooting a very icy, you-must-be-kidding look at her. Strangely, Auntie Minnie, who has seemed more glamorous and more American than any Flushing Korean, looks so outrageously tacky. Her bleached, rust-colored hair, puffed up with a serious teasing and set with generous hair spray, looks like a bronze medieval helmet. And she looks seriously fashion-challenged in her short, capelike mink jacket and bright purple leather skirt she has somehow managed to squeeze into. In fact, she looks like an aging Las Vegas showgirl.

Mom doesn't have the stomach to stand there and watch her being snubbed; she quickly looks away.

Finally, Auntie Minnie comes back out and strolls toward us. Mom just can't help herself.

"Why go in? You can't afford anything there," Mom says scoldingly.

"How you know I no can? I have money," she talks back defiantly. "You worry my money have 'GI bride' written all over?"

"Why do you always have to bring that up?" Mom snaps. Upset, Auntie Minnie speeds off ahead of us.

"Mom, why do you always say such mean things to her?" I ask. Mom doesn't answer. When we catch up with her, Auntie Minnie says she's going to the bathroom, and after that we will go home.

"Good!" Mom says.

As we ride the escalator down to the basement floor to use the bathroom, though, like an irrepressible weed, Auntie Minnie's mood perks up right away at the sight of the cafe by the nineteen-foot-tall, pink marble waterfall, where piped-in Muzak plays a sappy symphony.

"Oh, nice! Let's have coffee here before go home."

"Don't waste money on the overpriced coffee," Mom says, fast shooting down Auntie Minnie's idea. "We'll have a cup when we get home."

"Your coffee, *Unni*?! Only Maxwell instant! Here it real coffee. They make from original beans!" Auntie Minnie says, waving her hand.

"What do you mean, original beans? Some beans are copies?"

"Never mind, *Unni*," Auntie Minnie mumbles, looking thoroughly fed up. "You not know how to enjoy life."

After stopping at the bathroom, not to give Auntie Minnie a chance, Mom heads straight to the escalator and up to the ground floor, then through the revolving door out to Fifth Avenue, which is swarming with multitudes of people. I feel so stupid and furious hurrying after Mom. Auntie Minnie is right: It is partly Mom's fault that Dad ran off with another woman. Mom weaves life tight and dry. She only lives for tomorrows that will never arrive. With her, life is like the permanent sign on a bar window promising "Free Beer Tomorrow." But isn't now, this very moment, a "tomorrow"?

All the way back home, Auntie Minnie gives Mom the cold shoulder. I am just glad to be inside the warm car, after the long, freezing walk back to the garage. I can literally feel my frozen bones thaw.

When Auntie Minnie drops us off at the corner of Magnolia Place, Mom, now a little sorry, asks her to come in for coffee.

"Next time," she answers curtly. As soon as we get out, she makes a wide swipe around the circle and guns her blue Ford away into the cold night.

"It's the last time I go anywhere with her," Mom says.

Inah feels the unhappy vibes coming from me. When I walk into the kitchen, she asks me how it was.

"Don't even ask," I reply glumly. I wash my hands, fill the kettle with water and set it to boil.

"Why? Mom didn't like it?"

"You go and ask her if you want to know," I say. I take out the Ovaltine jar and my big brown mug and line them up on the counter. Michael hasn't looked up. He is bent over the dining table, inserting what looks like a tube into the neck of a plucked clean, bald-headed duck that resembles a Rubber Ducky with bumps. In the Chinese section of Flushing, you often see whole glazed ducks hanging on hooks behind the windows at some Chinese restaurants. I always find the sight a little disturbing. And I've never been into birds. Besides, we never eat duck, and there must be a reason for that. I also know that in Korea, ducks are symbols of marital harmony. I hate to think someone has taken the life of a duck's spouse.

"Where's Jessica?" I ask, wondering whether Inah has snitched on me to Michael, about what I said about him being gay.

"She's coming over later," Inah says. The kettle starts whistling. I mix the Ovaltine and take a long, slow sip. The hot, sweet liquid chases the chill down my spine, and my whole body shakes with satisfaction.

"Yunah," Michael says, looking up and showing not even the tiniest sign of a grudge.

"Hi, how's it going?" I say, avoiding his eyes, which always seem to read my mind. I pick up the mug to go up to my room.

"It's going OK. I am about to pump the duck. You two can give me a hand." I look at him and Inah, clueless. I have no idea what he means by pumping the duck. I shrug, put down the mug and follow Inah to the table. I am not that dense though. I can see Inah can easily do the job alone. I mean the duck isn't so humongous, but I decide to go along.

"Just hold it down by the legs," Michael says. Inah casually gets hold of one. I hold the other. In my hand, the cold leg feels rubbery and slippery.

"Yuck!" I say in disgust. Michael laughs and starts pumping a bicycle pump attached to the duck through a hose. He explains that the air, pumped in, will separate the duck skin from the meat. Slowly the duck starts ballooning up, transforming into a kind of obscene shape. I try not to look at it, but it is not that easy. Inah, struggling not to laugh, bites

down on her lips hard and holds her breath. Soon her face is
turning bright red, and all the facial muscles are getting distorted. Then our eyes meet. That does it. Her lips burst
open like the seams of a too-tight dress: "*Toot-toot! Prrrrrrt!*"
Inah doubles over in a hysterical laughing fit. She's shrieking and writhing and jumping up and down, all the while
trying to hold on to the duck leg.

"Stop it!" I scream. Inah looks up but after a quick look
at my tortured face, she plunges right back into her laughing
fit. Dismayed, Michael shakes his head at Inah laughing
and wiping the tears from her eyes. Suddenly, the bicycle
pump falls off the tube.

"Oh, holy duck!" Michael cries, looking down at the hose
and the pump in his hand. I can't take it any longer. I let go
of the leg, and right away, the hose attached to the neck
springs off, too. And before we know it, the slippery, naked
bird leaps off the table and sails off into the air like a
launched rocket. Wingless and featherless. Michael swiftly
lunges after it, catches it in the air, slips and ends up on the
kitchen floor, flat on his back, cuddling the bald duck in his
arms. Inah and I go completely bonkers. We run around the
kitchen in circles, shrieking and laughing and wiping tears
and holding our sides with our hands. Inah cradles her jaw
with her palms, as if she has had one too many jawbreakers.
Michael is still lying on the floor, cradling the duck, looking
completely calm.

"Michael!" Inah calls scoldingly.

Michael closes his eyes and launches into an Irish lullaby: "Loora, loora, loora. Loora, loora, lie! Loora, loora,
loora, that's an Irish lullaby."

Mom walks in to see what is going on. Her face is shiny
with the cold cream she has massaged on to take off
makeup. Seeing Mom, Michael bolts right up, scrambling

off the floor, and, with a completely straight face, presents the duck to Mom with two hands and a deep bow. Mom doesn't know what to make of it. She looks at it and then at Michael. Obviously, she's shocked the way it is being handled. As it is Mom thinks "Americans" lack a sense of hygiene. For one thing, they keep their shoes on inside the house.

"No way I am going to eat that," Inah says, having recovered from her laughing fit.

Later, we rinse it and do the whole thing all over again and help Michael glaze the pumped-up duck. We then take it out to the pantry and hang it to dry on a hook shaped from a wire hanger over a pan placed on the floor to catch the drip. Inah and I go down to the basement and bring up the electric fan.

"At least the duck's got a good, pampered afterlife," Michael says, turning on the fan. The wind will dry it faster, but it will still take hours.

After Mom goes to bed, Jessica Han comes over. With Auntie Minnie's stash of Jim Beam whisky, Michael makes us quasi-Irish coffee with a high cone of whipped cream on top, and we play crazy four with black beans. From the "Irish coffee," our faces turn tomato red. Inah and Jessica act like their brains are rattled. They come up with one stupid joke after another involving animals. Then every time Michael goes out to the pantry to check on the duck and empty the catch-tray, we troop after him and get into a laughing fit all over again. We find the duck hanging in the pantry with the fan sending the wind up incredibly hilarious. "It committed suicide," Inah says, "indignant at the way we treated it." We quiz Michael about whether it is a male or a female and how can one tell? Michael can't believe how silly we are.

THIRTEEN

Sunday morning, I find Mom standing at the stove, stirring a thick pine nut porridge in a stainless steel pot.

"Mom, who's that for?" I ask, greedily sniffing at the delicious smell of pine nuts.

"Wash up and get dressed. I want you to take this to Auntie Minnie. Poor thing, all alone," Mom says, ladling the hot porridge into the thermos.

Auntie Minnie has been recuperating at home after surgery to remove a huge fibroid mass growing in her uterus. She found a doctor who used the latest laser surgery technique and traveled all the way to New Orleans to have it done by him. Two days ago, Mom and I went to pick her up at La Guardia airport when she came back. They wheeled her out of the plane on a wheelchair, still all doped up on a prescription narcotic painkiller. She looked like a sick hen with her dilated, out-of-focus eyes, and she could barely spit out a word. And then as soon as we installed her in the back of the car, Auntie Minnie slumped sideways and fell into deep, soundless, motionless sleep, scaring the hell out of us. We thought something was wrong.

"Make sure she eats it," Mom says, putting the cover back on the thermos.

"How come you're not taking it to her yourself?"

"I will be late for church. Go with Inah if you don't want to go alone." After Mom leaves, I go up and ask Inah. She says sorry, she has to do laundry.

"Take a bus," Inah hollers to my back as I close her room door. It's not that cold, so I decide to walk. Auntie Minnie lives behind Queens Botanical Garden. It's a good fifteen-minute, fast-paced walk. It's a typical winter morning. Gray and damp. Everything flat, washed out of color. The sky, dull silver. The crowds are even thinner down Main, where Chinese and Korean grocery stores and restaurants give way to Middle Eastern grocery stores and spice shops, video stores and Indian sari shops. I make it in ten minutes.

When I come back from Auntie Minnie's, Michael's green storm boots are sitting at the foyer. He hasn't been around since the Peking duck night. Several days ago at dinner, Inah casually mentioned that Michael got accepted into a famous culinary institute in the San Francisco area and would be leaving sometime in February. Mom, who really likes Michael, seemed real sorry to hear that; she kept saying, too bad. I feigned indifference, but, strangely enough, I felt kind of betrayed.

On the way to my room, I stick my head into the kitchen. Apparently they haven't heard me coming in. They are standing side by side at the counter. Inah is slicing something on the cutting board, and next to her, Michael is expertly beating eggs in a bowl. He then kind of pauses and leans over Inah's shoulder.

"Ooh, Inah!" Michael says in mock horror. "I can see you're going to make a hell of a good cook! Look, how thick you cut the mushrooms!" He then playfully pokes Inah in the side. Inah, shrinking, giggles a little girl's giggle. I feel blood rush up to my head. I'm such an addle-headed idiot. So what about Inah's face? Michael genuinely likes her. I know that if Michael weren't so gorgeous, I wouldn't have such a hard time believing it. I just want to slip away quickly, unnoticed. But just as I turn, a sneeze comes, and, trying to stifle it, I end up almost gagging. Michael's and Inah's heads turn at the same time. Inah quickly averts her eyes. She looks pissed. She probably thinks I have been spying on them.

"Yunah," Michael says, quizzically scanning my red face. There isn't a hint of embarrassment in his beautiful, breeze-cool eyes.

"I am sorry, I didn't know you were here."

"Oh, don't worry. I am about to flip some mushroom omelettes. If you want one, just say so."

I am not hungry and I don't even like mushrooms. I mean, mushrooms are some kind of fungi, aren't they? They can't possibly be good for you. Without waiting for my answer, Inah takes out paper napkins and forks and knives and sets the table for three. From the way she keeps quiet, I know I am an unwelcome intruder. I notice a freshly brewed pot of hot coffee sitting at the coffeemaker.

"Well, I'll have some coffee. I love it when it's fresh and scalding hot." I pour myself a half mug and sit down. I am self-conscious, and even I can barely stand myself. I wish I hadn't backed out of the trip to Manhattan this morning with the girls from school.

Michael brings the first batch of omelettes on a plate and puts it down in front of me. I notice how his fingers are so long and skinny and pale, plantlike. I feel so stupid. Of course, Inah can see it. It is useless to try to hide it. It's written all over me. I can't stand it. I am making a fool of myself and Inah.

"How's Auntie Minnie?" Inah asks, breaking the omelette on her plate with her fork. I absentmindedly pour a river of ketchup over my omelette. Michael looks at me and the ketchup-bathed omelette with alarm. I take a big gulp of the scalding hot black coffee and think I am going to die.

"All right, I guess," I say, cringing as the hot coffee makes its way down, burning the pipe. "She made me watch this video of her surgery. Before the operation, they insert this thing attached with a tiny camera through a hole cut right below her belly button and kind of poke around inside, looking at the liver and stuff. You can hear the doctor saying that her liver seems a little swollen, flicking at it with the rod or whatever that's in there. Auntie Minnie thinks it's real funny. Remember the expression Mom often uses? Telling Auntie Minnie that her liver is swollen when she gets extravagant. Don't look up a tree you can't climb? Be yourself?" I know I am being gross. Inah looks at me like she can't believe it. I don't dare to look at Michael. I go on, deadpan.

"Anyway, after removing the fibroid," I go on obnoxiously, "cutting around it with the laser—it's like a blowtorch, you can see the flesh burn off—the doctor holds it up for the camera. As if it's some kind of archaeological find. It's a big, solid mass. The size of a big grapefruit. Kind of round and waxy and flesh-colored. And it's got these red blood veins all over. Auntie Minnie asked for it as a keepsake. It's sitting on the kitchen counter in a big kimchi bottle, soaked in alcohol. When you go see her, don't forget to take a look at it."

"Yunah?! Gross!" Inah blurts out and screws her face up. "Thanks a lot. I can't eat now."

"Me neither," I say, meaning it, putting down the fork. "Sorry, Michael." Michael looks me full in the eye, as if trying to figure me out. I notice he is sitting in Dad's seat.

PART FIVE

On the train to Rome, Inah's out cold. In her wrinkled, out-of-the-backpack clothes, and tanned dark, she looks even dingier than she did the day at the Venice airport. And the way she sleeps, curled tight, arms folded, her head squished against the sunlit window, she reminds me of a wounded animal, bracing herself for more attacks. Incredibly tense and yet inexplicably vulnerable.

Last night, back from Siena, Inah hinted, in her usual oblique way, at what might have happened at Oxford. I don't know what prompted her. It was probably the fight we had: Imagine how it must have stung her, all the horrible words I hurled at her.

It seems that while at Oxford Inah befriended a girl from Canada. They lived across the hall from each other, and over time, developed a close friendship. Inah refused to elaborate on it, but it was clear that something horrible happened to her. The way Inah spoke of her made me think that she was no longer alive. That was the end of the story, if it was a story. Inah had already decided how much to tell me beforehand, so there was no point for me to push her for more. It would have seemed nothing more than a prurient curiosity on my part, anyway. And after all, there are many ways to tell a story. By omitting, adding, editing, twisting and glossing over, you can always stitch a story together. As long as it contains a truth, what does it matter, I thought.

That's all, Inah then said: That's all. Of course it wasn't. Knowing her, whatever had happened must have shaken her up badly. She wouldn't admit that was what ultimately caused her to abandon her studies, but I think it did precipitate what happened later. Inah began to struggle again. Then, bit by bit, her life just spiraled out of control. I can see that. It must have been all the more difficult because she thought (as we did) she had put behind all the stumbling years and reached a place where she could somehow manage life with some semblance of peace. Unless it had reached a point where she simply couldn't go on, Inah would not have taken off like that. Naturally, she couldn't tell Mom. Not then, anyway. Imagine the way Mom would have reacted to her decision. So Inah must have agonized over it. Alone. It couldn't have been a decision she had made lightly. Not by any means.

By telling me what happened, Inah, I thought, was trying to reassure me. Now I wonder if she did it because she got sick and tired of looking at her image reflected in the mirror I held for her. And I wonder if I was ever really conceited enough to think that I would be able to rescue her. No, I don't think so. It was Mom's idea, and somehow, I bought into it. Or rather, I needed to believe what Mom believed. And it is only now, on the train to Rome, that I finally realize the very obvious: No one can save Inah except herself. (Who can save anyone from life?) And if only instinctively, she has always known that. She may still be lost, but at least she's fighting and struggling to stay afloat. It should be a sign of hope, not of trouble. And if she's determined to do it her way and on her own, no matter how difficult it is and however long it takes, then I should help her as best as I can.

It's only that sometimes, in her struggle to stay afloat, she looks to us as though she is drowning. And from her instinctive desire to protect her, Mom feels she has to intervene. It's impossible for Mom to be a spectator and wait until Inah asks for help. Not when she thinks she's holding the rope that will pull her out before drowning. But Mom has to throw the rope away and let go. Give Inah a chance to learn to survive on her own. So much of our heartbreak stems from Mom's inability to let go. But she will have to try. It will be very hard, for it will feel like giving up, but it really is the only way. She has to let go of her and hope for the best.

So it is with new resolve and something like a sense of relief that I arrive in the Rome Isadora Duncan called "a wonderful city for a sorrowful soul." Happy to be released to become one of its free-floating, anonymous particles. I am probably imagining it, but Inah, too, seems almost gleeful at the thought of getting rid of me soon. Bit by bit, like old scabs, she sheds the strange focused urgency that tightly gripped her in Florence and emerges tender and more sure-footed and less maudlin. Maybe it's simply being back in Rome, for no matter how temporarily, it's here where she makes her home.

Inah stays with me at the hotel (I checked in because she seemed reluctant to invite me to her place), and we spend several surprisingly good days. Every morning, bitten by the Korean Spartan bug and determined to make up for lost time, she hurries me out of the hotel, a small, nondescript building that stands near the foot of Via Maggio. She feels like it's her town. I find it amusing and almost touching, the proprietary pride she displays shamelessly. She's eager for me to discover that something which makes Rome so special. The Rome that effortlessly appeals to one's sense of beauty and joy and the "now" and bestows on one a sense of bliss.

Under the Roman sky, a gilded fountain of light, we walk miles and miles every day with our blistering feet. Zigzagging through Old Rome and darting around the city, cramming in all the tourist sites. We eat too much gelato, drink too much coffee, and wolf down too many greasy slices of pizza, sold by the weight. And I mourn our fast dwindling days together in Rome. To think that it could be this easy. . . .

TWO

After Michael leaves for San Francisco, intent on burying him in memory, we avoid talking about him as we do about Dad. But it's hard not to notice the bottles of half-used vanilla and almond extract that lie inside the pantry like pieces of memory, pushed all the way into the back by Inah and me. And then, late at night, comes the sudden craving for Michael's ginger sherbet or rice pudding, lemon soufflés or heavenly chocolate custards. So often, walking into the kitchen, my nose catches that imaginary whiff of grated rinds of oranges and lemon, and my mouth waters. At a moment like that, I can almost see it, too, the gelatin texture of ginger sherbet Michael used to pour into ice-cube trays and the counter that used to be crowded with flour and sugar bags, chocolate crumbs, stains of egg yolk and spilled milk. I miss Michael's voice saying, "Just a pinch of salt," or "We're going to let it cool for a few minutes."

But suddenly, spring is back in bright yellow forsythias

and yellow and white daffodils. Freed from the long winter's siege, Ash Avenue, shedding its hunkered-down look, slowly wakes up, ruffled with shabby brown patches of lawn and overgrown hedges and cracked sidewalks. It stays that way, desolate, even more so than in winter, until trees burst out in blooms all over, in clumps of hazy clouds. First magnolias, and then cherries, and then dogwoods. So dazzling are they in the sunlight that my eyes seem to turn watery just looking at them. I begin to notice, too, how people walking down the sunlit sidewalks past the flowering trees all look slightly dazed and feverish. And Inah comes and goes, with that vague, absorbed look on her face. Subdued and quiet, except when she battles Mom over her choice of college. Then one day, a cold spring rain falls, dousing the blossoms and temporarily muting the brilliance; I come home from school following the sidewalk dizzily strewn with wet, foot-crushed petals and sniffing (as Dad used to) at the air, pungent with a sweet-sick smell.

Soon after, May hurtles in, as though prompted by the rain, bringing with it a string of perfect dry spring days, filled with quiet, sunny afternoons. In the blue sky, winds push white clouds along. Time seems to stretch on and on like an elastic band. On afternoons like that, when our shabby stretch of Ash Avenue looks exactly like the spring when we moved here, it's almost easy to believe that everything will be fine. Even without Dad. If there's anything that still seems to miss his presence sorely, it is the backyard garden, where the peonies bloom and dip hardly noticed. New baby green bamboo shoots are coming up like crazy, pushing through the old, sickly yellow leaves that look like moth wings clinging tenaciously. In a couple of years, the bamboo will probably take over the whole area by the fences, and then it will be too late to do anything about it.

It's earlier than usual when Mom starts her six-day workweek at the travel agency. Inah, suffering from hay fever, pops red bean-sized Sudafed pills like M&M's. I get fat on the steady diet of junk food Mom buys in excessive quantities at a new price club she regularly raids with Auntie Minnie with militant zeal (along with 42-roll packs of toilet paper and 36-roll packs of paper towels). In the bathroom mirror, my face starts to look like a fat white turnip. I am haunted by a vague fear that things are getting out of control, slowly racing to a crashing point.

The only person who's happy is Auntie Minnie. She's got a boyfriend, a Bayside Italian who owns a small hair product distribution company. She met him at a trade show. (Remember she swore off men for good after her divorce?) So now she rarely comes around or stays over. When she remembers to call, she sounds ecstatically happy; she's having the time of her life. Her boyfriend even took her to Atlantic City in a white stretch limo trimmed with lightbulbs. Imagine! She knows, too, that he is two-timing her with a young Hispanic divorcée and is leasing her a beauty salon somewhere in Jackson Heights. So what, she says. I am too old to let jealousy get in the way.

One Saturday evening, she finally brings him over so Mom can check him out for her. Uncle Frankie, whom Auntie Minnie unabashedly introduces as "Prankie," turns out to be a stereotyped-to-death Italian, prone to flashy gold chains and an open shirt. But Auntie Minnie matches him just so, with her own loud clothes and enough makeup "to paint a whole canvas by rolling her face over it," as Mom puts it so tactfully. In Korean, of course.

They end up staying hours. Joking and kidding each other, making fun of Bayside Italians and Flushing Koreans, telling jokes about the Mafia and Moonies, and roaring with their heads tilted back. Uncle Frankie keeps calling Auntie Minnie "Connie Chung," as a compliment, of course, and she returns it, declaring, "He handsome or what? Like Alpha Chino!" And for some unfathomable reason, she keeps slapping him on the legs and arms as if she were trying a punching bag. The whole time, embarrassed and shocked, cringing and wincing, and trying not to break into a laughing fit, Mom and Inah and I sit there, catching flies with our open mouths. It's the best time we have had in months.

Then one day, just like that, Dad is back in Flushing. Inah and I are in the kitchen making *ramyun* for lunch the Saturday afternoon when the phone rings. We figure it's Mom, and Inah picks up the phone: "Hello?!" Obviously it's not her, because Inah spends the next long minute mostly silent, blurting out just a couple of barely audible *nehs*, yeses. She's all flustered, and for a second, she even looks like she's hyperventilating. Finally, she puts down the phone and slowly sinks into a chair, looking as if she has just been hit in the head with a sledgehammer. Her face is still flushed crimson red.

"Don't tell me. It's Dad, isn't it?" I ask. Inah nods slowly. "Was he calling from Chicago?" She shakes her head. "Then where was he calling from? Tell me!!"

"Dad's in Flushing," she says. "He was calling from the pay phone at *Woo Chon*." *Woo Chon*, the Cow Village, is a Korean restaurant on Kissena Boulevard. I can hardly believe it.

As long as Dad stayed in Chicago, we somehow managed, holding our emotions in check. Maybe it was the distance that made it seem not quite real. But his sudden presence in Flushing is like a declaration of war.

Mom erupts like a volcano that has been lying dormant. That evening, she comes home from work and raids all the dresser drawers and closets. Standing at the doorway, Inah and I watch as she ferrets out Dad's things and flings them to the top of the bed. We don't dare interfere.

"Why did I ever marry your father? Why? I had to be crazy. Everyone tried to stop me and I didn't listen!" Mom howls, flinging out Dad's sweaters and pajamas. Sighing and drawing a quick cross across her chest, Inah mutters, "Here we go again!"

Inah and I hardly listen as Mom narrates that old story we've heard dozens of times. Every time she's mad at Dad, she brings it up. And each time, we notice, the story goes through a slight revision. She will conveniently omit some crucial facts. For example, she will never mention that it was she who doggedly pursued Dad, her high school art teacher. Nearly for five years after high school, all through college. Every day she used to go to Dad's studio above an art-supply store in downtown Seoul, where he also lived between the time he quit his high school teaching job to devote his life to painting and the time he went back to teaching at a college. When he wasn't in, she would wait for him for hours.

She didn't care then that Dad was an old bachelor with almost no prospects except a poor artist's life. And each time, Dad would try to talk to her, repeatedly reminding her that he was not only much older than her but also an unreliable, penniless artist without a single practical bone in him. He'd tell her that marrying him meant that she would never live an easy, bourgeois life. (Dad thought she was a spoiled princess.) But Mom, so in love, didn't care about any of that. Finally, he married her a year after she graduated from college and got a teaching job herself. It used to be a love-conquers-all story. Now she believes that the only love that remains true is unfulfilled or unrequited love.

Dad used to joke and tell us, with a wink and a nod, that he had married Mom just to stop her from bothering him. If she hadn't trapped him into a marriage, he would have been living a free and happy bachelor life in Korea. Sometimes, just to rile her up, he would hint that Mom hadn't even been the prettiest of the girls he could have married. Moreover, there had been a very beautiful girl who'd liked him very much and had later become a famous movie star. A household name in Korea. Freshly jealous after all these years, Mom would grill him who. But he wouldn't say it, making her fume for hours.

"Do you know your grandmother hated your father at the very first sight of him? She threatened not to see me ever again if I married him. And did I listen? So young and stubborn?!" Inah and I look at each other and shrug.

When the pile of Dad's things grows to a mammoth mountain on the bed, Mom chucks his Made in China slippers, which have been sitting there all those months at the foot of the bed, into a garbage bin. She then stuffs all the clothes and books into black garbage bags and fruit boxes and stacks them up high against the wall in the foyer.

THREE

A few days later, in the early evening while Mom's still at work, Inah and I pack some of Dad's clothes, a mink blanket and his tubular Korean pillow stuffed with rice-chaffs into two black garbage bags. We pile and tie them to a cart and set out for the half-basement apartment where Dad is temporarily staying. We are not exactly worried that Mom will find out. We figure she has probably been hoping we do exactly that, since she is all contradiction and nothing but contradiction.

When we reach the corner of Roosevelt, though, Inah suddenly gets cold feet. She isn't sure, she says, if she can face Dad. I know just what it is, too. Inah, such a damn Puritan, can't handle the fact that he has been living with another woman "mixing flesh" or "mixing bodies," the Korean euphemism for sex. (It shocks you like nothing else when it occurs to you for the first time that your parents "sleep" together. Your parents are not supposed to be sexual beings who entertain sexual thoughts, much less practice them.) It's not easy for me, either, but I deal with it by trying to avoid dwelling on it. It's such a gray area, anyway, and too much of a mystery, the worlds where adults navigate.

I threaten Inah, telling her that either both of us go or neither goes. Does she think I enjoy doing this? In fact, I hate it as much as she does. But Inah looks so unbearably miserable. She twists and pulls at her fingers. But I don't budge. We argue back and forth, standing on the crowded street corner with the cart parked between us.

"Please, Yunah! Why can't you go by yourself?"

"Why should I? Like I am dying to see Dad? Are you going or not going? Just make up your mind." Inah hisses, stamps her feet, wraps her head with her hands and squeezes it as if trying to stop it from exploding. "Shit, shit, shit!" she curses, kicking the curb. The air suddenly smells like smoky meat coming from the Korean restaurants. I stand there, thinking how I hate this time of day, just before the blue hour, when everything seems to overlap, and sounds and lights change their textures. I feel anxious, and I am furious at Inah.

"Forget it. Let's just go back home!" Grabbing at the cart handle, I spin around.

"All right! You win! Are you happy now?!" Inah squeals and snatches the handle back from me. She then rants all the way, saying how she hates everyone and every damn thing.

It feels really strange standing in front of Dad's apartment door. Inah is sort of right. It's probably a bad idea coming to see him like this. I don't think he will be happy to see us this way, either. I take a big breath, pull away the storm door and knock. I am going to count to ten, I tell myself, and if there's no answer by then, I will turn around and leave. I close my eyes and start counting, when I hear the door open. Startled, I look up and there's Dad, standing right there in front of me. I feel all the blood rush up to my head. Dad finally seems to realize it's me; his eyes go all dark. He looks as dismayed and as uncomfortable as I am.

Standing there framed by the narrow basement doorway, Dad looks almost gaunt and exhausted, as if he hasn't had a good night's sleep in ages. His bleary eyes sitting deep in the sockets are distant. And there is definitely an unfamiliar aura about him. An aura he acquired from another life that completely excluded us. I want to ask him why he did what he did. I want to ask him if he ever knew how we always thought him special and how we were so proud of him: for refusing to be molded and changed and fit; for staying so noble and high-minded despite a string of humble jobs he held to provide for us; for not becoming another Uncle Shin; for not wanting what everyone wants; for not grasping for the lowly and vulgar trophies of materialism.

But I don't ask him any of that. Instead, I quickly look away. It's hard to look him in the eye. It's so much harder than I expected. I feel as though it is me, it is us who have done something wrong and done him in. I glance back at Inah. She is standing at an angle, a few feet behind me, grinding at the cracked cement with the toe of her clunky black shoe. She has no idea how so unbelievably grateful I am to her for not having abandoned me to face him alone.

Dad's eyes slowly travel over to Inah. But she won't look at him. She holds her face stubbornly averted. Dad drops his eyes, stares at the ground for a second. I remember Dad coming home on a snowy night from the hospital where Inah was staying after the accident. He sat down for the dinner Grandma had fixed him, and he broke down and wept, holding his face with his hands. Even though I was very young, I knew he was hurting so much. It was the only time I ever saw him cry.

When Dad looks up again, his eyes are glassed over. With his brown and bony hand, Dad feels for his shirt pocket and takes out a cigarette pack. It's empty, because Dad crumples it in his hand. They look like white ivory buttons, the knuckles rising sharply through his skin.

"We brought you some of your things, Dad," I say, pointing at the bags on the cart. I have almost forgotten them. Surprised, Dad stares at the bulging garbage bags. He looks perplexed. As if he couldn't quite comprehend: his life lying there at his feet, reduced to two garbage bags. Dad slowly shakes his head. Then without saying anything, he rubs his stubbly chin. We all stand there, choking on the silence that sits like a fish bone caught in the throat.

Finally, Dad asks if we have eaten yet. I am disappointed. It's all Dad could think of to say after seven months of absence; if we have eaten yet.

"You haven't eaten yet? Dad will put these away and take you out to eat." He takes the bags inside. He doesn't ask us if we want to come in. That dark, small basement apartment is the only private space he owns in this world. The storm door bounces and shuts behind him with a subdued bang, shutting us out again.

I turn around to Inah, standing behind me. Then, as if we read each other's minds, Inah and I skip up the steps and start down the road. As fast as we can without running. It isn't until we reach the corner of Union and Roosevelt that I look back to see Dad hurrying down in a dark blue Windbreaker I haven't seen before. He catches up with us waiting at the light. Then, placing his hands on our shoulders, he gives our shoulders a squeeze. But I can't stand it: the feel and warmth of his hand. The light changes, and Inah and I start across, leaving Dad standing there, his hands in the air, rejected.

When we turn a corner, Inah launches into a loud wail. "Ung, ung . . ." She cries, bellowing shamelessly, like a child. I don't even try to stop her. The light is turning bluish. I remember how we used to go for walks with Dad on a beautiful spring evening like this.

FOUR

My last night in Rome, across the small rickety table at an outdoor restaurant on Via del Lavatore, amused, I watch Inah. The way she sits forward with her sharp elbows planted on the table like an eager student, and the way she so assiduously studies the menu, which she holds in front of her like a big, important book. I know she's comparing the prices and shopping for the best value for her money, pragmatic as always. (It's one of those tourist traps Inah shuns like poison, but she lodged only the mildest protest—I told her it's my treat.)

After a long while, she finally closes the menu, having decided on risotto with squid ink, the most exotic-sounding dish. She looks ravenously hungry. There's something endearing about her excited anticipation of food.

"No anti-pasti? No?" Our waiter asks after we order. He's gangly and as tall as a poplar tree and pale, more like a Northern Italian. "How about insalata?" He's persistent. I shake my head and smile apologetically.

"No problem," he says, playfully shaking his head, and then suddenly emboldened, asks me whether I am Japanese. (He never looks at Inah, not even once, as though she is invisible.)

"No, we're Americans," I reply.

"Eh?" he says skeptically. He thinks I am pulling his leg. He casts a quick, scrutinizing glance at me and shrugs and walks away. Inah predicts he will more or less ignore us for the rest of the meal. I don't quite get the logic, but it turns out she's right on the mark.

Food comes out fast, as if it is fetched from a conveyer belt. Inah's risotto with squid ink is too fishy for my taste, but she gobbles it up. A disheveled Italian man with a guitar is making the rounds of the tables, soliciting requests but not being very successful. He then stops at the nearby table of an American family of four, and after a short, lively discussion, suddenly and improbably, launches into a spirited "Rocky Mountain High." He has a terrible, jagged voice. Inah groans and says, "He can't sing for shit."

"And, duh, he's Italian," I say. Inah pulls her head down and giggles. Seeing her giggle with such childish delight, I am again filled with remorse. I could have tried harder. I should have been more patient. I will never be able to take back all the terrible words I said to her. I will kick myself for months. But there's no more time to make up for anything. Tomorrow I will have to leave her and fly back home. Just as I start feeling that I am finally succeeding in pulling her out of the shelter where she takes refuge.

"Look at it this way, Yunah," Inah says, as if she has read my mind. "At least, from now on, you don't have to be embarrassed if anyone asks you if you've been to Rome and seen the Spanish Steps, the Trevi, the Pantheon, et cetera, et cetera."

"Well, who's going to ask?" I know she's trying to cheer me up.

"You never know. A waitress at Dojo, for example."

"Yeah, right." Ha, ha. "Just don't forget the stuff you want me to take back home," I remind her.

"I will go get it in the morning."

"Fine. Just don't make me miss my flight."

"Well, if you like, we can go get it after dinner," Inah suggests unexpectedly. "It won't take long. We'll take a bus."

"Sure, why not," I say, trying not to sound too surprised. The day we arrived in Rome, she left me at the hotel and went over to her place in Trastevere to pick up some clean clothes. I assumed I would leave without ever seeing her place.

Inah is glad to leave before the man with the guitar makes his way to our table. We walk to Piazza Venezia and catch a bus just leaving for Trastevere. It rumbles across the bridge over the Tiber, which is surprisingly narrow and picturesque, and we are soon on Viale di Trastevere, a wide, bustling boulevard crowded with shops and stores housed in nondescript modern buildings. The change is so sudden and startling that it's like crossing the East River from Manhattan to Long Island City.

After a few stops along the Viale di Trastevere, we get off the bus. Up a couple of yards from the bus stop, Inah steers me into a street with a narrow sidewalk. Lined with low, old, brick buildings, and crowded with small lively restaurants and stores, it looks and feels just like one of the streets in the Village or Little Italy. From that slightly run-down and cramped look to the dingy sidewalk. As if reading my mind, Inah says, with a slight hint of disgust in her voice, that Trastevere used to be a backwater but it has become a Yuppyville and is now considered a fashionable place to live.

"Sounds just like New York," I say, smiling because she sounds so territorial. "But it's lively. It should be safe." She doesn't say anything to that. I can feel her mood change.

"This is it," Inah says, stopping in front of a scuffed brown door of a gray six-story building that houses a small pizzeria on the ground level. With a key she pulls out from her backpack, Inah lets us into the musty hallway, and we climb the foot-worn stairs to the third-floor landing, lit by a single lightbulb hanging from the ceiling like a small, dying moon. For some reason, Inah won't use her key. Instead, she rings the doorbell, which unexpectedly sounds like an insolent bleat of a hog. After long seconds, from inside comes the scraping sound of footsteps, and the door opens just a crack and a head pokes out.

"Oh, only it's you, Inah," says a girl's voice in an accented English. From what I can see, she seems about our age and rather short. It's the dark circles under her big brown eyes that give her round face a strangely fierce, birdlike look. And she's one of those people who can pass for anything: Italian, Greek, Spanish, Indian or Middle Eastern. She floats me a quick, darting glance over Inah's shoulder and quickly pulls her head back in and disappears behind the door.

"Will be back in a sec," Inah says, slipping inside after her. I crane my neck, hoping for a glimpse of the apartment, but Inah quickly shuts the door behind her. As I stand there waiting for Inah, the whole thing hits me as a little bizarre. It bothers me the covert and furtive way Inah and the girl behaved. Inah didn't even bother to introduce me to her or ask me in. And the girl seemed almost hostile. I didn't like her darting eyes, either. It was as if she were hiding something. What is going on? I am flooded with suspicion.

It occurs to me that Inah might belong to some kind of

cult. And I wonder if this place is one of the safe houses run by it. It all seems to make perfect sense. For a moment, I even doubt the story Inah told me about why she left Oxford. It didn't account for why Inah's living at this run-down place with this mysterious girl. That's it. I place my ear to the door, but all I can make out is the intermittent murmurings of their voices. I try the doorknob and give the door a quick shove, but it doesn't budge. I debate whether I should ring the bell or pound at the door. Just then I hear footsteps approach the door, and I quickly step back. The door opens and Inah walks out carrying a frayed khaki-cloth rucksack, sagging at the bottom with the weight.

"Remember this?" Inah says, pointing at the rucksack.

"Can't believe you still have that," I say, stealing a quick look at her face. But she looks perfectly innocent. I wonder if I am getting paranoid. I have yet to learn to trust Inah.

"We bought it together at an Army-Navy store in Manhattan," Inah reminds me again as if she can't believe that I remember it.

Suddenly, I feel a pang of something like nostalgia. Of course I remember; I remember everything. Isn't that the problem: remembering everything and not being able to forget anything? Inah probably hasn't a clue how I miss those days. Whenever she came home for Christmas from Antioch, she would bring with her a long list of things (she was always making lists even then) she couldn't get in Yellow Springs, Ohio. And then, like an annual ritual, after Christmas, we would spend a day in Manhattan, rummaging through the shelves of used books, racks and bins of used clothes and boxes of old records and used CDs. We loved the same books and songs and movies then, and shared the excitement of discovering a great new book or song over long distance.

It always seemed freezing and gray. In my head, I still carry an image of Inah from those days, walking next to me, hunched and shivering in her thin dark blue pea coat in the mauve light of winter dusk, and chattering her teeth behind a long, purplish knit scarf and now and then uttering her trademark dry observations like chicken droppings.

"We went to see *The Buddha of Suburbia* that night at the Public Theater," I say to assure Inah that I remember. "It was a BBC miniseries, wasn't it, adopted from the Hanif Kureishi novel you liked?" Impressed, Inah nods. Later that night after the movie, we rushed down to Tower Records on Bleecker Street, hoping to get hold of the David Bowie title song of the movie. We had to have it right then and there. We thought it was one of the best songs we had ever heard. But we couldn't find it.

A couple of years later, I finally got hold of a David Bowie CD with the song on it and mailed it to her. She was then in San Francisco working for a nonprofit organization called Food First, whose lofty mission was feeding the world's hungry. I remember it was about the time that Inah's slow drift started.

Inah pushes open the door, and we file back out to the street of the warm night. The misty air hangs thick with smoke and cooking smells.

"Inah. Do you remember the song? From that movie Ashley Judd starred in. 'Trying to hold on to the earth . . .'"

"You mean *Ruby in Paradise*?"

"Right, that's it! 'If I close my eyes, I'm afraid I won't wake up; If I stop and listen, I'm afraid I hear too much . . . solid gold question mark, twenty feet tall . . .'" To my surprise, the rhythm comes right back to me, too. I used to love that frenzied flurry of pounding beats toward the end of the song. It always gave me an urge to run out into a downpour.

"I used to listen to it all the time and feel sorry for myself," Inah says. "Maybe it's just the song for the young and confused. I don't know. . . . Music always makes you sad anyway."

"Don't you think you gravitate to sad music because you are sad to start with?"

"Maybe . . . ," Inah mumbles, looking uncomfortable. She wants to steer clear from any subject that might lead to a discussion of her life. We lapse into an awkward silence. I think about what Inah said; music always making you sad. I wonder if it's because we always remember the first time we hear a certain song. The place we were, the people we were with, the time of the day and the light and how we felt then. And every time we hear that song, we relive all that. That's why we listen to the same music again and again in the hope of recapturing that first emotional experience. And isn't it always sad to remember something that's past and gone? And isn't the same true with life? Isn't so much of life, after a certain age, about trying to replicate what's past and gone? To recapture the magic of a place and time that no longer exist? But the truth is that we can never experience the exact same thing twice. And that's what's so sad about life.

"So what do you listen to these days?" Inah asks after a while, trying to lighten up the mood.

"Andrea Bocelli? I guess I'm getting old." Inah hoots deliciously. "I'm not kidding, Inah! Mom has been reminding me that I will be thirty next year by Korean age."

"And I won't be?"

"She even says things like how in Korea, no man will touch an old miss like me with a ten-foot pole."

"Like it's a great loss," Inah says drily. At the scrubby piazza up the street, someone starts singing through a static speaker. It sounds like a sudden bleat. And then we hear peals of laughter. They must be having that singing contest again, Inah says. We walk down the rest of the street in silence, chasing our separate threads of thought.

"What did you say the girl does?" I ask Inah when we are at the bus stop.

"Who?" asks Inah absentmindedly. Then she glances at me curiously. "You mean Nidra Phookan? I told you she's a doctoral candidate at Oxford. She's here for her research."

"I don't think you told me anything about her," I say, hating my apologetic tone. "What is she? Indian?"

"She's English," Inah answers in an offhanded way, looking away, annoyed.

"She seems a little strange," I say, fishing for more information. I know I am pushing, and I hate myself for it. I am as hopeless as Mom.

"She's fine. She's just not the most sociable person in the world," Inah says in a tone that says that's the end of our discussion of her. After a while, though, she adds, "Don't worry, it's not at all what you think." I never get to ask her what she meant by that because just then a bus comes. I know enough to drop the subject.

Back at the Piazza Venezia, we are the last and only passengers to get off the bus from Trastevere. The warm air still feels as thick as syrup. The huge and curiously ugly Victor Emmanuel II monument in the white floodlight looks as if sculpted out of a snow mountain. Slowly, we head for the Trevi.

It's well past eleven, but the narrow streets converging into the Trevi are still clogged and buzzing with crowds. The ice-cream store is still bright with lights. The terraces around the flood-lit fountain are swarmed with tourists, happy and laughing, wistfully throwing coins over their shoulders. The Italian boys with slick, moussed-back hair and slippery smiles, the ones who come every night to hang around and check out girls, are still here, too, smoking and laughing at the doorways and around motorcycles parked up the narrow steep side streets.

We stand there for a while, watching the happy crowd milling about, and then continue on to Via della Dataria. The deserted street stands hushed and strangely eerie in the dark. Outside the arch entrance to the Palazzo del Quirinale, the motionless guards look like stone statues dressed up in uniform. Inah looks at me dragging my feet and says, "Will race you to the piazza for a piggyback ride."

"I can't. I'm totally pooped."

Lugging the rucksack, Inah sprints up the hill anyway. Halfheartedly I trot up after her and then kind of get into the spirit. I slip off my sandals and speed up the hill. The stone feels warm and hard on the balls of my feet. Inah disappears over the piazza just as I reach the foot of the steps. I crawl up and tiptoe my way to the obelisk, where she is bent over, catching her breath. But before I can jump her, she quickly spins around, shrieks, and runs off, startling a couple who are making out by the balustrades behind the police box. After racing to the other end of the piazza, Inah stops, turns around and leans against the staircase, so she can keep an eye on me. In the light, her sweaty face gleams like half-fired pottery. I casually stroll toward her.

"Shoot!" Inah squeals and sprints for the stairs that lead to Via Maggio. Still, I manage to catch her arm.

"OK. You win!" she hollers hoarsely, collapsing, and gasping for breath.

"Bend over," I order. Inah takes off the rucksack and obediently bends over, turning her bony back into a slippery bow. I step back and then, kicking my heels, jump onto her only to slip right back down. Inah turns her head, looks at me and bursts out laughing. I try again and slide off again, landing on the ground on my butt. It's so pathetic, she can't stand it any longer. Laughing and holding her sides with her hands, she staggers off.

"Come back!"

"No, stop it!"

"Don't be silly! I am not doing anything," I say, still sitting on the stone, all sweaty and sticky. Finally, I pull myself up on my wobbly legs. Inah comes back and bends down again on all fours, making it easy for me. I climb up and straddle her skinny back. She hands me the rucksack and wraps her arms around my legs and stands up, lurching under the weight. She then gingerly picks her way down the steps and trots along as I paddle her sides with the sandals. Suddenly, just before the carabiniere station, she picks up speed and runs past the row of parked police cars, screaming in mock horror. I am certain she is going to stumble and fall any minute and send us both down the steep sidewalk. Tumbling like broken dolls. I quickly jump off and slip the sandals back on. Inah shoots ahead down the hill, screaming, "Aaaaah! . . ." Acting goofy.

Watching Inah's extra-large white T-shirt shrink away in the dark like a flag of surrender carried by a ghost, I feel something like hope; I become a water bowl filled to the brim. If I move too fast, the bowl will tip, and the water will spill out all over. And then I will never be able to stop crying.

Inah looks up from a doorstep and holds out her hand, and I pull her up. Her hand, unexpectedly soft and supple, fits just so into mine. For a second or two, she leaves her hand in mine. I can't hold it any longer; the water bowl tips, spilling out all over.

"Yunah?!" Inah whines. "Why do you have to ruin it?"

"Sorry, can't help it."

We walk down slowly, hot and exhausted. In the mist down the street, the neon-lit letters of our hotel look like gigantic free-floating fireflies in the summer night. I don't want the moment to end even though I am scared to death to feel hopeful again. But it's worth it. Every fleeting second. We live riding the waves and the drifts of time. Without ever knowing the ending. And sometimes, as Inah once said, what we have now has to be good enough.

FIVE

Warm rain falls lazily and soundlessly the afternoon we
drive to Princeton. Dad at the wheel, with his new haircut
and in a black dress shirt, couldn't look lonelier. And Mom,
next to him, sits as still as a stationary shadow, close to the
door, as far as she possibly can be from him without leaving
the car. Outside, the grainy world rolls by in still pictures.
Elizabeth. Bridges. Cars. Trucks. Docks. Containers.
Cranes. Refineries. A barbwired prison. Newark. Planes
taking off like gray birds. Rumbling the leaden sky. Rain.
Inside, necessity, struggle, needs, and soggy silence. Mom's
face, which I steal a glimpse of in the rearview mirror now
and then, is sad and sad and sad. Sadness drips and drips
and fills the car, and we are all slowly drowning in it.

Inah and I assumed all along that there would be some
kind of dramatic, clear-cut ending to Dad's affair, a defining
moment, but there wasn't any. One day, he just moved back
home with his blanket and tubby pillow and the clothes we

had once delivered in two black trash bags to his basement apartment in a shopping cart. He also went back to his old job at Uncle Shin's trading company in Manhattan. Inah and I asked no questions. Neither Mom nor Dad tried to offer us any explanations, either. We didn't want them, anyway. It seemed more bearable that way. We just pretended everything was fine again. He came back. Wasn't that good enough? We were a family again. Remember? Koreans are nothing without family, Uncle Shin always said.

But we are also old enough to know that it's not as simple as picking up a paper towel and wiping up a coffee spill. Nothing is so innocent anymore. Every little gesture and every remark is suspect. The new carefulness. The awkward moment of silence. We notice them with guilt. And we can't help but remember. Despite ourselves. Memories, we are finding out, have a way of haunting and taunting. Like shadows in the corner, the regrets and the hurt will linger on. For now, we can only try to make adjustments. Because after riding out the swells, who can tell which shore we will wash up on?

But the worst of it all is that we will always wonder what happened to Dad's affair. Did it just run its course and come to a fizzling end? Was that why he came back to Flushing? Or was it to resolve what had been dragging on unresolved? In an excruciating limbo. Maybe he didn't know himself. He had simply gotten tired of his illicit life in a strange city. Maybe the isolation and the guilt started taking a toll on him. Passion, or whatever it was that had given him the absconding feet in the first place, had proved to be not nearly enough. In the end, he realized what colossal courage he had to summon. To begin a new life. To start all over again. That it was not so easy to discard the old life and go on. That his choices are few. Maybe at some point it occurred to Dad how he had simply exchanged one trap for another. Get rid of the old shoe. A new shoe will eventually wear out, too. Every life eventually disappoints.

I know for a long time Inah and I and Mom will hear that little voice of doubts. We will wonder again and again whether Dad's decision to come back to us was his next best choice, the choice of reason rather than that of heart and whether he will hate himself for that and resent us for denying him a chance of happiness. And Inah and I will wonder whether Mom took him back in for the sake of Inah and me. Sacrifice is the most sacred word for Korean parents. Divorce was never an option she would have considered. It would be the worst kind of failure for her. A flawed life is always better than a failed life. Koreans are nothing without family.

The Princeton campus is nearly deserted, with most of the students gone for the summer. In soundless drizzle and dusklike light, we walk around, stopping at the rain-slicked paths cutting through mint green lawn and looking at the beautiful old buildings carved in gray stone—as still as in a painting, majestic and grainy in the gray veil of rain mist. It's a new old world. So removed from the grime and shabbiness of grinding daily life in Flushing, it's a finely visualized version of Mom's American dream for Inah and me. Mom, who came to America afflicted with an incurable "Ivy League" disease, points out buildings, a fountain, sputtering lamps, a sculpture, and lingers at the edge of well-tended, freshly cut lawns, trees thick with the shawls of summer foliage, her permed hair turning frizzy in the rain. Looking so wistful. Dad stabs the soggy Princeton guide into his back trouser pocket and lights a cigarette.

Inah drifts away, not wanting to give Mom a chance to

start all over again. It was Mom's idea to begin with, to come here today for our belated tour of the Princeton campus. But it's more of a denouement. And like so many things Mom does, an exercise in futility. For Inah is all set to go to Antioch College in the fall. Mom and Inah fought and wrangled over her choice of college like two merchants negotiating a lifetime deal, as if their lives depended on it. In the end, Inah, attracted by its work-study program, chose the small progressive college in Yellow Springs, Ohio, over schools like Vassar, Princeton and Yale.

"But why shouldn't Inah go to Harvard or Yale if she can?" Mom would ask, truly perplexed whenever I tried to convince her that Inah was making the right choice; she should be proud instead of being so upset. Inah may be stubborn, but she's smart and thinks for herself. It was Inah who was going to college, after all, and Mom should let her make the choice.

"Mom, not everyone can or should go to Harvard or Yale! They could ruin you, don't you know that?" I once said, exasperated, and Mom kind of looked at me as though I was trying to put one over on her. "And Mom, attending Harvard or Yale no longer carries such a cachet. As it is, Harvard Square, I've heard, is overrun with Korean kids. There are enough of them literally to form a whole new tribe. And you know the types, Mom, the Korean kids who go to Ivy League schools. They come out all the same, as if out of cookie cutters. They all want to become doctors, lawyers and investment bankers, as if there aren't enough of them already. And then they marry, have kids and move to suburban homes with lawns and two-car garages. They become Republicans and Christians with hearts that they rarely use. They live selfish lives. It's not for Inah. And it's not the kind of life she wants to live. Don't you want what's best for her?

I know you do. Just let her make her own choice." Mom, never into irony, was too caught up in it to take my tongue-in-cheek comments with a grain of salt. She didn't think it was funny at all. She said we were all turning out just like Dad. Idealistic. One by one, we all disappoint her.

For a change, Inah was positively impressed by my performance. She thought it was one of my best Saturday-night rants ever, and she even grilled me about where I lifted those lines from. I was a little proud of myself. I felt I had finally risen to the occasion.

We slowly trace our way back to the Blair Arch. Mom stops and looks around one more time, as if she can't accept the fact that all of this will be wasted on other kids. She turns to me and asks, "Yunah, what do you think? Isn't it so nice?!"

"Uh, very," I mumble, avoiding her searching eyes. I can tell she's still treading the water of hope. She's even wondering whether she has been barking up the wrong tree. Maybe, after all, I, not Inah, just might fulfill her "Ivy League" dream. There's still hope—I have another year to decide, as Inah skipped a grade ahead of me. It's sad to think how gladly Mom will sell the house to pay for it, too. But why not? Weren't we the reason our parents came to America? Even though for her and Dad it meant starting all over again at the bottom. Eager to transform themselves into ladders for us to trample on with our feet to reach the sky. And they would consider it a privilege and an honor, not a sacrifice. And whenever it became tough going, Mom reminded herself that Confucius's mother had moved twelve times for her son's education. It doesn't sound like a big deal, she'd tell us, more to convince herself than us, but remember there were no jets or trains or buses or cars in those days. She probably heaped everything on a cart or a donkey and traveled for days. Through torrential rain, blinding blizzards, mud slides, flooded roads, swollen rivers and whatnot. Mom stubbornly refuses to believe that we don't want to be burdened with that kind of epic sacrifice.

We pass through the arch and cross the street to Palmer Square, empty and quiet except for birds whistling in thin, clear notes from the trees and a half dozen scraggly pigeons cooing about. Through the rain drifting down in fine sheets of mist, streetlamps sputter on like green liquid moons, and the windows of the elegant shops at the square bloom in warm orange glows. The few people we see on the street all look as though they have stepped out of the pages of L.L. Bean catalogues. They seem exotic, breezy, self-absorbed and casually territorial, and there is an air of entitlement about them. This is their world. So orderly, so pristine and so cold. I just can't place Inah or myself into this neat, too neat picture. Inah would never fit in. And I know I would feel like a phony.

We wander down Witherspoon, narrow and sloping away, carrying its quaint old buildings into a wall of rain fog below. You can tell it's not Flushing just from the absence of the harsh fluorescent lights, I tell Inah, nudging her at the elbow, and she simply snorts. Mom says, it's clean. We turn around and walk back up the street, past a cafe. Dad asks if we'd like coffee before heading home. Mom looks at us, not wanting to be the one to nix the idea. At least not today.

Sitting with my parents and Inah at a tiny round table inside the warm cafe, I know I will always remember the afternoon here: the fragrance of the hot cappuccino frosted with steamed milk in the yellow plastic cup; the sad coffee ring in Mom's thick white china mug, where dark American coffee sits, getting cold; Mom and Dad, sitting across from us, together yet separate. All these years we have rarely had a moment like this. As family. Mom was always busy. She had no time for frivolous things. Even on weekends, she always had her church to go to, home visits to make, laundry to do and grocery shopping to go and kimchi to make. It was always just Dad and Inah and I when we went to the Catskills, Bear Mountain, the Poconos and Harriman State Park. Mom will never know what's it's like: to be driving on a winding road that reveals new scenery at each bend; passing a small, quiet village with a fire station where an American flag flew on top of a pole; hiking up a steep mountain road in the Catskills to reach a waterfall; discovering an old, stained Korean doll at an antique shop in the Poconos; huffing along the musty hiking trails in the woods, marked by ribbons tied on tree branches. She doesn't share with us the memory of the textures of the soft, electric green moss on the trunks of fallen trees, or of the dark blue summer evening at Blue Mountain Lake outside the closed general store where our childhood came to an end.

And Dad, who always tried to replicate for us his boyhood experiences in Korea, where he grew up wandering about the fields and hills, chasing dragonflies and locusts and picking wild berries, who wanted us so much to experience the kind of wonder and joy he had felt in nature—getting so excited detecting a flickering sense of recognition in us—always seemed to end up frustrated for not quite being able to explain the intangible and undefinable yearning he felt; now he sits here looking so somber, his hair going gray, feeling excluded and left behind.

It's sad but true that Mom and Dad will never, ever, be part of this America. After the cup of coffee, they will go back to their old life in Flushing, where wounds are still fresh and all the relics of their struggling immigrant life are waiting to reclaim them. It is for Inah and it is for me that a new world waits. Inah, even with her scarred face, will have chances to forge a life no matter how difficult it may turn out to be: in the middle of what Mom calls "real America," if only unconsciously meaning "white America." Mom wishes that we dissolve into that white America, that we fit in. Mom thinks this will happen if we go to the best schools, if we speak English better than Americans. But that's not enough, we already know that. Hasn't Inah already started on a path that will never make Mom happy?

SIX

Auntie Minnie, renting a beach house on Long Beach Island with Uncle Frankie for the summer, calls and invites us down, saying Mom and Dad need to spend time together without us. Of course Inah and I say yes immediately. We have no idea where Long Beach Island is except that it's somewhere off the Jersey shore. But we couldn't care less. The effects of Dad's affair are still lingering like a long, bad cold, and we feel ready to go anywhere, even if it is to Timbuktu. Just to get away from home.

Inah and I pool our savings and scout what Inah calls "the Third World aisles" at Woolworth's and Caldor's on Roosevelt Avenue, stocked mostly with cheap and flimsy Made in China things. We pick up one-piece swimsuits, clear plastic beach sandals, straw visors and suntan lotions, all on a summer blowout sale. And then we go to the library and take out a whole stack of books to take with us, salivating at the prospect of spending days on the beach with them.

But Inah wholeheartedly hates it, this thoroughly middle-class beach town, although it is probably no better or worse than the other zillion ragged beach towns dotting the Jersey shoreline. It's true that there's not a whole lot to do here (except to lie on the beach all day, being roasted in the sun) or places to go without a car. There's the town's main drag, a sandy road running lackadaisically more or less parallel to the shore, its sidewalk lined with a ragtag of salt-eaten, sun-faded, single-story commercial buildings facing the ocean. On the ocean side of the road, looking out to the beach, about a dozen or so boxlike beach houses stand on dark wooden stilts, like old hobbled birds perching on badly gangrened legs.

And for some weird reason, they have more blue Ford pickups here than any place on earth. On heat-stunted afternoons when Inah and I walk up the beach and wait to cross the street for ice-cream cones, they come up the sandy road toward the intersection, where the town's only traffic lights hang, swaying in the sea breeze. They are almost always driven by sun-cooked white men (with optional baseball caps) carrying plastic coolers and fishing gear in the flatbed back. And it's the summer everyone's in the Asbury Park state of mind, because their car radios are always blasting Bruce Springsteen's "Born in the U.S.A." Every time a pickup passes us by, we hear drumbeats and electric guitar pouncing and pouncing, momentarily drowning out the quiet of the heat-dazed afternoon. We feel the damp, salty sea air pulsate and vibrate and ring, and hear Bruce Springsteen's tattered throat spitting out words like clumps of blood: "Got in a little home town jam / So they put a rifle in my hand / Sent me off to a foreign land / To go and kill the yellow man. . . ."

Then, just because we look as conspicuous as two sea-

gulls on a mountain road—two yellow girls in bikini tops
and shorts waiting to cross the street—the "jerks" always
holler through the blasting sounds of music, "Agghhhhh!"
Inah, unable to resist it, holds up her hand and gives them
the finger as they make a showy, ear-splitting, screechy left
turn and disappear toward the bay. Later, though, crossing
the street, Inah bitches and blames me for asking for it by
parading around in short-shorts or hot pants, with my white
buns peeking out in half moons.

"Here, give me your tough-shit card, Inah, and I'll punch
it for you, OK?" Fuming and slapping her heat-stretched
plastic sandals, Inah tears down the street, past Bamboo
Garden, the tacky Chinese restaurant, a bar with a pitch-
black interior, a deli, a pizzeria, a drugstore and a check-
cashing place. And I feel inexplicably sad.

But then, Inah and I are sad all the time. Even here, far
from home. Especially around dawn, when the angry, constant roar from the sea pulls us out of comatose sleep. Half-
awake, we lie in our beds under the trundling ceiling fan for
what feels like hours. Listening to the constantly churning
and crashing sea and watching the pockets of night linger in
gray and blue outside the windows. Submerged in vague
despair that feels more like sorrow. When we've had
enough, we stumble out of bed, groggy and swollen and
heavy from too much sun from the day before. We throw on
the still damp bathing suits under big T-shirts and toss the
suntan lotion bottles, books, the Walkman and beach towels
into the straw bag, and slip out of the house, down the rickety steps to escape to the beach.

It's always subdued, the early-morning walk to the
beach. Especially those mornings after we heard, not by
choice, through the flimsy wall, Auntie Minnie and Uncle
Frankie make love in the next room. The muffled sounds of

their grunts and moans will follow us to the beach like the smell of fish that lingers on your fingers long after you touch it. We trudge along in silence all the way to the empty morning beach, lying in long, yellow, rippled sheets, gilded by the sumptuous morning light. Vaguely feeling doomed. Our heads all messed up with Dad's affair and the strange things adults do. So casually and negligently.

As a rule, Inah and I never talk about the affair (how would we find the beginning of the thread?), but we're thinking about it all the time. Helplessly. Wishing we didn't know so much: all the latest sordid details we eagerly snatched up from the kitchen hallway, wincing and nail-biting, as they passed from Mom's venomous tongue to Auntie Minnie's pricked-up ears.

That's how we know that Dad's lover is back in New York and has been coming around to Uncle Shin's company, trying to see Dad. One morning, to his dismay, Dad found her waiting for him at the entrance of his office building. "Wearing a low-cut, slinky gray silk dress and high heels," according to Mom. Imagine! She got into the elevator with him and followed him upstairs to the office. Uncle Shin tried to escort her out quietly, but she refused to leave, saying how she wasn't going to be shooed away "like a leper!" In the end, thick-set Uncle Shin had to hustle her out, literally pushing her back as she yelled and spat out strings of curses over his shoulder to Dad.

"That woman" was out to embarrass Dad in front of everyone, Mom said indignantly, spitting out each word with a tongue of fire. Well, he deserves it. What did he expect, getting himself involved with "a woman like that"? If he thought he'd escape from it unscathed, he's a fool. Swallow it when it's sweet and spit it out when it's bitter? It's good for him to be humiliated a little. He will think twice before he does this kind of thing again. That's what Mom said, who isn't a Christian for nothing.

What did Dad do while all this went on? While she shouted that she wasn't going to go away quietly and accused him of being a liar and worse? In the office full of eyes and ears. Did he sit slumped behind his scratched steel desk, its cracked, bubbly Formica top crowded with cheap imitation jewelry samples from Korea and China? Mortified and shamed and, worst of all, his face lost? Suffering the indignity? Hating himself? Feeling like a coward? Surrounded with such ugliness. Frozen in the flood of greenish fluorescent light. Unable to escape. Dad must have closed his eyes and tried to imagine himself a Buddha sitting on top of a burning pyre in self-immolation. It, too, shall pass, for life is a mere passing of wind. But he couldn't have blocked out the curse-ridden threats issuing from his lover's painted mouth. We know that in Korean, they would have sounded so much worse, so biting and potent.

Mom's spiteful, unhappy voice drums in our heads as we lie on the sun-crushed beach, the coarse sand, the color of orange squash in the sunlight, where children play with beach balls sectioned in bright red, blue, yellow and white, and all we can do is just try to stay afloat in a dreamlike state. Gazing out through squinty eyes to the hazy horizon lying placidly far, far away, dwarfed by the immense, monotonous, drowsy summer sky. Or just lying about being roasted and pricked by hot needle-pin rays of the sun. Carrying on long and confused and separate conversations in our heads. Trying to shut out the noisy thoughts of the other. Trying again and again not to dwell on things, not to feel the sadness and the dull, hot pain inside that stays on like a low-grade fever. Feeling stuck in the ugly beach town and the ugly beach house with Auntie Minnie and Uncle Frankie but not wanting to go back home, either.

Sometimes, it takes all my energy just to stay still on the damp and sandy beach towel, to keep the mind blank. But it's impossible to shake off the feeling of being lost in a still mass of fog. It's as though we are just waiting for it to clear up so that we can see clearly for once.

When the noise inside her head gets to be too much, Inah takes out the Walkman, greasy with finger smudges, and listens to loud music through the earphones. I don't know why, but the steady and monotonous and repetitious beat of the music—as persistent as the sounds of the sea—that comes off her Walkman depresses me even more. To drown out the noise, I close my eyes and slowly recite "Sunflower Sutra" in my head, over and over again, hoping that in time it will carry me to the closest possible state of Nirvana.

Then around noon, Uncle Frankie and Auntie Minnie come down to the beach, carrying their collapsible beach chairs and the sweating red plastic jug. All of a sudden, it's a flurry of activity and a carnival of smell: suntan lotion, perfume and cigarette smoke mixing in the salty sea breezes. Out of her pink straw beach bag, Auntie Minnie pulls out our lunch in brown bags: peanut butter and banana sandwiches on stale white bread, and bags of potato chips and sweating grapes.

Now and then, after lunch, Inah lets Uncle Frankie cajole her into going for a walk. Auntie Minnie and I follow them with our eyes as they grow smaller and smaller up the shimmering beach among the crowd of sunbathers, beach towels, parasols and chairs. After a while, Auntie Minnie will turn to me mindlessly building up and break-

ing up a sand dune with my hands, and ask me how I am
doing.

"OK, I guess."

"OK, I guess," she repeats, to let me know that she
knows I am being less than honest.

Because we dread going back to the house, we stay behind
on the beach and linger until the winds pick up and the
plaintive summer sky starts churning in apricot and peach
and the clouds turn yellow and sulphur and violet. Inah's
mood always progresses from bad to worse then. We bicker
over stupid little things like who will carry what. Then,
fueled by sudden, stupid rage, Inah storms off, racing across
the emptied-out beach, where the sunlight is intense and
yellow and speckled like gold. Carelessly dragging the
damp, striped beach towels along the sand, and recklessly
swinging the red plastic jug half-filled with the warm
Orangeade diluted by the melted ice to the color of piss.
Kicking up a sandstorm with the heels of her bare feet.
Bracing against the syrup-textured sea wind.

"Inah!" Struggling after her, I scream and curse in full
throat for making me carry all the chairs. "Wait! Asshole."
Ignoring my howls and hisses, Inah climbs up the sand
dune and down and is gone. And I feel like crumpling the
whole world with my hands. Overcome by inexplicable
anger and helpless despair, I hate everything. The beach
house with the flimsy walls and dime-store furniture with
cigarette burns and nicks and scratches, where we lounge
about on the itchy polyester, gray-and-peach "Comfort Inn"
couch; sleep on the lumpy mattresses that hold the smell of
all the people who passed through hot summer after hot
summer; eat and drink out of the cheap plastic bowls and
cracked plates and chipped enamel coffee mugs kept inside

the moldy, musty cupboards; and take showers in the slimy stall crawling with black dots of mildew.

But most of all, I hate my body. Standing stripped and naked on the sea-blue-tiled bathroom floor, where soggy towels lie in a crumpled pile, I can barely look at the awkward body inside the long mirror. The browning arms and legs, sticky from the coconut suntan lotion with its sweet smell that will linger even after the shower. Sunburned and peeling shoulders, round and sloping. The swimsuit-covered part as white as a fish belly. The strangely unfamiliar face framed by the hair matted from the sand and sea salt and wind. It seems all wrong somehow: too heavy and too big, more than I can carry and manage. I hate it enough to want to die. Later, standing under the scalding hot water in the shower stall, I cry and swear that I will never, ever marry.

But like a miracle, we somehow get over the miserable hour. There is even a certain relief when we walk to the Bamboo Garden with Auntie Minnie and Uncle Frankie (it's where they take us out after too many dinners of cold cuts and rolls). At the restaurant, sitting at the round table loaded with the usual spicy Kung Pao chicken, glutinous Moo Shoo pork, bland-as-hell Buddha's Delight and greasy chow fun, Inah and I manage to smile at the lame jokes Uncle Frankie comes up with to cheer us up. But we must still look miserable, because he declares that he knows just the cure for our maladies, and before Auntie Minnie can stop him, verbally prescribes it—boys. Aghast, Auntie Minnie elbows him in the side, furiously signaling to him with her eyes to remind him how insensitive his remark was in front of Inah. Uncle Frankie heaves out a few embarrassed dry coughs. But Inah sits there perfectly collected and serene, striking a cool pose with the inscrutable expression of a stone Buddha. A little red in the cheeks from the complimentary sweet plum wine she sneaks from Auntie Minnie's glass.

At the end of the meal, Inah even provides a brief comic relief. Holding up the fortune strips she pulls out from the soggy fortune cookies like entrails from a fish belly, she reads out spontaneously manufactured fortunes: "'Where there is no wind, the grass does not move,'" or "'When in doubt, take the middle road.'" Garbling the lines half-remembered from *The I Ching* or some such book, and keeping a perfectly straight face. It invariably makes clueless Auntie Minnie wonder if that means good luck at the blackjack table that night. And, for a moment, it almost seems that everything is normal.

SEVEN

If there's anything we look forward to, it is having the beach house (we hate so much during the day) all to ourselves at night. We anxiously wait for Uncle Frankie, his shirt front unfurled, and Auntie Minnie, drenched with lilac-scented perfume and dressed in a halter top dress or some such floral thing and beaded sandals, to emerge from their room for their night out. They usually head out to Beach Haven to the south or Seaside Heights to the north, where there is, we are told, more nightlife. When they feel particularly lucky, though, they will drive down to Atlantic City to play blackjack and poker, which means they won't be back until three or four in the morning and will wake us up with their early-morning lovemaking.

"How do I look?" Auntie Minnie asks us, pirouetting and then, for some reason, patting down her damp-looking neck.

"Perfect!" I screech.

"Don't change a thing," Inah adds. Auntie Minnie knows, though, that we are simply anxious to get rid of them, and she gives us that look.

"Beautiful. So beautiful you will make Sophia Loren jealous," Uncle Frankie says, winking at us and hurrying Auntie Minnie out the door. (We hear her asking him who is this Sopi Loren as they walk down the stairs outside.)

Soon, crushing the gravel, Uncle Frankie's car backs out of the driveway, and they are gone. We run to their bathroom and slather Uncle Frankie's Noxzema shaving cream all over our sunburned arms and legs. Afterward, we switch off all the lights in the house and go out to the deck facing the sea and lie down, side by side, on the two saggy, creaky chaise longues, their salt-eaten, dented aluminum frames held up together at the joints by duct tape.

It is the only bearable time of the day, when we lie there in the dark, feeling mint cool in the sticky, sea-borne breeze, listening to the night sea that stretches away, toward black nothing, forever, and watching the dark blue sky, buzzing and ringing with stars, like the palladium in the Museum of Natural History. After a while, we know, we won't be able to think even if we tried.

One evening, after Uncle Frankie and Auntie Minnie leave, Inah rummages through the basket by the gray-and-peach Comfort Inn couch in the living room and excavates a thin paperback from a stack of old magazines like *Redbook*, *People* and *Sports Illustrated*. Someone must have left it behind many summers before; the yellowing pages are warped and curled. It's a French novel called *Bonjour Tristesse*, by Françoise Sagan. Inah holds it up and reads out loud the description of the novel on the partly ripped and buckled egg-yellow and baby-blue cover: "'The classic bestseller about amoral youth on the French Riviera.'" It sounds simply too delicious to resist.

We take it out to the deck and, taking turns, read the book out loud to each other in the dim yellow deck light. It's a fast read, as easy to down as a syrupy summer drink. It's about shallow rich people with insatiable appetites. It's about a carefree summer that a spoiled seventeen-year-old French girl, Cecil, spends in the sun-drenched French Riviera with her playboy father and his girlfriend, Cyril, which ends tragically.

"'Bonjour, tristesse!'" Inah reads the very last sentence, closes the book and adds her own epilogue in her cynical voice: "And, of course, they lived happily ever after!" And then, inspired, if only in a sad way, we stare out at the dark sea, churning and crashing ashore in an endless repetition. Helpless as unwelcome thoughts crowd their way into our heads.

"Let's celebrate!" I jump up from the chaise longue. I go inside and filch one of Uncle Frankie's unfiltered Lucky Strikes from an open pack sitting on the kitchen counter. I return to the deck and display the cigarette and a matchbook. "Look what I've got."

"Oh, shit," says Inah, delighted, surprising me as she often does with her puzzling lack of judgment. She sits up and cups her hands for me to light the cigarette. I take a puff and hand it to her. She holds it pinched between her thumb and forefinger like it was a joint and takes a long drag, imitating the narrow-eye look of a seasoned smoker. Then she breaks into a coughing fit and giggles. I get up and turn off the deck light. In the dark, we sit hunched on the wrecked chaises and take turns at the strong cigarette. It is strangely mesmerizing to watch the red disk of light crackling on the cigarette end as it burns its way up in the dark.

After a while, we feel dizzy and collapse into the chaises,

which sag underneath, creaking sadly. The breezes carry a faint whip of cigarette smoke and drying Noxzema shaving cream, which I have been unconsciously and obsessively rubbing off all night, shedding it like dead skin in thin, floury rolls.

I wonder what it will be like after Inah leaves for college at the end of the summer. It will be just Mom and Dad and me at home. Then I wonder what Mom and Dad are doing now. It has been only a week, but it already feels like such a long time ago, the Friday afternoon that Dad drove us down here from Flushing. The traffic was bumper to bumper all the way down on the Garden State Parkway. I remember suddenly noticing how Dad looked so old. It was after we got off the parkway. We were driving through local roads, where the scraggly and deserted-looking commercial buildings were enduring the sluggish afternoon, submerged in deep pools of black shadows. The bright, late-afternoon sunlight was blinding, and both Inah, watching out for the Manahawkin Bay Bridge sign, and Dad, driving, were squinting hard. Maybe it was the new band of gray hair above his ears. It was as if the years had caught up with him all at once.

I asked him (I still don't know what made me) how come he didn't paint anymore. My question seemed to surprise him. He said, "How come?!" As if he himself wondered about the very same thing. He then said he was not an artist anymore. In fact, he had stopped being one a long time ago. Just as a tree doesn't grow by itself—it needs an inspiration to grow: nutritious soil, wind, sun and rain—an artist doesn't grow out of thin air. That he was more like a transplanted tree, its roots shriveled away, unable to adjust to the new soil. That he wouldn't know what to do even if someone seated him down with the best brushes and paints and canvases money could buy.

"But Dad, you are not just any tree," I said. "You're a special tree." Dad just smiled. I remember how sad he looked.

Inah flicks on the flashlight and shines it on the empty night ocean, where the sound of waves are now like howls of the wind. Suddenly, it seems all so clear. I know that I will have to be the one to stay close to home and to our parents, to make up for Inah's absence, and also for Dad's loneliness. As for Mom, I know she will survive. No matter what.

EIGHT

The morning Inah leaves for college, I wake up with butterflies in my stomach. Then, afraid to open my eyes, I keep
them closed. I can tell it's going to be another hot day: The
air in the room is still, and not a breeze blows in through the
open window. I slide back under the sheet, lie there, sweaty,
full of dread and half-awake, drifting along in the muffled
sounds of morning: Dad's footsteps in the backyard; water
hitting the bottom of the watering can; and the dull, chop-
ping sound in the kitchen downstairs. I think about all the
summer mornings that started just like this, with the same
muffled sounds that promised another uneventful summer
day ahead filled with the usual chores and boredom. But it
isn't one of those mornings. In a couple of hours, Inah will
be leaving, and it will never be the same again.

I hear Inah run up the stairs and go into her room. She
comes back out and from the top of the stairs shouts to
Mom in the kitchen downstairs, "Mom! Am I taking an

iron?" After she races back down the stairs, I finally quit the bed, slip into cutoff jeans and a tank top and go down. The hallway smells of freshly cooked rice: sweet and soft and warm. I walk out barefoot to the porch. The sun is burning through the morning fog, and it already feels like a steam bath. The sky is white and shimmery. And Dad loading the trunk of the car parked at the street curb looks fuzzy and grainy. He's driving Inah to Yellow Springs, Ohio.

Carrying a duffel bag, Inah comes out. She flashes me a quick, lopsided smile and heads down to the car, navigating her long, lean legs. When she comes back up, I follow her back inside to the foyer and help her carry a box Mom packed with bottles of kimchi and containers of *banchan*, the side dishes she has prepared for days.

"You're going to stink up the whole dorm the first day," I say. Inah just shrugs. She's thrilled and excited at the prospect of her new freedom but is trying hard not to show it too much.

At the breakfast table, Mom, afraid of a moment of silence, talks nonstop, bombarding Inah with questions: "Are you sure you packed everything? If you forgot anything, just buy it instead of calling long distance to ask me to send it. It's cheaper that way." Inah nods. "And don't skip meals, make sure you eat on time." Mom's still upset that she can't go with Inah to the school. Inah didn't want her to.

"Don't worry, Mom," Inah says, nicely for a change.

"Why do you have to go so far away?" Mom says. "There are so many schools here."

"It's not that far," Dad says.

"Then how come I can't just take a subway and go see her?"

I briefly debate whether to make a joke about Yellow Springs—in Korea, they say you go to *Whangchon*, Yellow

Spring, after you die—and then decide that even as a joke, it won't go over well with Mom.

Dad straightens up his back and shuts the trunk. The dull thud sends cold shivers down my back. I can barely breathe. Dad gets in the car and starts the engine. Inah turns around and gives Mom a quick hug, averting her face. Inah, once such a solicitous, perky and feisty kid, has grown up and is leaving home an aloof, cool and detached teenager who hates demonstrativeness and has no use for emotional frills. I am afraid Mom is going to hold on to Inah and won't let go. But she releases her easily, if only to spare Inah the sight of her tears. For a second, Inah's hand lingers on Mom's arm, and then she seems to decide it's better not to get her started.

"I'll call, Mom," Inah says. Mom nods and just barely manages to say, "Just take good care of yourself. That's all I want." I open the car door for Inah.

"Bye, Inah." I wrap my arms around her. Her still damp hair from the shower smells fresh. Like scents from the woods. "I'm going to miss you."

"Bye," Inah says calmly. "Don't fight with Mom." I laugh and push into her hand my parting gift. Inah looks at the small box wrapped in blue-and-silver paper. It's a silver antique picture frame with a snapshot of us as two-year-olds when we were still perfect twins with big smiles permanently pressed on our unmarred, jade-smooth faces. I spent hours in the hot, dusty attic, going though stacks of old pictures from Korea, sitting inside the moldy shoe boxes, vanished by Mom, curling and sticking in the dust and humidity of the attic, like old memories waiting to be rescued and pasted together.

"Don't open it until you get to Ohio," I say. Inah nods

and looks at the box again. Dad honks. Inah turns around and climbs into the car next to Dad, and I close the door. For a second, I am almost frantic with fear. I can't imagine Inah not being around. And what will it be like for her in Ohio? Will she fit in? What if she gets sucked into Middle America and dissolves without a trace? We are immigrants' children, we are supposed to be biodegradable. But still.

Dad makes a wide U-turn and honks one more time and drives down the street. Inah rolls down the window and waves. Smiling. In the sunlight, she has that puzzled look of a child being sent away. Mom can't take it anymore. She turns around and heads up to the porch. I stand and watch until the car turns the corner into Kissena.

Finally, I turn and look at Mom. She is standing at the doorway, partly bleached in the morning sunlight. Looking like a figure in an overexposed black-and-white photo. When she sees me, she wipes at her eyes and throws open the door and goes inside.

I look down Ash Avenue one more time: standing in the heat, empty and quiet and a little misty where it ends and opens to another world. Slowly, I walk up the steps, past the rosebushes, where the last flowers of the season are in lackadaisical bloom, in commiserating white clumps. I wait a while, to give Mom time to grieve by herself, and then open the door.

The house feels cool and dark and strangely empty, like a big fruit, its inside carved out hollow. At the corner of the foyer, a worn pair of sneakers and a pair of see-through plastic beach sandals Inah left behind sit quietly, like lost goods. In the kitchen, I find Mom sitting at the table crowded with half-finished breakfasts. She is holding her hands tightly together, as if in prayer. She looks up when I walk in, almost relieved to see me. I pull a chair next to her and sit down.

The quiet is overwhelming. In the huge vacuum Inah has left behind, Mom is utterly lost. She doesn't seem to know what to do with herself. I put my arm around her; Mom quickly crumbles like a sand castle and breaks into a sad sob. She really wanted to go with Inah to help her unpack and settle in and see the dorm and the campus so that she could at least later picture her in it: going to classes, walking around, sleeping and waking.

"Mom, please. Don't be sad. Inah's only going to college. I know it's not to Harvard or Yale."

"I don't care about Harvard or Yale," Mom says, sobbing and wiping at her eyes with the back of her hand, wide and squarish with long, nubby fingers. Just like Inah's and mine.

"Then why are you so sad? It's not like she is gone forever," I say, trying to squelch the fear that's trying to rise up again.

"You don't know? Poor Inah! With that face . . ." Mom buries her own face in her hands and sobs hard. "Every time I think about it. . . ."

"I know, Mom. . . ." I think about all the years Mom tried to make Inah believe that it's the mind, what's inside that counts, not the looks. But she always knew that out there in the world, face, physical beauty, counted a lot more than she was willing to admit. It goaded her, the thought that Inah would never experience the kind of pleasure, joy or reward most women take for granted. It was the reason she pushed Inah so relentlessly. She wanted so much for Inah to succeed, to be compensated for all that would be denied to her as a woman. Oblivious as to how her devotion and drive seemed to us to have less to do with Inah or her well-being and more to do with Mom's sense of guilt and the pain she carried with her. But it doesn't make any difference now. Mom will always live a life of regret. And no matter what, it will be hard for Inah and for the rest of us, too. All we can do is just to go on. Grappling. Scooping up whatever joy along the way.

How I wish I could assure Mom that, growing up, Inah and I had our own share of happy days just like every other kid. But time adds pigments to memories, and I am not sure if that's true. If it's true for Inah. Anyway, it won't be much of a comfort to Mom. For now, her heart is just breaking and breaking. Mom is grieving because Inah has flown the coop and she can't protect her anymore.

NINE

Knowing that there's nothing Inah hates more than saying good-bye in public, I ask her just to put me in a taxi. But
she insists on taking me at least to Termini railway station,
if not all the way to the airport. I relent because there's no
time to argue: Our two weeks have dwindled to a mere couple of hours, and suddenly, we are being chased by time.
With Inah taking the luggage, we go downstairs to check
out. The roly-poly middle-aged desk clerk—he looks just
like Rodney Dangerfield—claims that Saturday is a good
day to leave Rome. In the same malevolent, thick-tongued
English in which he warned us every morning, as we left the
hotel, about pickpockets, gypsies and dark people from
other countries.

"All foreigners, no Italianos, these pickpockets. You
know why? Italianos are spoiled! They like to go straight to
the bank." He'd then rub his stubby fingers. "More money
in the bank. Ha-ha-ha!"

We walk down to the corner of Via Maggio, cross the street and hail a taxi. I know that a city is nothing but a state of mind, but still, it's as though Rome suddenly has made an about-face: The perennial sun is missing from the sky, and the city looks dull in soupy, gray air. I feel a little embarrassed. For all the shameless flattery I've uttered.

In the taxi to Termini, remorse and sheer helplessness keep both of us quiet. Then, because it's the only thing I can do, I try to give Inah money—the money in the envelope Mom slipped into my jeans pocket at Kennedy, asking me to take Inah to Korean restaurants and fatten her up. I don't know how much it is, as I have never bothered to open it. It's still inside the same white drugstore envelope, the kind Mom buys in a bulk of one hundred for weddings, graduations, birthdays and funerals, as if money, so vulgar and dirty, has to be cloaked and hidden. Inah adamantly refuses to take it. We push the envelope (now a little worn off at the corners and edges) back and forth, acting just like Mom, who fights relatives and friends to pay at restaurants, sneaking away from the table and rushing to the counter with the money in her hand, as if she's playing out some kind of social ritual of strategic importance. Inah and I used to swear, too, that we would never become like her.

We are early. Inah helps me carry my suitcase and her rucksack—we have finally gotten rid of Mom's hideous suitcase—to the platform where the Termini-Leonardo da Vinci airport train stands idling. The sun has burned through the morning haze, and there's a golden, fuzzy spectral ring around everything, like an aureole. I leave Inah with the luggage at the platform to get a train ticket from a ticket-vending machine. When I return, Inah is standing exactly the way I left her, but even more stiff with dread.

After Inah helps me put the luggage away, I decide not

to prolong the agony for her and to say good-bye. At least I can do that much.

"I'm going in, Inah. Don't wait around," I say. Inah nods, visibly relieved. Maybe she has been expecting a long, sentimental sermon and tears. We hug. All morning I have been rehearsing in my head just what to say at this very moment, but with my arms around her, I can barely remember or pull out a word. I wish there was more time, but Inah doesn't want me to stay any longer. In fact, she can hardly wait to be alone. I can literally feel her ache to be released.

"Inah, I am . . ." I swallow the lump in my throat. "I am sorry we fought."

"Don't, Yunah . . . ," Inah says miserably. "Don't start." Loosening her arms around me, she pulls away.

"Are you really going to be okay?" I manage to ask. Inah nods and turns her head away. "Promise me just one thing. Please!" Inah looks up, searching my eyes. I know what she thinks, but I won't make her promise such a thing; it's too hideous. "Get an email address, so I can write to you?" Inah's face breaks into a wan smile. I pull out the envelope and quickly push it into the open palm of Inah's unsuspecting hand, dangling at her side. In the morning at the hotel, I slipped the letter I wrote in Florence into the envelope. Inah angrily protests to my back as I board the train.

Completely exhausted and drained, I sink into a seat by the window and close my eyes, crushing the lids tight. I just can't bear to look out the window and see her walk away. Alone. So many people in the world but always alone. . . . Keeping my eyes shut, I wait and wait. Fighting the urge to look out.

I don't know how much time has passed. Startled at the rapping sound on the window, I open my eyes. It's Inah. Outside the smudged train window. Standing on the sun-blasted platform, looking like a cutout figure with phosphorous edges. Has she been standing there all the time? Inah lifts her hand, shielding her squinting eyes from the sun, trying to see. Her scarred face looks puffy and sallow, like an old oiled-paper.

"Inah?! Why are you still here?" I shout through the smudged window. "Go! Go! I told you not to wait!" I point toward the Termini exit and wave her away with my hand. Inah nods but doesn't move. She says something and smiles, pulling her scarred mouth in a crooked angle. Inah then lifts her hand that has been shielding her eyes and waves like a child. She hesitates, uncertain if I saw her, and then she finally turns around, wiping at her eyes with the back of her hand. Inah, you *babo*, fool, don't cry. Through the tremor of tears, Inah slowly turns into a blurry figure. How small and lost and defenseless she looks. Then I don't see her anymore. She's gone. I cry like nuts.

A middle-aged French couple come and take the seat across from me. I am grateful that they aren't Americans from my confession-crazed, bare-it-all, shame-as-fame, talk-show-bazaar country. They would want to know if I am all right, offer me a wad of Kleenex and try to comfort me. Instead, they go on talking in their snorting, guttural language. As if it were exactly what they expected to see on the train to the airport. One more foolish girl crying her heart out over a short-lived romance in Rome. The train lurches forward.

I keep my swollen eyes to the window. A mirror to the world. The gray, hazy sky stretches like a tarpaulin over the outskirts of Rome. It is strangely satisfying to see that even Rome is not immune to ugliness and urban blight. The apartment buildings, gloomy, paint-slapped cement boxes with graffiti on the walls, remind me of home. For a moment, I am almost giddy with the fact that I am going home.

I hope one day Inah, too, will feel just as giddy and grateful to be coming home—home, to which we are all tethered by an invisible thread called love. I know she will, for we never forget where we come from. By then she will have realized how much we love her, everything of her. In our own deficient, even self-serving ways, but as best as we know how. Only then will she return. Hungry for that bone-deep and suffocating love.

How I would like Inah then to have a home that she can call her own. A place she can return to at the end of a day, to rest and to refresh and to recuperate. Where at night, she can shut the windows, turn off the lights and go to bed, and in the morning, wake up and open them again. I will then get a print of the Horace Pippin painting of the Victorian living room she loves—with the armchairs draped with antimacassars, a round table with a vase flowing with flowers and curtain-pulled windows framing tree branches and wisps of clouds outside—and hang it up on her living-room wall. And when spring comes to Flushing, we will go back and go for a walk again with Dad. Down Ash, past the Chinese house on Syringa Place and down the blossoming Cherry. Just as we used to do the first spring on Ash Avenue. Mom will take out the pale green celadon plate she brought back from Korea the summer Grandma died, and wait for us at home with peeled and sliced apples arranged on it like flowers.

But take your time, Inah. Everything can wait. For everything changes and heals and fades away over time. For time, which we measure by seconds and minutes and days and months, and distance, by yards and miles, are only imaginary obstacles. In our minds, we overcome all distances and

time. I will always be there with you: a constant companion.
You won't be alone. Remember what Colette said: " . . . a
woman can never die of grief . . . she grows supple in the
practice of suffering and dissimulation. . . ."

So go wherever your heart leads you. Go and gaze at the
turquoise Mediterranean Sea. Roam Greek islands and
watch sunlight play magic on white, geometric buildings.
You have already walked the thronged, chaotic streets of
Calcutta and gazed up at the immense night sky over
Rajasthan and sat under the bo tree. You have immersed
yourself in beauty, poverty, ugliness, richness and loneliness,
and yet you're not healed. So if you must, lose every bound-
ary. If necessary, forget everything. Every language, even
Korean, the language full of an untranslatable trove of
words to express love, joy, anger, sorrow and pain. You can
even invent a new one to express them.

Don't come back until you are aching with longing. By
then, you will have lived all those feelings and emotions a
thousand times over. You will come home, not wiser or happier, but at least with a little bit of peace in you. Until then,
try to hold on.

ACKNOWLEDGMENTS

My deep gratitude and thanks go to Judith Curr, the publisher of Atria, for her warm and kind support; Suzanne O'Neill, my wonderful editor, for her wisdom and tireless work; and Joanne Wang, my superb agent, for her indefatigable efforts. And many thanks to Charles Palella, Barney Rosset and Astrid Myers for their discerning eyes, and the Tuesday pool nights; and Lewis Frumkes, the director of the Writing Center at Marymount Manhattan College for the support he gave me, beginning with my first book. I am also forever indebted to my great teacher, Cynthia Ozick. And I am truly grateful to my family in Korea and America for their nurturing love and unending faith.

Finally, Jennifer, wherever you are, I hope you are happy. Thanks for giving me the first inspiration for this book.